FISHBOWL

MATTHEW GLASS

CORVUS

First published in Great Britain in 2015 by Atlantic Books,
an imprint of Atlantic Books Ltd.

10 9 8 7 6 5 4 3 2 1

A CIP catalogue record for this book is available from the British Library.

Trade Paperback ISBN: 978 1 78239 261 3
E-book ISBN: 978 178239 262 0

Printed and bound by CPI Group (UK) Ltd, Croydon, CR0 4YY

Atlantic Books
An Imprint of Atlantic Books Ltd
Ormond House
26–27 Boswell Street
London
WC1N 3JZ

www.atlantic-books.co.uk

FISHBOWL

FISHBOWL

1

THE PITCH TOOK less than twenty minutes. Robert Leib listened without interrupting, dividing his glances between the slides in front of him and the two young men sitting on the other side of the table.

When it was finished, he leafed silently back through the presentation. They were in Leib's conference room in a sprawling, stone-clad office building on Sand Hill Road, the strip outside Palo Alto favoured by the venture capital firms that had provided the funds to blow open the age of the internet. Just 200 yards in one direction was the office of Sequoia Capital, 300 yards in the other direction was Andreeson Horowitz, both of them early backers of some of the biggest names on the net. Leib Roberts Berkowitz, or LRB, as it was known, had made a string of successful tech investments that had brought Robert Leib and his two founding partners immense wealth.

Leib was a short, tubby man in his fifties with receding hair and a trim, greying beard. He wore a blue polo shirt and a pair of khaki chinos.

He stopped on one of the slides.

'This user growth,' he said to the man who had done the talking during the pitch. 'Chris, this is all verifiable, right?'

'No. We just made those numbers up.'

Leib smiled for a second. Chris Hamer was thirty-one, a tall Californian with blond hair and a mischievous glint in his eye. Leib had invested in one of Hamer's previous ventures and made a moderate amount of money. But this venture wasn't Hamer's, and the stakes, Leib knew, wouldn't be moderate.

He was much more interested in the other person sitting at the table, Andrei Koss, a pale young man with curly dark hair who had sat through Chris's pitch with an air of indifference or impatience or something, anyway, which Leib wasn't accustomed to seeing in the founder of a start-up when his company was being pitched for hundreds of millions of dollars. Like every other investor in the valley, Leib had been interested in meeting Andrei Koss for quite some time. Just back from his annual salmon fishing trip to Scotland, the venture capitalist hadn't hesitated for a second when he got a call from Chris Hamer asking if he could bring Koss to talk to him.

Leib closed the slide deck. 'You know, the general assumption is that you guys would never look for venture capital. You've got the revenues to fund your own growth. So this is interesting, but, frankly … you don't need me.'

'We're here,' said Chris.

'Yeah, but you don't *need* me. When someone comes to me for money they don't really need, I get offered terms I don't really like. So I'm thinking to myself – what are these guys doing?' Leib smiled again. 'Why would they invite the vultures through the door?'

Chris grinned. 'There's a bunch of development we need to do and we think for a year or two we're going to need additional funding to get through that.'

'What kind of development?'

'Stuff.'

'What kind of stuff?'

'Work on the platform. Work on the site. The usual stuff, Bob. It's not one single thing. We've got a bunch of projects in mind. We've decided, rather than doing them piecemeal over however long that would take, let's get the funding and deliver them all right away.'

Leib's eyes narrowed for a moment, then he glanced at Andrei, who hadn't said a word since shaking his hand. 'How old are you?' he said.

'Is that material?' asked Andrei.

'Is it immaterial?' said Leib. 'You're the CEO of this company and you're asking me to invest. I'd like to get some sense of how much experience you have.'

'I'm twenty-three,' said Andrei.

'And according to what I've just heard, you own fifty-eight per cent of this company?'

Chris reached towards the slide deck in front of Leib. 'The full share structure's in the presentation—'

'That's right,' said Andrei.

'Well,' said Leib, 'the first thing I should say is, congratulations. I mean that. From what I know, from the buzz, from what you've just shown me, you've built an extraordinary business in … how long is it?'

'Three years.'

'Extraordinary,' said Leib.

'Thank you,' said Andrei.

Leib sat back in his chair, hands behind his head. 'Andrei, what are you trying to do with this thing? What's the vision?'

'Deep Connectedness, Mr Leib.'

'I've heard that you use that term. What does it mean?'

'It means giving people a way to come together wherever they are on the globe. It means creating the most efficient way for them to find others who share their interests, create a connection, share their knowledge. I want to give people the means to come out of their circle of friends, out of their neighbourhoods, out of their communities and find people they would never have found before. That's the new world, Mr Leib. Clusters of people with shared values, shared ideas, wherever they are on our planet.'

'Your website does a lot more than that. Why don't you just post a list of names for people to contact?'

'People don't respond to that.'

'How do you know?'

'I tried it.'

Leib suppressed a smile. There was a sense of certainty about the 23-year-old that chimed with what Leib had read in the newspaper reports of him. He was blunt, but Leib guessed he was honest. It was obvious he didn't have much in the way of social skills, but then when had he ever met a great programmer who did? Leib would have been worried if he'd turned out all smiley.

'And the model of advertising you use? Controversial, isn't it?'

Chris grinned. 'Anything revolutionary is controversial.'

'The way you get people to buy stuff ...'

'It's not my role to say what forms Deep Connectedness can take,' said Andrei. 'It's not my role to tell the world what it can do. My role is to help the world do what it wants to do most efficiently.'

'Is that how you see it?' asked Leib.

'What other way is there to see it?'

'Didn't I hear there was a district attorney investigating to see if she could stop what you're doing?' Leib had had his staffers put together a summary of everything in the public domain about the business ahead of the meeting, and knew exactly what the Santa Clara district attorney had threatened.

'Old news,' said Chris. 'She's backed off.'

'Sure, but my question is, how sustainable is this?'

'That's a judgement, Mr Leib,' said Andrei. 'At present that's not quantifiable.'

'But you're asking me to judge.'

'With respect, sir, that's your job, isn't it? Isn't that what venture capital firms do. You weigh risk and allocate funds, correct?'

Leib smiled. 'That's what I do.'

'Then I guess that's what you're going to need to do here.'

Chris pulled a tablet computer out of his bag. He swiped it and quickly typed a few letters, then slid the tablet across the tabletop to Leib. 'We thought you might want to get an experience of the functionality.'

The venture capitalist glanced down at the screen and found himself looking at someone's home page. A picture showed a slim, fortyish man on a riverbank with a fishing rod in his hands.

Another showed the same man holding up what must have been at least a fifty pound salmon.

'Who's this?' asked Leib.

'Just someone,' said Chris. 'He's kind of a salmon enthusiast like you are. We set up an account in your name and put your interest as salmon fishing. He's obviously seen your profile and thinks it might be cool to talk.'

'My profile?' said Leib sharply.

'The one we created. It's all public knowledge. We just took a few facts off your profile on the LRB website.'

'That doesn't say anything about salmon fishing.'

'I added that,' said Chris. 'Bob, anyone who knows you knows that's the only interest you have in your sad life.'

Leib stared at Hamer mistrustfully.

'Bob, talk to him. How's it going to hurt? He's sent you a Bait. Just click on it.'

Leib saw a button labelled, 'Take my Bait?'

'Bob, I really think you ought to try it out.'

Leib hesitated. Then he clicked on the button.

Words began appearing in a message box: 'Hi, Bob. How are you doing?'

'What's his name?' asked Leib.

'It's on his page.'

Leib looked. Paul. Still he made no move to respond.

Chris sighed. 'Bob, we're going to shut down this account the minute we're done here. You can watch us do it. Talk to the guy. It's not going to kill you. We have four hundred million people who do it every day.'

'What do I say?'

'Talk to him. Pretend he's sitting right here. Just be natural. He's just a guy who likes salmon fishing.'

Leib hesitated again. 'OK,' he murmured. He typed. 'Hi, Paul. I'm well. How are you?'

'Good. I'm fishing here in New Zealand. Just getting ready to go out for the day. Had a great day yesterday. Eleven beauties.

None of them under twenty pounds. One of the guys landed a sixty pounder.'

Leib gazed at the words for a moment. Then he typed. 'Sixty? Really?'

'I kid you not.'

'What are you catching?'

'Chinook. Down here they call it quinnat. Best chinook fishing in the world. Most unspoiled fishing left on the planet. You ever been to NZ?'

'No.'

'Bob! You should. It's awesome. Better than Alaska.'

'Have you fished Alaska?' typed Leib.

'Plenty of times. Kenai. Karluk.'

'Karluk? I've been there too. Remote Alaska is awesome.'

'Bob, I could tell you a story or two about Karluk. You know, a couple of years back they had a September blizzard up there.'

'I heard about that.'

'You heard? I was there! But let me tell you, Bob, New Zealand is something else. There's this great spot I know on the Hurunui River. You should come down here and try it. You really should. I know a bunch of guides who can take you places where there are fish like you've never seen before. And there are some great lodges. Real luxury places. If you want to bring a bunch of guys, you'll live like kings. I'll send you a link with some information.'

'What are you talking about?' asked Chris.

Leib looked up, suddenly conscious again of Chris and Andrei watching him. 'Salmon fishing in New Zealand.'

'Have you ever been there?'

'No.'

'Do you think you will?' asked Chris.

'Maybe. Maybe it's time I tried a new place. I've never done Southern Hemisphere. Paul says New Zealand's even better than Alaska. He's going to send me a link and I'll—'

Suddenly Leib stopped.

Chris laughed. 'How long did that take, Bob? Two minutes?

What would you spend on a trip down there? Ten thousand dollars? Twenty?'

Leib didn't reply. In two minutes, as Chris had said, New Zealand fishing had been sold to him in a way that an advertisement or a brochure could never have succeeded in doing. Bob Leib felt that he was in the presence of something immensely, almost scarily powerful. And did he want a part of it? Even more than when Chris Hamer and Andrei Koss had walked through his door that morning.

'You can see the results of the larger deals we've done.' Chris opened the slides in front of Leib again. 'They're only the beginning. We're currently working on deals with—'

'How much are you looking for?' asked Leib, cutting across him.

'Three hundred million.' Chris said it quickly. He had pitched companies before, but nothing like this.

'For?'

'Five per cent of the company.'

Leib ran his hand thoughtfully over his beard. 'Three hundred million for five per cent. So after three years of operation, and with the numbers you've shown me, you value yourselves at six billion dollars.'

'No,' said Andrei. 'I value us way higher than that, and I'm not the only one.'

Leib raised an eyebrow.

'It's customary for the vultures, I understand, to get a premium.'

Leib laughed. 'That's because of the risk, Andrei.'

Andrei didn't reply.

Leib looked at Chris. 'Who else are you talking to?'

'No one. That was my advice to Andrei. We're speaking with you. If you can do the deal, we do the deal.'

'Is that how you see it, Andrei?'

Andrei nodded. 'Chris says you know the space. He says you'll bring wise counsel as well as funding.'

'Do you want wise counsel?'

'I'm only twenty-three.'

Andrei's expression was deadpan. Leib didn't know if he was making a very dry joke or simply stating what he took to be obvious.

Leib put his hands behind his head again and gazed at the two young men. Then he sat forward. 'LRB won't put three hundred in by itself. But I could potentially put that together through a syndicate with another couple of funds. We'd lead. We'd put in a hundred and fifty to a hundred and seventy-five. The rest would come from the others. How would you feel about that?'

'I told Andrei that was how it would likely work,' said Chris.

'And?'

'We'd need to have right of refusal over the other funds before you approach them.'

'That could work. So … three hundred million for five per cent? Is that what you're asking?'

Chris nodded.

Leib looked at Andrei. 'Let's be clear. Andrei, is that what you're saying? You're prepared to sell five per cent of your company for three hundred million.'

'Yes,' said Andrei.

'And a seat on the board. We'd need a seat on the board.'

'Yes.'

There was silence.

Chris could barely breathe. Meetings where the venture capitalist did the deal right then and there were the stuff of legend. Usually it took weeks of negotiation and hair-splitting.

Leib gazed at the screen of the tablet computer again.

'OK,' he said. 'Provided we can see the usual documentation and my guys can do the standard due diligence—'

'Sure. Whatever you want—'

'Just listen, Chris. Provided we can do the usual due diligence – *and* with one condition that I'll come back to in a minute – I'll put together a syndicate that will put in three hundred million for five per cent of this company, with the proviso that we have an option in twelve months to take another five per cent at the same valuation.'

Chris started to smile.

'No,' said Andrei. 'That's too much.'

'What's too much?' asked Leib.

'Another five per cent at the same valuation in twelve months is too much.'

'Andrei,' said Chris, 'don't you think we should—?'

'If you want the option, Mr Leib, then it's four per cent for three hundred million today and your option is for two per cent in twelve months for another three hundred million.'

'That doubles the valuation in twelve months,' said Leib.

'I estimate we're worth more than that already.' Andrei shrugged. 'If you don't agree, you don't have to take up the option.'

Again, Leib suppressed a smile. He quickly ran the numbers in his head, watching Andrei as he did it. He was increasingly impressed with the young man. Suddenly he rose from his chair and reached forward to shake Andrei's hand. 'Done!' When he sat down again, he raised a finger in the air. 'Now, I said this deal was dependent on one other condition. This has to be sustainable. You say the DA's given up looking at you?'

Chris nodded.

'That's what I heard too.' Leib smiled slightly. 'I don't give a fuck what some little DA in Santa Clara says.' He gestured towards the tablet computer, where the final few lines of his conversation with Paul were still visible on the screen. 'How can you guys guarantee me that *that* is legal?'

2

THE JOURNEY THAT led Andrei Koss to Robert Leib's office had begun three years earlier, a couple of miles away in a student dorm at Stanford University. The autumn quarter that year brought together four juniors in a two-bed double in Robinson House, one of the accommodation blocks on Sterling Quad. Andrei was majoring in computer science. His roommate was Ben Marks, a psychology major from Baltimore. In the other room in the suite were Kevin Embley, a beefy Chicagoan majoring in economics with a more than passing interest in programming, and Charles Gok, a tall, gangly physics major with a bad case of acne.

Andrei was the youngest of three children of a Russian emigrant couple who had left Moscow for Boston when he was four. His father was a professor of linguistics at Harvard and his mother a hospital pathologist. There was no trace of Russian in Andrei's accent. Standing slightly below average height, and a little awkward in his movements, he had won every high-school award going in physics and maths. He had been coding since he was twelve and his decision to major in computer science was more or less pre-ordained. While still at high school, he had written a clutch of internet apps, one of which had garnered a few users and which he had sold to a software developer for $200,000.

Andrei, Ben and Kevin knew each other from their first two years at Stanford. Charles was new to all three of them. As the four juniors settled in that fall, they spent their time in the common room between the two bedrooms, where four small desks jostled with a sofa and a couple of chairs under a changing but persistent scum of soda cans and take-out containers. The only thing that differentiated it from any other common room in any other dorm in America was a large aquarium that stood against one wall, stocked with tropical fish. Ben had always had an aquarium since his father had bought him one when he was in the third grade, and he had kept the tradition at college. People dropped by to feed the fish, often with articles that no self-respecting piscine would even have sniffed at, which for some reason became a cult activity in the house. Ben fought a constant battle against would-be fish feeders bringing pieces of pizza and chicken nuggets.

Of the four, Ben was the most socially successful. He was five ten, dark-haired, with an air of calm self-assurance. Charles was quiet, introverted and shy, and most people agreed that an arranged marriage was probably his best shot. Kevin, who fought a constant although not particularly vigorous battle against chubbiness, made up in enthusiasm for what he lacked in attractiveness.

Andrei had been having an on-again, off-again relationship for the past year with a sophomore called Sandy Gross who was on the public policy programme. There were times when Sandy was strongly attracted by Andrei's uncompromising intelligence and frankness, and other times when those same qualities could be almost unbearably infuriating. He could be caring and affectionate, and yet the next time she saw him his mind might be occupied by some programming problem to the point of insensitivity. When he was on to a problem, he would work at it for days until he cracked it. Even then, there was something about Andrei's resolve, his determination to shut everything else out and solve the problem, that Sandy found compelling. But she was by no means sure that the relationship would last, or that it would even be healthy for her if it did.

Andrei loved epic historical movies and had a borderline obsession with them. Otherwise, his only interest was coding. He had an almost inexhaustible capacity for work and the ability to code for ten, fifteen, twenty hours at a stretch, sitting at his desk with headphones in his ears, a Coke can by his hand, gazing at his computer screen as his fingers tapped the keyboard, oblivious to whatever chaos might be happening in the common room around him. Someone once likened him to a hamster because of the way hamsters can run on a wheel all day long, and his multi-hour stretches of coding accordingly became known as wheelspins. He would come off a wheelspin exhausted but wired by the ten to twenty cans of Coke that he would have drunk, and ravenously hungry. Invariably he would see if anyone wanted to go with him to Yao's on University Avenue, his favourite noodle bar, where he would order a double helping of chicken and prawn fried noodles.

Andrei rented his own server space for $100 a month to host his creations, but apart from the one app he had sold he hadn't had any great success. The idea would start off with some kind of problem that he wanted to solve, and his focus, like that of most software engineers, would be to find the leanest, most elegant way to solve it. His pitfall was that he didn't pay much attention to the appearance of the product or the experience for potential users. None of that stuff interested him – or not enough to keep him from being distracted by the next problem.

Kevin Embley had done some coding himself and had a good share of talent as a programmer. Occasionally he would help out with something Andrei was working on, sitting beside him with his own pair of headphones, at his own screen. When the occasion arose he could wheelspin as long and as hard as Andrei. Mostly, though, Kevin pursued his own cyber interests. He had a habit of constructing personas on social networking sites. These weren't a matter of a few pseudonymous comments in a chatroom with the face of a cartoon character as a picture, but elaborate confections with so much personal detail that anyone would think they were authentic. He would invent a name, borrow – as he termed it – a photo of someone in Brazil or Poland or some other random country, deftly merge it into images he had borrowed from somewhere else, construct a personal story and then try to connect to someone he knew vaguely or had once met, and see where the exercise took him. He would work on it for weeks, often developing a web of intense online relationships, refining his persona and adding more fabricated photos, and then suddenly delete himself when he had had enough.

Andrei didn't find this kind of thing particularly interesting, but Ben found the psychology fascinating, the way one could test how other people would behave by using the character Kevin created. After they had got to know each other in their freshman year, he and Kevin had spent long sessions at Kevin's computer debating what one of his personas should do and say next and what effect it was going to achieve.

This was the mix that came together in the common room in Robinson House that fall. Out of this chance combination of four young men and their interests, two things soon happened that would have consequences beyond the imaginings of any of them.

The first of these things was that Kevin decided to strike up a pseudonymous relationship with Dan Cooley, a junior who roomed on the floor below them in Robinson House. He never thought too hard about the reasons – it just seemed like a fun idea. According to his home page, Cooley claimed to be a fencer, although as far as Kevin knew he wasn't active in any sporting society and was generally regarded as a certified loser.

It would have been easy to pose as a woman, but Kevin didn't do that. That would have been shooting fish in a barrel. Instead, he created 'Jeff Milgrom', a college senior who was supposedly at Northwestern University – with the face of someone in Trondheim, Norway – who was into fencing and Japanese haiku, and set up a home page. Dan took the bait. Through him, 'Jeff' – or Kevin-with-Ben-watching-over-his-shoulder – met a bunch of other wannabe fencers.

In the online discussions that ensued about the sport, Dan said he used Nike fencing shoes. In fact, he said he wore them all the time, and was always saying how great they were. No other brand could compare. Kevin and Ben were bemused by the intensity of his Nikephilia. They still weren't even sure that he fenced. The next time they saw him, they surreptitiously checked out his shoes – Nikes on his feet. They decided on a small experiment: to see if they could convert him to Adidas. Victory would be declared the day he ditched the swoosh and appeared with the three stripes of the German manufacturer's shoes.

Soon conversations about sneakers were taking up a considerable portion of the communication going on between Dan and 'Jeff'. Kevin and Ben competed in creating arguments that might appeal to Dan in favour of Adidas and denigrating Nike. Kevin created links to false articles on web pages he designed to look like the *New York Times* and the *Washington Post* alleging horrific abuses at factories producing Nike goods.

Inevitably, news leaks out in a college dorm. It wasn't long before the whole of Robinson House – with the exception of Dan Cooley – knew what was going on. Bets were being laid as to whether and when Dan would succumb. A daily Sneaker Watch was mounted.

Even Charles Gok, who paid about as much attention to what was happening around him as the average nuclear physicist – he must have walked past Kevin and Ben huddled around Kevin's computer a hundred times before he twigged to what was going on – eventually became aware of it. When he did, he sat down in the common room the next time he found them huddled, a serious expression on his face. 'Guys, this is wrong,' he said, subconsciously rubbing his own pair of Nikes. 'This is very wrong.'

'It's sneakers, Charles,' said Ben. 'We're not messing with his values.'

'You don't call these values?'

Kevin laughed.

'Andrei?' said Charles. 'What do you think? They should stop this, right?'

Andrei turned around from his screen, where he was in a chatroom for fans of epic movies. 'Any of you guys ever hear about a Spanish film called *Aguila Roja*?'

There were shakes of the head around the room.

'I got a guy from Colombia here telling me it's the best epic movie ever made.'

'Dude,' said Kevin. '*Aguila Roja*? Are you telling me that's better than *Troy*? Better than *300*?'

'Do you know *Aguila Roja*?' asked Andrei.

'No.'

'Then how do you know it isn't?'

The three other guys looked at him for a moment. Then Kevin started to laugh.

In Andrei's head, the second of those things had just happened.

In the chatroom Andrei was visiting, a heated debate was taking place about the ten greatest epics of the twenty-first century so far. The discussion had reduced itself to a dance on the head of a pin about whether *Gladiator*, which was released in 2000, was technically a twentieth or twenty-first century film, and had got to the point where datings of the Gregorian versus the Julian calendars were being cited, when someone with the moniker 'Guy from Colombia' had come online and said, 'Who cares anyway?' By far the greatest epic movie ever, he claimed, was *Aguila Roja*, released in Spain in 2011. Just about everyone online ridiculed the opinion, and soon ridiculed the person, even though, as far as Andrei could tell, no one else had even heard of the film, let alone seen it.

Andrei was a fairly regular visitor to the chatroom and knew – in a cyber sense – just about everyone who frequented it. It wasn't a place for dilettantes, and the level of knowledge was quite high. Every so often, someone new would appear but they would face a fairly hostile reception, a kind of baptism by fire, and would rarely come back. Almost everyone in the chatroom was US-based, and the vast majority of films they discussed were from Hollywood. There was one French guy who regularly banged on about French movies the others had rarely seen, but mostly he was ignored, suspected of being from some cultural institute promoting French cinema.

Guy from Colombia probably had a financial interest in the film he was talking up, thought Andrei – but maybe he didn't. And even if he did, that didn't mean he was necessarily wrong. He had tried to respond to a couple of the attacks and then exited the chatroom. There was a good deal of unpleasant humour at his expense. But he was gone, and once gone, there was no way to find him.

Everyone had immediately assumed Guy from Colombia was talking out of his ass, just because they hadn't heard of him or his film before. So had Kevin. He had simply laughed.

But how did they know?

Andrei got hold of a pirated download of *Aguila Roja* and watched it that night. In his opinion, it was far from the best epic movie of the twenty-first century, or of 2011, or of the month or probably even of the week it was released. If Guy from Colombia was serious that it was the best epic ever, then he was an idiot.

But Guy from Colombia, and Kevin's laughter, left Andrei with a deep, nagging feeling of unease. He didn't know if the person's name was Guy, or if he was describing himself as a guy from Colombia. But, either way, what if there was a guy from Colombia who wasn't an idiot? Or a guy from Mexico, or Scotland, or Omaha? Or a girl? In other words, what if there was a really smart, really bright person who had interesting things to say about epic movies but didn't happen to stumble into that chatroom? How would Andrei ever know that he or she existed? How would they ever have the chance to exchange ideas?

There were media other than chatrooms that brought people together. Group pages on social media sites, specialist blogs, home pages of associations and societies. But each of them covered only a subset of the people you might want to connect with, and if you were using those media, the chances were that they included the group most like you. The chatroom he frequented was a case in point. It was cosy, unchallenging. There were disagreements, often intense ones, but everyone knew each other and knew the kind of things they were going to say. A kind of shared understanding of where the limits were – the same assumptions and cultural references. But surely, if you had an interest, the most stimulating people would be the ones who were most unlike you except in the interest that you shared. Surely *they* were the ones who would provide the most challenging and thought-expanding conversations.

It was possible to find experts and academics, of course, through simple internet searches, but those weren't the people Andrei had in mind. And social media had search facilities, but then you were restricted to the population that used a particular network. And people listed so many interests, or listed them so broadly, that the chances were you'd miss the few genuine specks of gold those searches might turn up in the false glitter of everything else.

The problem was obvious, so obvious that Andrei couldn't believe he hadn't been struck by it before. If such people existed – not experts, not academics, not authorities on a subject, but smart, thoughtful people submerged in the general population who just happened to share one of your interests and might have something interesting to say about it – then how would you find them?

3

THE QUESTION GNAWED at Andrei. He just couldn't let it go. The itch got stronger and stronger. Eventually, Andrei did the only thing he could do. He forgot about classes, he forgot about Sandy, he forgot about meals – and coded.

Days later, at the end of one final, stupendous wheelspin, Andrei took his headphones off, put them down beside his keyboard and looked around. The common room was empty. It was dark outside. He had no idea of the time and was only moderately certain he knew what day it was.

On the desk beside his computer stood a good number of empty Coke cans. Andrei pulled the ring on the last unopened one and put it to his lips.

He could hear the bubbling of the water in Ben's aquarium. He watched the fish as he sucked on the can, and felt the sweet, warm fizz of a Coke that had been out of the fridge way too long.

Some of the fish swam in the upper part of the tank, others in the lower part. It always struck Andrei how they layered. He watched one, an orange and white fish with a snub white nose, drift from one side of the tank to the other.

He needed a name. The website he had created was ready to go live. Between wheelspins over the last few days he had kept telling himself that he'd have time to think of a name but now the coding was done, and he still didn't have one.

The website was far from perfect. The search algorithm underlying it was crude, at best. And there was a list of about a hundred other improvements he could make and features he could add. But the core of it was done, enough to show the concept, and if people didn't like it, there would be no point in spending the time doing any of the other things he had in mind.

But he had to have a name. He couldn't launch without one.

Andrei's gaze moved around the room. It was worse than a pigsty. He wondered for a moment how come the trash didn't pile up so high that it physically submerged them. Presumably someone cleared it out from time to time. Who? He knew that he had never done it.

He began to scrunch up the Coke cans. He finished the one he was drinking and scrunched that as well.

He was hungry and exhausted, as he always was after a wheel-spin. He wanted to launch this thing and then go and get something to eat and maybe grab a couple of hours of sleep or go to a class and then come back to the computer and see what had happened, see if anyone had taken a look at the site and what they had to say.

He had to have a name.

Andrei found himself gazing at the aquarium again. He watched the orange and white fish. Or maybe it was a different one. There were at least four in there that he could see, now that he checked. They all swam somewhere between the middle and the upper part of the tank. Were they even aware of the fish that stayed at the bottom?

Suddenly their predicament seemed to be a metaphor for the problem he was trying to solve. Maybe it was all the caffeine and the sugar in the Coke speaking, but, in Andrei's mind, there was an uncanny parallel that had the almost unreal crystal clarity of an idea conceived by a mind that had had way too little sleep. It may have been only a four feet by three aquarium on the other side of the room, but it was a microcosm. The fish swam around in different layers, sharing the same water with the bits of pizza and chicken nuggets raining down on them from above – but did any of them know that the others in the other layers even existed? Some swam above, others below. Separate existences in a common world. What if the orange and white fish could have spoken to the little grey fish that always seemed to be drifting around amongst the various objects embedded in the sand? Wouldn't each have had things to say, perspectives to share, which would have amazed the other? What was it like to look up all the time? What was it like to look down? But how could they communicate, even if they wanted to? How could they exchange ideas and insights and … OK, they were fish. You could draw the analogy too far. But as the fish were to the aquarium, so were people to the world.

But the name? Aquarium? Aquarium.com? It was flat. It had no ring to it.

Then it hit him. Fishbowl.

Fishbowl.

Somehow, it was perfect.

Only one thing wasn't. Andrei did a search and found that the domain name was taken under every suffix he might conceivably use: TheFishbowl was taken as well. So was AFishbowl. Now that Andrei had hit on it, he felt as if he had always had that name in mind. Nothing else could capture the concept he wanted to express. He had to have it, without paying the tens of thousands or even more it might take to buy it, and without waiting the weeks or months it might take to negotiate for it. He wanted it right now. He was ready to launch.

He went quickly back to the domain name search box and searched the suffixes again. Impulsively, he added a second 'l' to the name. Fishbowll.com. He did a search. No one had it! A minute later, he had registered it.

His fingers could barely keep pace with his mind now. They flew over the keyboard. He hit a key – and the site was live.

'Check out this new website I've just launched,' he wrote to his email address book. 'Fishbowll.com. That's right, you didn't misread. It's got two l's at the end. If you like it, let other people know.' He hit Send, then he shut down and looked around, alone in the common room. He jumped up and went to his room. Ben Marks was snoring. He opened the door of the other bedroom.

Kevin and Charles were both asleep. He was too excited to stay still. 'Anyone want to go to Yao's?' he yelled.

There were groans.

'Come on. I'm hungry.' He waited. 'Guys. Come on! Yao's! Noodles! I'm buying.'

'Dude,' came Kevin's voice, 'do you have any idea what time it is?' There was a crash of something falling on the floor, then a rustling, and then Kevin's voice again. 'It's six o'clock. I don't think Yao's is open.'

'It's a list,' said Ben Marks that afternoon, after he had looked at the site.

Andrei nodded.

'It's a list,' he said again. 'Andrei, it's just a list.'

'It's a list of just about everyone in the world,' said Andrei, with only mild exaggeration.

'I know. It's amazing. I don't know how you did it.'

'Do you want me to explain the algorithms?'

'Do you think I'd understand?'

Andrei gazed at Ben for a moment. 'No.'

Ben laughed. 'Look, what I don't understand is, what am I supposed to do with it? How am I going to use it?'

Andrei looked at him uncomprehendingly. 'You can find anyone you want. Anywhere in the world. Anyone with any interest you want to talk about.'

'Dude,' said Kevin, waving an antique fly swat that had somehow found its way to the common room and now resided there. 'I got eight hundred thousand names.'

'Great!'

'Yeah, but eight hundred thousand!'

'What did you search on?'

'Eggs.'

Ben laughed. 'Kevin, you've got to get a life.'

'I just wanted to see.'

'But eggs?'

'And you got eight hundred thousand people?' said Andrei. 'That's awesome.'

'The first name I clicked on was a guy in, like, Australia who's got some thing about caterpillar eggs. The next one was some woman in Canada who has this thing about swan eggs. Then there was the guy with this very kind of waxed beard who did something with quail eggs. Actually, the beard was quite interesting.'

'Eggs is too general,' said Andrei. 'You should have specified.'

'Yeah, so that's what I did next. Goose eggs.'

Ben kicked his legs in amusement. 'Goose eggs! Kevin, what is this sickness?'

'And what happened then?' asked Andrei seriously.

'Seventeen thousand.'

'See?'

'Seventeen *thousand*. Dude, seventeen thousand names. And they're not ranked, they're not ordered.'

'You can search by country.'

'At least let me know who's hot.'

'How am I going to do that?'

Kevin shrugged. 'Do something with their pictures so I don't get the guy with the beard every time.'

Andrei frowned. 'So you're both saying … you get too much?'

'Way too much,' said Ben. 'Too much choice. You know the classic experiment – show someone six brands of jelly, and they'll choose. Show them twenty-four, and they're paralysed. I look at this thing … I don't know where to start. I don't know *how* to start.'

'Start from the top.'

'But there's no ranking. Is that a ranking, the order?'

Andrei shook his head. 'The order's random.'

'Then why don't I start from the bottom?'

'You could.'

'Or from the middle?'

'You can start where you like.'

'That's the problem!'

Andrei frowned again. 'You think it needs to be ranked?'

'You need something,' said Ben. 'I don't know if it's a ranking but … something.'

Kevin beat the fly swat thoughtfully on the armrest of his chair. 'Dude, you've got to do something. There's no way into this thing. You've got this list. A gazillion people. It's scares the shit out of me. It's fucking awesome.'

'I think you mean awe-inspiring,' said Ben. 'As in dread.'

'Exactly. I'm in dread.' He looked at Ben. 'Is that a word?'

'I don't know.'

Andrei looked over at Sandy Gross, who was sitting on his desk, shaking her head. Andrei had neglected her completely once he had started coding, but she had taken the arrival of the email announcing Fishbowll's launch as a sign that he had surfaced from his wheelspin and had come to see him, only to find that he could think of nothing but his new website and how people were reacting to it.

'You too?' asked Andrei.

'I might use this for a sociology project,' said Sandy. 'Once.'

'So you wouldn't log in again?'

'Not unless you were paying me.'

Andrei frowned. Fishbowll didn't have the capability to do a ranking of the names that came up, at least not yet. He had thought of developing a ranking algorithm but had decided against it. Not because he couldn't do it – there were a couple of ways he could think of to provide a ranking, although both would require a vast amount of programming time and considerably more server space than he had available. No, there was another reason. If he gave a ranked list, the same few names would get clicked on each time, and most likely they would be recognized experts in their field – names anyone could find by doing a crude internet search. That wasn't the vision he had for the site. He wanted it to be a place where you would find Guy from Colombia. A place where you could expand your experience, a place where you would discover people you would never otherwise come across, people who shared your interests but from whom you could also learn about other practices, places, cultures, norms. People with amusing waxed beards, for example.

In order to do this, what Andrei had built was a lean, compact website, with no fuss or fanfare, in keeping with his lean and compact programming style. It consisted of a total of three pages.

The login page was simple and uncluttered. 'Fishbowll,' it said, 'is a place where you can meet people anywhere in the world to connect about the things that really interest you. These may be interests you already have or interests you want to find out about. Go ahead and try. In the Fishbowll, the world's your oyster.' At the bottom of the page was a button that said, 'I want to connect.'

When you clicked on the button, a second page came up. It asked you to type in the interest you were looking for. The bottom half of the screen gave you the option to search the world, by continent, or by country. Below that was a Go button. Click on that, and, once the search was done, the resulting list appeared on a third page with up to a hundred names – or a series of pages, considering the thousands of names the searches generated. Each person on the list was identified by name and country. Click on a name, and you were directed to their home page in whichever social networking site they used. What you did then was up to you.

Behind this deceptively simple façade – when you clicked on the Go button – you activated a program that scanned every social networking site of any significance globally, in order to produce a list of people who self-identified as having your chosen interest. But if that was all that it did, the program would have been only a minor advance on search facilities that already existed, adding quantity but not quality to the results. The unique part of Fishbowll, the truly brilliant innovation that Andrei Koss had produced in a breathtaking frenzy of technical creativity – which would later be improved, refined, expanded, but would always remain at the heart of the website – was a set of algorithms that identified, from a person's home page and every other accessible piece of information about them, the top three things they really cared about – not from what they listed as their interests, but from the content of their activities . It identified the things they talked about, posted pictures about, argued about, inquired about. The list that resulted was of people who were genuinely committed to the interest you had typed in, tested not by what they claimed – for whatever reason – that they were interested in, but by what they had actually *shown* they were interested in.

Andrei also ensured that any interaction people would have through Fishbowll would be captured and stored on the website's server so the program could continuously refine and update its identification of their interests.

But it had to be a site people wanted to use, and from the reaction of the people sitting in the room it didn't look promising.

By the end of the first day, about forty people had registered on the site – either friends of Andrei or friends of friends. And he was getting the same message from them. *Thousands of names. Great. Now what am I meant to do with this thing?*

There were a few more registrations the next day. But the number went down, the exact opposite of what should have happened if the site was going to go viral. People weren't recommending the site to their friends. Worse, as Andrei could see from the data on site visits, those who had registered weren't coming back.

Everything moves fast on the net. It doesn't take months of negotiating to rent a store front – equally, it doesn't take months of waiting to see if a business is a failure.

The verdict was swift. By day three it was over. Fishbowll, in the form initially conceived by Andrei Koss, had failed.

4

ALTHOUGH HE HAD told himself that he would waste no more time with the website if people didn't like it, Andrei continued to obsess over Fishbowll. There was something about the idea behind it that just wouldn't leave him alone. He couldn't help feeling that at the core of what Fishbowll was about there was something that had genuine and significant utility out there in the real world, in orders of magnitude greater than anything he had done before. There had to be a value in having a means to explore the things you most cared about with people from radically different backgrounds who cared about the same things. He believed people would want that. He also believed that it was a good thing in itself. Surely the more people saw that others who were apparently different from them in every way actually had something in common with them, the more people would come together.

Andrei also felt that the time had come for him to stick with something. He could have made a lot more money from the app he had sold, he knew, if only he had been prepared to work more on the cosmetics. Other people who were prepared to do that – people who would never have had the idea for it in the first place – had made that money instead. And other things he had done, he knew, had failed because he was only prepared to do the stuff that came easily to him: solve the programming challenges, and not the stuff that didn't excite him. Well, if he was ever to interest people in anything he coded, that would have to change. What was the point of coding anything if no one was interested in it?

And if he was going to change, why not now, when he had this idea for a thing that he really believed people might want?

But how? What should he do with the site he had created and which now languished unused on his server space? He pondered the problem during classes. He cornered anyone who had looked at Fishbowll and was foolish enough to come within earshot. No one had much in the way of ideas except ranking. But ranking, Andrei was sure, wasn't the answer. A ranked list was still just a list, highlighting the same experts and authorities that any other search would turn up, which wasn't what he had set out to do. Plus, if the top few people on the list refused to engage – which they would, surely, after the first few hundred people had tried to contact them – the list would be worse than useless.

Charles Gok was so caught up in his world of theoretical physics that he had never actually gone onto the Fishbowll site. Ben and Kevin would probably have forgotten about it if Andrei hadn't continued to badger them. They were more caught up in the experiment with Dan Cooley, who was still resolutely wearing the Nike swoosh. Ben was starting to become uneasy about the experiment and was beginning to think it was time to concede defeat, but every time Kevin caught a glimpse of Cooley wearing Nikes, in the quad, or in Ricker dining hall, where most of the students from Robinson House ate, he felt it as a personal slap in the face. The whole of Robinson House was watching. Kevin was determined to see the three stripes on Cooley's feet and was using all his considerable hacking skills in a final push for victory. Dan Cooley was now the lucky recipient of a series of bonus offers available only to first-time purchasers of Adidas sneakers, delivered direct to his inbox.

Opinion in Robinson House was divided over the legitimacy of this tactic and a number of bets were declared void.

Andrei, meanwhile, felt as if Fishbowll was going to drive him crazy. The same ideas for the website kept going around in his head, and none of them seemed right. He was getting to the point where he felt that he would somehow have to force himself to stop thinking about it if he was going to stay sane.

'Maybe give us a selection,' said Ben in exasperation, when Andrei had cornered him and Kevin in the common room again. 'Not the whole list, just a few names.'

'Then it won't be comprehensive!' objected Andrei.

'Andrei, we can't cope with comprehensive! How many times do I have to tell you? We're timid little creatures of limited brain-power. It's too much!'

'How big a selection?' asked Andrei.

'I don't know. Ten. Twenty. Something we can get our heads around.'

'How do I choose them? And don't say ranking. *Don't* say ranking. Ranking's not the answer.'

'Then do it randomly!' said Kevin, who was just as sick of Fishbowll as Ben, and even more exasperated by Dan Cooley's recalcitrance to every blandishment he could think of. 'Dude, give us ten, randomly selected. OK? That's it! I'm getting dinner. Who wants to come?'

'I'm coming,' said Ben. 'Is Charles around?'

'Who knows?'

'Charles ...?'

They waited for a moment.

'OK,' said Kevin. 'Let's go.'

Kevin and Ben headed out. Andrei followed them, shambling down the corridor and down the stairs disconsolately.

They went down to the quad and headed for Ricker.

'Do you really think that's what I should do?' said Andrei as they walked. 'Cut down the long list and just give a selection of names?'

Kevin sighed. 'Dude! Please! Enough!'

'I'm saying that instead of these gimungous lists,' said Ben, 'you should give us a randomly selected list that we can handle. Ten names. Whatever.'

'Put a gender filter in,' said Kevin. 'At least make it so we can choose the girls.'

'It's not a dating site!' retorted Andrei.

'Dude, every place you can connect with on the internet is a dating site.'

'That's too depressing.'

Ben shrugged. 'Ben's right, Andrei. Look at Dan Cooley.'

'What's he got to do with it? Has he developed a dating site?'

Kevin laughed. 'Only way he'd get a lay.'

'Dan responds to Kev—I mean *Jeff*, because he thinks Jeff's interested in him.'

'You think he's gay?' said Kevin, his face suddenly lighting up. 'Maybe I can offer him some kind of discount on Adidas sneakers for, like, gay buyers.'

Ben looked at Kevin incredulously for a moment. 'I'm not saying he's gay. What I'm saying is, Dan responds to Jeff because he thinks Jeff's interested in him. It makes him feel special. Once you feel special, you respond.'

Andrei had no idea what that had to do with Fishbowll. 'When you get a name on Fishbowll, it's obvious why you're interested in that person – because you share the same interest.'

'But why that person and nobody else in the five million names on your list?' said Ben.

Andrei shrugged.

'Exactly. You don't know. Look, Andrei, it's got to be a journey, and the journey has to start with some kind of impulse.'

Andrei stopped and stared at him. 'What does that mean?'

'I don't know, exactly. It's just ...'

'Dude, everything's a journey,' said Kevin.

'Everything should be a journey,' said Ben. 'This should be a journey of discovery.'

'It is!' said Andrei impatiently. 'You choose a name and you connect and you see what happens. What's that if it's not a journey?'

'Well, if that's the journey, people aren't taking it. It's like—'

'It's like they're in the departure lounge and they've got ten thousand flights on the board and who knows how the hell which ticket to buy?' said Kevin.

'Normally, you've got a ticket by the time you're in the departure lounge,' replied Andrei coolly.

'Andrei,' said Ben, 'whether you're in the lounge yet or not is not the point.'

'What is the point?'

'The point is no one gets on the plane! They see your list but they don't choose a name. And then they don't even come back to the site.'

'And that's their problem!'

'It's not their problem, Andrei. It's *your* problem. If you want them to use— Oh, sorry.'

They had stopped as they argued, and a couple of girls wanted to get past on the pavement. They stepped back and let them through.

'Put in a gender filter,' murmured Kevin, as they watched the two girls go.

'It's not a dating site!' cried Andrei in exasperation.

'Look, the gender filter's not important,' said Ben. 'It's the sense of journey. And the sense of being ... wanted. I don't know. Somehow, if you can get that, maybe you can do something with this.'

Andrei was staring after the girls.

'Andrei?'

'You like one of them?' said Kevin, glancing at the girls walking away from them. 'The one on the left, she's kind of hot.'

'I ...' For a moment Andrei continued to stare. Then he turned.

'Hey!' said Kevin. 'Aren't you coming to eat?'

Andrei was heading back to the quad.

'You want us to bring you something back?' called out Ben.

Andrei had broken into a kind of run. He turned a corner, and was out of sight.

'Well that was ... odd,' said Kevin.

Ben nodded.

'Should we go after him?'

'Why?'

Kevin shrugged. 'I don't know.'

Ben punched him on the shoulder. 'Come on. Let's eat.'

They went on to Ricker. Inside, they picked up trays and joined the queue. A few places ahead of them in the line was Dan Cooley. It had become second nature for them to glance at Dan Cooley's feet whenever they glimpsed him.

Three stripes!

Kevin and Ben looked at each other, expressions of incredulity breaking out on their faces.

'Hey, Dan,' Kevin said, taking a couple of steps forward, around the queue. 'Nice sneakers.'

Dan nodded.

'When did you get them?'

'I just bought them.'

'Cool. But aren't they Adidas? You like Nike, right?'

Dan looked at Kevin curiously, his mouth gaping a little, wondering how Kevin Embley, who he had spoken to maybe twice in his entire life, knew about that.

A few other people in the queue and at nearby tables were grinning.

'Don't you like Nike?' asked Kevin.

'I … changed my mind,' said Dan. The look of confusion on his face had grown deeper. He glanced around. Quite a few people were laughing now. A whisper was running around the dining hall. 'What's going on?' he said.

'Don't you know, you butthead?' yelled somebody from a table. 'Kevin's the guy you've been talking to sneakers about!'

Cooley stared. Now there was utter silence in the dining hall.

'Are you Jeff?' he murmured.

Kevin stared back at him.

Dan Cooley dropped his tray. 'There are rules here against that kind of thing, you know!' he yelled, and he ran out of the dining hall in his new Adidas sneakers.

There was laughter again.

'Dude, is there a rule against that?' whispered Kevin.

Ben shrugged.

Kevin glanced around. People were looking at them now. 'Shit,' he whispered. 'This doesn't feel good.'

5

SOMETHING HAD HAPPENED inside Andrei's head on that walk to Ricker. The arguments and conversations that had been brewing for so long inside his mind had formed a thick, fermenting mist that had seemed to be getting denser and darker, but suddenly all the murk and muck were blown away in one gigantic, cleansing explosion and he was left with pure, piercing clarity.

He got it. He absolutely got it. A gigantic list of names was way too impersonal, and way too intimidating. People wanted to connect with *people*. Not only did they want to connect with people – and this was the point he hadn't got until somehow Ben's words had flicked the switch in his head that had set off the explosion – they wanted to connect with people *who wanted to connect with them.*

So how did you give them that experience? That was the question.

Somehow, the answer was immediately there, as if it had been in his mind all along.

Andrei got to work, coding effortlessly, completely in the zone. At some point Ben and Kevin came back to the common room. He was oblivious to them. After a while, they gave up trying to tell him what had happened with Dan Cooley, almost fearful of what might happen if they did manage to disturb him, as one might be fearful of waking a sleepwalker.

Andrei kept the site simple and lean. When one opened Fishbowll as a user now, you were still asked what interests you wanted to share with others; you were still asked to choose between people from the whole world, a continent or a country. But then the site did something completely different. It asked whether you wanted to see the people who wanted to meet you, or whether you wanted to take a chance on seeing if anyone else wanted you to meet them.

If you clicked on the first option, a screen came up showing reduced-size screen-grabs of nine people's home pages. You could get a page view of the screen-grab by putting your cursor on the image. Under each image, in keeping with the piscine theme of the website, was a button saying, 'Take my Bait?' If you clicked on that, the home page enlarged to full screen, with a message box in the lower right corner to write to the other person.

If you clicked on the second option, up came a screen of nine reduced-size screen-grabs to which you could send a 'Take my Bait?' message of your own.

Andrei chose nine as the number of contacts, not out of any strict scientific rationale but because it seemed like the right kind of number – enough to give a meaty menu, but not too much to make it impossible to choose. A set of three by three screen-grabs also worked well on the screen. Every way he looked at it, this new format seemed to answer the objections everyone had raised. It was a selection of people – not a list of thousands. It made you feel wanted – these people had expressed a desire to meet someone just like you. It was the start of a journey – taking a Bait was the first step into the unknown.

The coding was simple to do. Everything seemed to flow – vision, design, code. A couple of inspired wheelspins and it was done.

But there was still a problem – no one was registered on the site, so there would be nobody to send Baits to anybody else. The first users who clicked on the option to meet the people who wanted to meet them would find ... nobody. And if they found nobody, nobody would ever come back.

So certain was Andrei that the site had to look as he now conceived it that he knew he had to come up with a solution. It turned out to be relatively simple. Rather than finding people who had registered and actually expressed a desire to meet others with a similar interest – which, one day, when there was a critical mass of users, the program would actually do – the program would initially search social networks and come up with a random selection from the thousands of people it identified with that interest. These would then appear with the 'Take my Bait?' tagline under their screen-grab. Obviously they had never asked to meet anyone, so if they were sent a message taking the Bait they didn't know they had sent, a tagline was added above the message that wasn't visible to the sender: *Fishbowll is a great new place to meet people from around the world who share your interests.* [SENDER'S NAME] *from* [COUNTRY] *thinks it would be cool to chat with you because* [HE] [SHE] *is interested in* [INTEREST THE SENDER SPECIFIED] *and has heard that you are too. Register on Fishbowll and talk to* [HIM] [HER] *today.* Next to this would be a Register Now button that would direct the user to the Fishbowll registration page, following which a screen would appear with the sender's home page and a message box.

In short, each of the people communicating would be under the impression that it was the other who had wanted to communicate with them first.

Obviously, out of the ensuing conversations between the two people, it might emerge that this piece of engineering had taken place, but Andrei imagined that in many cases it wouldn't and, if it did, would usually be put down to a glitch in the system. He knew there was a deceit involved, and Andrei thought hard about whether it was justifiable. He was utterly convinced that if the site was going to work, people had to feel that the other people they encountered *wanted* to talk to them, and until he got the necessary number of users on the site, there was no other way to create that impression. Andrei believed that people would want the functionality he was developing, and if it took a slight deceit to introduce it to them in a form they would use, he decided that that was an acceptable compromise. He rationalized it as a small, necessary and excusable evil with the potential to create more than enough good to outweigh it. Besides, it was a temporary measure. Once the site took off, he would be able to identify people who really did want to send a Bait.

Andrei had all kinds of ideas for ways to refine and improve the site as it grew and as user data began to come in, and he knew that a whole series of other ideas would occur to him as those ideas were put into practice. But there was one other element that was built into the design of the site from the start. Retained from the first version of Fishbowll, it was perhaps the feature that would turn out to be the most important thing about the site after the 'Take my Bait?' concept itself. Any kind of interaction was captured and stored. When two people connected on Fishbowll, even if they were accessing it through their social networking home pages, everything they subsequently did with each other – their chat, the pictures they posted, the videos they sent – was held on Fishbowll servers.

Andrei's motivation in doing this was to ensure that Fishbowll could always produce the most relevant and current view of a person's interests. But it also meant that, in theory, everything a user ever said or did could be retained, archived, and searched.

There was no specific rule against the experiment that Kevin and Ben had carried out on Dan Cooley – but it was a clear breach of the Fundamental Standard, the two-line statement of general personal responsibility that governed student life at Stanford. In extreme cases, a breach of the Standard constituted grounds for expulsion from the university. The Office for Judicial Affairs, which had oversight of student discipline, regarded any alleged infraction with the utmost seriousness.

As Andrei immersed himself in the reconstruction of Fishbowll, events moved quickly against Kevin and Ben. Only a week after Dan Cooley was found wearing Adidas sneakers in Ricker dining hall, a disciplinary board was convened to consider the case.

It was clear that Kevin would have to take the lion's share of the blame. It was his computer that had been used: he had set up the account, he had typed every keystroke, had posted every picture and had carried out a number of frankly illegal acts of hacking, which, if discovered, would leave the board no choice but to involve the police. There was only one way for Kevin to partially exonerate himself, and that would be to claim that Ben had told him what to do.

Kevin and Ben discussed this possibility and received the views of a number of other students – only some of which they sought. No one thought it would be a particularly smart move, not even for Kevin. Stanford was an elite institution and regarded itself very much as such. It seemed pretty certain that a Stanford disciplinary board would react worse to an apparently pliant and manipulable dupe who was unable to distinguish right from wrong when instructed by someone else than to a smart, self-motivated and curious junior who had gone a little too far in an innocent prank. If they were going to throw someone off campus, it was more likely to be a dupe than a prankster.

Kevin and Ben thus agreed that while Kevin took the blame for originating and executing the exercise, Ben would present as someone who knew from an early stage what was going on and, if guilty of anything, was guilty of not intervening to stop it. The board wouldn't take kindly to his moral failure, but the fact was that by the time the experiment came to an end most of Robinson House and quite a few people outside it had been guilty of the same lapse. Since the board, therefore, couldn't very well expel Ben without expelling a good percentage of the junior class with him, they thought this would protect him from the worst of the vice-provost's wrath. Kevin's fate would depend on the way he presented himself. Contrition was key.

A friend of Charles's had been up before a disciplinary board for a minor misdemeanour and they lured him to Robinson with promises of women and drink – only one of which eventuated – and got him to help out with a trial run. The night before the board, the common room resembled a lawyer's office the night before a trial, with Charles, his friend, Ben, and even Andrei breaking off from his Fishbowll coding to fire questions at Kevin.

It worked. Or perhaps some members of the board, guilty of a student prank or two in their own student days, secretly admired Kevin for his skill and originality in mischief-making. They put him on probation, asked him to sign a pledge to refrain from accessing any social networking sites for the next twelve months, and required that he see a counsellor. Ben, who felt chastened by the experience and wondered how he could have lost his moral compass to such an extent as to have allowed himself to get involved, received a stern rebuke but was let off without formal punishment.

Both of them were also required to apologise to Dan Cooley in front of one of the university officers and to hear his account of how the experience had affected him. Ben had already sought Cooley out to offer an apology.

It was about the best they could have hoped for. That night, Kevin organized a party in the suite. The whiff of alcohol soon attracted a crowd and the party spilled out of the door. Through it all, Andrei sat at his computer, headphones on his ears, in the last stages of coding. The building could have gone down around his head and he would have carried on tapping.

With a flurry of final touches, Fishbowll 2.0 was ready.

At around 2 a.m. that night, in early November, as the party was winding down around him, Andrei pressed the button to go live. He sent a message to his friends and acquaintances telling them about the new Fishbowll and asking them to try it again.

Then he opened the site once more, just to see what it would look like to someone who had never visited it before. A simple, uncluttered login page appeared in front of him.

WELCOME TO FISHBOWLL

A dating site for the mind

6

TWELVE HOURS AFTER Fishbowll went live for the second time, seventy-five people had registered and Andrei was getting positive messages in his inbox. By the end of the second day after launch, there were 200 users on the site, three times the number that the first Fishbowll had ever achieved.

By now, Andrei knew, the circle of users must have spread beyond his friends and acquaintances. Fishbowll had floated out into the open ocean of cyberspace, where the fact that Andrei Koss had developed the site was no reason to look at it. By the weekend, the 1000-user mark had been breached. A fortnight after launch, 40,000 users were registered.

Andrei watched the figures rising. Fishbowll was going viral.

He analysed the numbers. On average, each user who sent a Bait did so to 3.1 people, of whom, on average, 2.2 registered and responded. Of the 2.2 who responded, 1.7 in turn sent their own Baits to new users within forty-eight hours. Fishbowll had all the hallmarks of exponential growth, in which each new user in turn helped attract more users to the site, fuelling a surge in usage.

Every night Andrei checked the user numbers and yelled them out to whoever happened to be in the common room. Sometimes it was only to the fish in the aquarium, but not often. Kevin and Ben, with a Dan Cooley-sized hole in their leisure activities that was just waiting to be filled, soon became involved.

They loved the site – so much so that they wondered whether the design really could have come from Andrei, who had never previously shown any insight into the features that would ring a user's bell. But he had succeeded in doing that this time. The escalating user numbers proved it, as did the comments on Fishbowll that could be found in proliferating numbers by doing a simple internet search. On social networks, in chatrooms, in blogs, a small but growing group of fans was buzzing about Fishbowll. They loved the experience of finding others who shared their interests in places they would never have thought to look. They loved the idea of sending a 'Bait' and getting 'Hooked'. But there were other things they wanted. They wanted the site to produce better, more filtered Baits so they would end up with even more specific contacts. They wanted to be able to talk to more of those contacts than only one at a time. They wanted to be able to set up a Fishbowll home page that would be visible to others, which was something Andrei had never anticipated, imagining that people would continue to use their home pages on their existing social networks. And there were other demands. Everyone seemed to want a new functionality.

Andrei was wheelspinning as fast as he could just to keep the site running. With each step change in user numbers the program creaked, and its appetite for server space escalated. He was continuously coding to make the program more efficient. Sandy Gross would drop by, take one look at him sitting at his desk with his headphones on and a Coke in his hand, and leave without even bothering to try to catch his eye.

One night, Kevin pulled up a chair and asked if there was anything he could do, and Andrei was soon parcelling out chunks of coding to him. Wheelspins now involved the two of them sitting at screens at adjoining desks, headphones in ears, a slew of Coke cans on the floor between them, breaking off only to crunch a problem and then get back to work. In the meantime, huge amounts of data were being generated about user behaviour, which would have been invaluable if only someone had had the time to analyse it.

Ben didn't know much about programming, but he had a year of statistical techniques for his psychology major under his belt, and he was more than capable of giving himself a crash course in the methodologies he didn't know. But it wasn't only dry statistical analysis that was needed.

'We need a community,' Ben said to Andrei, soon after he got involved.

Andrei looked at him blankly. 'It's a dating site for the mind, Ben. We bring people together, we don't shepherd them.'

Ben shrugged. 'The users need a place to talk about the site.'

'They can email us.'

'No, they need to talk to each other. They're doing it anyway. They've set up pages on other networks.'

'That's good.'

'No, it isn't. They should be doing that on our network.'

'We're not a network, Ben. We connect people on other networks.'

'Well, they want more. I spend hours searching for their comments in all kinds of places.'

'You haven't done too badly.'

'There's stuff I'm not hearing because I don't happen to come across it. Why should we deprive someone of their right to be heard because I don't happen to type in the right set of keywords?'

Andrei looked at Ben thoughtfully.

'They have a right to be heard, Andrei. And if they have a right to be heard, we have an obligation to provide a forum for them to speak.'

'Yeah,' said Kevin, toying with the communal fly swat. 'And it will give them a stake, make them feel involved. It builds loyalty.'

'Plus,' said Ben, 'when there's something they want, or something they don't like, we'll hear about it first.'

They talked about it. Every spare minute now, they talked about Fishbowll.

Andrei wasn't persuaded by Kevin's argument. Loyalty, he thought, would be a function of the efficiency and user experience offered by the site. If that wasn't enough to make people want to come back, he didn't want to try to lure them by offering some kind of false sense of community. And he didn't think that would work anyway, not for long. But what Ben had said gave him pause. It was a serious point. What responsibility did he owe to his users? Less than a month in, there were over a quarter of a million of them now. Andrei's idea had been for a slim, functional site where people found other people – and that was it. He hadn't looked beyond that. But over the past couple of weeks he had had a growing feeling that this vision wasn't adequate for the beast that Fishbowll was becoming, and that the responsibility he had assumed in putting Fishbowll into the world was far greater than the responsibility of writing a piece of code and putting a user interface in front of it. He hadn't thought it through – hadn't had the time – and he didn't know what shape that responsibility would take or how far it would extend. In fact, there was something scary about even contemplating it. He hadn't anticipated this, but he knew he couldn't simply ignore it.

Sandy agreed with Ben. Some kind of community space on the site was needed. Andrei listened to her carefully. The female mind, he felt, was a closed book to him, and Sandy was about his only way of getting a peek inside. Only 38 per cent of his users were female. That wasn't high enough. He needed to understand what they wanted – he needed to understand what everyone wanted.

'All right,' he said to Ben, eventually. 'How would this community work?'

Ben shrugged. 'We'd have, like, a discussion page, I guess, where anyone could log their comments.'

'Once we start, they'll tell us how they want it done,' said Kevin. 'Let's listen to them. Dude, we're not trying to control what they do. This isn't Apple, right?'

Andrei grimaced.

'Exactly.' Kevin thought of himself as a libertarian and got on his high horse at the first whiff of control. 'Let's listen to the users. We should give them anything they want as long as nothing we do makes the world a worse place.'

'OK, let's give them a place to talk,' said Andrei. 'See if they want it. If they want it, we'll build it out. Let's do it.'

'What do we call it?' asked Ben.

'Good question.'

Andrei looked at the aquarium that had inspired the name of Fishbowll in the first place. On the sand at the bottom, in amongst the seaweed, was a scattering of objects for the fish to swim around. Some of them were the conventional things usually found in fishbowls, like a miniature wreck, and some were not so conventional, like a tourist model of the Golden Gate Bridge that someone had tossed into the water while Ben wasn't looking. Amongst the conventional items was a cave made out of some kind of brown stone.

'The Grotto,' said Andrei, still gazing at the aquarium. He looked up. 'You live in the fishbowl. You want to talk to your peers, dive down to the grotto.'

'Cool,' said Kevin.

Over the next couple of nights, Andrei created the Grotto. He announced its launch on Thanksgiving morning with a message on the Fishbowll login page. Within hours, it was unusable because of the sheer number of people trying to get into it.

The technical issues surrounding the Grotto were soon solved. Andrei dug into his savings – even further into his savings – to rent more server space. But it soon became apparent that having the Grotto wasn't as simple as Ben had suggested. Someone had to tend to it. It wasn't only comments that were posted there – questions turned up, suggestions, demands for a response from Fishbowll. A group of early Fishbowll users soon came to inhabit it, spending what seemed to be all of their time there. They were passionate and demanding about the site.

Andrei didn't have time to spend in the Grotto, and neither did Kevin, who was more often than not wheelspinning beside him. Imperceptibly, Ben became Grotto Captain and the online spokesman for Fishbowll. Complaints came in about users abusing others in the Grotto. Ben asked Andrei if he wanted to write a user policy. Andrei, heading into a wheelspin, asked if Ben could do it. Ben researched the user policies of half a dozen social networks and produced a Fishbowll version. Next came demands for a privacy policy, and Ben wrote that as well.

Out of the Grotto gushed streams of ideas for improvements and additional functionality for the website. Andrei, Ben and Kevin, whose class attendance time had plummeted, would spend hours in the common room debating them.

In the end, everything had to get past Andrei. His objective was to empower people to connect in the most efficient way possible. Out of this objective grew two technical tests that any new idea had to pass: simplicity and connection. Alongside these, a third test evolved informally in the long discussions in the common room: not making the world a worse place. As long as a suggested functionality didn't reduce simplicity and connection or manifestly make the world a worse place, Andrei was prepared to consider it. Allied to this philosophy of inclusiveness, one of the defining characteristics of the early Fishbowll was a willing-ness to allow users a meaningful voice in influencing the development of the site, an approach supported especially strongly by Kevin.

The first couple of months of Fishbowll's existence saw some of the other classic features of the website created. The demand from the Grotto to have home pages on Fishbowll was over-whelming, and this capability was soon provided. The functionality to set up group pages – or Schools, as they were námed, in keeping with the fish theme that was now running through the naming of everything on the site – was also developed, as was the ability to nominate oneself as a 'Fish' of someone else, receiving all posts relating to the shared interest that person made. This soon led to each person seeing on their website: 'How many Fish do I have in my Net?'

Kevin wanted this score to be publicly visible. 'Dude, we could give titles!' he said. 'Like, if you've got a hundred fish, you're a snapper. And if you've got a thousand fish, you're a tuna.'

'A tuna?' said Ben.

'Tuna are awesome fish. And if you've got ten thousand fish, you're a marlin. And if you've got a hundred thousand fish, you're a … great white!'

'A predator?'

'Dude. A hundred thousand fish. That's a great white.'

'Some people might see that as racist,' said Ben.

'Come on. A great white shark? Everyone loves great whites!'

Andrei held back from making the numbers visible to others, much less creating a category of predators with three rows of teeth. He feared it would evolve into a form of ranking by another name, and ranking was something he had avoided from the start.

To aid connection, he still wanted the journey to begin in a fairly random way so that the users would find themselves talking to people they would never have found otherwise. Later, in response to a growing clamour in the Grotto for improved filtering, he would relent and create two options when people wanted to send a Bait: 'Sorted' and 'Go Fishing', so people had a choice between more specific or more general lists. As the search algorithms became more sophisticated, he added 'Most Like' and 'Most Unlike' Baits, so that people could contact others from similar or different backgrounds.

Fishbowll acquired a logo as well. A friend of Ben's who was majoring in art history had connected with a Panamanian guy who shared his interest in the silverpoint technique of the Flemish Renaissance artist Jan van Eyck: they were both doing a thesis on the very same drawing. Ben's friend had dropped by the suite to tell Andrei how much he loved the site and found himself hanging out, as a lot of other people did, while Andrei wheelspun at his desk. He picked up a pizza box and started doodling on the lid. Two hours later, the result was on the login page.

Stanford students were, naturally, big users of the site. By the end of the quarter, coming to watch Andrei wheelspinning in Robinson House had become almost a pilgrimage for the most enthusiastic of them. In its last issue before the undergraduate housing was closed for Winter Break and the student exodus reached its peak, the *Stanford Daily* carried an article titled: 'Is the next Next Big Thing happening right here in Sterling Quad?' The writer, a liberal arts major, came to the suite and Andrei broke off from his screen to answer a few questions.

It was obvious she didn't understand the technical details behind Fishbowl so he didn't talk about them. She asked how many users he had on the site. Andrei replied that he wanted to find a way to bring people together, and whether a thousand people or a million people wanted to use the website, as long as some people found it useful, it was fine with him.

If he *had* given the number, Stanford would have discovered that after six short weeks Fishbowll had grown from the tame little creature Andrei Koss had launched on the world into a beast with a staggering 600,000 registered users, of whom an eye-watering 92 per cent visited the site on a daily basis.

The suite broke up for Winter Break. Charles Gok, for whom Fishbowll was merely a distraction as he made his way through the increasingly crowded common room to and from the physics lab each day, only had to travel as far as Los Angeles. Kevin went home to Chicago. Ben went back to New Jersey. Andrei got on a plane to Boston.

As the plane took off, Andrei felt something inside him take off as well. Maybe it was watching things grow smaller on the ground, but suddenly he felt himself looking at what he had done over the past couple of months as if from a height. Things had been happening so fast and with such intensity that he had had no time to try to understand it all. He had sat the exams for the Fall Quarter on the back of a couple of nights of intense cramming, and he knew his grades weren't going to be what they should have been. He really needed to think.

He decided that for the next two weeks he wasn't going to do any work on Fishbowll. He was going to step back and try to understand this thing he had created and which, in a few short weeks, seemed to have taken over his life.

And it wasn't only time that Fishbowll was taking, it was money. The site was chronically short of server space and there was only so much he could do by streamlining the architecture. He had already put in most of the savings he had in the bank from selling his app. If Fishbowll's growth continued at anything like the rate it was showing, a significant additional investment in server capacity would be required merely to keep it standing.

Back home, he told his parents about Fishbowll for the first time. His brother and sister were visiting for the holidays as well. He showed them the website. When he opened it, his sister, Dina, who was doing a PhD in chemical engineering at Princeton, started laughing. 'That's yours?' she said.

Andrei bristled a little, wondering what was so funny.

'I joined up last week.' Dina grinned. 'Leo,' he said to their brother, 'have you joined yet?'

Leo shook his head.

'What do you guys at Wharton do all day? Come on, this is the most awesome thing I've ever seen.' She turned back to Andrei. 'It's yours? You really wrote this thing?'

Andrei nodded, still not sure if Dina was pulling his leg.

'Mom, Dad, this thing's unbelievable. You've got to take a look at it. How many users have you got, Andrei?'

Andrei shrugged. 'Around half a million. A little more.'

'Half a million?' said Leo. 'In how long?'

Andrei shrugged again. 'A couple of months.'

'That's unbelievable!' said Leo.

Dina hit him on the arm. 'See? Join up already!'

Andrei's parents glanced at each other, wondering what their children were so excited about 'You're taking care of your school work, right?' said Andrei's father, waggling a finger at him.

'Sure,' said Andrei.

Naturally, Andrei couldn't quite keep his hands off his keyboard over the holiday, and he used the opportunity to fix a few aspects of the site's functionality that had been bugging him for a while. But he did force himself to step away and think about it as well.

Dina and Leo wanted to know more about the site, how he had got the idea, how he had developed it, what plans he had for it. Andrei wished he could have answered the last question. He took long walks along the icy streets around his parents' house in Brookline and tried to figure out what he had got himself into. Was Fishbowll a figment, a fancy, a programming whim, or, as he was beginning to feel, a revolutionary means of providing a radically deeper level of connection in a way that might change the world? Or was he just turning into a completely deluded fantasist?

As the old year ticked into the new, Fishbowll had 793,000 registered users. Three days later, Andrei was on a plane back to Stanford.

Even if he wanted to walk away from Fishbowll, or set it on the back burner while he concentrated on school, he wasn't sure that he had the right to. He had offered it to people and they had taken it up. Almost a million of them. They depended on it now.

He could sell it and let someone else – someone with the time and the money that was needed for it – take it to the next level. Even now, with the growth curve it had generated, he might well get something for it, perhaps even a seven-figure sum. Not bad for half a semester's work. He had school work to do and his future to think of, as his parents had reminded him, and just as a site's user base could rapidly grow, so it could rapidly fall. He was lucky enough to be at one of the world's great universities. He had a course to finish and he was barely more than halfway through it. He had neglected his studies badly since Fishbowll launched. If he kept going with it, he knew that Fishbowll was going to demand more of his time, not less.

And even if he wanted to keep going, was he the best person to do it? If Fishbowll had even a tenth of the importance that he believed it did, was he capable of building it as it needed to be built? And could he do it by himself?

As he flew went back to Stanford for the Winter Quarter, Andrei knew he had to make a decision. In fact, a number of decisions.

7

IT WAS KEVIN who organized the party to celebrate Fishbowll's millionth user – if hauling a heap of alcohol into a dorm and letting it be known that there was going to be a party could be called organization. The user count ticked over to the magic seven digits about two hours after the party started. Kevin jumped on a desk and announced that it was a 63-year-old lady from Saskatchewan who was interested in Scottish terriers. There was silence. No one knew what to make of that. 'I'm joking!' yelled Kevin. 'It's an eighteen-year-old girl in Rio who wants to know about fellatio.'

By the time they woke up the next day, the user count had ticked up another couple of thousand, and the million milestone already felt as if it was in the past.

'Let's go to Yao's,' said Andrei.

'For breakfast?'

'Kevin,' said Ben, 'it's twelve o'clock.'

They went to the noodle place. Andrei knew just about all the waiters by name. Lopez, a short Mexican waiter who had his arms piled with plates, nodded in the direction of a free table at the back.

'I wanted to tell you guys something,' said Andrei, after Lopez had taken their order and they were waiting for the food to arrive. 'I've been to see a lawyer.'

Kevin glanced knowingly at Ben for a second, then looked back at Andrei. 'You're selling Fishbowll, aren't you?'

'Why do you say that?'

'I knew you would,' said Kevin.

'Really? You think someone would buy it?'

'Dude, are you serious?'

'You think it's that good?'

'I don't need to tell you,' said Kevin. 'You know it better than me.'

Andrei shrugged. 'You get a buzz, the numbers go up. Then they go down.'

'Not this one. This is the real deal, Andrei.'

Andrei looked at Ben. 'What do you think?'

'I don't know,' said Ben. 'I don't know what makes a website work. But I can tell you, if you go to the Grotto, you've got a shitload of people who believe in this site. I mean, *believe*. Evangelical. It's scary.'

'Guys,' said Andrei, 'this site just sits on top of a whole bunch of social networking sites. It's like a network that connect other networks. A meta-network, if you will. It just connects home pages.'

'Not so,' said Kevin. 'People have their own Fishbowll home page now.'

'Some people. And if they stick to those, it just creates another silo. The point is to trawl the different networks – that's what gives the step change in connection.'

'And your point?' said Kevin.

'How long until one of the networks starts doing this themselves?'

'Why are they going to do that?' demanded Kevin. With all of two years of an economics major, he regarded himself as the business guru of the group. 'Dude, think about it. The whole point of their model is to keep people in their network. The walled garden. *Your* point is to put connectivity across those networks. Like you said, Fishbowll is a meta-network. It's like the brain. The social networks, they're like regions in the brain. Each one of them can only do so much. But connect them, and look what you can do.'

'And someone else will recognize that,' said Andrei. 'Maybe I should sell now before that happens.'

Kevin sat forward. 'What's going on? Has someone made you an offer? Has someone—?'

He stopped. The food had arrived.

'Thanks, Lopez,' said Andrei, as the waiter put down their plates.

Lopez smiled. 'Sure.'

'Well?' said Ben, when Lopez had gone. 'What's the offer?'

'There's no offer,' said Andrei. 'I'm just thinking. How defensible is this business? If I can do it, someone else can do it.'

'But they haven't,' said Kevin.

'But they will.'

'You're the first mover. That's why you've got the numbers you've got.'

'I've got a million. We need a billion.'

Kevin grinned. 'Give us a couple more weeks.'

Andrei took a forkful of his fried chicken and prawn noodles. 'Why shouldn't I sell the site?'

'What have you been offered?'

'Nothing, believe me. But let's say I was. It might be at its peak value right now, before someone tries to take us out.'

'You'd be giving it away.'

'Depends how much I was offered.'

'Whatever you're offered! Hell, sell it to me!'

'Kevin, you have nothing.'

'I'll give you an IOU.'

Andrei turned questioningly to Ben.

Ben frowned. 'I'm not a businessman. I don't know what it's worth. As to whether the big guys are going to eat you alive … I don't know. You'd think they would. But Kevin's got a point. There's a conflict. They don't want people going outside their network – and that's the core of what we do. They want to keep people in. All I can say is, psychologically, people have a hard time doing the opposite of what they've been committed to doing, even if that's what they say they want to do. But I don't know if that's the same for business.'

'It is,' said Kevin, with all the assurance of the junior economics major.

'I don't think it's a flash in the pan,' said Ben, 'but if you think now's the time to sell, Andrei, then I guess you should.'

'Dude, shut the fuck up!'

'It's his, Kevin. It's his choice.'

'He'll sell it to some corporate who'll just ruin it. Is that what you're going to do, Andrei? Sell it to some fucking big corporate like Homeplace? Then make them pay you a billion. At least make them pay for ripping the heart out of what we've created.'

'You're being melodramatic,' said Andrei.

'Am I?' Kevin looked as if he was about to leap up and tear his shirt off. 'Am I really? Then why are you selling to them?'

Andrei didn't reply. He ate a forkful of noodles. Then another. 'Fishbowll's about connection,' he said eventually. 'That's all. It's about inspiring people to connect in ways that are unexpected and exciting and important and can change the way things happen, the way they think.'

'Dude, I totally get it. So why are you selling—?'

'I'm not selling!' said Andrei impatiently.

'So why did you go to a lawyer? Why are you telling us—?'

'I want to know how committed you are,' said Andrei, cutting across him.

'And a lawyer's going to tell you that?'

'No. You are.' Andrei looked at each of them in turn. He said the words again. 'I want to know how committed you are.'

Kevin slapped his fist, knuckles down, on the table beside his bowl of noodles. The tendons stood out in his wrist. 'You want my blood?'

'Ben?'

'Andrei, this is the coolest thing I've ever been near. It's the biggest psychological experiment you can imagine, seeing how people use this network, seeing how they respond to what it offers, seeing what they say, what they feel, what they think, and I've got a seat behind the one-way window. I'm not going to ask you to hold on to it just for that, but—'

'Dude, he's committed,' said Kevin. 'All right? We're both

committed. And you know what, I was thinking over the break … since you're asking about commitment, and if you're telling us the truth and you're not going to sell, then I guess this is a good a time as any to say it …' Kevin coughed. 'Maybe you should recognize that. Our commitment, I mean.'

Andrei didn't reply.

'We both put in, Andrei. I'm not saying we contributed what you did. I'm not saying we had the idea or brought it to life. But I think, if it hadn't been for us, I'm not sure if Fishbowll would still be in operation. There were times over the last couple of months when I think you would have gone down without us.'

'So you want me to pay you?'

'No. I'm just wondering whether we shouldn't have some kind of … you know, some kind of a share.'

Andrei glanced at Ben.

Ben put up his hands. 'First I've heard of it. We haven't discussed it.'

'Dude, I'm just being honest,' said Kevin. 'I've been thinking about it. That's what I think.'

Andrei was silent for a moment. 'What are you going to do about school?' he asked.

'What are *you* going to do?' replied Kevin.

'I'm going to try to get through this quarter. I'm going to try to juggle things that far. Then I'll see.'

'What comes first?'

Andrei picked up a napkin and took a pen out of his pocket. He listed a set of dates: 1 February, 1 March, 1 April, 1 May, 1 June. Alongside each date he listed a user number, rising to hit 10 million by the last date. 'If we can track that growth curve, this comes first.'

Ben smiled. 'If you don't hit those numbers, you'll do more, not less.'

Andrei pushed the napkin across the table. 'I want to know if you guys are prepared to be in.'

'Dude, we told you we're in,' said Kevin. 'What part of "in" don't you understand?'

'Then going back to what you said before, I want you to have part of the company.'

'What company?' said Ben.

'The company I went to the lawyer to set up. This is getting big. I agree with you, Kevin – I couldn't have got this far without you, and I'm not exaggerating when I say that. It's going to get more crazy, not less. We haven't even seen the start of it.'

'So you're saying … you want to give us a share?'

Andrei nodded. He had no idea how he was going to manage his school work for the rest of the year, but he had no intention of selling Fishbowll, even if he could get some money for it. That wasn't why he had built the site. He had seriously asked himself if he was the best person to build the site and he had come up with the answer that he didn't think anyone else would understand his vision of connection the way he did. And that meant that if he wanted that vision to come to life, in all of its power and its purity, he had to keep building it. If he sold it, it would never be the Fishbowll it could be, and his vision would never be realized. Whoever bought it would prostitute it to advertising, like every other site on the net, to make as much money as they could.

But he couldn't do it by himself. That was something else he had decided very clearly. He had started something, and he had no idea where it was taking him. Already, after two months, Fishbowll was bigger, more diverse, more demanding – different, in almost every way – than anything he could have imagined when he began. It way too lonely to be doing this alone. He had felt that in the plane home, out of San Francisco, and he had felt it even more strongly coming back. He needed help. He needed brothers in arms, and those brothers were Ben and Kevin. He needed the way Ben listened, the way he thought. It was Ben who had come up with the idea for the Grotto, Ben who had said the things on the way to Ricker that had finally set off the explosion in his head that had made Fishbowll work. And he needed Kevin, who was as much of a wheelspinner as he was. He wanted them to be in, in a way that was strong and permanent. And if there was ever going to be any money in Fishbowll, he wanted them to have part of it too.

He had no problem with Kevin having asked before he had had the chance to make the offer. After the work he had put in, Kevin had every right.

'Ben,' he said, 'we wouldn't be here without the things you said to me. Kevin, you're a Stakhanovite.'

'What's that?'

'It's the old Soviet term for a hero worker, the guys who did more than anyone thought possible. We would have crashed and burned in week two without you. I want you to have fifteen per cent of the company each. But I'm going to need you to put in some money. We need more server space. I'm putting in everything I've got, every last cent I've saved. Can you find something? I don't know, talk to your families. Say, fifty thousand each.'

'How long will that take us through to?' asked Kevin.

Andrei glanced at the napkin with the numbers he had written. 'September? I figure we're also going to have to pay someone to help with the coding, and that should cover that as well.'

Kevin considered it. Obviously, Andrei wasn't going to divide the company equally, with each of them getting 33 per cent. Andrei had had the idea, he had made it happen, he had put in the initial funds for server space. He deserved to have more. Kevin hadn't settled on a share for himself that he thought would be fair. Twenty would have been nice. Ten would have been low.

Fifteen per cent of the company for $50,000 valued the business at somewhat over $300,000. Kevin believed in Fishbowll and its potential – $300,000 was nothing. If they did things right, he calculated that it would be worth a whole lot more than that.

'I'm in,' he said.

'Can you get fifty thousand?'

'I'll tell my parents any lie I have to. I'll tell them I got a girl pregnant.'

'Tell them something they'll believe,' said Ben.

'Funny. Very funny.'

'Ben?' said Andrei.

'I'm not sure. My folks don't have that much spare cash. Stanford's stretching them to the limit.'

'Call them. I want you in. You guys should get your own attorneys. I don't want you to feel there's any problem in the future. I've got my guy to draft an agreement, but we should make sure everyone is happy that this is absolutely fair.'

'I'm OK,' said Kevin. 'I'll talk to your guy.'

'I'm OK with that,' said Ben.

Andrei nodded. That was what he wanted to hear. He had felt he had to recommend that the others get their own lawyers, but if they had taken him up on the suggestion, he didn't know if he would have gone ahead with the deal. If they didn't have trust amongst the three of them at this stage, he didn't think it would work.

Andrei put out his hand. 'Welcome to Fishbowll, gentlemen!'

'Dude, we are going to make something awesome,' said Kevin.

Andrei nodded. 'I hope so.'

Ben and Kevin talked to their parents. Ben was able to raise only $30,000 and received 9 per cent of the company. Kevin produced $50,000 and received 15 per cent. The legal papers were signed a week later. Andrei Koss, Kevin James Embley and Benjamin Shapiro Marks became the founding owners of Fishbowll Inc., incorporated in Delaware.

Two weeks after the papers were signed and the money was handed over, Fishbowll hit a wall.

8

OUTSIDE THE SUITE in Robinson House, no one knew what was happening. Users only ever saw nine names at a time, out of lists that usually reached into the thousands, and often many thousands. So if those lists were reduced by 40 per cent, or 60 per cent, or even more, it wasn't apparent to them. But Andrei had detected that the list numbers had contracted dramatically.

A little more investigation revealed that names from Homeplace, the world's biggest social network, were no longer coming up on Fishbowll searches.

In an all-night wheelspin, Andrei and Kevin independently checked the relevant coding to see if a bug had crept in. Considering the tiers of functionality that had now been layered over the original Fishbowll search algorithm, it was possible that a piece of coding had been introduced that inadvertently had the effect of excluding the names. There was nothing. When they were finished – with a couple of dozen empty Coke cans scattered on the floor between them – they looked at each other wearily, knowing that they were going to have to check it all again.

Ben appeared, looking obscenely fresh after a full night's sleep, and asked what they had found.

'You know,' he said, when they told him they had drawn a blank, 'I was thinking, what if it's not us? What if it's them?'

'Homeplace?' said Kevin. 'They've got a bug? Is that what you mean?'

'No, I mean, what if they're keeping us out on purpose?'

'Keeping us out?' said Kevin incredulously. 'Dude, you think Mike Sweetman even knows we exist?'

'Well, maybe not us. I mean, maybe they're keeping everyone out. Anyone who's accessing them. Could they do that?'

Andrei and Kevin exchanged a glance. It was possible. There was constant tension between social networks, which wanted to keep people within their sites for as much of their online time as possible, and search engines, which wanted their users to be able to search social networks from outside. Technically, it would be a relatively easy thing for the networks to shield themselves from the web crawlers that the search engines – and Fishbowll, as well – used to access them. A cold war existed between them, with the potential to turn hot at any time. There was an unspoken understanding that Mike Sweetman, the CEO of Homeplace, and the CEOs of the other social networks weren't going to shield their services entirely. But it was a step that was just waiting to be taken.

And, naturally, if the war had broken out, as in any conflict there was going to be collateral damage.

There was a glum silence.

'If Homeplace gets away with this, every network is going to do it,' said Kevin eventually.

'But we don't just look at social networks, right?' said Ben.

'Dude, ninety-eight per cent of our names come from social networks. We're a meta-network. You can't be meta if you've got nothing underneath you. The social networks cut access – we're dead.' Kevin glanced at Andrei. 'Should have taken the money when it was offered.'

'I never had an offer,' said Andrei impatiently.

Charles Gok came out of the room he shared with Ben. Normally he walked straight through the common room, ignoring the wheel-spin or the discussion or whatever Fishbowll activity happened to be taking place. But this time he stopped. Even Charles could sense that something was wrong. The room was silent. Andrei, Kevin and Ben were just sitting there, looking miserable.

'Guys,' he said. 'You OK?'

They nodded gloomily.

He sat down. The silence continued.

'OK,' he said. 'This is fun.'

More silence.

'I'm going to go get breakfast on the way to the lab. Anyone want to come?'

'Not me,' said Kevin.

Andrei shook his head.

'Later,' said Ben.

Charles got up. 'OK, well, I'm going to go get dressed, and if anyone wants to, like, come to breakfast, that's cool.' He paused. 'OK,' he said, and he went back to his room.

The silence continued.

'So what the fuck do we do?' said Kevin. 'Do we just sit here and let them kill us? I just put fifty grand into this thing. My parents think I've got a girlfriend who's pregnant with twins.'

Ben laughed. 'Twins!'

'Dude, I don't know if I'd be so cheerful. You put in thirty. Well, that thirty will be a big fat *nada* if this doesn't get fixed.'

Ben's face changed. 'Can't we get it back? We only put it in, like, two weeks ago.'

Andrei sighed. 'Most of it's committed. I got a great deal on server space for paying up front.'

'And Kevin's right? Are we dead?'

'We have one and a quarter million users,' said Andrei. 'If we had a billion and a quarter, we'd be fine. But a million and a quarter ... that's not enough. We need access to social networks. That's our oxygen, Ben.'

'Shit,' said Ben. 'Isn't there anything you can do? You know ...'

'What?' said Andrei. 'Write some code that gets around whatever they've put in place? Hack into them? Is that what you mean?'

'I don't know. Is that what I mean? Well, OK, maybe we should do that.'

'I don't know if that's a very sustainable way to build what we're trying to do here,' said Andrei.

'But if it's necessary for survival? Would it make the world worse?'

'To hack into Homeplace?' A bout of hacking always appealed to the libertarian in Kevin, regardless of the justification. 'To give our users the full level of connection they had before? No, I don't think it makes the world worse. I think it makes it a hell of a lot better.'

'If it means we don't survive in the long term because of legal issues,' said Andrei, 'then it does make the world worse, because we're not in it. A world without Fishbowll is definitely worse than a world with it.'

'And dead men don't get sued,' said Kevin pointedly. 'Dude, we're going to be road kill. We're going to be dead before Mike Sweetman even knows we existed.'

Andrei frowned. 'You know, my father is no businessman, but he knew a few. Back in the nineties, he saw the way guys in Moscow made billions. He often says to me that timing is the most important thing. You wait, you wait … and then you do what you have to do.'

'What does your dad teach again?'

'Linguistics.'

Kevin raised an eyebrow.

'Kevin, he's an academic. He's not good at doing stuff, but he's very good at analysing stuff. And he's seen some people operate. You don't know what Moscow was like in the nineties.'

'So without the homespun Russian philosophy,' said Ben, 'what exactly are we going to right now?'

'Well, first of all,' said Andrei, 'we don't know that Mike Sweetman has done anything to shut down access. It's a possibility. It's also a possibility that there's a bug in our program.'

'Andrei,' said Kevin, 'we've been all over our—'

'And secondly,' continued Andrei, 'if he has done something, we're going to know about it soon enough. Or, as my father would say, *Slukhom zemlya polnitsya*.'

'Which means?'

'We'll hear about it.'

They did. A day later, the world's biggest search engine announced what the blogosphere was already saying: it was being blocked from Homeplace. Immediately, the cannons were lined up. The usual hackneyed transparency arguments on one side were launched against the usual hackneyed privacy arguments on the other side. Fishbowll watched as the heavyweights of the internet world argued principles when everyone knew that the real interests at stake were their ability to attract users, learn about their preferences and sell advertising. Transparency suited the search engines; privacy, the social networks. How much of each the users actually wanted didn't seem to figure at all.

Every blogger on the net and every tech pundit on mainstream media weighed in. Politicians had their say. Soon the dark forces of the internet were attracted to the fray and a number of denial-of-service attacks, designed to overload the targeted services and render them unusable, were launched at companies on both sides of the divide, with each side accusing the other of fomenting the unrest. A previously unheard-of group claimed responsibility with a plague-on-both-their-houses statement and issued a manifesto prickling with anarchist ideology.

Everyone had been expecting a skirmish like this to happen for so long that no one seemed to ask the one question that should have been first to everyone's mind: why now?

As the conflict settled into an edgy stalemate over the next few days, Andrei monitored the list sizes generated by Fishbowll searches. They ran steady, at 30 to 50 per cent of the sizes before the crisis had broken, suggesting that other social networks were watching before acting, waiting to see the outcome of the conflict. The more ardent users of Fishbowll had noticed the absence of Homeplace contacts. Questions were being asked in the Grotto. Andrei told Ben to let them go unanswered. Those who knew about the way internet searches were constructed would already have worked out that Fishbowll must have been affected. Everyone else, which was the vast majority, was unaware of it. User growth on Fishbowll was continuing at the same rate as before.

Homeplace still hadn't formally admitted to what it was doing, but it faced the possibility of a backlash from its own massive user base. Mike Sweetman had a record of taking so many liberties with their data and trying to dominate their usage of the internet in so many ways that no one trusted that anything he did was in their interest. Those users were also users of search engines, and the search companies were hoping they could persuade them that search would become ineffective if transparency levels were allowed to fall so low.

But perhaps the threat that had most impact on Sweetman wasn't anything that had developed in response to the internet but a century-old judicial weapon that government had in its locker to wield, if provoked, against overmighty business.

There was a lot of unease in certain political circles that social networks were creating monopoly positions on the net, locking users into their services in ways that users didn't understand or found it almost impossible to opt out of. Antitrust law gave the Department of Justice the power to act against monopolistic practices and it had already let it be known that it was monitoring the behaviour of the largest social networks. Cutting access by search engines to Homeplace would only move it closer to action.

There was never any formal admission that officials of the nation's law enforcement arm met Mike Sweetman in those weeks after he blocked access. It was possible that the Justice Department's increasingly pointed public statements were sufficient. In any event, three weeks after Andrei had first noticed the Fishbowll's list sizes contracting, Homeplace took down its blocking program. Immediately, Fishbowll's list sizes were back to normal.

The search engines trumpeted it as a victory for transparency on the net. Their shareholders trumpeted it as a victory for their share price. Andrei, Kevin and Ben thought they had merely been lucky bystanders. They learned better the next day.

9

'ONE HUNDRED MILLION,' said Andrei.

Ben and Kevin stared at him.

'*Dollars?*' said Ben.

'No, rubles.'

'Mike Sweetman's offering you a hundred million dollars?' said Kevin.

Andrei nodded.

'When did this happen?'

'He called me this morning.'

Ben and Kevin glanced at each other.

'What did you say?' asked Ben.

'What would you have wanted me to have said?'

Ben frowned. 'I don't know.' He drew a deep breath. One hundred million dollars. His stake would be worth $9 million.

'How long have you been talking to him?' asked Kevin.

'I haven't,' said Andrei. 'He just rang me today. I've never spoken to him before.'

'Has he seen our figures?'

'No.'

'Our user numbers?'

'No.'

'Seriously?

'He hasn't seen anything.'

'And he's offering you a hundred million?'

Andrei shrugged.

Kevin shook his head in amazement.

They were at Yao's. Lopez stopped at the table. 'Everything OK?'

'Fine,' said Andrei.

'You're not hungry?' asked Lopez, nodding towards their barely touched food.

'We're just talking.'

Lopez shrugged. 'You know, me, when I want to talk, I don't order a plate of noodles first.'

Ben laughed. 'We're going to eat.'

'OK. Mr Yao, he won't be happy if I take those plates back full.'

'We won't send them back full, I promise,' said Ben.

Lopez looked at them doubtfully and then moved on.

Kevin turned to Andrei, hunched forward over his plate. 'What the fuck did you say?' he hissed. 'Come on! What?'

'I said no. What do you think I said?'

'You said *no*? You didn't even tell him you'd think about it?'

'I said no.'

'Dude, you said no to a hundred million dollars?' Kevin leaned back. 'What the fuck are you doing? He can crush us. Isn't that what he just showed? You know what? I think that's what that blocking was about. Us!'

'I agree. It's possible.'

Kevin clenched his teeth and looked from side to side, resembling some kind of rodent trapped in a cage. 'It was about us! Fuck! We never realized! It wasn't about the search engines at all. It was about us!'

'That's how it would appear.'

'Just to show us that he could crush us.'

'No,' said Andrei.

'Andrei,' said Ben. 'I think Kevin's right. That's what he was showing us.'

'No, I don't think he was trying to show us,' said Andrei. 'I think he was trying to do it.'

'Crush us?'

64

Andrei nodded.

'What makes you say that? Did he say it?'

'No, but he offered me a hundred million dollars. Guys, if you can crush someone, you don't offer them a hundred million dollars. That's way too much, don't you think? Even for a guy like Mike Sweetman. If that's what you think you'll have to pay, you wouldn't just show them – you'd go ahead and do it.'

Ben raised an eyebrow. He had always known that Andrei was very cool, very rational. Sometimes he felt that he lacked a certain degree of emotion. Suddenly, he saw the power in that coolness and rationality.

'Don't you think so?' said Andrei. 'If you really feel you can crush them at will, then you offer some desultory figure, saying, basically, you're not worth the effort I'd have to go to to destroy you.' Andrei picked up a forkful of noodle. 'If he'd offered me ten million, I probably would have said yes.'

Neither Kevin nor Ben tried to persuade Andrei to accept Mike Sweetman's offer. Each of them had his reasons. Like Andrei, Kevin was encouraged by the sheer size of the offer. He began to think that Fishbowll might end up being worth a lot more than Mike Sweetman's number. Ben, on the other hand, was more detached when it came to the question of Fishbowll's value. He had never really thought about what Fishbowll might be worth and was happy to accept Andrei's judgement on that. He also didn't think he had much of a right to try to influence Andrei one way or the other. Unlike Kevin, who understood the programming behind Fishbowll and who had therefore played a large part in its development, Ben felt that he contributed far less and was simply lucky to be a part of this extraordinary thing. He would be happy with whatever he eventually got out of it. He was fairly certain that would be a lot more than the $30,000 he had managed to scrape together from his family, and whether that was the frankly staggering sum of $9 million for his 9 per cent share, or more, or less, wasn't something he was too concerned about at this point. He had managed to become part of Fishbowll, he wanted that to continue, and he knew that would be unlikely if Andrei sold it to someone else.

Over the next few days, there were moments when Andrei did find himself suddenly thinking: Someone offered me a hundred million dollars! And I turned it down! It would have been easy, very easy, to call Sweetman back and take the offer. He would have $76 million for his share of the business. For a semester's work.

But he didn't call Sweetman back. Andrei really believed the offer showed that Sweetman had tried to take them out, risking a move that he hadn't dared to make before, and only pressure from elsewhere had prevented him from succeeding. Perversely, that gave Andrei faith in Fishbowll's viability. It also meant that Sweetman saw the type of service Fishbowll was offering either as a huge threat or a huge opportunity. Either way, it gave Andrei faith in Fishbowll's value. He didn't know if Sweetman had been offering high or low – Mike Sweetman had been known to pay over the odds in the acquisitions Homeplace had made as it became the world's leading social networking site, and a couple of his deals had been at prices that hadn't only raised eyebrows but made people laugh out loud. But even if Fishbowll was worth only half of what Sweetman had offered, or a quarter, it was still worth a significant sum. And, anyway, that wasn't the most relevant point. Andrei had barely begun to make Fishbowll what he thought it could be. He wasn't going to let someone else get their hands on it now.

The episode also made something else clear to him. People were watching Fishbowll.

Despite the fact that by now he had close on a million and a half users, and a Grotto full of people yelling and screaming about what they wanted out of the site, somehow it had still felt like a world in itself – as if Fishbowll and its users existed in some kind of quiet, protected space, unnoticed by anybody else. Not even the interview with the *Stanford Daily* had changed that feeling. It was a student newspaper, the 'journalist' had been a liberal arts major. That interview hadn't felt as if it was something out there in the real world. But this was. Suddenly the real world was all around him, imposing itself. It was as if some false, illusory walls had collapsed and suddenly he could feel the cold wind of reality blowing in his face – a wind that had actually been blowing all the time.

Out there, people were *watching* Fishbowll. Not only were they watching but they were prepared to hit, and hit hard. Mike Sweetman had been prepared to go to war with the search engines to take him out.

In a way, it was a compliment. A very, very dangerous one.

Andrei wished now that he had never given the interview to the *Daily*. Fishbowll's explosive growth had happened without any publicity, and it seemed to him that was the best way to do it. Rightly or wrongly, he connected Mike Sweetman's attempt to strangle them with that nterview.

But the genie was out of the bottle. And the truth was, even if Andrei had never spoken to the *Daily*, it would have jumped out by itself. The buzz around Fishbowll was like a brushfire fanned by the wind, visible as a glow even from a distance away.

People were becoming aware of it. People who had their ears to the ground of the internet for all sorts of reasons.

At around 11 a.m. on a day in late February when Andrei, Kevin and Ben should have been in class but were Fishbowlling in the common room, there was a knock on the door. The visitor was a slim, trim man in his thirties, wearing a suit. He asked if this was the office of Fishbowll Inc.

Kevin laughed. 'Dude, no one's ever called this an office.'

The man repeated his question, unsmiling.

'I guess it is,' said Ben.

'I'd like to speak with your chief legal officer.'

10

THE MAN WAS an FBI agent called John Dimmer who worked out of the Palo Alto resident agency. After he had established that there was no legal officer in the company, and after he had identified which of the three young men in the common room was Andrei Koss, he asked Andrei if there was somewhere private that they could go.

For want of anywhere else, Andrei took him into his bedroom. As they stood between two unmade beds in a room that could have done with an airing, Dimmer took an envelope out of his pocket and explained that he had brought it over personally because he knew this was the first time the company had received one of these and the FBI didn't have a named officer to send it to.

Andrei took the envelope hesitantly.

'It's a National Security Letter,' said Dimmer. 'Do you know what that is?'

Andrei shook his head.

'It requires you to hand over data on a number of specified internet address holders.'

'What do you suspect these people of doing?'

'That's none of your concern, Mr Koss. This request is part of an investigation into international terrorism or clandestine intelligence activities, which gives us grounds to issue you with this letter. That's all I can tell you. Read the letter. I'll wait. You may want to consult an attorney, but I'll answer any questions you have.'

Andrei opened the envelope. He took out two stapled pages. The first one had the FBI shield printed at the upper left corner.

Andrei read over the pages.

'Let me go over the main points for you,' said Dimmer. 'This is serious, so it's important you understand them. You are legally required to provide this information. You do have the right to challenge this request in court, but I can assure you that this letter meets the requirements of the relevant federal legislation and executive order and you will not win. Note carefully the information you are required to provide. We are not asking for content, only the transactional information on these account holders – activity logs, header information, etcetera. Note also, and this is particularly important, that you may not disclose the contents of this letter or even its existence to any person other than if required to provide the data requested or to obtain legal advice, and anyone to whom you do disclose it is bound by the same requirement. If you do disclose it to any other person for purposes of fulfilling the request, I may require you to give me their names. It is also your duty to inform them of this non-disclosure requirement. Do you understand this, Mr Koss?'

Andrei nodded.

'The penalties for breaching the non-disclosure requirement are severe and you would be prosecuted.'

'How long do we have to give you this stuff?' asked Andrei.

'Like it says right there on the second page. Fourteen days.'

Andrei hadn't taken that in. He hadn't taken quite a lot in. His mind was still trying to process the fact that he was embroiled with the FBI over an issue of national intelligence.

'Do you have any other questions?'

'I can consult an attorney about this, right?'

'Yes. Like it says on the second page, your attorney will be bound by the same duty of non-disclosure. He'll understand that when he sees the letter. Something else I want to make sure you understand – when you send the data we've requested, you need to hand it personally to me or use a secure delivery service. It's in the letter but I want to make sure you've got this. Do not use the routine mail. Do not use email and attach it. If you have any questions for me, you can call me, but do not mention this letter on the phone. Calls are not secure. You can say that you want to discuss something and that will be enough – we'll arrange a meeting. All this stuff is in the letter, but I'm saying it in case you don't think it's serious. It is serious. If the substance of this request is disclosed to subjects of the investigation as a result of a telephone call that is intercepted, the lives of a number of people may be at risk. You will also be subject to prosecution. Do you understand, Mr Koss?'

'Yes.'

Dimmer gazed at him for a moment. 'OK. Unless you want to do this stuff yourself from now on, you need to nominate an officer to receive these things. You're going to be getting more of them.'

Dimmer left. Andrei sat on his bed. He felt as if someone had just punched him hard in the stomach. The wind of reality that he had felt blowing in his face a few days earlier when Mike Sweetman had made him his offer had just got a whole lot colder.

He read the letter again, this time trying to take in each of the points. Then he sat back and closed his eyes.

Eventually he got up and went out into the common room. Kevin and Ben watched him. Wordlessly, he put the letter down on the desk. 'Read it,' he said. As they did, he got on the phone to their lawyer.

The lawyer Andrei rang was the one who had drawn up the agreement between the three founders. He knew nothing about National Security Letters and sounded as if he didn't want to, but he said he could find them someone who did. The following day, Andrei and Ben went to see the attorney he had suggested. On reading the letter, Kevin had let out a blast about Fishbowll becoming an agent of the government, and Andrei didn't think it was going to be productive to have him in the room.

The attorney looked at the letter and explained that, as the FBI agent had said, it was a lawful demand that could be made by the government without need for a court order. He asked what kind of business they were in and when Andrei told him what Fishbowll was, he nodded knowingly. He explained that, as the letter stated, they were required only to provide transactional data – dates, times, email addresses, IP addresses – but not the content of any communications.

'Is this common?' asked Andrei.

'The government issues about one hundred thousand of these a year.'

'*One hundred thousand?*'

'In the business you're in, you're going to see a lot of these.'

'Should we challenge it?' asked Ben.

'Do you have grounds?'

Ben looked at Andrei, who shrugged.

The lawyer described the grounds for challenge. 'Be aware that the government will contest your challenge as high as it needs to go. It does whatever it can to avoid precedents that could impair its ability to use this instrument. It will involve you in considerable expense. But that doesn't mean you can't win if you have grounds and you're determined. There have been cases where the government has had to back down or modify its demands. But it's a long and very costly process.'

Ben and Andrei glanced at one another again. The company's finances were thin enough as it was.

'What do most people do when asked for this data?' asked Ben.

'They hand it over.'

'Homeplace? Would they be doing that?'

'I would imagine that occasionally, in some exceptional case, they might haggle with the FBI, but mostly they would probably hand it right over.'

'The FBI agent said they'd win if we challenged.'

'He would,' said the lawyer. 'Unless you have grounds to challenge, this is perfectly legal, remember. This is above board. You may not like it, but right now it's the way our justice system works. No court needs to authorize this. But remember, it's only the transactional stuff you have to give them.' The attorney smiled for a second. 'As you probably know, the government has its own ways of getting at the good stuff.'

Back at Robinson House, Kevin predictably blew up again. But Andrei didn't see an alternative. Instinctively, he didn't want to hand over the data, and felt that he was compromising himself. He had heard so much about the way the government's intelligence agencies operated that he had no idea if they really had a case against the suspects they were supposedly investigating, or if it was just a fishing expedition. But he couldn't imagine that he would win a court challenge, and he didn't see the point of wasting Fishbowll's dwindling reserves of cash on a quixotic attempt to avoid a foregone conclusion.

The problem prompted a number of lengthy discussions. It made them determined to ensure that Fishbowll's security would always be as strong as it could be in order to prevent any unauthorized gathering of information on their users, to the extent that that was possible. But this instance wasn't unauthorized,and not even Kevin had an answer to the simple reality that the law required them to comply. All he could say was that it was wrong.

Andrei thought they needed to understand what Fishbowll was there to do. Was it there to challenge the law? Did it have an ideology it wanted to promote? While Kevin blustered, Andrei talked through the questions with Ben. Eventually, Andrei decided that Fishbowll was neutral. It had to be neutral. If people wanted to challenge the law, it was a medium for them to do it – the medium, not the message.

In the end, Andrei handed over the data to Dimmer, still feeling conflicted about it. He told the agent that in future Ben would act as the officer to be contacted for National Security Letters. It wasn't long before more of them arrived.

11

AS FISHBOWLL GREW, the three founders struggled to keep up with their class work. The academic authorities at the university had got to know about the website and while they had no power to stop anyone working on it – and had their own interest in seeing a successful tech start-up emerging from Stanford – they let Andrei, Kevin and Ben know that they were expected to maintain their studies. Amongst themselves, the three young men had agreed that they would each do the minimum required to get through their courses until the end of the academic year. Every other waking moment was devoted to Fishbowll.

The common room of the suite in Robinson was an engine house. Andrei and Kevin would be deep in coding, Ben would be analysing user statistics, responding to questions in the Grotto or dealing with inquiries coming from the press, which were becoming increasingly frequent. Andrei didn't want to talk to anyone. Ben became the unofficial spokesman for the company with instructions to keep the press at bay. A couple of other programmers Andrei knew from his class at Stanford, and who he was now paying to work on Fishbowll, were often crammed into the common room as well. People wandered in and out, wanting to be part of the buzz. Being college students, they engaged in long philosophical discussions about Fishbowll – its place, its purpose, its principles – and drinking games. One fuelled the other, and vice versa. While Fishbowll's dealings with the FBI remained a secret shared only by the three founders, every other topic was fair game.

When Andrei had his headphones on and a clutch of Coke cans beside his screen – which was most of the time – he ignored the chaos around him. When he took the headphones off, he joined in. The mantra in these all-in talkfests was not making the world a worse place. Despite the myths that would later develop about which of the three founders had originally articulated that slogan, none of them could actually remember who had said it first or what they had been talking about at the time. But over the last few weeks it had become the touchstone for the company and its fellow travellers.

The numbers kept growing, running far ahead of the figures Andrei had scribbled on the napkin at Yao's. The early users who had taken to the Grotto had established themselves as a kind of self-appointed advisory community through the sheer depth, intensity and fanaticism of their debate over every feature and change in Fishbowll, no matter how minor. They had developed a group page within the Grotto that they called the Cavern and although there were no enforceable rules about who could go there, it was quickly made clear to interlopers that they weren't wanted. No one knew exactly how many of them there were, but in the common room at Robinson House they became known as 'the 300', after one of Andrei's favourite epic movies. Their comments crowded out almost everyone else on the Sunken Wall of Atlantis, as the site for public comments in the Grotto was known. Although the three Fishbowll founders had never met any of them, they felt as if they personally knew the more prominent members of the group. They were almost phantom figures inhabiting the common room alongside them, especially for Ben, who spent much of his time responding to their comments.

There was Karl Morrow, for instance, who was always angry. Even when they made some kind of change that he had been aggressively demanding for weeks, he was angry. Ben devised a measure of the degree of Karl's anger called the Morrowmeter and he tracked it whenever an idea was under discussion. It was generally agreed that, as a rule, the angrier Karl was, the better the idea. At the other extreme of the spectrum was Barry Diller, or the Dillerman, as he was dubbed in the common room. The Dillerman had a reputation for finding a way to defend everything Andrei did. Some of the 300, never shy of conspiracy theories, aired suspicions that the Dillerman was actually Andrei himself, especially since he said he was from Boston, which was Andrei's home town. Whenever they were testing some new innovation on the site, Andrei only had to ask Ben what Karl Morrow and the Dillerman were saying in the Cavern in order to hear the two extremes of the spectrum.

But as Fishbowll's growth exceeded Andrei's projections, so did something else.

It had been surprisingly easy to say no to Mike Sweetman's offer of $100 million, but now Fishbowll ran the risk of going out of business for want of a couple of hundred thousand. They were burning through cash almost twice as fast as Andrei had anticipated. One night, Andrei took a look at the numbers and did some new projections. He estimated that if Fishbowll kept growing on the same trajectory, by May they would have exhausted the funds they had put in and the company would be broke.

Andrei didn't think he would be able to get anything from his parents, who had shown no inclination at Christmas to encourage what they considered to be a distraction from Andrei's school work, despite Dina's and Leo's attempts to persuade them that it was much more than that. It was pretty clear that there wouldn't be more forthcoming from Ben, who hadn't even been able to raise the full starting sum. Kevin's family was wealthier but even with another fifty or a hundred from Kevin, how much longer would that keep Fishbowll in business? There was Sandy, of course. He could try to tap her family for funds, but he had the sense that would only be putting off the inevitable. Logic dictated that the site eventually would need to be able to generate money in order to keep going.

At some level, Andrei had always known that, but somehow he just hadn't engaged with it in his mind. He hadn't expected the moment to arrive so soon.

There was an obvious solution to the problem, of course.

Andrei baulked at it. His aim was to make Fishbowll as efficient as possible – allowing advertising on the site would do the opposite. Measured against the twin technical tests that he used to assess any new functionality – improving connection and retaining simplicity – it failed on both counts. He believed it would contribute nothing towards connection, and would reduce simplicity. And even if it didn't, the idea of advertising nauseated him. Site after site in social networking, in search, in so many other functions on the net, had started off with apparently good intentions and ended up as not much more than vehicles for intrusive advertising steered by the rape and pillage of user data. He hadn't founded Fishbowll to join their number.

Kevin, on the other hand, had no opposition to the prospect. He had always expected advertising to be the ultimate revenue generator for Fishbowll and had no philosophical problem with the idea. From his libertarian standpoint, he regarded advertising as a form of expression that was as legitimate as any other form of expression in a free society, and it would be up to Fishbowll's membership to accept or reject it. Ben, who saw Fishbowll as a massive social experiment, suspected that advertising would inevitably affect the way it developed – but that would be interesting in itself.

Sandy, like Kevin, saw no problem either. Her father was an oil company executive and had reconciled his own genuine sense of social responsibility with the dirty reality of the industry that funded his lifestyle by adopting the view that, while the world certainly needed changing, all you could do in the meantime was work with it as you found it. As she grew up, Sandy rebelled against that suspiciously convenient accommodation and had called her father a hypocrite on more than one occasion. Yet now that push came to shove in regard to her boyfriend's nascent business, she turned out to have more of her father in her than she might have suspected. Her attitude was briskly pragmatic: 'You have to survive,' she said to Andrei. 'So? You let in advertising. As long as you know why you're doing it, you can still retain your integrity.'

But Andrei wasn't so sure. That was probably what Mike Sweetman had told himself at the beginning, he thought, and look what had happened to him. Homeplace had become a byword for the appropriation and exploitation of user data.

As Fishbowll's financial position worsened, the issue came to dominate conversations in the common room. Everyone who turned up had an opinion, often reflecting the fact that they had the luxury of not actually having to make a decision. But for the three founders, the need to find funding was real.

Since Andrei was so reluctant to allow advertising, they tried to think of other ways of raising cash. Kevin came up with the idea of creating virtual goods and selling them. 'For every School we've got,' he said, 'there's probably some kind of virtual goods we can create and sell. Take the Saddam Hussein memorabilia group. We could create, I don't know, avatars of Saddam or 3-D cyperspaces of his palaces and sell them.'

'Aren't people already doing that?' said Ben.

'It's just an example.'

Andrei stared. 'We've got a Saddam Hussein memorabilia group?'

Ben nodded.

'And they're selling avatars?'

'Dude, check out the Grotto,' said Kevin. 'Half the place is a bazaar.'

'When did people start doing that?' demanded Andrei

Kevin laughed. The libertarian in him loved the filthy, opportunistic, entrepreneurial Wild West that the Grotto had become. 'Probably about as soon as we set it up.'

The problem with the idea, which Kevin himself immediately pointed out, was that they would be competing with a large array of other sellers that had already moved into the marketplace they had inadvertently created. He doubted they could generate revenue quickly enough to solve their cash crunch. Besides, they would have to hire people to monitor what was happening in the Grotto, identify the opportunities for virtual goods, and create them, and that would add more cost just when they were struggling to keep going. It was such a great idea, it might eat them alive before they ever got to see it work.

Rather than trying to create virtual goods, Ben suggested simply taking a cut of the transactions.

'Dude,' retorted Kevin, 'you're turning into the government!'

'No, we provide the Grotto, so it's like we're providing the real estate and we're taking a rent—'

'We're taking a sales tax!' said Kevin, picking up the fly swat and whacking the armrest of his chair with it.

'It's a service fee.'

'It's a tax. No! We're not taxing anybody. We're creators, not taxers!'

Andrei agreed. He then came up with the idea of developing virtual money for the transactions in the Grotto, taking a fee for issuing and managing the currency. Kevin didn't think that was much better than Ben's idea. 'Dude, you're turning us into the Fed! If you guys want to do stuff like that, why not just charge a membership fee?'

'Don't be an idiot,' said Andrei. 'No one's going to pay a fee.'

'We could say we're not for profit. We could ask for donations.'

Andrei gazed at Kevin suspiciously. Of the three of them, he was the least likely to propose that idea.

Kevin laughed at the preposterousness of his own proposition. 'And you can kiss goodbye to any of the development ideas we've got. We'll be lucky to raise enough to keep going.'

'I don't know,' said Ben, 'it's possible—'

'Dude, someone else will start up and do exactly what we're doing for free, because they'll let in advertising. And not only will they make a shitload of money, they'll build a better, faster, smarter service for their users, and nobody's going to fork out anything for the slow, shitty service that we'll be offering. Anyone who does this is going to let in advertising, because that's the only way to make this thing work.'

There was silence.

'I like the currency idea,' said Andrei.

'That's because you thought of it,' muttered Kevin.

'We'll call it Fish Food. Fish Food comes in all shapes and sizes.'

Kevin shrugged. If he had to choose between Ben's idea and Andrei's, he preferred Andrei's, but only marginally. But in any event, like his own virtual goods proposal, it would take time to get going, and would impose more costs up front.

'Maybe we should take an investment,' said Andrei, when they found themselves hashing over the problem again a couple of days later and another few thousand dollars down in their bank account. Apart from Mike Sweetman's $100 million offer for the whole company, he had had some calls from venture capitalists asking if they could come and talk to him. Some of them had even made preliminary offers over the phone.

'Sure,' said Kevin. 'And you know the first thing they're going to say to you? How do you monetize this business? And if advertising isn't part of it, that's the first thing they're going to ask for. At least this way we have control. We don't hand it over to a bunch of corporate suits. And we can be smart about this. I'm not talking about banner ads. I'm not talking about anything that's going to deface the site. Say you log on to your home page and you get a message about a some selected aspect of your specific interest. You know right away it's about something you're really interested in. It's giving you knowledge as much as trying to sell you something – it's giving you information you need to know because of your interest. It's a service as much as anything. This doesn't have to be the same as everybody else. We can do it in a totally Fishbowll way.' Kevin leaned forward. He waved the fly swat for emphasis.

'Do you know what we have here, Andrei? We have *the* most targeted list of audiences for advertisers in the history of the world. This is fucking awesome or awe-inspiring or whatever the word is. Most sites, you know, people say what they're interested in, and you try to target like that. Or on the basis of searches they've done or stuff they've previously bought.' Kevin snorted. 'Like advertising for what you bought yesterday isn't closing the door some time after the horse has bolted! How dumb is that? But *we* can generate data on the things people care enough about to actually go and find like-minded people. Things that they're going to be interested in today, tomorrow, next week, and interested enough in to spend some money. That's gold-plated, Andrei. Advertisers will pay a shitload of money to get to those people.'

Andrei wasn't blind to that fact. The very power of the data he was generating, paradoxically, increased his reluctance to let in advertising. It seemed almost too powerful, the responsibility of using it too great. Where would it lead?

He started work on the Fish Food idea. But even as he did, he knew Kevin was right about it. Even if he could get it launched quickly, and even if Fish Food took off, the revenues were going to be a slow build. But there was nothing slow about what was happening to their bank balance. The pace at which it was emptying was frightening.

He could find an investor, but an investor, as Kevin said, would only demand that he start advertising. The result would be the same – the only difference would be that he would have given away a chunk of the business and the control that he currently had.

Yet still Andrei couldn't bring himself to do it.

But the bank balance didn't lie, and it was giving him less and less room for manoeuvre. A few nights later, after looking over the latest dismal figures in the company bank account, he walked into the room he shared with Ben. Ben was buried in a psychology text, a rare moment of academic work. Andrei sat down glumly on the edge of his own bed.

Ben looked at him. 'Hey,' he said, then turned back to his book. He read for a moment, then looked up at him again.

'We've got six weeks left,' said Andrei.

'Until what?'

'Until we don't have any money.'

Ben closed the book.

'Six weeks, and then we can't pay for the servers.' Andrei shrugged. 'That's optimistic. It might only be five.'

'That doesn't sound good,' said Ben.

There was silence. It hung thick between them.

'What about Fish Food?' asked Ben eventually.

Andrei shook his head.

'You don't think it's going to work?'

'Not quick enough.' Andrei frowned. 'Do you think we should go with advertising?'

'Do we have a choice?'

'That's not what I asked. Do you think we should?'

'What's the alternative?'

'We could stop. We could say, OK, we came this far, and that's it.'

'And then what?' said Ben. 'Sell it?'

'Maybe. Maybe just stop.'

Ben gazed at him in bemusement. 'And the money we put in ...?'

'I know.' Andrei sighed. 'Look, I know what Kevin wants. His mind's made up. If it was up to him, we'd start tomorrow. I want to know where you stand. Should we let in advertising or not?'

'You've got the majority share, Andrei. You can do anything you want with the company.'

'I want to know what you think, Ben!' Ben's opinion made a difference to Andrei in a way that Kevin's didn't. Ben thought about things, he considered them on their merits. Kevin always ended in the same position from which he had started.

Ben was silent for a moment. 'I'd prefer not to,' he said at last, 'but we've got to recognize reality. Our first principle is not to make the world worse, right? Well, let's assume that without advertising we go out of business. So we stop, like you say. Let's forget about the money we put in. The question is, is the world a worse place with a Fishbowll that has advertising or with no Fishbowll at all? Because those are the alternatives, right?'

'If we go out of business,' said Andrei, 'someone else will do it.'

'Right, and let's assume they'll allow advertising. Or we could sell it to someone who will, which is effectively the same thing. So, for the sake of this argument, there are really only two options. One, Fishbowll with advertising that we control. Two, a Fishbowll copy or a sold Fishbowll with advertising that someone else controls.' Ben shrugged. 'If those are the only options, then doing two definitely makes the world a worse place, because I think it's fair to assume that anyone else controlling Fishbowll would not be as responsible as us.'

'But that still leaves the world a worse place than Fishbowll with no advertising.'

'But that's not a realistic option, Andrei.'

'That just means option one is the least worse. It makes the world worse by less than option two. We didn't say that our objective was to make the world a less worse place. It was not to make the world a worse place, period.'

'Maybe the least worse is the best you can do right now.' Ben leaned forward. 'Andrei, you've put this thing into the world. You can't take it out again. If you try, someone else will put it back there. So it's a question of us or someone else. And I think, if that's the question, it's a no-brainer. Having someone else do this rather than us makes the world worse. So that means we've got to go with advertising.'

Andrei didn't reply.

'We don't have to do it like everybody else. Kevin's right. We don't have to be like Mike Sweetman and wring every last drop out of the stone. We can do just enough to keep ourselves going, if that's what you want. And in the future, if Fish Food works, we can stop. This isn't irreversible, Andrei. Maybe it's just a tempo-rary thing we need to do. I think if we explain it like that, people will understand. I think even the 300 will understand. Karl

Morrow will hit the roof but, then, when doesn't he?' Ben grinned. 'The Dillerman will find a way to make it seem OK.'

'Even the Dillerman will have trouble on this one,' murmured Andrei.

'You might be surprised. People know the reality. It takes money to keep going.'

Andrei sighed. A deep, long, troubled breath. He didn't have to do it like Sweetman or any of the other net entrepreneurs who had sold their ideals, as he saw it, for a fistful of cash. He could do it any way and to any degree that he chose. But still he felt that something was happening, a line was being crossed, and, once crossed, whatever Ben said, it couldn't be crossed back.

'OK,' he said eventually. He put his head in his hands and nodded a couple of times. 'OK.'

Ben watched him. 'We don't need to sell our souls.'

'I guess not,' said Andrei quietly.

'The thing is,' said Ben, 'I don't know how we even do this. How do we make this happen? You say we've got six weeks' cash left?'

'Five, to be safe.'

'Where do we start? Do we go out and hire somebody? How do we start getting the money in, in five weeks? Do you know how to do this stuff?'

Andrei shook his head.

'Does Kevin?'

'I doubt it.'

'I don't think we've got the time to make it up as we go along.'

'I know,' said Andrei.

Ben looked at him questioningly.

'There's a guy who's been bugging me,' confessed Andrei. 'Somehow he got my number. He's been calling me for weeks.'

12

ED STANDISH FIRST learned of Fishbowll when his nephew, an engineering senior at Duke University, came home for the holidays and raved about the site over Christmas lunch. Standish was a Dallas-based advertising executive for a firm called 4Site, which had developed a lucrative practice helping internet start-ups build and target their advertising offerings. At forty-six, he was accustomed to dealing with twenty-something tech guys and had honed a keen sense of what worked on the net.

That Christmas night, when the kids had gone to bed and his wife had collapsed in front of the TV, he opened Fishbowll, registered, explored the site and found an advertising-free service. When he went back to work two days later, he did some research about the website, took a closer look at it and tried to figure out what income stream they could have. He wasn't able to come up with anything. Unless he was missing something, or unless they had backing from a deep-pocketed investor who had no interest in getting a return on his money – a mythical creature, as far as Ed Standish was aware – that was an unsustainable situation. Ed then wondered if they had already done a deal with another agency, so he did a search of the trade media to find out if it had been reported. Then he did some calculations about Fishbowll's revenue potential under various assumptions, and immediately wondered how 4Site could get a piece of it.

He got an assistant to ferret out Andrei Koss's phone number and started ringing. The first couple of times Koss answered, then he didn't. Standish kept trying, on average, a couple of times a week. If Koss was ignoring him, he figured, at least he knew who he was. He wanted to keep reminding him. At some point, Koss's attitude might change, and Standish wanted to be the one he thought of.

He would have kept going for a year if necessary. But he didn't need to. Koss rang him.

Mentally clearing his diary of anything that was in it, Standish said he could be in Palo Alto the next day. He asked Andrei where he wanted to meet.

Andrei gave him the name of the first place that came into his head.

Standish stood on University Avenue with the 4Site colleague he had brought with him. They were both dressed in open-neck shirts and chinos. Standish was a little overweight with receding reddish hair. The other man, Andy Merritt, was dark-haired, good looking and young. Ed Standish knew that he himself looked an unlikely type to specialize in dealing with tech start-ups, and liked to have someone who fitted the stereotypical mould at a first meeting to set the tech guys at ease.

'You sure this is the place?' said Merritt doubtfully.

Standish looked at the name on the door. Yao's. 'This is it.'

In they went. They found Andrei, Kevin and Ben sitting at a table with the remnants of a meal in front of them. Standish wondered if this was some kind of weird power play on Andrei's part, to have him turn up like a supplicant while they were eating.

The truth was, while they were meant to meet at one o'clock, Andrei had got hungry and had headed down for lunch at twelve.

Standish introduced himself and Merritt and then sat down.

'Do you want to order?' said Ben, looking around for Lopez.

Standish shook his head. 'We're fine. Andy, you OK?'

'Sure,' said Merritt.

'Let's talk,' said Standish. He started by congratulating Andrei on Fishbowll and said that 4Site had a team that tracked developing companies in the internet space and Fishbowll was the most exciting thing they had seen in years. 'Everyone at 4Site is dying to work with you guys.'

'What control will we have?' said Andrei by way of reply, jumping straight to one of the two main things on his mind.

Standish looked at him blankly for a moment.

'Over the kind of advertising we do,' said Andrei. 'You said on the phone we'd have control.'

Standish smiled. 'It's something we'd work out together. Like I said on the phone, this has to be win-win for you and your users. The kind of advertising you put on the site has to enhance the experience. It's something your users have to value. We know how important that is. We'll have time to discuss that.'

'What if any advertising we put on the site can only detract from the experience? What if they come to the site because they want a site where there is no advertising?'

'Well, Mr Koss,' said Standish, quickly abandoning his plan for how he wanted to direct the conversation and deciding to go along with the stream of questions coming at him, 'if that's the case, then you don't want us. But I doubt that's the case.'

'You don't know our users.'

'What I do know is that not a single website that I'm aware of – and you can correct me if I'm wrong – has ever been abandoned by its users because of advertising. I don't know of a single case where it's had negative impact of any duration. A lot of hot air, but nothing real. Do you know of any examples, Andy?'

The younger advertising executive shook his head.

'People are realistic now,' said Standish. 'They expect it. They know the internet doesn't come for free.'

'Andrei's got very high principles,' said Ben.

'That's good,' said Standish. It wasn't the first time he had had to deal with a start-up founder agonizing over introducing advertising to his site. Most of them got over their qualms pretty quickly. 'Look, it may be, Andrei, that you're thinking this is some kind of betrayal of why you started Fishbowll. And I understand that. But the bigger betrayal, I think, is if you're not businesslike, if you let your principles – which I respect – get in the way of making sure that you can provide the best possible service for your users, or, even worse, your survival. You've got to raise money in order to do that. Let's face it – that's the reality. We're here to help you do that in the way you're comfortable doing it. We're not here to try to make you put anything on the site that doesn't work for you. In the long run, that's not smart. Even if we earn a little more today, that means we all earn a whole lot less tomorrow. I don't like to think of it as who has control, as such. We work this as a partnership. That's how we at 4Site always work. Our experience is that that gives the best results.'

Andrei watched the advertising man silently, wondering just how much of what he was saying was bullshit.

Standish smiled again. 'Look, I haven't even told you what we offer. Let me take a few moments to tell you. We think your site has incredible advertising potential for specialist companies seeking their unique audience. We have a few slides we can look at to show you what I mean.'

Standish gestured to Merritt, who reached under the table and extracted a set of thin, bound folders from a bag. Standish pushed aside the plates on the table and handed them out.

Standish opened a copy of the file. 'Skip the first couple of pages – just the usual company wadding.' He grinned. 'Yadda, yadda, yadda. OK, let's look at page four. Now, I don't know what the other agencies you're talking to have been telling you, but I'm not going to sit here and tell you that you are going to be the number one choice for every company under the sun. A Coke, a Bud …' Standish shook his head '… you're not a great channel for them. Maybe when you're really, really big, when you can put a billion eyeballs on their ads … great. But, right now, for me, it's about specialized services and goods. We think you're an unparalleled venue for that kind of client – and this is not exactly niche. If you look at the next page … we're talking about an annual worldwide advertising spend for clients of that type of upwards of a hundred and fifty billion dollars.' He chuckled for a moment. 'Not that you'll get all of that – at least not at once.'

'I think we could figure out what kind of company we'd appeal to,' said Andrei.

'Fair enough. I'm sure you could, probably better than me. But you need to get to them. How do you do that? That's where we come in. You're going to spend a lot of time and need a lot of people and spend a lot of money if you try to get to that kind of client yourself, especially as an unknown website. Just getting to their VP of marketing or their advertising agency will be a challenge. What do you think they do when *another* internet start-up calls up? What you'll struggle to achieve with ten calls, we can get in one. I know that, because that kind of clientele is our sweet spot. We have the knowledge and the network and the experience and the resources to identify and target those clients and bring them to you in a way that would take you years to replicate if you had to do it yourself. And I'm guessing, if I'm right, that you don't have years.'

Andrei didn't reply.

'What's the deal, Mr Standish?' said Kevin.

'Good question. I know this is going to sound kind of cheesy, but the most important part of the deal for you is what I've just said. 4Site's network and experience. We work with net companies, amongst which are many start-ups. We know the challenges you'll face and we know how to solve them. I skipped these before, but go back to the first couple of pages and you can see some of our credentials.'

Ben and Kevin flipped back. Standish noticed that Andrei didn't. He decided to ignore the credentials and move on to the next subject that he guessed was on Andrei's mind.

'There are financial aspects, of course. That's summarized on page six. We'll guarantee revenue to you of a million dollars in the first year, with a rising guarantee depending on performance over years two and three. Also, our deal includes an introductory commission for the first twelve months of twenty per cent rather than the normal rate of twenty-five per cent. That helps you get established and gets your cash flow going. I'm guessing you guys may not be too familiar with advertising models but you've probably already found out from the other agencies you're talking to that twenty-five per cent is pretty much a norm and twenty per cent is a genuine discount. Now, of course we don't know your user numbers or time on site or any other metrics so on the next page you can see what we've assumed. As long as we're in the ballpark, we're happy to honour these terms.' He smiled. 'Actually, we'd love to honour these terms.'

'How much is upfront?' said Andrei.

'How much of what, Andrei?'

'How much of the million you guarantee?'

'We normally pay that quarterly.'

'Quarterly in advance?'

Standish shook his head. 'Over the year, we expect you to be considerably ahead of the guarantee. What we do is top up quarterly to – in this case – a quarter of a million dollars if you don't make the numbers, and we'll take that back when you make up the ground. That gives you certainty over your cash flow, which is helpful to most start-ups. What we would expect here is for the next quarter or two, we would be making up the payment and then later, when the revenues get going, we'll adjust that back. What you can be sure of is getting your quarter million minimum each quarter.'

'But not in advance?' said Andrei.

'Is that important, Andrei?'

Andrei frowned for a moment, wondering if he had given too much away. Then he said, 'The other agencies we're talking to are prepared to consider that.'

Merritt glanced at Standish. The older man's face showed no reaction.

Andrei turned a page in his file and glanced at the numbers. 'We're considerably ahead of the numbers you've assumed.'

'Great,' said Standish. 'You'll do even better. The million guarantee, Andrei, is a minimum to give you some certainty as you plan. Now, I don't how much the other agencies are offering you but a million in this circumstance is a considerable sum – by far the highest offer I have ever made to a new start-up – and 4Site is happy to do that because of our belief in your business. Even on the numbers we've assumed – and you say your numbers are even better, and I believe you – and even with our reduced commission, you should do a lot better. I'm estimating at least two to three times better. If you don't, we take the hit.'

'How long does the contract run?' asked Andrei.

'Three years.'

'Is that exclusive?'

'That's exclusive.'

Andrei nodded. He got up. 'Thank you.'

Standish looked up at him in surprise. 'What's wrong?'

'I wanted to know whether you were serious.'

'Andrei, we're offering you a million-dollar guarantee over the next twelve months. I think that says we're serious.'

'Do you know how long three years is in internet time? Three years is a lifetime.'

'Andrei, sit down, please. We're serious. We think Fishbowll has enormous potential and we thought you'd want a partner who was prepared to commit to a substantial involvement. That's why we said three years. But if three years is too long, I'm sure we can manage something else. Sit down. Please.'

Andrei sat. 'The numbers you've assumed in your presentation, the numbers you have for our users and visits and time on site, we're over double that on every one of those.'

'How far over double?'

'Significantly.'

'That's awesome.'

'I want to be fair to you,' said Andrei. 'I understand that if we're going to do this, you have to have some time to benefit from the investment you make. I think an eighteen-month deal is fair.'

'You know, eighteen months is quite a short timeline, once you set up and start to roll out. I think if we could do two years—'

'Eighteen months from go live,' said Andrei. 'That's a clear eighteen months. And the one million – we're over double the numbers you assumed, so let's guarantee that in the first six months, not the first year. And I don't like this quarterly thing. I'd like half up front, the rest at the end of the six months.'

Standish watched him, absorbing what he was saying.

'After that, you have another twelve months before we look at the contract again and I'd expect a guarantee of two million over the following year. And your commission – fifteen per cent, not twenty. We get control over what kind of ads we do and how we do it. If you object, then you can terminate. That's fair. We keep whatever you've paid us, you walk away.'

'We do need to collaborate on the way we do the ads, Andrei. Like I said, that's something we do know quite a bit about.'

'Well, we can talk about it. But we have final say. If we have an irreconcilable difference, you can walk away.'

'And what happens at the end of the eighteen months?'

'We'll see. If you've done a great job, why wouldn't we stick with you?'

Standish took a deep breath. 'OK, let me make sure I know what you're saying.' He flipped over his file and began to jot down bullet points on the back. 'Eighteen-month deal … Exclusive … Guarantee of a million in the first year—'

'Six months.'

'Sure, sorry. Guarantee of a million in the first six months, two million in the following twelve months … Fifteen per cent commission … Control of ads …'

'And the first million – half up front and half after six months,' added Andrei. 'Don't forget that.'

Standish nodded, making a note. He gazed at the list. Merritt peered at the page and pointed at a couple of things, then looked at him meaningfully. Standish ignored him. 'I think what you're asking for on the commission is … that may be a little too steep. I'm going to have to go back to my board with this. I need a little something.' He looked up. 'What if we split the difference? Seventeen and a half?'

Andrei shrugged. 'Make it eighteen.'

Standish smiled, crossing out fifteen and writing eighteen. 'OK. I am *pretty* sure I can get this past my board. But I need to know something. If I do that, if I get my board to agree, do we have a deal? What I can guarantee you is that if my board agrees to this, they won't renegotiate it if you come back with something else. And they're not going to let it hang out there. They won't allow 4Site to become part of some kind of negotiation where you're talking to other parties and you're playing us off against someone else. If I get you these terms – and these are great terms for you, Andrei – that's it. That will be 4Site's bottom line, and you'll have twenty-four hours to agree. After that it will be off the table, and if we do offer you anything again, it probably won't even be as good as the terms I started with.' Standish paused, looking to see Andrei's reaction. 'Now, I can talk to my board first thing tomorrow. I can have a draft letter of agreement with you end of day. That means you'll have until the end of the following day to agree – then it's off. And it's going to be our bottom line. I'm not joking.' Standish put out his hand. 'On these terms, do we have a deal?'

Andrei gazed at him.

'Yes or no?'

Andrei nodded.

Standish smiled, shaking his hand.

'Send me through the draft,' said Andrei and he got up. Ben and Kevin got up as well.

The two 4Site executives watched them leave the restaurant.

'What an arrogant prick,' muttered Merritt.

Ed Standish laughed. 'What would you have said if he'd gone for three years? That he was a stupid prick?'

'He worked you over, Ed. Eighteen per cent? We've still got to sell this to the board.'

'Easiest sell I've ever done.'

'They'll kill us. What was wrong with you? He was begging for the money up front. Couldn't you see that?'

'Of course I could see that.'

'You could have got him to sign up for anything as long as you were dangling that half million in advance. I would have—'

'What, Andy?' demanded Standish sharply. 'What would you have done? Tried to screw every last dime out of him? And how long is he going to stick with us then? Do you understand the potential this website has? Have you thought about it? This is the best fucking deal 4Site has ever done. It would be the best deal at twice the price.'

Merritt snorted.

Standish chose to ignore that. 'You want to eat? I'm hungry.' He looked around for a waiter. 'All I'd like to know,' he said, as he waited for Lopez to come over, 'is what we have to do to invest in this company.'

Outside, on University Avenue, the three founders of Fishbowll walked away.

'Whoa!' whooped Kevin, fists in the air. 'Dude! Awesome!'

Andrei stopped. Suddenly he was trembling. His heart was thumping.

'Where did you learn to do stuff like that?' demanded Kevin. 'I would have said yes to the first deal.'

'That was pretty damn impressive, Andrei,' said Ben.

Andrei shrugged. He didn't know where he had got the idea, or the courage, to do what he had done. All he knew was that the first deal was no good because he had to get money up front. A guarantee of money in arrears was no use to him, and if he wasn't going to get that, nothing else mattered. Once he had decided to push back over that, he had just kept going and pushed back on everything. He was just as astonished at himself as the others were. And it had felt easy.

'My father always says, "Push hard",' he said. '"Push hard and then harder." Always get up and make them call you back.'

'Is that more of that oligarch stuff?' asked Kevin.

Andrei nodded.

'What about giving him that extra half a per cent? We could have got seventeen and a half. You gave him eighteen.'

'If you can, make people feel like a winner.'

'That's from your father as well?'

'Yeah. Make them feel like a winner – or else make sure you have a very big man you can call on.'

Kevin and Ben laughed.

'He's never applied any of this,' said Andrei in a tone of bewilderment, still wondering at what he had just done. 'It's talk. When we bought our house in Boston, he paid the exact price they asked.'

'Dude, who cares? What else did he teach you?'

'Nothing. That's it.' Suddenly Andrei frowned. 'That was pretty good, wasn't it?'

'That was awesome.' Kevin whooped again. 'You are the negotiator.'

As they headed back to Robinson, Andrei thought about what had just happened. He had learned a lesson. When people came to him with an interest in Fishbowll, he could push them hard. Very hard.

But he had winged it. He had gone into the meeting totally unprepared – hadn't even taken the obvious precaution of talking to another agency. He had only Ed Standish's word that 25 per cent was the standard ad agency commission. He had no idea if a million dollars was a large guarantee or a small one. And now he had reached the end of his father's crude and theoretical teachings about success in business.

By the time the three of them were crossing Sterling Quad back to the dorm, Andrei's sense of wonder at what he had just done had been replaced by a sense of foreboding. They were amateurs. They were three clowns who had turned up for that meeting and somehow come out of it without being recognized for what they were. There was so much, Andrei suspected, that he didn't know, that he didn't even know enough to know that he didn't know it.

13

THE HALF A million dollars from 4Site arrived a fortnight later. Andrei sat at his screen, checking the bank account every ten minutes until he saw it arrive. He yelled to the others. Kevin let out a whoop.

The first advertisements were on Fishbowll within four weeks, almost six months to the day after the site was launched. When users logged in, they saw a button titled, 'Sponsored Bait', with a tag underneath: 'Check it out to see if you get Hooked!' The button gave no idea of what was being advertised. Embracing Ed Standish's idea that advertising, if possible, should complement and even enhance the user experience, Andrei had worked to find a form of advertising that would reinforce Fishbowll's central vision – the taking of a journey into the world of your interests where the destination was unknown. He guessed that if people didn't know what was being advertised, but were certain that it would chime with their interests, they would be more likely to click to find out what it was about.

Andrei had announced the move in a post in the Grotto. He had thought hard about the attitude to strike and had talked it over with Ben, who knew the mood of the Grotto better than anyone. They both knew they were going to face a backlash, especially from the 300. Although Andrei wished he didn't have to do what he was doing, Ben thought the backlash would hit harder and last longer if he was apologetic about it. People would feel that if they shouted loud enough he might relent. He decided therefore to be positive and upfront. He also decided to announce the move only the day before it was implemented. A prolonged debate before people had the opportunity actually to experience the advertisements for themselves would inevitably be fuelled by misconception and fear, and would play into the hands of people opposed to advertising or to change in general – which, Andrei knew, would be just about everyone.

'Fellow Fish,' he wrote, 'tomorrow we are introducing Sponsored Baits on Fishbowll. The reality is that if we are to continue to provide our service, and make the improvements you are telling us you want, this is something we have to do. Our aim is to bring you messages from highly selected and trusted partners about things you are genuinely interested in, many of which will include special deals available to Fishbowll users only. The Sponsored Baits will be clearly identified – you don't have to click on them. If you do click on them, and if you're not interested in what they are offering you, tell us, and we'll tell them! If you are interested, tell us about that as well. Most of all, keep telling us what you think of Fishbowll and how we can improve it. Happy swimming, Andrei.'

The users did tell them. The traffic in the Grotto reached record highs and the 300 erupted in a storm of verbiage. The Morrowmeter was off the scale: 'Sponsored Baits?' ran one typical message. 'Why not call it what it is? Fishbowll sells out like all the others.' 'How are they targeting those ads?' said another. 'What about privacy? I'm outta here.' 'Shame on you, Andrei Koss. You're no better than the others.' And so it went on. The Dillerman valiantly fought Andrei's corner: 'Guys, what do you expect? If the site we love is going to survive, it's gotta have a revenue stream. Andrei's doing it in the least bad way. Let's help him out. Click on these Sponsored Baits to make sure he gets the cash to keep going!' A shitload of abuse was poured over the Dillerman's head but he and a small number of supporters kept writing similar things. Some messages even turned up that were actually positive: 'I love Sponsored Baits! I found something I didn't even realize I need. I'm totally Hooked!' Those messages were met with the suspicion that the people posting them secretly worked for Fishbowll. Andrei denied that in a second post he issued a few days after the Sponsored Baits appeared. He also reassured users that although their data was used for targeting purposes, as was standard practice on all networking sites and in keeping with the privacy policy that Ben had drafted – largely by copying the policies on those other sites – no actual person at Fishbowll had access to that data, which was analysed by a totally automated set of algorithms.

Naturally, a School soon formed of people whose interest was in stopping Fishbowll sending Sponsored Baits. Its membership surged to over 100,000 but there were never more than a couple of hundred active members, and the frequency of their protests soon fell away. For a brief period there was a larger than usual number of deregistrations, then growth of the site returned to normal. Apart from a few lunatic free-netters, as Kevin described them, who left the site to find the next outpost of cyberspace where they hoped the realities of the world would never impinge on their dream of getting something for free for ever, the rest of Fishbowll's membership seemed to accept reality, albeit not always with the best humour. The heat gradually went out of the battle, and sponsored Baits became an accepted feature of the Fishbowll seascape.

When it was over, Andrei was amazed at how easy it had actually been and how transient and negligible was the response to what he had done, despite the volume of noise that it had generated. Just as the experience of Mike Sweetman's attempt to crush Fishbowll, which he connected with the *Stanford Daily* article, made Andrei forever wary of the press, his experience of introducing advertising to Fishbowll – the first major risk he had taken in the site's functionality – left a lasting mark. It made him sceptical of the significance and sustainability of user opposition, no matter how loud it sounded at the start. It didn't exactly make him feel that he could do whatever he liked, but it definitely inclined him to be willing to do more than he might have thought was possible before that experience.

In the meantime, it rapidly became clear that revenues generated by advertising would exceed the minimum $1 million guaranteed by 4Site for the next six months. Recognizing the degree of targeting they could obtain, and seeing the first results come in, the companies 4Site approached were soon prepared to pay rates per click that were five or even ten times the fee on other networks, a trend amplified by the scarcity of advertising opportunities on Fishbowll and the auction mechanism Andrei devised to award them. Initially, each user or School page received only one Sponsored Bait per day from companies offering a product in the relevant area of interest. The limit was Ben's idea, which he saw as a means of protecting the user experience. Ed Standish at 4Site resisted the concept at first, but soon came to see its value, not only in protecting the Fishbowll user experience but stoking demand and achieving premium pricing for the ads. An automated winner-takes-all auction at midnight each night determined whose advertisements would take the slots the following day.

Over time, the approach was refined. Some users clicked on the Sponsored Bait button more than once in a twenty-four-hour period, obviously seeking more ads. But in the course of any one day they saw the same ad each time, and if the same advertiser won the auction for the next day, they would see the same ads again. Standish, who was spending just about all his time on Fishbowll, thought this would frustrate the users as well as being a wasted opportunity to involve more advertisers. Andrei therefore developed a functionality that meant that if a given user clicked on the Sponsored Bait link for a second time in the twenty-four-hour period, a different Bait would appear. If they clicked a third time, a third Bait would appear, and so on down to the ninth slot. The auction process now offered not only the prime slot but the eight additional slots as well. Revenues tripled.

The statistics were relentlessly analysed. Some users consistently worked their way through all nine Baits for the day; others rarely clicked and if they did, they clicked once or at most twice.

Geography mattered as well, with users from developing countries consistently clicking on more Baits than users in the US and Europe. It seemed they were using the Baits as entertainment or information in their own right, while US and European users saw them more as advertisements. Andrei developed a further improvement in the functionality that allowed advertisers to bid at different rates for users by country, age group and gender.

All of this required a huge amount of work. Andrei, Kevin and the team of programmers, which now consisted of three additional Stanford undergraduates, worked through gruelling sequences of wheelspins to get the advertising functionality launched and then to keep improving it. Under Andrei's direction, they focused tirelessly on maximizing its efficiency and integrating it seamlessly into the user experience. Ed Standish sent through a weekly financial report detailing Fishbowll's earnings, but those were the numbers Andrei was least interested in. Now that he had a million dollars guaranteed for the next six months, he didn't think about the money from advertising at all. It was the user metrics that fascinated him, the problems they raised, the opportunities for improvement that they signposted, and the elegance of the solutions he could devise. It was an area rich with programming possibilities, and the technical discussions he had with Kevin and the other programmers were some of the most stimulating since he had started Fishbowll. Andrei spent hours at the screen, taking the most technically demanding parts of the coding for himself, headphones on, Coke can to hand, coding alongside Kevin and the other programmers crammed into the common room in Robinson House.

It was around this time that Andrei began to think more deeply about Fishbowll. By now, user numbers were heading towards 10 million, covering just about every country on earth. To be a part of the lives of 10 million people was not something trivial. Fishbowll meant something to them, and those meanings had all kinds of shades. The feeling Andrei had had when Mike Sweetman had offered him $100 million and when John Dimmer had handed him their first National Security Letter – there had been fifty by now – was still fresh. Fishbowll had a place in the world, and that place was not simple; neither was it entirely under his control.

From the beginning, and especially from the time that he had taken off to fly home to Boston and forced himself to step back and look at what he was doing, Andrei had thought about what Fishbowll was for. But now he found himself pondering it more searchingly, recognising that it was something he needed to understand explicitly. What did Fishbowll mean? What was it trying to achieve?

He began to write down his thoughts in a series of black note-books in which – ironically for someone who had founded a tech website – he scribbled his ideas longhand. It was in this period of extraordinary activity and mental ferment, around the time that advertising was introduced, in these notebooks written in his neat, dense script, that the fundamentals of Andrei's philosophy of Fishbowll developed.

In its essence, Andrei saw Fishbowll as a tool with which to slice through the superficial barrier of place so as to enable anyone to engage with anyone else, anywhere, about the handful of things that most mattered to them. He began to conceive of the world and its population not as a set of physical agglomerations but as a set of clusters – of ideas, views, values, aspirations – spanning the planet, and Fishbowll as a means of bringing them together in a way that had never been possible before. Andrei began to envisage these clusters exerting an effect on the real world, dissolving misapprehensions by groups of people about others and creating a series of shared, global identities based on values and interests rather than on nationality, ethnicity or other artificial constructs of affiliation over which an individual is able to exercise little if any choice. He began to conceive of overcoming these artificial constructs as the great challenge for humanity, and of Fishbowll as playing a central role in beating the challenge. In short, he began to see Fishbowll not only as a way for people to connect but as a radical, revolutionary form of connection that would change the way people understood themselves and thus the way in which they understood others around them.

At some point in this period he began to use the term that would be associated more than any other with Andrei Koss: Deep Connectedness. To Andrei, this was the thing above all others that Fishbowll offered: the act and reality of connection; depth in both extent and meaningfulness.

Andrei saw Deep Connectedness, as he began to conceptualize it, as an important and fundamentally good thing. He carried in him a sense that Fishbowll had been born in a kind of original sin – that secret deceit, long since discarded and not admitted to anyone, that he had had to employ in order to ensure that in Fishbowll's first weeks and months, when registration numbers were low, people thought they were being sought by others. Andrei was by no means a mystical person, but he felt that there was a strange symmetry in this, that somehow such a fundamentally good thing as Fishbowll could only come about through something that had an inkling of evil in it. And if there was such an inkling in it, then only by ensuring that Fishbowll remained fundamentally good could that founding evil be counterbalanced.

But that didn't mean that he saw Fishbowll as a vehicle to challenge law or authority. He was confirmed in the view that he had developed after the first meeting with John Dimmer: Fishbowll was a medium, not a message. The radical good at the heart of Fishbowll was Deep Connectedness and all that it made possible, not any kind of ideological objective espoused by Fishbowll itself. It was for others, facilitated by Deep Connectedness, to espouse their ideologies and test them in the crucible that Fishbowll helped provide.

Similarly, money in its own right was no objective. As Fishbowll took shape, Andrei saw the money that it could generate as purely instrumental, not an end in itself. Raising revenue would be necessary in order to run the service efficiently and to provide the opportunity to continuously improve and develop its functionality. Deep Connectedness was the goal – money earned by the website was nothing but the means.

The black notebooks scribbled in his small, impatient handwriting covered the same ideas over and over again, refining, clarifying, extending. Andrei came out of this period with a much more elaborate and sophisticated theory than he had had before, tying together his understanding of human history, the possibilities opened up by the internet, mankind's future, and a vision for the role in all of this that Fishbowll could play.

Kevin, meanwhile, unbeknown to Andrei or Ben, was pursuing his old interests again. In doing so, he was about to throw out a challenge to Andrei's new concept of Deep Connectedness in a way that Andrei had never foreseen.

14

IT WAS BEN who discovered what Kevin was doing. He came into the common room one day while Kevin was by himself at his screen, with his headphones on. Suddenly Kevin laughed out loud.

'What?' said Ben.

Kevin still hadn't heard him. 'That is so bad!' he said to himself.

Ben went over to see what Kevin was laughing at.

On the screen was an image of a man in a light blue wetsuit with a black body panel and a bulge at the groin that looked as if he had packed a cucumber and a pair of cabbages down there.

'What are you doing?' demanded Kevin, suddenly aware of Ben looking over his shoulder.

'Who's that guy?'

'No one.'

Ben peered closer at the message above the picture. 'Who's Tonya?'

Kevin shut the screen down.

'Kevin,' said Ben. 'Who's Tonya?'

Tonya, it turned out, was a 34-year-old South African whose passion in life was swimming with sharks – the bigger and scarier the better. Or it would have been, had she existed. Kevin had concocted her out of snippets of photographs he had found in various places. With all of Fishbowll at his disposal, he just hadn't been able to resist the temptation to fabricate a personality. Or two. This, of course, was in direct violation of the terms of the probation the disciplinary board after the Cooley Affair had set down for him – but then so was just about everything else he had been doing since the day the board had handed down its sentence.

Kevin had learned that one doesn't have to know much about something in order to sound credible. Past experience with other fabricated personalities had taught him that all that was needed was to listen carefully and play back to people what they had already said, or what someone else had already said, in a way that was slightly different to the original, or which seemed to express an opinion based on personal experience. Add a few choice snippets from a five-minute internet search and people would think they were dealing with an expert. In other words, give people what they expected to hear, and they wouldn't look any further.

He was soon talking authoritatively about cage-diving with great whites in the waters around Dyer Island near Cape Town, Tonya's favourite location. Thanks to his choice of face and body for Tonya's photos – Tonya liked wearing very skimpy bikinis – quite a few sharks of the human variety showed remarkable interest in her messages.

Kevin hadn't been able to resist trying a Cooley experiment with a guy called Ian, a 44-year-old businessman from Seattle who was a fan of O'Neill wetsuits and was always raving about how great they were. Kevin, through Tonya, had decided to try to convert him to Xcel suits. He waged the campaign both through the School group page and in personal messages with him. 'Try it,' Tonya urged him. 'Try an Xcel.' Then she added: 'I bet it will show off your packet like no other suit.'

Ian did – and then sent her the picture of himself in an Xcel wetsuit with a vegetable-stuffed crotch that elicited the fateful, ill-timed laugh just as Ben had walked through the door.

Ben was genuinely angry at what Kevin had done. They had been rightly censured for what they had done to Dan Cooley – in retrospect Ben saw how damaging it could have been to Cooley, and he was deeply ashamed at having been involved. But there was a lot more at stake now. He and Kevin shared responsibility with Andrei for a website, and that website wasn't some student gimmick or prank. The kind of deceit that Kevin was practising, as he saw it, ran counter to everything he thought Fishbowll was for.

By the time Andrei reappeared in the common room that day, the other programmers were there as well. Other people came and went. Ben waited until the programmers and everyone else had gone that night, and only he, Kevin and Andrei remained – then he told Andrei what had happened.

Andrei wasn't happy about it, either. Kevin said he had done it in order to understand the user experience.

'You don't have to create a false personality to do that,' snapped Ben. 'Just be yourself. No, you're right,' he added acerbically, 'that wouldn't interest anyone.'

'Very funny.'

'About as funny as what you've been doing! This is supposed to be about people connecting, not figments of your sick imagination.'

Kevin turned to Andrei. 'Look, half the people out there are probably using pseudonyms. We've never tried to stop them. And why should we? If someone is more comfortable connecting behind some kind of mask of anonymity, then who are we to stop them? Andrei, it's a dating site for the mind, right? That's what it says on the home page. Your words. If it's a dating site for the mind, what difference does it make what the rest of you purports to be? Arguably, you reveal your mind more fully if you're not encumbered by your own true appearance.'

'Casuistry,' said Ben.

'Why?' demanded Kevin. 'We haven't banned anonymity, right?'

'This isn't anonymity, Kevin. When you're anonymous, everyone knows you're anonymous.'

'All right, we haven't banned pseudonymity.'

'This is more than that,' said Ben. 'It's fantasy. How many of these personalities have you got going?'

'Tonya. She's the only one.'

'She's not. How many? How *many*?'

'Two.'

'Two now!'

'There's Tonya and there's this ... he's, like, a kid who collects colonial Spanish coins.'

'And?'

'That's it. I swear.'

'Don't swear when you're lying.' Ben turned to Andrei. 'Whatever he says, double it. That's what they teach us about addicts.'

'What's the addiction?' demanded Kevin.

'You will get your ass *so* busted if the OJA hears about this. You'll be out of this university for ever.'

'And who's telling them? You? Lighten up, Ben.'

'I will not lighten up! You did a freaking Cooley on one of them. You're an officer of the company, and not only are you pretending to be someone you're not, you're *manipulating* them as well!'

'Them? Who's *them*? Dude, one Cooley. That doesn't make a *them*. And it didn't seem to worry you when we did it with Cooley.'

'It was wrong! It was wrong and I regret it.'

'Oh, now you're so self-righteous.'

'You're an officer of the company!'

'Officer of the company? Lighten the fuck up, Ben! Don't take yourself so seriously.'

Ben shook his head, too exasperated for words.

'Andrei, you can't ban what I did,' said Kevin. 'You know that as well as I do. We can say we don't want people putting pseudonyms on our site, but then we just look like idiots because they'll do it anyway. If that's true, we should embrace it. This is cyberspace. If you choose to inhabit it, that's what you're going to encounter. Anonymity, pseudonyms—'

'Lies,' said Ben.

'We can't fight it,' continued Kevin, ignoring him. 'It's a dating site for the mind, Andrei. And if the mind creates one kind of personality or another, it's still that same mind. That's perfectly honest. And if that mind can free itself to think or say things it wouldn't think or say when tied to its real physical body or its physical existence, then I say it's even more honest.'

'That is so full of shit,' said Ben, 'I don't even know where to start.'

'Why don't you start by listening to what I'm saying instead of replaying your own prejudices?' retorted Kevin angrily. He was making up the rationalization as he went along, but he found that it was actually making sense to him.

'Don't say there's nothing physical in this,' said Ben. 'It's a fantasy. If this was purely about the mind, you wouldn't attach any physical characteristics to yourself.'

'Yeah, and people are really going to respond to that.'

'I think you've got a fantasy about being Tonya.'

'Dude, I do not have a fantasy about being some South African shark-swimming freak.'

'So why create her?'

'Maybe I created her because somehow … Look, maybe it's like that's the way I become fully identified with that thing.'

'Swimming with sharks?'

'Yeah, in this case, swimming with sharks. That personality, that construct, somehow maximally puts me in touch with that.'

'Even if you really did swim with sharks? Which you don't, of course.'

'Well, even if I did, maybe that construct would somehow enable me to connect with the experience even more fully. Who are you to say it wouldn't? Maybe it's an important part of connection.'

'And maybe pseudonymity is an open invitation to obscenity and abuse.'

'No doubt it is! Have you seen what's out there on the School pages?'

'Exactly! See?'

'What? That it's *already* there?'

Ben glared at him. 'I think you've just got a fantasy about wearing a bikini,' he muttered. 'Have the guts to wear it at least.'

'Very funny,' retorted Kevin. 'I don't know what you're so pissed off about.'

Ben found it hard to say himself. He was the one who had watched – sometimes even egged him on – as Kevin had made up personalities in the past. As Kevin had said, he had been part of the original Cooley experiment. But something about the thought of Kevin doing it on Fishbowll, on their network, made him wildly angry.

Ben looked at Andrei. He hadn't said a word as Kevin and Ben fought it out.

Kevin looked at him as well. 'What I'm saying is that we can fight a battle to stop people doing this, but that's a battle we're going to lose. But my point is, we shouldn't even want to fight that battle. It's a bad battle. It's a persecutory battle. I don't want to persecute anyone – the pseudonymous or the non-pseudonymous.'

Ben rolled his eyes. 'There's no equivalence. It's outrageous to say there's equivalence.'

'Well, I think there is. Here's Charles. Let's see what he says.'

Charles Gok, who had just come in from working late in the physics lab, stopped in the doorway. Since the common room had become the worldwide centre of Fishbowll, he rarely spent any time there. Sometimes the others forgot he even lived in the suite.

'Grab a beer,' said Kevin.

'Kevin, I don't drink,'

Kevin put one in Charles's hand anyway. 'We need your opinion.'

Charles hesitated. The atmosphere in the common room was heavy with tension. 'I'm not sure I've got one,' he murmured nervously.

In a few sentences, Kevin told him what he had been doing and summarized the discussion they had just had. Ben watched sceptically.

'Well,' said Charles, after a pause, 'it does feel kind of spooky, thinking you're talking to this Tonya woman in South Africa when you're actually talking to Kevin in this hellhole of a common room in Robinson House. But, you know, I guess, on the other hand Kevin's right. It must be happening all the time. If you can't stop it, then I think you have to embrace it.'

'It's one thing to embrace it,' said Ben. 'Even if I agreed with that, it's another thing to … you know, we're officers of the company! This is not something we should be doing.'

'Absolutely it is!' said Kevin. 'If we embrace it, we embrace it. That means we do it. We above everybody else should be doing it.'

'That's going a little far,' said Andrei.

'All right, at least we shouldn't *not* be doing it. If one of us wants to do it, and we can't, then basically we're saying this is wrong. And that's not what we're saying. What we're saying is this is part of cyberspace. This is part of what it is to be here. And if one of us wants to participate in that aspect of cyberspace, then we do.'

'That's not what we're saying,' said Ben. 'That's what *you* are saying.'

'If we're really embracing it, we should be transparent about it. Right, Charles? That's what you're saying, isn't it?'

Charles stared.

'Who appointed him the expert?' demanded Ben, saving him from the ordeal of answering.

'Let's admit this is happening,' demanded Kevin. 'Let's admit it's part of what a dating site for the mind is, and not deny it. We don't have to say we encourage it – fine – but we should be prepared to point out that we accept it.'

'Now you want to publicize it,' said Ben in disbelief.

'It's nothing to be ashamed of. That's the point, dude.'

'Whether we can stop it or not, officers of the company shouldn't do it.'

'That's hypocritical,' retorted Kevin.

Andrei glanced at his watch, a habit he had when he wanted to get away from a conversation and think about something. Ben and Kevin recognized the sign.

'We need to talk about this again,' said Ben ominously.

'Whenever you want,' replied Kevin, rising to the challenge.

The matter simmered. It was the first issue that had significantly come between the three founders since the inception of Fishbowll. Advertising was something that each of them had known they would have to face at some point, and by the time they had faced it there had been little choice anyway, and none of them had been implacably opposed. But this, with Kevin and Ben entrenched in opposite positions, threatened to cause real damage.

Discussions became increasingly irritable and ill tempered. They were all sitting their end of quarter exams, for which they were spectacularly under-prepared and which they all feared they would fail, which didn't help their mood. Kevin became increasingly extreme in defence of his pseudonymous activities, elaborating a strong libertarian argument that challenged the imposition of any kind of censure or control on any of the various ways one could represent oneself on the site. Ben felt just as strongly that pseudonymity, while something that couldn't necessarily be eradicated, ran counter to Fishbowll's primary objective of providing a place for people to find meaningful connections, and therefore the less of it there was, the better. Andrei listened to the arguments, using them to test his own bias and trying to understand how all of this fitted into his conceptualization of Deep Connectedness, or whether that conceptualization needed to change.

Eventually, Andrei spoke to Ben alone. Talking with him helped Andrei develop his thoughts and he had got into the habit of having long, open-ended conversations with Ben in a way that he never did with Kevin.

'You know everything Kevin said to you was post-hoc rationalization,' said Ben. 'He wants to act out these fantasies and he's looking for some kind of respectable-sounding argument to justify it.'

Andrei nodded. 'Maybe.'

'He shouldn't be doing this stuff.'

'That's a different question,' said Andrei. 'His motivation may be personal, but that doesn't mean his principle isn't right. Look, my first response was the same as yours. Instinctively, I thought, no, he shouldn't be doing this. But I've been trying to find the fault in his argument. Who are we to say what guise a person can and can't adopt? You're the psychologist, Ben. We all use masks, right?'

'Andrei, come on. This isn't Psychology 101.'

'If other people are doing it, why shouldn't Kevin, just because he's an officer of the company? So to me, this isn't about Kevin. It's a question of whether we should allow it in general. We've said from the very beginning that we don't police the Schools, they police themselves. And, overall, from what you tell me, they're pretty effective at it. We give them the tools to exclude or moderate and they're doing that pretty well. And if they don't want to, that's their choice. We give them the space, they can build whatever kind of house they want. Right? That's the principle we agreed on.' He paused. 'Kevin's right. We have to assume there's lots of people operating under pseudonyms right now. And if that's the case, then we accept it. Or else, like he said, we fight a battle that we're never going to win. And, like he said, we probably shouldn't even be trying to win it.'

'I'm not saying we can stop it. I'm saying we shouldn't encourage it.'

'But let's pretend we could stop it. Say we could prevent people using pseudonyms. Should we? To me, that's the question here, Ben.'

'Andrei, Kevin used the pseudonym to manipulate someone.'

'Would it make a difference if he did it as Kevin instead of Tonya? Would that make it better? If manipulation is the issue, the pseudonymity is irrelevant. People tell lies all the time online to manipulate people even if they're not using a pseudonym. Should we try to stop them lying as well?'

'They're more likely to lie if they're using a pseudonym.'

'How do you know? They may be more likely to tell the truth.'

Ben sighed. 'Look, this isn't just a lie. This about who you are.'

Andrei shrugged. 'A matter of degree.'

'I don't think so.'

'It comes down to, what are we trying to dictate? *Why* are we trying to dictate? That was never my intention with Fishbowll. Fishbowll is, "Here's the functionality to give you Deep Connectedness. Go use it." That's enough. That's our job.'

'I'm not arguing with that.'

'Well, in that case,' said Andrei, 'surely it's a matter for people to find their own way to express what they are in this space. Like I say, I reacted like you, but as I've thought about it I've begun to kind of like it. I kind of like the thought that people can find different ways. If you want to be who you are, sure, go ahead – the majority of people will do that. But if there's some reason that you can express yourself better and find connectedness better under the guise of someone else, then why not? It's kind of liberating.'

'What about the person on the other end of that connection?'

'That person may be a pseudonym as well.'

'What if they're not?'

Andrei shrugged. 'As long as they're aware this might be happening … Ben, you think this is a distortion of Deep Connectedness. I did as well. But now I'm thinking, maybe it's a stronger form of Deep Connectedness, a deeper one. That's why this is really important. As a matter of principle, I think we need to conceptualize Deep Connectedness broadly, not narrowly. A narrow conceptualization will leave us always where we are, and I don't think we've explored the bounds yet. I don't think we've explored anywhere near the bounds. I kind of feel like … this thing is taking us on a journey. When I launched it last November, did I have any idea that it would look like it looks today? Did I have any idea I was about to flunk my exams because of it? And in another six months … I've got no idea what it's going to look like then. I've got no idea where we're going, Ben. All I can say is there'll be things that'll challenge us. There'll be things that make us uncomfortable. But if we're going to take this journey, then I believe we have to be open to that. To have a broad conceptualization of Deep Connectedness means that we have to be willing – even wanting – to be challenged by new forms for it, and to be willing to accept them. That's what this thing has really taught me. It's challenged the narrowness of my conceptualization and dared me to broaden it.'

'But nothing we do should make the world a worse place.'

'Absolutely. So let's ask the question. Does having pseudonymous people on the site make the world a worse place? I don't think it does.'

'I do. What if having pseudonymous people makes some people not want to use the site?'

'What if it makes others more likely to use it?'

'What if those who don't want to use it because of pseudonymity outnumber those who do? That would reduce the level of connectedness, wouldn't it? And that would make the world worse.'

'That's an unknown. We can't quantify that and, anyway, the reverse might be the case. So then the point is, we can't prevent it – which mean we have to accept it. You're the one who told me that sometimes we can only do the least worst thing.'

'But we can at least not encourage it.'

'I agree with that. I don't think we should take a position on anything, either for or against, except on the freedom to connect. But let's look at what that means. We shouldn't encourage people to use pseudonyms, but we shouldn't encourage people *not* to use them, either. It's their choice. To be consistent, we have to be neutral.'

'Doesn't having an officer of the company using pseudonyms encourage it?'

'No more than having an officer of the company not using a pseudonym. And each of us has an account, right?'

Ben buried his face in his hands, shaking his head. He couldn't fight the logic. This was Andrei all over: cool, rational, ruthlessly consistent.

Andrei watched him. Between them was the unspoken recognition that Andrei owned a majority of the company, and whatever he decided was the final word.

'It's not personal,' said Andrei. 'You're not going to leave over this, right?'

Ben looked up in surprise. He hadn't even thought of leaving.

'I need you, Ben. But I need Kevin too. He's a Stakhanovite. Ben, I'm going to say yes on this. We've got to be consistent. But no hard feelings, right? All of us, we argue for what we believe is right. That's really important. We have to be able to do that and then make a decision and keep going.'

'What if the decision is one that one of us can't accept?'

'I hope it never comes to that.'

There was silence.

'No hard feelings?' said Andrei.

'There's a little hard feeling.' Ben shrugged, then forced a smile. 'I guess it'll go.'

Ben was a natural listener and conciliator. Whereas Kevin, having been thwarted, would have marched off in a huff, Ben's instinct was always to find a means of accommodation.

'Well,' he said eventually, 'I think if we're going to have this pseudonymity, we should be transparent about it.'

'I agree,' said Andrei.

'People need to know when they're seeing a pseudonym.'

'No. That defeats the purpose. And how would we enforce that? But people do need to know that they might come across pseudonymous people. We have to acknowledge that. Then it's their choice. If you don't want to deal with that, don't come to Fishbowll.'

'So what are you going to do? Do you want to post a statement in the Grotto?'

'I'm not sure yet.'

'I don't think we should come out and say one of the founders of the company has been posing as a South African shark swimmer.'

'I wasn't thinking of that. I'm still thinking about how to do it.'

Andrei took some more time to decide. Kevin continued his life of multiple personalities, although Tonya came to an end – Ian of the Xcel wetsuit and the large packet started pestering her for a video call and suddenly it was all too complicated. Tonya posted a farewell note to the School and quietly disappeared.

A few days later Andrei said, 'Guys, have a look at the new home page.'

At first they didn't notice anything. Then they saw a line in small font at the bottom of the screen.

In the Fishbowll, you may encounter avatars, pseudonyms and even real people.

'What do you think?' said Andrei.

'Cool,' said Kevin.

Ben let out a sigh. 'Is this live?'

Andrei nodded.

'We're going to get a shitstorm in the Grotto.'

'They won't even notice it.'

'They notice everything.'

Outside the Grotto, other people noticed as well.

15

IN JANUARY OF that year, around the time that Kevin and Ben were joining Andrei with shares in Fishbowll and putting the first investment into the business, Chris Hamer set off on a trip into the Australian Outback.

Tall, gangly, with a shock of blond hair, Hamer, then twenty-eight, was already a veteran of three internet start-ups, one of which he and his co-founders had sold for $120 million, netting him a fortune of $18 million. While waiting for his next big idea to hit him, he lived in LA and spent his time as a professional investor funding other internet start-ups.

Hamer was the son of a successful Los Angeles lawyer and had attended the prestigious Harvard-Westlake School, and then Princeton. He had emerged from the experience a curious, widely read, highly intelligent and strangely cynical character. The website from which he had made his money, FriendTracker, was an application that piggybacked on social networks to follow the activities of your friends and give other friends the ability to rank them as being positive or negative for you, using an algorithm to provide an overall score for friendliness or antagonism – or betrayal, as FriendTracker characterized it. It was like *National Enquirer* come to life. Bust-ups as a result of FriendTracker became common, loudly trumpeted on a FriendSmash! page specifically dedicated to fights and garnering huge publicity. The page was Chris's invention, as was the idea for the site itself. He thought the whole thing was hilarious and demoralizing in equal measure, confirming him in his jaded view of modern society.

In theory, there was as much potential for FriendTracker to highlight the depth of genuine friendships and the selflessness at the heart of them, but all anyone cared about was conflict and deceit. Duplicitous or jealous friends found ways to use the tool to manipulate their rivals and stab other friends in the back. Chris found even more hilarious and demoralizing the eagerness of advertisers to get on the site, and of a syndicate of Ukrainian investors to take it off his hands when he was getting bored with it.

He couldn't believe the site had lasted as long as it had. He had thought it was more of a gimmick than a long-staying business and had been proven right by its subsequent decline. Chris felt no guilt about that. The group of investors who had bought FriendTracker thought there was additional value to be had, which meant, in a way, they were trying to screw him. He thought it was overvalued as a result of the publicity over the fights it generated, which meant that he, in the same way, was trying to screw them. Turned out he won and they lost.

The whole thing, in retrospect, was an exercise in cynicism, starting from the idea at the heart of it – exposing the shallowness of apparent friendships – through the hype it engendered, to the ludicrous price he extracted for it.

But while Chris's cynicism was about the nature of people in modern life, their gullibility and hypocrisy, the things they did, valued and believed in, he wasn't remotely cynical about the businesses that served – or as he put it more bluntly, exploited – their needs, a number of which he invested in. He was a sharp and insightful observer of the internet space. To Hamer, the cutting edge of the internet was a scything mass of startling and original ideas, many of which would fail, but some of which would survive to shape the world for decades, if not centuries, to come. Constantly in search of intellectual stimulation, he was obsessed by the incessant invention and newness of what he saw, fascinated by its development. And by the potential to make truly stomach-churning amounts of money, while having what he considered to be the most fun that it was possible to have. He was always in search of new ideas that would allow him to do that.

The world Chris Hamer inhabited was thus an ever-changing cloud of oddly capitalized cyber names that blew in and then blew away, only rarely sticking. Every week, if not every day, he heard about something that was supposedly the next big thing. Most of those names, he knew, would be forgotten by the time he heard about the next one. But when he did find something that was interesting enough to pursue, when he found that one-in-a-hundred idea that seemed to have a genuine spark of originality and relevance, and when he did hook up with a team of truly capable start-up founders, Chris Hamer had a lot more to offer than mere cash.

Hamer had the priceless experience of having lived through the start-up experience three times over. He had twice seen his creations fail and take significant sums of investors' cash with them, and he had made every mistake it was possible to make. He knew the pitfalls of rapid growth – the difficulties of scaling up, as it was known in internet circles – that could kill a start-up dead or at least hamper its development to such an extent that a copycat site had the chance to get going and overtake it. He knew the ways and means of venture capitalists and the numerous devices by which they could end up controlling the company you thought you owned and showing you the door. Gregarious, inquisitive, energetic, Hamer had a wide network in the internet world and his network in the venture capital community was equally extensive. He knew just about all the major firms on Sand Hill Road and, more crucially, had the ability to get a meeting with a good number of them. His mix of cynicism and intelligence appealed to the venture-capital crowd, many of whom shared those character traits. Chris himself didn't have tens of millions to put in, so he tended to get involved with start-ups at an early stage, when a few hundred thousand dollars could make a difference. When the time came for a bigger cash injection, his connections into the VC world were invaluable.

Chris, however, did have one foible. Like many others made cynical by the contemporary world, Hamer had an almost naive belief in the redeeming power of primitive lifestyles, and had the money to buy his way into tasting those lifestyles for himself, cutting himself off from everything at home in order to immerse himself fully in the experience. Previously he had spent periods living in the Amazon rainforest and with Laplander reindeer herders. During the three months he had just spent travelling, camping and living with Aboriginal communities in the searing heat of a Central Australian summer, he was completely oblivious to events in California. When he returned to Los Angeles that spring, he kept hearing the name of a new website called Fishbowll.

He didn't check it out right away. He had a backlog of stuff to catch up on and there were other names people were mentioning to him as well. For some reason it kept slipping his mind. He thought the spelling was silly, too, kind of kitsch and try-hard, and he didn't think he'd want to get involved with people who thought that was cool. It was only when he was asked what he thought of Fishbowll for the third or fourth time by people whose judgement he respected that he finally sat down and typed the name into his computer.

To his surprise, he liked the home page. Clean, simple, uncluttered. A fish with big, interested eyes staring out from a stylized bowl. Underneath it the tag: *A dating site for the mind.* Chris was intrigued. Then he noticed the line on the bottom of the page. *In the Fishbowll, you may encounter avatars, pseudonyms and even real people.*

His curiosity was piqued. What was that about? Was this a social networking site, a virtual world, or a game?

They met at Mang, a fancy Vietnamese restaurant in Palo Alto where Chris often ate when he was in town. The restaurant specialized in serving small dishes for sharing and Chris ordered for the four of them as Andrei, Kevin and Ben watched.

By now, eight months after Fishbowll had been born, Andrei was receiving calls fairly frequently from people saying they were interested in investing in the site. Since the 4Site deal was sufficient at the moment to fund Fishbowll's growth, he wasn't interested in having anyone invest, so most of the calls were short. He did meet a couple of people out of curiosity but found them not particularly knowledgeable and got the feeling they could have been investing in potato chips as long as the chips were being sold on the internet. He walked out of one lunch even before the cocktails arrived. But when Chris Hamer called, he listened. Hamer wasn't exactly anyone's notion of an internet god, but Andrei knew about FriendTracker. Here was someone who had actually done something in the internet world, not just invested money in the self-interested hope of walking away with a fortune reaped from somebody else's intellectual property. Not that FriendTracker had been the world's most outstanding site. Andrei suspected that the algorithms underlying it had been fairly crude. What he liked about Chris, when they met at the restaurant, was that he admitted it himself.

'I kept telling them,' said Chris, throwing back one of Mang's signature mango mojitos and looking around for a waitress to order another, 'the algorithm was primitive. What else do you expect? What was neat was the way we got people to use the site anyway so we could get their feedback to evolve it. To be honest, the whole thing was just a huge Beta all the way through, just a work in progress.' He broke off as a waitress approached. 'Miss, can I have another? Guys? Yeah? OK, another one all round.' He looked back at Andrei. 'I was kind of proud of that. You know, I think if we'd kept it going, by today, I think we'd have had a pretty good bunch of algorithms.'

'So do you regret selling?' asked Kevin.

'I got a shitload of cash for it.'

'Maybe you could have got more if you'd got the algorithm right.'

'Maybe. But what was it? A site where you could see if your friends were shitting on you. Dude, life's too short. I don't want to be setting myself up here to give you advice but, guys, what you've got to ask yourself is, are you doing the single most important thing you can possibly be doing? I'm not saying there is a one most important thing, objectively, for all people to do. Everyone's going to define that in a different way. To some people, the most important thing is to change the world. To some people, it's to have a good time. To the Aboriginals of Central Australia, it's to honour the Dreamtime. As long as you're not hurting anybody, define it as you will. But you've got to look at yourself, and say, "Me, Andrei Koss, or Kevin Embley, or Ben Marks, does Fishbowll give me the best shot at doing the most important thing that I want to do?" Because if it doesn't – and a site to see if your friends are shitting on you was fun but it absolutely was not the most important thing in the world – so if it doesn't, then sell the hell out of that thing and go do something else. Seriously.' Chris sat back as the next round of mojitos neared. 'That's what I'm saying.'

Kevin nodded. 'Cool.'

Chris looked at Andrei. 'What are they offering you for Fishbowll?'

Kevin and Ben looked at him as well. They would have liked to know.

'I don't know,' said Andrei.

Chris stared at him for a moment, then laughed.

'I don't know.'

'You mean you don't ask?'

Andrei shook his head.

'Well, shit, that is funny.' Chris shook his head disbelievingly. 'You don't even ask?'

'I keep telling him he should find out,' said Kevin.

'What about you, Ben? Don't you want to know?'

Ben shrugged. 'Andrei's got seventy-six per cent of the company.'

Chris picked up his glass. 'Here's to not even wanting to know what your company's worth!'

Andrei looked at him quizzically.

'I'm not mocking you, Andrei. I'm admiring you. Most guys, the first thing they do when they sniff a little revenue is spend their time talking to VCs. Spend so much time, they usually stop doing what got them that far in the first place, and that's the end of the business. Pick up your glass, Andrei Koss. That's a toast I've never made before.'

Andrei warily picked up his glass.

'To you guys,' said Chris, glancing in turn at each of them. 'To not wanting to know what your company's worth.'

Andrei sipped silently from his mojito and put the glass down. Chris glanced at him, then launched into a story about one of his other start-ups.

The food came in a succession of dishes that Chris described and explained. He did most of the talking that night. At twenty-eight, with the things he had done and the places he had travelled, he had so much more to talk about than they did. He told them about the time he had just spent with the Aboriginals in Arnhem Land, and his time two years earlier in the Amazon. And there were stories about the big names in the internet world he knew. He did a little name-dropping for Kevin and Ben's sake. Andrei hardly said a word, just sat there watching and listening.

That evening, Chris didn't ask much else about Fishbowll. He didn't think Andrei was going to tell him anything and he wondered if he might frighten him off. He really didn't know what to make of the pale young man sitting opposite him, who was silently dipping into the dishes arriving at the table. There certainly wasn't anything kitsch and try-hard about him, as Chris had expected from the website name. And the fact that he hadn't bothered to ask what people were prepared to offer for the site was somehow deeply impressive. If anyone else had said that to him, Chris wouldn't have believed it, but for some reason he suspected that in Andrei's case it was true. Chris was intrigued, deeply intrigued, both by Fishbowll and its founder. He wanted to know more about Andrei Koss and his vision for the website.

Yet he had no idea what Andrei was thinking or whether he had any interest at all in prolonging the conversation with him.

He didn't know Andrei well enough yet to realize that if Andrei had had no interest in what he had to say, he would have got up and left.

So it was a genuine surprise to Chris when Andrei called him a couple of days later and asked if he could talk with him again. Although he had no plans to go up to the Bay Area, Chris immediately said he was going to be in Palo Alto for a meeting early the following week and could make time to see him. This time, rather than suggesting a place, he asked where Andrei would like to meet. Andrei named the first place that came into his head.

16

IT WAS HAMER'S first time at Yao's. He could see that the waiters knew Andrei well. Chris ordered kung pao chicken. Andrei didn't even need to say that he wanted the chicken and shrimp fried noodles.

'I'm running what appears to be a large and growing business,' said Andrei matter-of-factly as soon as the orders were taken. 'I'm twenty-one years old and I'm well aware that I have no experience that prepares me for this.'

Chris nodded. He was impressed both by Andrei's insight and his honesty. At the same age, still in college and running his own first start-up, he had messed things up precisely because he had lacked both. He was also interested in the way Andrei had made a statement of apparent humility come out more as an assertion of control. Chris had seen a lot of guys running start-ups. The more he saw of Andrei Koss, the more interested in Fishbowll he became.

'It's not that easy to find disinterested advice,' said Andrei.

'And you think I'll offer it to you?'

'You're the first guy I've met who hasn't tried to buy my company.'

Chris laughed. 'Full disclosure. You know I'm an investor.'

Andrei nodded.

'OK,' said Chris. 'Well, let me see how I can help you. What do you want to know?'

'I want to know what I'm not doing that I should be doing. I want to know what I am doing that I shouldn't be.'

'Good questions. I had to go through two start-ups before I learned those lessons.'

'I'll pay you for your time,' said Andrei quickly.

Chris laughed again.

'I don't expect any favours.'

Chris leaned forward. 'Andrei, you'll be doing me the favour. But I need to know some numbers. I need to get some sense of the scale of what you're doing. How many users have you got?' He saw Andrei hesitate. 'It's confidential, I promise. But, full disclosure again, I may use the numbers myself to decide whether to make you an offer of some cash. I won't divulge anything to anyone else.'

Andrei hesitated a little longer. 'OK,' he said. 'Thirty-two million.'

'How long have you been running?'

'Eight months, more or less.'

'That's good.'

'They have an extraordinarily high usage rate. And we have an exceptional geographic and demographic diversity, which generates a lot of demands. I've got a thousand things people are asking for.'

'And the things you want to do?'

'I've got a thousand of those as well.'

Their dishes arrived.

'Tell me your vision,' said Chris, digging into his kung pao chicken.

'It's there on the website.'

'Tell me in your own words.'

'They are my words.'

'Andrei, just tell me.'

'Connectedness,' said Andrei. 'Most social networks put you in touch with people you know, and if you're lucky, through them you might connect with other people. That's still a relatively contained and insulated subset of the total group you may want to connect with. Group pages and chatrooms are full of people who get attracted to something momentarily and aren't committed. I want to provide an avenue to find your way to people who you would want to talk to, because they're interested in the things that are really important to you, but who you would never normally find. And I want you to be able to do it right now, today, this instant, and not have to wait for chance connections through friends of friends of friends that probably won't even ever happen. I think of it as Deep Connectedness – taking you wherever and to whoever you want to go to in the world.'

'The other night I asked you if it's important,' said Chris. 'I asked if it's the most important thing you could be doing. And you're telling me there's this Deep Connectedness you're trying to facilitate – which I totally get and which I think is totally cool – but my question is, how important is that?'

'World changingly,' said Andrei without hesitation.

Chris smiled. 'That's what everyone always says. I've seen guys setting up an internet site to sell socks and they think they're going to change the world. I tell them, "Dude, it's socks. I already wear socks."'

'But you don't already have Deep Connectedness. This is new. It's something that makes the world a new place. We still see the world as divided up by place. That's a way of thinking that comes out of old communication, where you're limited by physicality.'

'Is it? The telephone's been around for over a century.'

'And that wasn't enough to change it. Why? Because I may have a phone, and I may be able to connect with any number in the world – but I don't know who to call. There's no one helping me find out. The places we live, those are accidents. They're not the real things that unite or divide us. The things that do that are ideas, values, aspirations. And they're not limited by place. These clusters, these communities of ideas, exist between places, outside places, but they're real communities, or they're starting to be, and if we can create the connections, they'll be even more real. They'll be larger, fuller, deeper. They won't be limited to the elites. The way the world groups itself is changing. Give it Deep

Connectedness, and it'll change even faster. That's what Fishbowll does. That's what Fishbowll is for.'

Chris was silent, watching him.

'You don't think this has the potential to be world-changingly important?' Andrei frowned. 'Maybe I've got this out of proportion. You know, for the last eight months it's just been Fishbowll, Fishbowll, Fishbowll, morning, noon and night.' He paused again. 'Maybe I've lost perspective.'

'No,' said Chris. 'I don't think you have. It's not socks. It's so not socks. I was just testing you a little, Andrei. Probably for the first time in my life I'm looking at a start-up where the founder is telling me it's going to change the world and I find myself thinking, he's right. And that is not a small thing, dude.' Chris smiled. 'That is a fucking monster thing.' He picked up his Coke glass. 'To the fucking monster thing that is Fishbowll.' He clinked Andrei's glass and drank. 'Two more questions. Thirty-two million users. What do you project by the end of the year?'

'Seventy to eighty million.'

'Growth projections are never right. They're either too high or too low. Historically, over your eight months, where have you been? I'm guessing you've been too low.'

Andrei nodded. 'Back at the start of the year I wrote my projections on a napkin. Right here – right at that table over there. Ben still has it. Every month he brings it out. He tells me it's nice to have some evidence that even Andrei Koss can be wrong.'

Chris laughed.

'But the year-end projection I've just given you takes that into account.'

'No, it doesn't. You think it does, but it doesn't. Not as far as infrastructure planning is concerned. Plan for a hundred, minimum. If you're prudent, a hundred and twenty million. Do you have the infrastructure to serve that?'

'Not yet.'

'Will you have it? Andrei – and I speak from personal experience that I can tell you about some day, if you don't mind me weeping into my beer – the thing that will kill you quicker than a coyote chasing down a roadrunner is if your server speed slows and if your site starts to go down. If Fishbowll gets a reputation for that, you may as well turn it upside down and empty the water out right now.'

Andrei stared at him.

'I'm serious. That's where you need redundancy. If there's one thing you should go do this afternoon after we finish, it's go find yourself more server capacity. Don't sit down and code. Get on the phone and find yourself server space. Get your infrastructure ready. Now, the second question. Have you got any revenue?'

'We've got a deal with 4Site.'

'Who are they?'

'An advertising company.'

'What are they like?'

'There's one guy who's cool. He's kind of old but he gets it. The other guys I've met think they know it all.'

'What kind of a deal have you got? This is confidential, I promise.'

'They get eighteen per cent commission and guarantee one million revenue this year, double next year.'

'That's good. Is it exclusive?'

Andrei nodded.

'This deal runs for how long?'

'Eighteen months.'

'You'll have outgrown them by then.'

'I know,' said Andrei. 'But I thought we'd need that long to figure out how the advertising model works. This isn't about making as much money as we possibly can. If we have to have advertising, then it's about using it, as far as we can, to enhance the user experience. My aim is to use the contract period to experiment with the approach. And we have a guaranteed income, which was important for us. We were running out of cash. We'd be dead now if we hadn't done that deal.'

'I'm not saying it's a bad deal,' said Chris. 'Eighteen per cent is about as low as I've ever heard. Who negotiated that?'

'Me.'

'I'm impressed.'

'Don't be. I was lucky. My father knew some oligarchs. He's Russian. I'm Russian, too. I mean, I was born in Russia. I'm American now, of course.'

Chris looked at him in confusion. 'And the connection is …?'

'Don't worry about it,' said Andrei.

'Are you talking about Russian oligarchs? Is there some kind of Russian mafia involvement here?'

Andrei cracked a rare smile.

'Because I've been involved with some unsavoury characters, but if that's what we're talking about, Andrei, I'm out of my league.'

'Nothing. There's nothing. Forget I said it.'

Chris peered at him for a moment. 'All right. Tell me about Ben and Kevin. They own part of the company?'

'Kevin owns fifteen per cent and Ben owns nine.'

'And you have the rest?'

Andrei nodded.

'What does Kevin do?'

'He codes.'

'You can pay a programmer.'

'I do. Four. Kevin's not like that. Kevin keeps it all going. If there's a problem, he works at it until it's done. He's a Stakhanovite.'

'A what?'

'It's an old Soviet term for a hero-worker. Someone of super-human productivity. Kevin's a Stakhanovite.'

'Well, every start-up needs one. And Ben?'

'He's a psychology major. He helps … I don't know, figure stuff out. He also analyses the data.'

'So that's it. You three guys and the four programmers you pay?'

'That's it. Do I need more? I don't know if I've got the money for more, especially if I've got to scale up for a hundred million users.'

'Then you need to find it.' Chris sat back. ' You *need* to find it. I can't believe you're still surviving as you are. Andrei, I share the vision. I get it, I totally get it, and I love it. It's awesome. The world is on a one-way journey to a global future and it's only a question of who gets to lay the road. It may be that when the history of this is written, Fishbowll will have a chapter all to itself. But when I look at it from a business perspective, I think, if you get it right, you also have the most extraordinary thing on your hands. You have a set of users that are walking around with bullseyes on their backs. They're not just selected for their interests but self-selected, and not just for their interests but for the interests they really, really care about. If advertisers have wet dreams, this is it.'

'I know,' said Andrei. 'We find that we have a little of what we call interest-tourism, where users just type in some crazy thing to see what comes up. Mostly it's new users and they do it a couple of times and that's it. But for the others, we're getting pretty good now at analysing usage patterns – who people talk to, how often, on what topics – to figure out how committed a user is to a particular interest. I think we're starting to understand that better than our users understand it themselves. Right now, advertisers bid a basic per-click rate at a daily auction, and that's adjusted up or down by a certain amount depending on a set of data about the individual user, like how long he's been registered, how often he visits, how much time he spends on the site. But that's still incredibly crude. I would say within a month we'll be able to adjust the per-click rate on the basis of a commitment score that we'll be able to generate from usage patterns, which I think will be incredibly predictive of propensity to buy. We're just trying to get the data to prove that right now.'

Chris slapped the table in delight. 'I love it! What you have is magic in your hands and you're working out the best way to use it. You're like a wizard, Andrei. You're learning your capabilities.'

'But Fishbowll's about Deep Connectedness, Chris. Advertising is there because we need it. I just want to make it as efficient as I can. It's wrong that an advertiser should pay the same per-click rate for two people who have a radically different propensity to buy. That's just wrong. It's not efficient. We can make it much more efficient than that.'

'Exactly. But you cannot do something like this and not be businesslike. Again, I could tell you a story right out of the Chris Hamer scrapbook. If you don't earn enough out of whatever you're doing to service it, to constantly develop it, to give your users what they want, and to make it run fast and smooth, someone else will. At your level, Andrei, the net has no place for altruists. Nature abhors a vacuum – the internet abhors non-profit.'

'I don't have to make a profit to do all those things.'

'Fair enough. Let me rephrase that. The internet abhors non-revenue. But let's not kid ourselves – that means big revenue, because your users are going to demand big things. And make no mistake, they *will* leave you if you don't deliver. First law of the net – if you don't, someone else will.'

'Don't what?'

'Anything!' Chris grinned, then he folded his arms, the smile still playing on his lips. 'I bet the social networks hate you.'

'Mike Sweetman offered me a hundred million for the site.'

Chris laughed. 'Hold your enemies close, right? So close you can stifle them. What did you say?'

'No.'

Chris laughed again. Then he shook his head. 'He'll come after you somehow.'

'He already has. He shut down access.'

That had happened when Chris had been in Australia, but he had heard all about it when he got back. 'The search engines stopped him, right?'

Andrei nodded.

'What's it got to do with you?'

'That hundred million offer … he made it the day after he was forced to open up again.'

Chris stared at him. 'Really?'

Andrei nodded.

'Interesting.' Chris ate some of his chicken, thinking about what Andrei had just told him. Its significance didn't escape him. 'Very interesting.' Chris had hardly touched the food so far and it was almost cold, but it was still tasty. 'This is good.'

'I'm no food critic,' said Andre, 'but Yao's is a fine noodle establishment.'

Chris watched him for a moment, wondering if this was an apparently rare Koss attempt at humour. 'So, what should you do?' he said, waving a fork with a piece of chicken on it. 'You asked my advice. First thing – and this may not be immediately relevant, but one day it will be, so hear me out – is that when you take venture capital, never be in a position where you lose control of the company. Even if you go below fifty per cent ownership, there are still ways for you to retain a majority vote. Dual class voting stock, for example. If you don't do that, not only do you risk losing control over the important decisions about the way things are done, you may even be forced out. It's not a pleasant experience, and I know. The VCs will tell you that you can't retain that control, but you can. You just have to make them hungry enough to buy in under those conditions. There are no rules when that point is reached – there's only panic to get a piece of the action. You've got to see it, Andrei, the greed of these guys and their raw, naked fear when they think they're going to miss out.' Chris grinned. 'It's a thing of rare and ferocious beauty, my friend.'

'How do I make them that hungry?'

'Build the business. Build it as you see the vision. What you have is potentially so compelling that the beasts of Sand Hill Road will come salivating to your door. The second thing, and this one is immediately relevant, is that you need someone to manage the infrastructure.'

'We don't own the servers, we rent them.'

'Of course you do. You still need someone to manage the relationship with whoever owns the infrastructure. Make sure they give you the service you need, the responsiveness you need. For those people, you're in a queue. You need to be at the front. And if you've got a problem, chances are you can figure out the solution a lot quicker than they can. If you get a reputation for slowness or time outs, you're dead.'

'Maybe Kevin could do that.'

'Tell me something,' said Chris, suddenly realizing he hadn't asked an obvious question. 'Are you guys at college?'

Andrei nodded. 'Stanford.'

Chris shook his head, smiling.

'What?'

'Nothing. Look, hire someone to manage the infrastructure. Don't try to do it ad hoc, Andrei. If you're lucky, you might get by, but if you don't, you're dead.'

'How much would that cost?'

'Depends how much stock you're prepared to put into the package.'

'Do you know anyone who might be able to do that?'

'I can ask around. Do you have the money for this?'

Andrei frowned. 'I'm not sure.'

Chris didn't say anything to that. If Andrei wanted him as an investor, he wanted Andrei to ask. 'The third thing – and again, it may not be right now, but it's going to be very soon – is to be realistic about what you three founders are able to do and what skills you need to bring in. You must be great programmers to have got to where you've got to, and you've got a great vision, but even when start-up people have business experience, when the business starts to accelerate, as yours is doing, they're unprepared. You can obviously negotiate, if your advertising deal is anything to go by, but that's not enough by itself. It's likely other business skills you'll need to import. Again, another one of my mistakes – not doing that early enough. Be realistic, but be ruthless, about where your skills lie and where your fellow founders' skills lie, and bring in those that you don't have. And the fourth thing – get good people to advise you. When you look for VC money, look for more than the cash, look for the kind of backers who have a solid base of experience, the kind of guys who are going to let you run the company but offer you wise counsel.'

Andrei looked at his watch. There was so much that he needed to get away and think about.

'Do you have to be somewhere?' asked Chris.

Andrei shook his head. 'What about the fifth thing?'

'What's the fifth thing?'

'What do I do about Mike Sweetman?'

Chris laughed. 'See if you can get a billion out of him.'

'I don't want to sell.'

'No? Not for a billion? Then there's only one other thing to do.'

'What?'

'The same thing he tried to do to you.'

Andrei gazed at Chris sceptically.

'Not today. Not right now. But you're in the big league, Andrei. You're swinging against guys like Mike Sweetman. The day will come when it's him or you. Whether you like it or not, you'll have to start thinking like that.'

A couple of days later Chris got another call from Andrei. Again, Andrei came right to the point. 'I'd like you to come be part of Fishbowll.'

'Really?' said Chris. 'To do what?'

'I don't know. All I know is we need someone who knows something.'

Chris laughed. 'I think you know plenty, Andrei.'

'Do what you like,' said Andrei. 'Spend as much time or as little as you want. Just work with us. I want you to buy a share of the company.'

'How much do you want me to buy?' asked Chris.

'Five per cent. For a million.'

'That's valuing you at twenty million.'

'Mike Sweetman offered me a hundred.'

'Yeah,' said Hamer, 'but Sweetman was trying to take you out.'

'He's not the only one who's offered me more.'

'I thought you didn't ask.'

'That doesn't stop people telling me.'

Chris laughed, wondering again if Andre's deadpan delivery was an attempt at humour or a simple statement of fact. 'Do you need another million to get you through the year?'

Andrei didn't. After the last conversation with Hamer, he had rented more server space and had analysed the financial position, taking account of Fishbowll's likely advertising revenue, which was running higher than expected. Even if he employed someone to manage the infrastructure, the numbers looked OK. 'I want you to buy a share because I want you to be part of us.'

'Andrei,' said Chris, 'I'll need to think about it.'

He ended the call. He did need to think about it – for a minute. Fishbowll was the most exciting thing Chris had come across since ... it was the most exciting thing he had ever come across. He was impressed not only with the Andrei's vision for Fishbowll but with the younger man's thoughtfulness and maturity and, even more importantly, with his apparent willingness to learn. Chris believed that, stewarded well, the business Andrei had founded had the potential to become an important company, earn serious money for its founders and investors – and change the world. Although he was realistic about that. One could change the world – but all that meant was that a new group of predators would emerge to rip the rest of the population off.

He just had to find a million dollars. He didn't have it in cash, and it meant sacrificing some potential profit that would be lost if he sold out of certain investments now, but with a few phone calls he had liquidated enough assets to raise the funds.

He called Andrei the following day.

'I'm in,' he said.

'Great.'

'Just one thing that's been bugging me. Who thought of the name?'

'I did,' said Andrei.

'Why the weird spelling?

'Fishbowl with one *l* was taken.'

Chris nodded. He should have worked that one out for himself.

17

ANDREI HADN'T CONSULTED with either Kevin or Ben before asking Chris Hamer to buy into the company. Ben had no problem with it. The meeting at Mang had left him with the impression that Chris was a guy who liked to talk himself up somewhat, but he was smart and experienced and Ben immediately saw the benefit Chris could bring. Kevin, the self-appointed business guru of the group, responded more defensively. He wanted to know what Andrei thought Chris could bring that they didn't already have. Andrei gave him a list. Then he wanted to know why Chris had to buy in. Andrei told him he didn't think Chris was going to work for them for a wage.

Kevin's resentment simmered. At first Chris wasn't around much. The legal work was done and the million dollars was transferred. The academic quarter came to an end. Andrei had managed to come through all his courses, although his grades had taken a significant hit. Ben and Kevin were just OK. They shared an unspoken understanding that they wouldn't be able to manage the same feat again in their senior year.

They also knew that they couldn't just disperse for three months over the summer vacation. They rented a big house in a family neighbourhood in Palo Alto, in a little street called La Calle Court, and deposited their stuff there. They put Ben's aquarium in the entrance hall, right opposite the door. Andrei went home to Boston for a week and then came back. Ben and Kevin, soon back in California as well, moved in. So did two of the programmers Andrei had employed. Friends and girlfriends and various other people came and went. Sandy Gross stayed on and off before leaving for a vacation with a bunch of girlfriends in Europe.

The first time Chris Hamer stepped through the door he thought it looked like a frat house – a frat house with a lot of computer equipment in the living room. He rubbed his hands. 'Cool,' he said. 'Where's the beer?'

It was a caffeine- and alcohol-fuelled summer of wheelspins and partying, the kind of weird, wild, unfettered period of sheer intensity that can only ever happen once, and which, if you're not careful, you can spend the rest of your life trying to recreate. The freedom to focus on nothing but Fishbowll was an exhilaration. Andrei, Kevin and the programmers worked twelve-, fifteen-, twenty-hour stretches and then collapsed. Then they'd get up and someone would have organized a barbecue and they'd party while a series of epic movies played on a big screen on a wall on an endless loop that someone had rigged up, and then Andrei or Kevin would drift back to his computer and pretty soon another wheelspin was in progress. Fishbowll grew, developed and improved at a dizzying speed.

Chris came back and stayed for weeks, egging them on. If he was supposed to be playing the role of the adult in this room of computer-drunk children, he wasn't doing much of a job of it. He had a million dollars on the line in this frat house, but the anarchy and sheer exuberance exhilarated him. He sensed that he was caught up in an exceptional concentration of creativity and one would mess with the magic only at one's peril. Within the apparent wildness of the whirlpool, things got done. Astonishing, innovative, extraordinary things. When Andrei and Kevin and the other programmers sat at their desks and put on their headphones, it was work. If someone disturbed them, Andrei would throw down his headphones and let out a Russian curse that might have meant nothing, as far as anyone knew, but never failed to quieten the room. It was no way to run a business, but this wasn't a business – it was Fishbowll. Let it run riot. It would have time to grow up.

Nonetheless, there was one aspect of the operation that Chris couldn't let run wild. He had found Andrei someone to oversee the infrastructure, an engineer called Eric Baumer who had worked with him at FriendTracker. Chris lured him to the job with a modest salary, options worth 1 per cent of the company and his insistent personal assurances that one day those options would be worth a lot more than anything FriendTracker had ever delivered. Eric was meticulous, methodical and had proven at FriendTracker that he knew how to apply those qualities to keep a service running in the white-hot crucible created by the combination of exponential growth and hastily written software architecture. But not even FriendTracker had featured a place as anarchic as the house on La Calle Court.

While Andrei was deep in the coding of Fishbowll, Chris took it upon himself to make sure Eric was paid and kept the site running. Eric worked out of his home office in Hayward, about fifteen miles away across the San Mateo Bridge. To avoid scaring the hell out of him, Chris kept him as far from the Fishbowll house as he could. Whenever they had to meet, they'd get together over noodles at Yao's.

Most of the time, however, Chris hung around the house, drinking beers, talking Fishbowll and enjoying the vibe. He hit on most of the girls who came through the door and had occasional success. He hadn't had this much fun since the early days of FriendTracker, and FriendTracker, he had always felt, had been a fad. Fishbowll was here to stay.

Andrei had decided that he wasn't going back to Stanford in the fall. He was trying to organize a leave of absence for a year before getting up the courage to tell his parents. They must have suspected what was going on, however, and they arrived one Saturday afternoon, marched through the battlefield of the living room, and locked themselves in a bedroom with Andrei. Everyone stood outside listening to a lot of shouting in Russian. Afterwards,

Andrei and his parents came out and only then, it seemed, did his parents take in the state of the house.

Andrei's father shouted some more.

They stayed in a hotel and Andrei met them the next morning for brunch. By then they were somewhat calmer. They had taken in the points he had made about the revenue Fishbowll was already earning, and the amounts he had been offered for the business had had time to sink in. He brought them back to La Calle Court and introduced them to Kevin and Ben and Chris and the two programmers who lived at the house. By this time, his parents had sufficiently relaxed to have a conversation with them. Kevin asked about Moscow in the nineties and Andrei's father, over a beer, told a few anecdotes that scared the hell out of everyone. Then his mother lined them up, programmers included, and for the rest of the afternoon she had the full half-dozen of them cleaning the house. By the time Andrei's parents left that evening to go back to Boston, they seemed to have accepted the inevitable. Andrei had assured them he'd get a leave of absence.

Kevin was planning to get a leave of absence as well. Ben, on the other hand, was intending to go back to Stanford for the fall quarter. He sensed that a leave of absence would probably turn into permanent absence, and he wanted his degree. He still wanted to stay involved with Fishbowll and he talked to Andrei about how they could make that work. He would put less time into Fishbowll and then see if he wanted to come back full time when the year was over.

Chris thought it was a good idea when Ben told him about his plan one night. They were lounging on a pair of deckchairs with a couple of beers, watching two friends of one of the programmers playing ping pong on a table someone had brought into the yard. Inside, an all-hands wheelspin was under way. Since neither Chris nor Ben were involved in the prodigious bouts of coding that went on in the living room, they had found themselves hanging out quite a lot over the summer. They had conversations about psychology and spirituality. Ben saw spirituality as the fulfilment of a psychological need. Chris saw it as a doorway into a deeper dimension of the mind.

Chris liked Ben and enjoyed their conversations, but didn't think Ben contributed as much to Fishbowll as Andrei thought he did. The analysis he did on the data could have been done by a statistical programmer for a relative pittance of a salary, and probably better and quicker than Ben did it. Ditto for the management of press enquiries by a trained PR person. Dealing with the National Security Letters that arrived regularly from the FBI was the job of a legal person, if only Fishbowll had one. But Andrei seemed to need Ben around, to have long, philosophical conversations with him about Fishbowll and its place in the world, as if Ben were some kind of muse. Privately, Chris doubted that whatever Andrei got out of that was worth 9 per cent of the company.

'At least Stanford will take me back,' said Ben. 'I'm not so sure about Kevin.'

'Why not?' said Chris.

'No, I'm kidding. They will – or they would, as long as they don't find out about what he's been doing.'

'What's the issue?'

'Didn't you hear about our disciplinary scrape? It was back in October.' Ben stopped for a moment. October. That had been pre-Fishbowll. It seemed like an eternity ago, yet it wasn't even a year. 'We … well, Kevin has this thing about making up personalities when he goes on networking sites on the net.'

'You mean he goes anonymously?'

'No, he makes up, like, whole personalities. Men, women, whatever.'

'Seriously?' said Chris.

'Oh, it's serious. He concocts photos to make home pages and creates this whole life for them. It takes serious work. This isn't just a matter of making up a user name. It's a work of art.'

Chris turned and looked into the living room. Four desks were pushed together and around them sat six guys at screens. Kevin was beside Andrei, eyes down, headphones on.

'Is this some kind of sexual thing?'

Ben grinned. 'You're asking a psychologist, Chris. What isn't?'

'So … what …?'

'No, it's not sexual. Not overtly. It's just a thing he does. He'd say it's a way of losing inhibition and allowing your mind to really express itself, a kind of fuller Deep Connectedness, if you will. Anyway, there was this guy called Dan Cooley in our dorm …' Ben paused. 'You sure no one's told you about this?'

'No one.'

'Well, there was this guy called Dan Cooley, and Kevin – and I, incidentally – did a kind of experiment. I'm a little ashamed of it, actually, but I don't think it worries Kevin at all.' Somewhat sheepishly, Ben told Chris about the Cooley affair and its denouement. 'He bought a pair of Adidas sneakers and they charged us with violating Stanford's Fundamental Standard. That's Stanford's Bill of Rights. It's about two lines long and you can make it cover anything you want. Anyway, Kevin said I had nothing to do with it. He took a bullet for me.'

'You were lucky.'

'Absolutely. He's definitely a good guy. We don't agree on everything – in fact, we don't agree on a lot of things – but … you know. Anyway, they gave him probation and counselling and they gave me a caution. Needless to say, everything he's been doing at Fishbowll has been a violation of his probation.'

'Which was?'

'You're not going to believe this.' Ben paused for effect. 'Not to access social networking sites for twelve months!'

Chris grinned. 'Dude! That is bad!'

'He can't help himself. He does the same thing on Fishbowll. He admitted two personalities to us. I'm sure he's got more.'

Chris glanced at Kevin again. Kevin was gazing with intense concentration at his screen in the living room. 'Andrei says he's a Stakhanovite.'

'He absolutely is. He's the most Stakhanovite guy I've ever met. So anyway, this thing he does, with the personalities, we had a big discussion about whether Kevin should or shouldn't be doing it on Fishbowll. He put forward an argument about rights and control and the liberating effect of personality adoption on Deep Connectedness. Very libertarian, which is typical Kevin.'

'And Andrei?'

'Andrei bought it. I personally would prefer to see us trying to discourage pseudonymity, but Andrei's view is that it's legitimate. And if it's legitimate, our role is neither to encourage or discourage. I mean, I think, as officers of the company, we shouldn't be doing it ourselves. But to Andrei, if we accept it's legitimate, and if we accept that we can't control it and can't prevent it, then it would be hypocritical to say that we can't do it. Consistency is very important to Andrei. He doesn't let emotion overrule rationality. He's a deductionist. If he has a principle, he applies it everywhere, no matter how much it hurts.'

Chris sucked on his beer and swallowed thoughtfully. 'Kevin's a libertarian, you say?'

Ben nodded.

'What is Andrei's philosophy, do you think? Apart from deductionism.'

'I wouldn't say deductionism's a philosophy. It's a methodology.'

'So what's his philosophy?'

Ben thought about it. 'You know, that's hard to say. I don't think Andrei has a philosophy *per se*. He measures things by efficiency. That's his yardstick of better or worse. If two conditions have equal measures of efficiency, he's neutral between them.'

'So he's OK if someone kills someone else as long as they do it efficiently?'

'No, I'm not saying that. The basics are obvious. He's a good guy. He's a very good guy. He's got a morality. But when it comes to the more discretionary questions – I'm not talking about murder or theft – then it's efficiency. Efficiency is his measure. For example, he was opposed to letting advertising on Fishbowll. We had a lot of discussion about it. He didn't want to turn into a Mike Sweetman or whatever. I mean, we had *long* discussions. But in the end, we decided we had no choice. So now we've accepted advertising. And what happens? He is totally focused on making the advertising better, totally focused on making it more efficient, both from the perspective of the user and from our perspective. And when you seeing him doing that, the way he does it … the focus, the clarity …' Ben shook his head. 'It's an awesome sight. And the thing is, it's not about the money. It's absolutely not. Have you seen our revenue numbers?'

Chris shook his head. Normally, as an investor, that was the first thing he would have asked to see. But, funnily enough, he never had. It just hadn't seemed relevant.

'They're awesome. I mean, totally awesome. What Andrei and Kevin have done with the advertising just blows your mind. Ed Standish says we're running at three, four times what he would have expected. But I swear to you, I don't think Andrei's even aware of that. And when he decides to do something that generates even more revenue, it's not because he thinks, I can extract more money here, it's because he's thinking, I can make this better, this can be more efficient. And you know what? That gets us *more* revenue. It's like this magic formula. It's totally win-win.'

'And you don't think,' said Chris sceptically, 'at the back of his mind, somewhere, there's this little voice saying, "OK, but we can earn some more money out of this as well"?'

'I don't,' said Ben. 'I really don't think so. I think he's thinking about efficiency.'

Chris took another mouthful of beer, considering what Ben had said. 'So if that's Andrei's yardstick, efficiency, what about not making the world worse? You can do things efficiently that will make the world worse.'

'Sure. He doesn't want to do that. That's a serious thing with him. If he thinks something's going to make the world worse, he's not going to do it, no matter how efficiently. But I don't think he's got a clear yardstick for what makes the world better or worse. That's just gut, whereas for him efficiency is quantifiable, so it's that much more concrete.' Ben shrugged. 'But you know, when it comes to the big moral stuff, what makes the world better or worse, that's all any of us have, really. We dress it up in all kinds of ways – religion, humanism, whatever – but in reality it's just gut. That's the yardstick. It's what you learn at your mother's knee.'

Chris was silent. He watched the ping-pong game. The ball went back and forth over the net. 'I haven't had much to do with Kevin,' he said eventually.

'He's a little … he was a little funny about you buying into the company.'

'I guessed that. You know, I didn't ask to buy in. Andrei asked me.'

'Doesn't matter to me one way or the other. Do we need someone who knows about running a business? Hell, yes. Is that worth five per cent of the business? I'm guessing it is, whoever's idea it was.'

'But Kevin doesn't think so?'

'I really don't know what he thinks now. We haven't talked about it in a while.'

'What does he do with these personalities he constructs?'

'Just chat, I guess. Clearly, he gets something out of masquerading behind these facades.' Ben laughed. 'If I ever need a subject for a doctoral thesis …'

Chris looked at the living room. Kevin hadn't moved. He was still fixed in front of his computer, staring at the screen. Chris felt there was something weird in what he had been told, as if he had just heard that Kevin liked wearing his girlfriend's panties. Not that it was odd to go online anonymously or under a pseudonym – but to make up a whole personality with the kind of detail Ben had mentioned was somewhat more than that.

But there was something that appealed to him about it as well, something that spoke to Chris's spiritual side. He could see that there could be something liberating, potentially empowering about leaving behind who you were and immersing yourself in the mind and body of another being that you had created. All native cultures have mind-opening ceremonies that take the participants out of themselves and lift them into another realm, and Chris had experienced them first hand on three different continents. There was something about what Kevin was doing that reminded him of that, albeit Kevin was doing it in a radically different way. Maybe, he thought, this was a digital-age version of the rites that every culture had produced in every age since the dawn of time.

'You said he concocts photos?' said Chris.

Ben nodded. 'You should see the work he does. It's amazing. He uses Facemaker or Photox or one of those programs, depending on what he's trying to do. But he's improved them. He's created functionalities that would blow your mind.'

'Awesome.'

'He did a Cooley, too. Got some guy to switch from buying one brand of wetsuit to another. Kevin – or Tonya, I should say, who was this South African woman Kevin invented who liked to swim with sharks – told him he'd show a big packet.'

Chris laughed.

'What can I tell you? The guy went out and bought it.'

Chris's laughter stopped. 'Seriously?'

'Seriously. I think it's a terrible thing to do, but that's Kevin.'

'And does he still go online as Tonya?'

'I don't think so. The guy with the big packet wanted to talk to her so he made her disappear. I guess we've still got him – or her – in our archive. Nothing ever goes away, does it?'

'No, nothing,' murmured Chris. He gazed at Kevin for a moment longer, then turned back and picked up a fresh beer. He put it to his mouth, again watching the ping-pong ball going back and forth across the table. *Click, clack* ... An idea was lodging itself in Chris Hamer's mind as he let the glass of the bottle linger against his lips. 'I wonder which brand of wet suit that guy's buying now.'

18

KEVIN'S PREDILECTION FOR impersonation played on Chris's mind. He couldn't decide whether it was brilliantly subversive or disgustingly childish. Probably both, as the most subversive things often were. Primitive cultures always had trickster gods and heroes, lovable scallywags who illuminate through prank. Chris thought of the myths and stories he had heard from Aboriginal Australians only months before.

A few days later, when Ben had gone to Stanford to arrange something about his upcoming return to the university, Chris suggested to Andrei and Kevin that they go to Yao's.

Lopez took their orders and they soon settled into their usual meals. Andrei got the fried prawn and chicken noodles, Chris had the kung pao chicken and Kevin the Vietnamese rice noodles.

'So tell me about Tonya,' Chris opened.

Kevin looked up at him. 'Who told you about Tonya?'

'Ben.'

'Well, it's nothing. She's gone.' Kevin dug into his noodles in a way that suggested he wasn't going to say anything else.

Chris glanced at Andrei, who was putting a forkful of chicken in his mouth.

'Ben said you guys had quite an argument about it,' said Chris, still trying to open the subject.

Kevin shrugged. 'Dude, we have arguments about all kinds of things. It's healthy.'

'I'm interested to hear the points.'

Kevin was silent.

'We can't stop people doing it,' said Andrei.

'That doesn't mean you should encourage it.'

'It's not an argument about what we can and can't stop,' said Kevin impatiently. 'Look, why do we have to tell you about this? It happened before you came. We had a discussion, we agreed on a policy. I don't see why we have to put the case to you like you're some kind of judge.'

'I'm not judging anything. I'm just interested.'

'Whatever.'

There was silence.

'Why do you say it's not an argument about what you can stop?' said Chris. 'I would have thought that's exactly what it is.'

Kevin sighed. He shook his head for a moment, then looked at Chris. 'It's a philosophical argument, Chris. OK? If people choose to behave like that in cyberspace, who are we to stop them? Who are we to say it's wrong? Cyberspace isn't physical space. Different space – different rules.'

'I thought the idea behind Fishbowll was Deep Connectedness between people.'

'And what if pseudonymity facilitates that?' riposted Kevin. 'You get more Deep Connectedness.'

'False Deep Connectedness.'

'Why? What's false about it? What would be false would be to try to force someone to do things in a way that you prescribe. They won't do it. Therefore you'll have less Deep Connectedness.'

'So it's better to have more Deep Connectedness, if some of it's false, than less Deep Connectedness, if it's all true?'

'I don't see the distinction,' said Kevin. 'Dude, I told you, I don't think there's such a thing as this false Deep Connectedness you talk about. That's a false dichotomy. It's your construct and I dispute it. The connection between me, as Tonya, and the other shark swimmers, if you want an example, was real. I was interested in shark swimming, I learned, I contributed, I developed, and maybe I helped them develop. Where's the falsity?'

'You had to make Tonya disappear.'

'Because someone wanted to take that personality from the cyber world – where she existed – into the physical world. Is that my fault? It's like taking a fish out of water. We have two worlds on this planet, water and air, and very few creatures can live in both of them. Well, in human cultures, we now have two worlds as well, the physical and the cyber. Some people are amphibians. Some choose not to be.'

'I'm not sure I buy the analogy.'

Kevin stabbed at his noodles. 'I'm not trying to sell it to you.'

'What do you think, Andrei?' said Chris.

'Dude, we had the conversation!' Noodles flew out of Kevin's mouth. 'This was before you. It doesn't concern you. We had the conversation and we decided what we were doing. We're not reopening it.'

Chris waited a moment. 'Andrei?'

Kevin rolled his eyes, shaking his head.

'I think Kevin has a good point,' said Andrei. 'The way the cyber world develops isn't set in stone. Social networking sites took a step forward towards Deep Connectedness. With Fisbbowll, I think we're taking another step forward and we're getting to a much deeper, more meaningful level. But to do that, we have to have a broad conceptualization of what Deep Connectedness might mean. We need to be inclusive. We need to offer as much as we can. Because what Deep Connectedness looks like when it fully develops – what the players in that world look like – I think that's something the cyber world itself will have to choose. It may look different in different places. It may look different on Fishbowll compared to some other site. That's because people would be using Fishbowll and other sites for different aspects of Deep Connectedness, which is totally cool. So, philosophically, I agree with Kevin. The cyber world will evolve as suits it best, just like the physical world. There'll be things that don't work and therefore disappear – evolutionary dead ends, if you will – and things that do work and survive. I don't know that it won't be, but I hope Fishbowll isn't a dead end. What I am pretty sure I do know is that the best way to make it one is if we sit here deciding how every-thing's got to be. That decision has to come from the users.' Andrei glanced at Kevin. Then he shrugged. 'That's my perspective.'

'I don't disagree with it,' said Chris. 'I don't disagree with what either of you have said. Kevin, the distinction I drew between true and false Deep Connectedness is an artificial construct, I agree. And by the way, I think it's great that you guys think about this stuff and debate it.'

'Like we need your approval,' growled Kevin.

'I also think that most people are so focused on their own selfish desires for whatever they can get out of what's put in front of them that they will pay very little attention to the way things are developing. So the way things develop ... I think that's going to happen blind.'

'Evolution is blind,' said Andrei.

'True. But not even evolution is as blind as we are. When social networking sites took off, if people had been told they could have a free site where all their data's exposed so any adver-tiser can hit on them, or they could have a site that might cost them a few bucks a year but their data would be completely protected and they'd never see an unsolicited message, what do you think they would have said? That's the trade-off, right? But look where we are. Now, what does that tell you?'

'That we're a sad species,' muttered Kevin.

Chris laughed. 'What I'm interested in is what would be the effect on Fishbowll if it became known that x per cent of profiles were ... I won't use the word false ... let's say pseudonymous.'

'They do know. It's right there on the home page. *You may encounter avatars, pseudonyms and even real people.*'

'Do people read that? Do they process it?'

'Did you?' retorted Kevin. 'Look, it's there. We're not people's mothers. Fishbowll's there for them. They do what they want with it.'

'I think it could have an effect,' said Andrei, 'if something happened to make it a real issue that there are people using

Fishbowll under pseudonyms. You know, if there was some kind of major crime or something that could somehow be linked to that.'

'Like people who *don't* commit crimes don't use pseudonyms,' said Kevin.

'Exactly,' said Andrei. 'I think the effect would be short term. I'm trying to build something for the long term. I'm looking ten, twenty, thirty years out. I want Fishbowll to be the true global dating site for ideas, the place you go to make connections. I want the clusters that are only potential today, because people can't find their way to others in their cluster, to become real. And that can only happen through Deep Connectedness. And if that's going to happen, like I said, it's going to happen in the way the cyber community wants it to. Which means we need to have that broad conceptualization, be open to what they want. If they want pseudonyms, it's going to be with pseudonyms. Or not. I don't know. I don't care. The only thing I do know is that it's not going to happen in the way three guys at Yao's says it has to happen. That might work for a few years, but after that, if we don't let our users mould our service in the way they want it to be, someone else will appear and fill that gap. I don't want to leave a gap. I don't have an ideological need that forces me to leave that gap.' Andrei looked directly at Chris. 'Do you?'

Chris laughed. 'I have no ideological need at all.'

'So we're good?' said Andrei.

'We're good.' Chris looked at Kevin. 'I wasn't questioning the decision, Kevin. I just wanted to understand how it was made.'

The next time Chris had a chance to talk to Kevin, he mentioned Tonya again. He said Ben had told him that Kevin had done a Cooley.

'Wow,' said Kevin, 'Ben's really been talking, hasn't he? Why are you so interested?'

'I'd like to see how it's done.'

'Why?'

'I just would.'

'Go take a class,' said Kevin.

'I don't think they have classes for this.'

'Bad luck.'

But Chris persisted whenever he had the opportunity, trying to get Kevin to show him Tonya's home page. Kevin said the home page was deregistered. They both knew he could recover it if he wanted to. Chris told him that Ben had said he used Photox and had actually improved it, and asked Kevin to show him what he had done to the program. Grudgingly, Kevin mentioned some of the technical details. Chris wanted to know more. Over time, Kevin's conversations with Chris grew longer. The chance to talk about his obsession got the better of him, especially as Ben, who had shared his early forays into psuedonymity, seemed to have had some kind of religious conversion against it. Kevin was still somewhat resentful of Chris, and he wasn't completely sure that Chris wasn't going to turn around at some point and ridicule him over his online personas, but eventually, one night, Kevin couldn't help himself. He pulled up a home page dominated by a picture of a grinning woman sitting in a boat with a great white rearing out of the water in the background. 'This is Tonya!'

Chris sat beside him, fascinated. He was full of questions about what Kevin had done, how he had conceived of Tonya's persona, how he produced the photos, how he had introduced her into Fishbowll. Kevin clicked through a few more photos that he had posted on the site. The same woman's face peered out, at a party, with friends, and, of course, on boats or in the water. A couple of pictures showed her bobbing at the surface in a shark cage, a big grin on her face and the tiniest bikini imaginable covering her butt. Chris couldn't believe Kevin had concocted those photos out of fragments of other shots.

By now, Kevin had lost the last vestiges of his suspicions about Chris's motives and was enthusiastically telling him how he constructed and managed his personas. Photoxing photos was only part of it. You had to get into the head of the persona. You had to know the kind of things they would they do, the kind of things would they say. It all had to be coherent.

'It's like being a novelist,' said Chris.

'A little, I guess. You know, there was a time when I was a kid that I wanted to be a screenwriter.'

'Really?'

'I never thought I could be an actor.'

That wasn't the last time they discussed his pseudonymous activity. They bonded over it. Kevin's residual resentment of Chris for being allowed to buy into Fishbowll drained away. He revealed other profiles to him, personas he had kept secret from Andrei and Ben. Chris kept asking him questions, wanting to know more. They spent hours at Kevin's screen, looking over messages that had come in for his personas, deciding how to act, what to say, what photos to concoct. Chris couldn't seem to get enough of it.

Then Chris said he wanted to develop a profile. Kevin shared his improved versions of Facemaker and Photox, and helped him do it.

19

BY THE END of September Ben had left the house to go back to Stanford for his senior year, taking his aquarium with him. One of the programmers had left as well, although the other one living at the house had got a leave of absence to stay on at Fishbowll. Chris was spending less time at the house and more in LA. On one of his trips back, he suggested to Andrei that they get an office. Andrei was resistant, but they needed more programmers and people with commercial skills. Were they all going to live and work in the house? Eventually Andrei agreed. Chris contacted a realtor who was recommended to him by the guy who had found him FriendTracker's office in LA four years previously.

In the third week of October, just shy of its first birthday, Fishbowll moved into its first office, a bare, 1,200 square-foot space over a frozen yoghurt shop and minimart on Ramona Street, Palo Alto. Desks came from a local second-hand office furniture store. Other stuff depended on whatever anyone wanted to bring in. But there was one thing that Andrei insisted on. He drove with Ben to a store called Fish Palace and together they bought a six-foot aquarium and stocked it with three dozen fish.

On the day they moved into the office on Ramona, Fishbowll consisted of eleven people: Andrei, Kevin, Ben, Eric Baumer the infrastructure guy, and seven programmers. Chris, who was a lot more than a passive investor, made it a round dozen. Ben would come into the office some days when he had time between classes and Chris was there when he came up from LA, although he and

Andrei often hung out in the house on La Calle Court, where Andrei and Kevin and one of the programmers continued to live.

Life in the office was chaotic. It was the scene of typically heroic Fishbowll wheelspins as the user base continued to grow and new features were added, but everything else was dealt with ad hoc by whoever had the time and inclination. Eric commuted from Hayward each day but talked mostly to Chris, even if Chris was in LA and Andrei was sitting three yards away from him. Ben was handling press relations, customer service, legal matters and just about any other outward-facing stuff from his student room at Stanford, fitting it in around his course programme, which didn't make for the most responsive approach to a workload that was growing exponentially as the website expanded. For three consecutive weekends the infrastructure was close to breaking, despite Eric's titanic efforts to keep the site running. Eventually he rang Chris in frustration and threatened to quit.

Chris got on a plane, came into the office and sat down with Andrei and Eric. He told Andrei that Eric didn't feel valued by him and that Eric thought Andrei had no idea what it was taking to keep the site running.

'Eric, that's not true,' said Andrei. 'You're a Stakhanovite.'

'I don't want to be a fucking Stakhanovite!' yelled Eric. 'I want to run a site that's got a better than even chance of staying up! We need to do stuff to the architecture so it doesn't suck up so much server space.'

'I know,' said Andrei.

'No. We need to do it now! Not after you've done whatever hundred thousand projects you've got in mind. Now, Andrei!'

'He's right,' said Chris. 'And you don't need to be doing that kind of stuff yourself, Andrei. You should be working on new stuff, groundbreaking stuff. You need more programmers doing this kind of thing.' He glanced at Eric. 'Can you excuse us for a minute?'

It was a nugatory request, because there were no partitions in the office and everyone was already listening to what they were saying anyway. But as requested, Eric got up and stalked off to sit symbolically on the edge of a desk a couple of yards away.

'You know what?' said Chris. 'Let's take a walk.'

He and Andrei went out and started walking up Ramona.

'You asked me to join Fishbowll because you wanted my advice,' said Chris.

Andrei nodded.

'And I presume you want me to be honest with you.'

'Of course I do.'

'OK, well, I think there are a couple of things that have happened. The first is, Andrei, you're running a business now. I don't claim to have all that much experience in that area, but when a guy like Eric, a guy who's been keeping this website running when I don't know how it's been possible to do that, given the features you keep adding … when a guy like Eric says he doesn't feel you listen to him, you need to take notice of that.'

'I don't know what he's talking about! He's a Stakhanovite. I've told him he's a Stakhanovite.'

'That's not what I mean. When it comes to the operational stuff, he talks to me.'

'What's wrong with that?'

'Well, I shouldn't be running your operations. Trust me – you don't want me doing that. Basically, Andrei, you need to decide what you want to do. What's your role? Do you want to develop the functionality, do you want sit there coding all day – and I'm not saying you shouldn't, because your ability to do that is what's got Fishbowll to where it is today – or do you want to lead this business? Now, I found Eric, and I found this office, but there's a million things that need to be done. We need more people. Someone's got to recruit them, Andrei. And the more people we recruit, the more time and ability it's going to take to manage them. Maybe we should get a CEO, and then you can focus on the coding.'

Andrei stopped on the pavement. 'Is that what you think? Is that what you came up here to tell me?'

'It's an option. Someone needs to lead this business. As a business. Not just do coding.'

Andrei folded his arms. 'You're right. I need to decide.'

Chris nodded.

'I want to lead this business.'

'That was quick.'

'I know what I want to do,' said Andrei.

'You might want to think about it.'

'No. I don't want to just do coding. I've seen what's been happening. I know we need more people. I should have done something about it. I need to step up to the plate.' Andrei looked at him. 'Or do you think I'm making a mistake?'

'Not necessarily. Not if you want to do it. But if you want to be CEO, then you need a manager to manage the management stuff.'

'Isn't that what Eric does?'

'Eric handles the infrastructure. I'm talking about … call it a chief operating officer. Someone who'll do the recruitment, manage the people, all that stuff. You can do what the CEO does – lead the company, set the vision, decide where the people focus their time and where they don't.'

'And code?'

'The *really* important stuff. Only that.'

Andrei started to walk on. 'A chief operating officer. You mean some guy in a suit.'

Chris sighed. He'd had his own troubles with guys in suits, but they had their role. 'We can get him out of a suit.'

'Why can't you be the COO?'

Chris laughed.

'Why not?'

'Trust me, you don't want me doing that. You want someone who knows how to really operate a business. Someone who loves to do that stuff, all the shitty little stuff, day in day out.'

'I don't want anyone in a suit in my office.'

'Then we'll get him out of it. And we'll get someone who knows what an internet start-up is like. But honestly, Andrei, if we don't get this person now, I fear for what's going to happen.'

'We're going corporate,' muttered Andrei.

'We're facing reality,' said Chris.

Andrei walked in silence. He knew that Chris was right. And he also knew that if he was going to lead Fishbowll as it continued to grow, if that was the challenge he was setting himself, he had to stop wishing it could forever be like it had been in Robinson House or La Calle Court. It was only a year since Fishbowll had started, but those days were already gone. It was childish to pine for them, childish to complain about going corporate. Andrei promised himself then and there that he would never complain about it again. If he did, everyone else would too.

'I know a headhunter who does a lot of recruitment for start-ups. She can help us get a COO. I can handle this for you, Andrei. It's just … you need to be happy that we need to do it. And I really think we don't have a—'

'I know,' said Andrei. 'Enough. I know. You're right.'

'So I'll go and talk to this headhunter?'

'No.'

'I thought you said—'

'No, you shouldn't handle this for me. I should handle this myself. I have to start to lead this business, isn't that what you're saying? If I can't do more than code the website, then I should hand over to someone else.'

'And you're sure you want to do that? A lot of start-ups bring in a professional CEO. The VC firms almost always demand it.'

'We haven't gone to a VC firm. It's my call.' Andrei paused. 'You really don't think I'm making a mistake?'

'You're a programmer. You have no experience of being a CEO. You have a massively growing business.' Chris grinned. 'Hell, I say, do it!'

'I'm serious,' said Andrei. 'Tell me if I'm wrong.'

Chris nodded. 'Seriously? I don't know if you're going to be a good CEO. But neither do you. And that's a good thing. I'd be a lot more worried if you said you thought you were going to be great. You're going to have to learn a hell of a lot, Andrei. Don't kid yourself.'

'I'm willing to learn.'

Chris grinned again. 'Right! Let's go and get you a damn good COO.'

'Give me the name of the headhunter.'

'Let's go and see her together.'

'I said I'd handle it,' said Andrei. 'I need to lead. I need to do this stuff.'

'Andrei, there are a lot of flaky start-ups out there. If she's going to get you a great guy, she needs to know this isn't one. Let me come with you. Trust me on this. That's the first thing you've got to learn, Andrei. What you can do yourself and when you need help.'

Andrei looked at Chris for a moment. 'OK. We should have a meeting with the guys. They need to know about this COO thing.'

'It's about time you all got job titles as well.'

Andrei stopped himself from grimacing.

'Fishbowll is going to be very big, Andrei. You're on the cusp. A year from now, you won't know this company.'

Andrei felt of surge of foreboding, almost fear. Maybe he shouldn't try to be the CEO.

Chris laughed. He put an arm around Andrei's shoulder. 'Buckle up, Andrei. It's going to be a hell of a ride.'

That night, Andrei and Chris sat down with Kevin and Ben at Yao's. Over a traditional Fishbowll noodle meal, Andrei told them that he had decided to hire a COO. Predictably, Kevin protested about guys in suits, but Chris made a strong case in support of Andrei's decision. By now the relationship between Chris and Kevin was close enough for that to make a difference to Kevin. Even so, he wasn't happy. He was even less happy when Andrei said they needed job titles and told them he was going to be the CEO.

'Original,' said Kevin.

'Ben, I thought we'd call you the CMO.'

'What's that?'

'Chief Mind Officer.'

Ben smiled.

'Kevin. I thought, maybe ... President of Getting Things Done. What do you think?'

'It's ...' Kevin shrugged, trying not to show that he actually liked the title. 'There are worse names.'

'And Chief Stakhanovite,' added Andrei. 'All the Stakhanovites in the company are in your tribe.'

'What about you?'

'If I'm a Stakhanovite, I'm in your tribe as well. Now, Chris ...' Andrei looked at him appraisingly '... for you ...'

'I don't need a title. I'm an investor. Occasionally, I might give you a little advice.'

'Exactly. You're the Primary Counsellor.'

'If you like.'

'And *Éminence Grise*.'

'You're going to put that on my business card?'

'Absolutely.' Andrei glanced at Kevin. 'Just because we have titles, it doesn't mean they have to be anything a guy in a suit would think up.'

The COO Andrei and Chris recruited was a 34-year-old called James Langan who had worked at a couple of big names in the internet world. Andrei met him three times during the recruitment process and thought he could get on with him. Langan, for his part, hadn't actually worked at a start-up but he visited the office on Ramona Street and thought he could deal with the environment. He joined with a grant of 1.5 per cent of the company's stock and an accrual scheme that would see him double that share if he stayed for three years.

By now Fishbowll was fifteen months old and had over 120 million registered users. Although the user number still wasn't public information, there were some pretty good estimates out there and Fishbowll, which had already been noticed by the tech media, began to penetrate the consciousness of the mainstream press. Numerous articles appeared on the company with pieces in *Newsweek*, *Time*, *The New York Times*, the *Los Angeles Times*, Britain's *Economist* and, of course, every tech publication. The idea of meta-networks as the next big thing in social media was gaining currency, with Fishbowll being cited as the first true example to have come into existence.

Andrei still avoided giving interviews but the company had no formal press policy. Ben spoke to journalists and Kevin was always happy to supply a libertarian quip if a reporter happened to get hold of his number.

That was one of the first things James Langan tried to bring under control. He ordered a no-speak policy without prior approval and hired PR firm Jennings Massey to handle the press until he was able to find a permanent spokesperson.

Ben was relieved. He found the press inquiries repetitive. Reporters wanted to talk to Andrei, not him, and some of them got quite hostile at the tenth time of telling that Andrei had no interest in talking to them. Ben was also conscious that things he said might have legal repercussions of which he wasn't even aware. Langan hired an in-house lawyer, which had the added benefit of taking the National Security Letters out of his hands. The number that the FBI now addressed to him was so large that all he ever did was hand them on to one of the programmers to pull the data, without even trying to verify if the request was legal.

More desks were bought and people arrived in the office to populate them. One Monday, three new faces appeared and set up camp in a corner of the increasingly crowded space on Ramona Street. Suddenly, Fishbowll had a customer service team, removing another of Ben's responsibilities. More software engineers arrived. A human resources and finance person joined, sharing a desk in one of the last available spots. Ed Standish from

4Site always seemed to be in Palo Alto for meetings with James and the commercial team that James had set up. With barely half the 4Site contract period gone, Ed jumped ship after eighteen years in Dallas and joined as the Senior Vice President for Advertising. James was already looking for larger premises.

Andrei, meanwhile, was learning what it was to be the leader of what was now perceived as one of the most exciting internet start-ups in years. He spent less time coding, more time allocating the company's programming resources among the almost infinite array of projects they could launch and providing guidance to the software engineers. Calls from investors came in regularly. Valuations in the hundreds of millions of dollars were being bandied about without any verified public knowledge of Fishbowll's user base or revenue figures.

Andrei began to be invited to conferences and meetings, but avoided them. Both Chris and James told him that he couldn't avoid public appearances for ever. He would have to learn to deal with the press as well. If he wanted to be the CEO, that was a part of the role that he would have to accept.

His relationships with the other founders of Fishbowll began to change. He saw less of Ben, who was coming towards the end of his senior year and was focusing strongly on his studies. In any case, Ben had less and less to do in the business as James built up the team, and rarely had reason to be in the office. Inevitably, there were few opportunities for the long, rambling conversations Andrei and he had shared so often in the first year of Fishbowll's existence. Kevin remained anarchic, libertarian, enthusiastic and Stakhanovite – all of which Andrei valued about him – but didn't have the same outlook on the business that Andrei did. Andrei couldn't afford to be anarchic any more. He now had thirty-four employees. They needed some measure of reliability.

Another change that happened was in the name of the website. Chris had always been bugged by the second *l* in Fishbowll and felt that, potentially, it even limited the growth of the company by giving it an alternative and somewhat juvenile feel. If they wanted to go public, the name wouldn't help. James Langan agreed. Two months after James arrived, he and Chris persuaded Andrei to buy the rights to Fishbowl.com from the organization that owned it. The price immediately shot up and Andrei ended up signing a cheque for $400,000. Fishbowll was formally renamed Fishbowl.

Andrei Koss, at the age of twenty-two, was CEO and majority shareholder of a company that he would have had no difficulty selling right then for a price anywhere up to $500 million, and which likely would go public within the next couple of years at a valuation an order of magnitude greater. He was surrounded by a growing group of incredibly smart and talented programmers working on the thing that still was – in keeping with the question that Chris had asked him the first time they had met – the most important thing he could imagine doing. His leave of absence from Stanford would lapse in the summer but any idea that he might go back – if he had ever had such a thought – was entirely gone now. Advertising revenues continued to grow at a rocketing rate. As the second winter of Fishbowll's young life turned to spring, there was no reason to suspect that anything might happen to prick the bubble.

20

IN RETROSPECT, THEY should have seen it coming. Competition to Fishbowl was already beginning. A couple of start-ups in the US and Europe were trying to reproduce the Fishbowl experience, and inevitably China had its own home-grown, heavily censored version spreading behind the Great Firewall. It was only a matter of time until a genuine heavyweight entered the ring.

Early in the spring, Homeplace, the world's largest social media site, issued an announcement that within a fortnight it was going to launch a meta-network of its own, making it clear that they must have been working on a rival service for months.

'Now Homeplace users will be able to find anyone, anywhere, who shares their interests,' Mike Sweetman was quoted as saying. 'Leveraging Homeplace's unparalleled reach and breadth, we are confident that we will bring more connections to more people in more places than any other meta-network could possibly ever aspire to do. Homeplace will always be the place where the whole world is at home.' In an interview on *Business Daily* that night, in case there was any doubt who he had in his sights, he added: 'It's time for the big fish to get into the pond.'

Chris came up the following day. He, Andrei, Kevin, Ben and James met at the house in La Calle Court. James hated coming out to La Calle Court, which still had the look and feel of a frat house, but it was the only place they could get any privacy now that the office on Ramona Street was bursting at the seams.

They sat around on a pair of busted-up sofas with beers and pizza. Chris had spent most of the previous day on the phone but hadn't been able to find out much more about the service that Sweetman was planning than had been announced in the press. The one positive, James said, was that Sweetman obviously regarded meta-networking as a serious business. That was valida-tion – with a capital V, as he put it – to anyone out there who still doubted it, and that included potential investors if and when Fishbowl chose to go public. The downside, which nobody needed to point out, was that if Homeplace was successful, there might not be any Fishbowl left to invest in.

Fishbowl's user base was approaching 200 million – but Homeplace had over a billion and, more importantly, over half of Fishbowl's 200 million were Homeplace members as well. Even if they stayed loyal, even if they didn't switch back to the new service that Homeplace was going to offer, growth from that quarter would probably stop dead.

Chris felt they needed to come out quickly and forcefully to differentiate themselves, focusing on the fact that Fishbowl was unaligned and independent, a true meta-network that didn't discriminate amongst social networks or other sources from which it drew its members. James was less impulsive. He agreed that Fishbowl's independence was its differentiator, but was less keen to make a noise until Sweetman launched and they could see the nature of the competitor they were dealing with. He couldn't imagine that Sweetman would create a truly free and unbiased meta-network to rival Fishbowl. Somehow, James was sure, he would be seeking to put Homeplace at an advantage against competitor networks. James wanted to wait and see how much damage Sweetman was going to do to himself. That would be more powerful than anything Fishbowl could say or do. Chris worried that if Sweetman didn't do himself any damage, and if Fishbowl didn't got its shots in first, its voice might be drowned out in the thunder of Sweetman's success.

Ben inclined to James's view. Kevin was with Chris. He looked at Andrei. 'What would your father say?'

'How to deal with a competitor?' said Andrei.

Kevin nodded.

'I think the custom in Moscow in those days was to blow up their offices.'

Fishbowl restricted itself to a bland acknowledgement of the imminent launch of a competitor and said that meta-networking was such an important development in global connectedness that there was certainly space for companies that offered different approaches – a compromise between Chris's plea to start differentiating themselves and James's suggestion that they keep their powder dry.

Within that part of the press and blogosphere that was interested in such things, speculation was feverish about Homeplace's plans. Sweetman was keeping the details of the new service under wraps, which only heightened anticipation of its launch. Fishbowl's response didn't satisfy many commentators. There was soon a chorus of doomsdayers saying that Fishbowl had seen its peak and no one would be willing to pay a dime for it now. As the pressure built, Chris came back up to Palo Alto to plead for a more aggressive line. James urged Andrei to hold firm, saying that all they had seen so far was hot air being blown out by journalists and bloggers.

According to the blogosphere, Homeplace, with billions in its war chest and a staff of programmers that could develop in a month what had taken Fishbowl a year and a half to produce, would outmuscle, outmanoeuvre and generally outdo the young upstart on Ramona Street. Mike Sweetman, who had built the most extensive social network on the planet, had never put a foot wrong. Andrei Koss, they were saying, should have sold out when he had had the chance.

For two weeks, Fishbowl waited.

Launch day was a blitz. Homeplace flew in just about every tech journalist on the globe to a monster party in San Francisco's coolest venue, the Grey Warehouse. A thirty-foot planet suspended above the stage lit up with the hitherto secret name of the new meta-network – Worldspace – at the moment that Mike Sweetman announced that it had gone live. Underneath it, to make the point, someone had placed a twelve-inch fishbowl with a single goldfish swimming around in bemusement.

Sweetman announced that he expected 20 million registrations by the end of the first day, and had put in place unprecedented server capacity to manage the demand. The next day, Homeplace claimed that almost double that number had joined up – in less than twenty-four hours, in an awesome display of its reach and brand power, Homeplace had garnered over 20 per cent of the number of users Fishbowl had achieved in the entire eighteen months of its existence. If Homeplace was to be believed, that number doubled again the next day.

Then the complaints started.

Every time anyone opened their Homeplace page, they were asked whether they wanted so sign up to Worldspace, and had to click Yes or No in order to get to their page. After the first couple of times, they started to get tired of it. Some people claimed they had been signed up despite having clicked No. And on the other side, if someone signed up who wasn't a Homeplace user, they discovered that registration with Worldspace automatically signed them up to Homeplace as well. The next time they tried to sign in to Worldspace, they were told that they had to sign in to their Homeplace page first.

Then people began to notice that the only 'snares' they received seemed to come from Homeplace users.

People thought the use of the term 'snares' was pretty lame. Unable to use the terms 'bait' or 'hook', which were Fishbowl signatures, this was the best that the thousands of supposedly brilliant people at Homeplace had been able to come up with. It contributed to a growing sense that the site was derivative and unoriginal, replicating Fishbowl without offering anything new.

The tech press was lukewarm at best, damning at worst. Analysts lambasted Homeplace for having done nothing more than copy Fishbowl. The blogosphere heaved with a sense of disappointment and anticlimax. After all the hype, Worldspace had no innovative new features. Fishbowl actually set a record for registrations in the month of the launch. While the publicity of the launch generated interest in meta-networks, it seemed that plenty of people were opting for Fishbowl, perhaps as a way of punishing Sweetman for Homeplace's dominance of the social networking world, or for the laziness and arrogance of Worldspace's shortcomings.

By the end of the first week, Sweetman announced that the automatic question asking whether Homeplace users wanted to sign up to Worldspace had been removed. He claimed that it had only been intended to be there for the first few days to raise awareness. He said that Homeplace was investigating claims of sign-up despite clicking on the No button. And he denied categorically that the only snares came from Homeplace users. Technically, that was true, but two days later he was forced to admit that snares from Homeplace users were given higher priority than those coming from other sources, which everyone knew amounted to the same thing. He pledged to create truly random lists, again doing no more than replicating what Fishbowl already offered.

James had been right. The spectacle of Sweetman making concession after concession had more impact than anything Fishbowl could have done. Now Fishbowl launched its publicity drive. If Andrei wouldn't do interviews, at least he needed to speak. A video release was issued showing Andrei talking about Fishbowl's record of independence and comprehensiveness and asking why Sweetman hadn't addressed the outstanding issue of automatic sign-ups to Homeplace by non-users of the network.

In a video blog the next day, Sweetman announced that the automatic sign-ups from non-Homeplace users had been a mistake, and that they had already been stopped.

In response, Andrei was quoted in a press release as saying that he was glad Homeplace had seen the error of its ways, but he wondered that if they did what Mike Sweetman had pledged, what exactly were they offering that Fishbowl hadn't been offering for almost two years to some 200 million users?

Sweetman used an interview with Bloomberg to reply that Worldspace users also had access to all the features of Homeplace, with a streamlined registration process that took no more than a minute.

'That proves what we've been saying all along,' Andrei was quoted as saying. 'Worldspace isn't a meta-network – it's a micro-network. It seeks to close people into a walled garden – we seek to break down the walls around the gardens so everyone can see each other. If you want the walls, go to Homeplace. If you want the view, come to Fishbowl. And, by the way, how many users does Worldspace have now? And how often do they visit the site?'

Rumours were spreading that Worldspace growth had stalled, and that many of its registered users were barely using the service. James Langan issued a press release offering to provide Fishbowl's figures on key metrics if Sweetman did the same.

Six weeks after its launch, Mike Sweetman announced a total relaunch of Worldspace, to be renamed Openreach. He pledged to make Openreach a genuine meta-network with the widest possible reach, and to introduce a host of new features that would leave Fishbowl trailing in its wake.

This time there was to be no monster party, no giant globe looming over a tiny fishbowl. Details of the revamped service and its new functionalities would be revealed at a press conference to be held on the Homeplace campus.

The press conference was scheduled for 3 p.m. on a Wednesday afternoon – a Wednesday afternoon that, it turned out, would be etched indelibly etched into America's memory. But not because of anything Mike Sweetman did.

21

THE EDGAR T Lacey Federal Building in Denver was an eight-storey block constructed in 1981 that housed regional offices of the Drug Enforcement Administration, Bureau of Alcohol, Tobacco and Firearms, Social Security Administration and a number of other federal agencies. At 12.14 local time that Wednesday afternoon, a bomb exploded inside a van that had pulled into the delivery bay under the building, tearing through the cafeteria on the ground floor while demolishing the entire back of the building and severely damaging a number of other structures in the surrounding blocks.

As wounded and dazed survivors emerged through the smoke and shredded paper billowing out of the wreckage of the building, a sniper positioned on a rooftop with full view of the entrance plaza began to shoot. The records would later show that it was four minutes before the first emergency services arrived at the scene and a further seven minutes until, in the confusion, a policeman saw an ambulance officer go down in front of his eyes with an apparent gunshot wound to the chest and radioed that the Lacy building was still under attack.

By this time the plaza in front of the building was littered with the bodies of bomb survivors, firemen, ambulance personnel and police officers. It took another three minutes for the crew of a chopper that had been scrambled after the blast to locate the gunman, and another four minutes for a squad of police special forces to divert from the Lacey, run up the stairs of the building and get onto the rooftop, during which time the gunman continued steadily firing at anyone in range. In the ensuing gun battle, one policeman died and another two were injured, before the gunman himself was finally shot dead.

The initial death toll from the bomb was 224, far exceeding the 168 deaths in the 1995 Oklahoma City bombing, with which it was immediately compared. In the cafeteria, which had been full for lunch at the time of the explosion, 118 died. The majority of the others perished in the upper floors and stairwells of the Lacey building as they collapsed in on each other, while five fatalities were recorded in surrounding buildings from the blizzard of flying glass that the bomb had unleashed. Outside, in his eighteen minutes of uninterrupted firing, the sniper had killed a further fifty-nine people and injured forty-seven. Over the coming days, the toll continued to rise as the most severely injured lost their battles for life.

In total, 309 men and women lost their lives in Denver that afternoon or in the days that followed.

The gunman was soon identified as Walter Hodgkin, a 32-year-old ex-Marine with three tours of duty as a sniper in Iraq, and a soon-discovered history of involvement in anti-government, pro-gun circles after leaving the military. It wasn't immediately clear whether the bombing was the work of Hodgkin alone – theoretically, he could have left the van in the delivery bay and then made his way to the top of the adjacent building before remotely detonating the explosive – or whether Hodgkin had an accomplice, possibly one who had acted as a suicide bomber. The size of the explosion left very little forensic material in the vicinity of the van, which had ignited a fireball in an adjacent truck that was delivering fuel oil at the time.

The question was solved a couple of days later when a memory stick turned up in the mail at the headquarters of the National Rifle Association with a video showing Walter Hodgkin and another ex-Marine, Andrew Buckett, talking about the attack they were planning to launch on the Lacey Building. In a clear and apparently self-conscious echo of Islamist suicide videos, they sat in front of a flag – a stars and stripes, in this case – each clutching an M16 and with red, white and blue headbands around their foreheads.

For the first fifteen minutes of the video, Buckett railed semi-coherently about the iniquity of the anti-freedom, anti-human rights, anti-American socialist Washington government. Then Hodgkin took over, calmly declaring that he and Buckett were launching the United Taliban of America. They had seen in Iraq and Afghanistan that the only way to wear down a great colonizing power was through the dedicated, unanswerable attrition of the suicide martyr. There was no power greater, he said, than the socialistic communist government in Washington and no colonization more oppressive or predatory than its rule over the once-free states of the republic. Therefore, in Denver, they were going to unleash on the Washington government a suicide storm that, he claimed, would be joined by a legion of followers inspired by their example and grow in power and ferocity until it engulfed the socialist oppressors of Washington, just as the flames that those same oppressors had unleashed had engulfed the temple of the holy martyr David Koresh in Waco.

The NRA handed over the memory stick to the FBI, but not before someone had made a copy of the file. Snippets of the video began to leak. Soon the faces of Walter Hodgkin and Andrew Buckett, sitting in full combat gear and clutching their M16s in what appeared to be a cheap motel room with the stars and stripes on the wall behind them, had became familiar across the world. The FBI refused to confirm or deny that the video was genuine. It was only as their investigation wound down that they released the full footage.

But that would be weeks later. On the Wednesday afternoon of the bombing, none of that was known. In the office on top of the frozen yoghurt store on Ramona Street, the Fishbowl staff, now forty-one strong, gathered in knots of fours and fives around computer screens and watched the stream coming live out of Denver in horror and confusion. Across town on the Homeplace campus, the press conference that had been scheduled to relaunch Worldspace, with no chance of receiving any airtime in the face of what had happened, was cancelled. All across the country, people were watching on television or computer or smartphone or any other device capable of showing the images from the Mile High City, slowly beginning to understand the scale of what had taken place. James Langan, who was a devout Christian but usually kept his faith strictly out of the office, went to a corner of the room and knelt in prayer. A number of people joined him, holding hands.

In the days afterwards, everyone at Fishbowl shared the shock of the nation, the disbelief, the numbness. They watched the president address the country that evening, his face solemn and grim, his voice choking at times as he spoke of the men and women who had died in the blast, of the brutality of a man who could stand and shoot at survivors and the public servants who had come to their aid. They joined up, like 34 million people the world over, to Fishbowl Schools repudiating what had been done and offering support to the people of Denver. They stood with the rest of the nation the next Wednesday at 12.14 p.m. Mountain Time and shared two minutes of deep, reflective silence.

And the following day, like the rest of the nation, they first heard the name Fishbowl mentioned in connection with the attack.

The rumour first surfaced in the blogosphere. Reports emerged that Buckett had been an active member of a Fishbowl School including both domestic extremists and radical foreigners that discussed resistance to the US government and had even used the site for instructions about bomb detonation. The rumour spread quickly into the Grotto. Someone notified James Langan. James walked over to Andrei's desk. There ensued a quick, hushed conversation. Every eye in the large, unpartitioned room was on the two men. But whatever conclusion they might have reached, they didn't have a chance to get there before two FBI agents came through the door.

The familiar figure of John Dimmer was accompanied by a woman who announced herself as Fay Carver, Special Agent in Charge of the San Francisco field office. There was nowhere for them to talk. This was going to be way bigger than a routine National Security Letter and, as the agents waited, Fishbowl's legal officer got on the phone to find a lawyer with expertise in federal terrorist investigations. The agents said it was only an initial discussion and they didn't think there was any need for a lawyer, and suggested that they all go to the field office in San Francisco. Andrei was prepared to talk to the agents, or at least to listen to what they had to say, while legal advice was being sought. James didn't think it would be smart to get themselves locked into an FBI interrogation room. In the end, they went to the nearest hotel, where the the FBI guys got a room. They sat, Andrei and James on one bed, the two FBI agents facing them on the other, while the Fishbowl legal officer perched on a chair by the window.

Fay Carver did the talking that day. Dimmer took notes. Carver asked if they knew anything about Andrew Buckett, Walter Hodgkin or the fact that Buckett, at least, had been a registered Fishbowl user and that Hodgkin may well have been one as well. The answers to those questions were negative. Carver and Dimmer looked as if they had expected them to be.

Then Carver said: 'Well, what we really want to say is, we're going to need access to anything you've got on these guys. Their home pages, their conversations, anything on the people they were conversing with.'

'We'll give you anything we're legally required to give,' said Langan. 'That goes without saying.'

'Well, there are two ways we can do that, Mr Langan.'

'Which are?'

'The hard way, where we get court order after court order extracting the information from you bit by bit, or the easy way, where you go ahead and give us what you know we're eventually going to get anyway.'

'How would I know what you're going to get?'

'Mr Langan, I don't think you understand. We need every-thing you've got on these people. We need to know who they talked to, who the people who talked to them talked to, who might have helped them plan the attack, who might do the same in the future. We're talking about bringing people to justice. We're talking about prevention.'

'And I'm talking about privacy. The way you make it sound, you expect us to show you every single thing anyone's ever said on Fishbowl.'

'You're talking about privacy. I'm talking about lives, Mr Langan. I'm talking about your obligation as a citizen of this country.'

'My obligation as a citizen of this country – and not only that, my obligation as a Christian – is to uphold its laws. That's your obligation as well, ma'am. And what I've just said is we will do exactly that. We will supply you with any information that the law requires us to do.'

'Don't you tell me what my obligation is, Mr Langan! Two hundred and ninety-eight people are dead. Services like Fishbowl are breeding grounds of terrorism, they're incubators of conspiracy. Now, if I were you, I'd say that this is the time to stand up and show a little responsibility and—'

'We'll do it the easy way,' said Andrei.

Everyone in the room looked at him.

'Andrei, let's talk about this,' said James.

'We'll do it the easy way,' said Andrei again.

To Andrei the decision seemed perfectly clear. He agreed to meet the FBI agents the following morning at the office of the lawyer the Fishbowl legal officer had found, in order to agree on the scope of the data and how it was going to be handed over.

That evening, Chris flew up from LA. He, Andrei, James, Kevin and Ben met at the house in La Calle Court.

Ever since John Dimmer had turned up in Robinson House with the first National Security Letter addressed to Fishbowl, it had been clear to all that at some point a Fishbowl user or School might be identified with some kind of horrendous act – although not necessarily as horrendous as the Denver bombing. There was no way that could be prevented. Amongst the Schools on Fishbowl were a good number associated with politically or racially obnoxious views. Andrei, Kevin and Ben had long ago agreed that, beyond issuing their user policy, it wasn't their place to try to pre-empt them. The question was, what was their obligation after the fact?

By the time he arrived at La Calle Court that night, James had received a phone briefing from the lawyer. A request for any information beyond the usual transactional detail available through a National Security Letter would require a court order, and the court order would need to specify exactly what data were required. The scope could not be unduly broad and if the investigators wanted anything else, they would have to go back to court for a further order. Fishbowl would have the right to challenge each order and could expect to win unless the FBI could show how the data requested was likely to be linked to the commission of the crime.

Andrei didn't want to get involved in that kind of process. He respected James Langan's judgement, particularly after his advice to hold back over Worldspace had proven right, but if that was the direction James was headed, Andrei felt that in this case he was wrong. He didn't want to get into a situation where the FBI was turning up with court orders and Fishbowl was challenging and dragging the process out over weeks, or even months. He wanted to give the investigators the information they were seeking, right away.

James and Chris disagreed. That night, unusually, they found themselves on the same side of an argument, both counselling that Fishbowl ought to be more circumspect and at least see what the first court order specified. Otherwise Fishbowl would be tainted as a place where privacy walls crumbled as soon as the cops came knocking. Kevin naturally agreed.

Andrei was unpersuaded. 'I think if we don't cooperate willingly and proactively, we're going to bring down more and more criticism on our heads. James, you heard what that FBI agent said today. Social networks are a place for conspiracy. A lot of people are going to be thinking that. We've always said we're not going to try to police what people are saying on the network. Well, if that's the case, the flip side is that we have to come down hard when we know someone has done something wrong.'

'Agreed,' said James. 'We should do exactly what the law demands.'

'If we're in possession of evidence, I want them to have it.'

'Shouldn't they already have it?' said Kevin snidely. 'What have those guys at the NSA been doing? Isn't that why the taxpayer pays them? So they can read our stuff illegally?'

'That's why the Feds are so pissed,' said Chris. 'They missed these two guys and they know they look like crap.'

'Andrei,' said James, 'if you do this, you create a precedent. Next time, if you don't do it, they'll say you're being obstructionist.'

'They'll say we're being obstructionist now, if we don't do it this time,' said Ben.

'Maybe. But it's going to be even tougher in the future.'

Andrei shook his head. 'We can make it clear that this is an exceptional moment and we're doing this out of civic responsibility.'

'And where does that stop?' said James. 'What if you can help identify someone who assisted someone to kill three people instead of three hundred? Do you open our data then? What if you can find someone who killed one person. Or assisted in a fraud? Or in a theft?'

'I hear what you're saying, but this atrocity is so big ... I think you need to look at it on its own. This isn't a murder, this is terrorism.'

'Andrei, I pray for the souls of those poor people, every night. I pray for their families. I seek in my heart for forgiveness of those two terrible men who did this, and I still haven't found it.

But as far as Fishbowl is concerned, as a business, what you're suggesting is a poor decision. We'll suffer because of it. And we don't need to do it, legally or morally.'

'Morally we don't need to do it?' Andrei was genuinely surprised that James didn't see a moral duty to provide any evidence they might have.

'Morally, we have a duty to our users. They consign the contents of their communications to us in good faith. They have the right to believe we'll protect their privacy unless required by law.'

'Andrei,' said Chris, 'you can be a leader without rolling over.'

'I don't think this is rolling over. And I don't think that if we do this, it makes the world a worse place.'

'I think it does because of the loss of trust,' said James. 'If people aren't going to express themselves freely because of fear that their content might be turned over to the police, what will that do for Deep Connectedness?'

'But what are they expressing?'

'Are you saying we're going to censor them?'

'No, absolutely not. The opposite. They're free to say whatever they want. But if people think they have a medium that allows them to conspire to carry out this kind of act with impunity, what does that do for the world? James, I just don't think we can not do this. Morally, there's an argument to say that if users expect us to do the minimum required by law, then that's what we do. Granted. But I think this thing trumps that. If anyone assisted Hodgkin and Buckett and we can help identify them, through whatever we can do, we should. In the second place, if we can help prevent someone who's setting up do this in the future, we should. And finally, for our reputation, we can't be seen to be obstructive. We have to be seen to be leading.'

'This is leading in the wrong direction,' said Chris.

Andrei shrugged. He knew by now what James, Chris and Kevin thought. 'Ben?' he said.

At first Ben didn't respond, intrigued by the fact that Andrei hadn't been persuaded by James's argument that if he did this, he would have to do it in the case of any crime. That was normally the kind of logic that Andrei would have fallen for. In fact, he would have expected Andrei to be the one articulating it.

'Ben?'

'What I want to know,' said Ben, looking at the others, 'is what happens if there's another bomb in another couple of weeks, and because we didn't provide everything we could, because we dragged our heels, the FBI wasn't able to stop someone they would have found out about? What happens, James, to our reputation then? More than that, what happens to the way we get held accountable?'

Andrei's phone rang. It was Sandy, who was on a field trip with her anthropology class. He went into his bedroom to answer it.

Sandy had just heard about Fishbowl's involvement and asked what Andrei was going to do. He told her about the discussion that was taking place at the house. She asked him if he wanted her to come home. He didn't see the need.

'It's a tough choice,' said Sandy.

'What would you do?' he asked.

'I'd …. I'd probably go with James and Chris,' said Sandy. 'But I haven't heard all the arguments. You know I'll support you if you go the other way.'

He came back.

'James was just saying,' said Ben, 'that in the case of the example I gave, we say we were doing what was required by law. It's the same as cops not going into a place without a search warrant, even if that means they don't find out about a terrorist plan that gets carried out the next day.'

'Even if another three hundred people die?' said Andrei.

James shifted uncomfortably. 'That's the price we pay for our constitutional freedoms.'

'Go tell that to the dead.'

'They're not dead, Andrei. Ben posed a hypothetical case. Hard cases make bad law.'

Andrei didn't find that persuasive. James didn't back down. Where would it end if they committed to give the government anything they asked for? At how many degrees of separation would they agree to stop? Andrei said they could impose their own limits on that when they spoke to the FBI agents. Chris argued they would be branded as obstructionist if they did that, and they may as well stick with the letter of the law.

The argument kept going, and they didn't find any way to bridge the difference. At around midnight James called it to a stop.

'We've said everything there is to say. Andrei, where are you now?'

'I'm where I was.'

'OK, sleep on it.'

'I don't think that's going to change anything.'

'We're not doing anything until the morning. We told the FBI guys we'd be ready for them at eleven. We're meant to be at the lawyer's office at ten. Whatever happens, Andrei, we don't do anything until we talk to him. No statement from anyone, right?' He looked meaningfully around the room. 'And I mean *anything*.'

Andrei glanced at his watch.

'OK,' said James. 'I'll see you in the morning.'

James left. Ben went shortly afterwards. Kevin and Andrei still lived at the house, and Chris often stayed there when he was in Palo Alto. They talked for another half-hour or so and then went to bed.

Andrei had never felt more powerfully the burden of being the leader of this company. It was in the global spotlight now, he knew, at the very centre of the biggest thing that was happening in the world. The decision on how the company should act was his. Others could advise but he had to decide.

At around two, unable to sleep, he called Ben. Ben answered the phone quickly. He didn't sound as if he had been asleep, either. It had been a long time since they had had one of their talks. Andrei went through his thinking, explained why he felt he had to act in the way he was proposing, even though everyone was telling him otherwise. Ben listened patiently, even though he had heard it all already.

'I'm not disagreeing with you,' said Ben. 'Andrei, what is it that's making you so strong on this? I would have thought, actually, that your instinctive reaction would be the same as James's. That's the unemotional view.'

'I'm not being emotional,' said Andrei. 'This is the best thing for the business, Ben. I really believe that. We're a big presence in the world. We're not three guys in a dorm any more. If Deep Connectedness is going to mean anything, if it's going to be something that stays and makes a difference in the world – I mean a difference for the better – then we have to take that responsibility seriously. Something terrible has happened. If we've done anything to facilitate it, anything at all, then we need to admit it.'

'And the privacy argument?'

'If people value their privacy above this, then Fishbowl isn't the place of them. I don't care about the user numbers. I don't care about how many advertisers we can attract. If people want Deep Connectedness without responsibility, then they need to go somewhere else where someone will give it to them.'

'And where's the limit? How small does the crime get before you don't let the government see whatever they want?'

'I don't know, OK? This is a stand-alone case. Let them use the legal process for everything else. But for this, this is an exceptional case. I just … Look, it would be really easy for me to say what James is saying. I think that's the easy way out. But I feel this sense of responsibility, Ben.' He paused. 'It's like I brought this thing into the world. I'm not trying to take anything away from you and Kevin, but …'

'I understand what you're saying.'

'So I feel, you know, I've got this special responsibility … If someone's used this thing that I created, that I put into the world, for something like what happened in Denver, then I think I've got to honour that responsibility. I've got to do more than just say, "I'll do what the law demands." Anyone can do that, but that's not the responsibility I have.'

Ben was silent.

'And I know there's a disconnect, saying I'll do it for this crime, but not for some lesser crime, and if you ask me where the boundary is, I can't tell you. But I feel that now, with this thing, I've just got this responsibility and I can't ignore it.'

It must have been hard, thought Ben, for Andrei to find himself thinking like this, that there wasn't some universal principle he could apply to everything, but that there was an exception that stood out instinctively for reasons that weren't copper-bottomed with logic. No wonder he was agonizing over it.

'Ben? What do you think?'

'You can argue it both ways, Andrei. In the end, this is your business. Like you said, you built this thing. I'm not going to argue with what you think you need to do.'

'But do you agree with it? I want you to tell me.'

'It's a justifiable position.'

'But so is the opposite, right? But then what about what you said? If something happens that could be prevented because we go slow on this, what happens then?'

'Sticking with the law is a defence, Andrei. James is right. It's a good defence. We sometimes pay a price for constitutionality. Look, I think you've made up your mind. I'm not saying it's a bad decision. I'm just saying that the other one wouldn't be, either.'

There was silence again. 'I just think I need to do this,' said Andrei eventually.

'And that's fine. Don't torment yourself, Andrei, if that's what you think, then that's what you should do. I'll stand behind you. The Grotto's not going to be happy.' Ben paused. 'Just get ready for what's going to hit you.'

The statement Andrei proceeded to write wasn't that long, but it took him hours. He drafted and redrafted it, balancing every word, trying to make sure it hit exactly the note he wanted and couldn't be misinterpreted. The statement started solemnly:

'Fellow Fish,' Andrei wrote, 'Fishbowl may have unwittingly become a medium through which one of the most heinous terrorist acts ever seen on American shores was incubated. We are not sure of this, but it is a possibility. I am as committed as I have ever been to Deep Connectedness. But Deep Connectedness is not without responsibility.' He went on to explain what he was planning to do and why. He ended by saying that he knew some people would be unhappy, even outraged, but that he hoped in time they would understand. 'Exceptional circumstances call for exceptional responses,' he concluded. 'If these days, after the tragedy in Denver, do not call for an exceptional response from all of us, I can't imagine what would. Like all of us, Fishbowl must honour its obligation.'

At around 6 a.m. he read it over for the last time. Then he posted it in the Grotto, logged out, and went to sleep.

22

THE PHONE WOKE him. James Langan's voice was apoplectic with rage.

'I just felt it was important for me to say something,' said Andrei – or tried to, a number of times, but he couldn't break into the COO's tirade.

'Do you know what this does? It admits liability! Not just for us, for the entire internet! For all of social networking! It's so … stupid! So unnecessary! We said no one was going to do anything until this morning! We agreed! You cannot do things like this! This is a business, Andrei! It's not a high-school hobby. Sometimes I don't think you get that. Look at the way you live. I am not coming to your house again! It's disgusting. I cannot think in that environment. If we need to meet outside the office, we meet somewhere else. And you need to get control of Kevin. It absolutely is not OK that he talks to the press whenever he wants. And it's not OK that he diverts engineers onto projects that we've already agreed we're going to stop. He only does that because you let him. We're working in chaos …' It went on. Frustrations that had been buried in James since joining the company burst out of him. Finally he pulled himself up. 'Where are you, anyway?' he demanded.

'I'm in bed. I was up all night.'

'Well, get over here. We need to get to the lawyer. We need to talk before the FBI guys arrive.'

When Andrei got to the office, James was still so angry he could barely speak to him. Andrei had thrown on the nearest clothes to hand, which were the same T-shirt and jeans he had worn the previous day. They got a cab and sat wordlessly side by side on the way to the lawyer's office.

The lawyer, a small woman in her forties called Angela Dustin, succinctly laid out the minimum level of cooperation that was required of Fishbowl by law. Andrei told her that he anticipated going beyond that.

'That's a matter for you, Mr Koss.'

'Would that prejudice us in the future?' asked James, not so much as exchanging a glance with Andrei.

'In what respect?' asked Dustin.

'In that we might be required to do the same again in similar circumstances.'

'From a purely legal perspective, no. That you have cooperated to a degree in excess of that required by law does not automatically and of itself create a new threshold that you could be required to meet in another instance, even if it were identical to this. However, I would normally not advise a client to take that path, because from a practical point of view it would considerably increase the pressure you would experience from law enforcement authorities in the future, and although this is not a strict question of law, these forms of pressure can be extremely difficult to resist. On the other hand, if you establish in the first instance that your policy is to comply with the requirements of the law and only those requirements, you create an expectation in the future that helps shield you from—'

Andrei got up. Dustin looked at him in surprise. 'When they get here,' said Andrei, 'I want you to tell them we'll give them anything they can reasonably expect to relate to the bombing, but nothing else. If we decide they're asking for something irrelevant, and they can't convince us otherwise, then they can get a court order and do it the usual way. And if they find anything in what we give them related to any other crime, they can't use it. That needs to be explicit. There needs to be some kind of agreement in writing or something. Can you say that to them?'

'I can say anything you like, Mr Koss. Whether they'll agree is another question.'

'Tell them that's the condition. If they want content, it's Denver. Nothing else.' Andrei turned to James. 'I'm going, I'll see you back in the office.'

At Ramona Street, Andrei sat on the edge of Kevin's desk as surreptitious glances were thrown his way from all over the office.

'Dude, nice work.' Kevin grinned. 'Loved the statement. I assume James is happy.'

Andrei ignored that. 'The FBI is going to ask us for data. The deal is we don't give them anything if we think they're just fishing for stuff, and they can't use anything they find to prosecute any crime but Denver. I want you and me to be the ones to deal with this personally.'

Kevin grimaced. 'You want me to work with the Feds?'

'I'm going to ask them to feed their data requests to you. If you think it's fine to give something, do it. If not, or if you're in doubt, talk to me and I'll decide. But be liberal with them. I want them to have what they need.'

'Andrei, I'm not the right guy this.'

'No, you're the perfect guy for this. But no obstruction. Don't play any games. When we decide to give them something, we give it to them. As quickly as we can. And we give them the complete data set that covers whatever we've agreed on. We don't get them to keep coming back saying they're missing this or they're missing that. They get what we agree to, period.'

'Dude, where's the fun?'

'Kevin, three hundred people are dead. We're implicated. Our reputation, our ability to continue as a business, depends on how we respond.'

'You know, you can have one reputation with one audience and another with another.'

'What does that mean?'

'The Feds are going to love you. But you should see the shitstorm that's going on in the Grotto.'

*

Predictably, the Grotto had erupted like an underwater volcano at Andrei's statement. While large segments of the press just as predictably accused social networks of being uncontrolled hotbeds of extremism and conspiracy, the 300 howled at what they saw as a betrayal of privacy. Karl Morrow reached heights of invective extraordinary even for him. Andrei's approach was outrageous. It was weak. It was deceitful, said those who attributed negative motives to everything they saw. It was entrapment, said the full-blown conspiracy theorists. The Dillerman stoically led a small group of supporters, but his voice was almost drowned out by the howls of anger in the Cavern.

It was accepted wisdom at Fishbowl that if they ever lost the Dillerman on an issue – if such a thing were possible – they would know without doubt that they were doing the wrong thing. Amongst some of the longer-serving Fishbowlers, it had reached almost the level of a superstition. People spoke only half-jokingly of the Curse of the Dillerman, according to which Fishbowl would disappear as a company if ever the Dillerman deregistered his account.

Andrei looked at the Grotto for himself. The overwhelming flood of opinion was negative, abrasive, abusive. He followed the debate for a couple of days and then ignored it. The voices in the Grotto represented only a tiny proportion of the Fishbowl member base, and most users never went near the place. More worrying was an *Andrei Koss can't be trusted* School page that was set up and drew over half a million users. Some of the comments on the page were so vitriolic that Andrei had trouble reading them. He wondered what these people thought he owed them.

But, more importantly, under the light and noise of the reaction, the statistics showed that users continued to access Fishbowl at the same frequency as before. And, needless to say, the critics who were protesting within Fishbowl were, after all, protesting within Fishbowl. Ben, with whom Andrei spoke a number of times during these days, said that he should take it as a positive. People don t protest if they don't care.

That was the line Andrei took when he posted a second statement in the Grotto. This time he checked in with James before he posted it. Relations with James had been frosty, to put it mildly, since Andrei had posted his first statement, but they both knew that the company couldn't afford an open schism in the leadership at this moment of crisis. Somehow, they kept working together, but only just.

James didn't even read the statement. 'Do what you want. Show it to legal. Or not. Up to you.'

The lawyer suggested a couple of word changes but said that since the new statement gave essentially the same message as the first one, it would make no difference to Fishbowl's legal position.

The statement started by thanking the protesters for their words and recognizing that they were loud because they were passionate about Fishbowl. Andrei then said that he had done what he had done only after long consideration and deep soul searching. He reassured them that anything the law enforcement authorities took from the material Fishbowl provided would relate only to the Denver bombing. He reiterated that it was something he would only ever consider doing in extreme circumstances, and he felt the circumstances after the Denver bombing were extreme. He would do it again in the same circumstances, he said, but only in those.

As it happened, the FBI data trawl turned up very little. There were conversations between Andrew Buckett and a number of other right-wing extremists, including some general musing about an American Taliban organization that presumably had morphed into the United Taliban of America in Buckett's twisted mind. But there was nothing that could be even tenuously construed as advance knowledge of the Denver plot or of sharing of any knowhow that might have enabled Buckett and Hodgkin to plan and execute it. On the other hand, more conventional lines of inquiry led to the arrest of two people who had been instrumental in helping Buckett and Hodgkin obtain ingredients for their truck bomb and in procuring the truck itself, which had been rented. It was clear they must have known that some kind of an attack was in the offing, although not necessarily that the Lacey Building was the target or that Hodgkin would take a sniper's rifle to the survivors.

The anger amongst Fishbowl's users spluttered on for a time but gradually died out. And the overwhelming majority of users hadn't protested at all. In all likelihood, they thought what Andrei had done was perfectly reasonable.

Once again, just as he had experienced when he had brought advertising onto Fishbowl, Andrei Koss had felt the storm wind of user anger blowing like a hurricane into his face and had seen it, like a hurricane, blow itself out meekly. He wondered just what one would have to do to make people get up and walk away. Not that he wanted them to. But he felt vindicated. By cooperating with the investigation, Fishbowl had been absolved of involvement with the Denver bombing in a way that might have taken many months, or might even have been impossible if he had complied only with the letter of the law. Not only that, for anyone who believed that social networks were breeding grounds of conspiracy, Fishbowl had shown itself to be prepared to face up to its responsibility.

But there were other people who weren't so sure that the responsibility had been faced – or that it was even up to the people who ran social networks to decide how to do that.

23

SENATOR DIANE MCKENRICK of Arizona was a three-term veteran of the upper house and a leading member of the right wing of the Republican Party. Daughter of Ed McKenrick, a firebrand Arizona attorney general who had gone on to serve as a reactionary justice of the state supreme court, she was an alumnus of Yale law school and had been a partner at the Phoenix law firm of Witherby, Hollins, Franck before entering politics. Now aged fifty-nine, McKenrick was chair of the Senate Committee on Homeland Security and Governmental Affairs and was widely thought to be positioning herself for a tilt at the Republican nomination for the presidency the following year. Her long experience in security affairs gave her a solid claim to the role of commander in chief – especially important for a female candidate – and her reputation as a hawk would reassure a good portion of the party base. Like any putative presidential candidate, what she needed was something to stamp her identity solidly into the national consciousness.

Nothing would do that better than taking resolute action in defence of the United States against terrorism – even if it was home-grown.

The senator had watched events following the Denver bombing closely. The Homeland Security Committee had received a closed-door briefing from the most senior officials in the FBI, and she already planned to convene public hearings into the intelligence failure that had allowed two ex-Marines, apparently well known in extremist right-wing circles, not only to plan but to execute the most deadly terrorist attack on American soil after 9/11, and had made an announcement to that effect. But the hearings would have to wait until after the FBI and the other agencies involved had completed their initial investigations. That would mean a delay of at least a couple of months. By then, the raw shock of the bombing would have receded and, outside Denver and the beltway, the nation's attention would have moved on. And she would be investigating investigators, not people implicated in the actual crimes. McKenrick expected to receive a good degree of coverage for the hearings, but nothing like the attention she would have received if she could have held them right then, and if she could have had in front of her committee people with some responsibility for what had happened.

The allegation of the link with Fishbowl thus caught her attention. She had heard only vaguely of the company, and it had probably stuck in her mind only because of its ridiculous name, but McKenrick had sat on hearings in the past into the security implications of social media. Supporters of social media cited the role it had played in helping democracy movements bring down repressive regimes in places as far-flung as Tunisia and Thailand. She saw this enthusiasm as naive. They saw democracy – she saw destabilization, and the potential for similar activities by extremist minorities against democratically elected governments. If what was being said about the usage of this Fishbowl website by the Denver killers was true, it was as if her prophecy had come to life.

When McKenrick was told that the CEO of Fishbowl had posted a statement saying that Fishbowl might have unwittingly facilitated the planning of the atrocity, she read it in disbelief. In the senator's opinion, admitting that something like that might have happened without pledging action to stop it in future was an outrage. For that reason, it was also a gift. A gold-plated, diamond-encrusted gift. So much so that she couldn't believe anyone connected with one of these companies would ever do it. She got her chief of staff to call Fishbowl and make sure it was genuine. Apparently it was.

An opportunity like this didn't come along every day. The senator felt as if she almost had a duty to see if she could make something out of it, to tie social networks to terrorism and raise people's awareness of the true magnitude of the threat they posed. And burnish her security credentials on the national stage along the way. If the Fishbowl involvement in the Denver bombing exposed a chord of anxiety in the American people about lack of control over social media, and if she could touch that chord while it was still raw, she might go from a name known in Arizona, Washington and the arcane world of the intelligence establishment to a name known across the country.

McKenrick had a long discussion with her senior staffers. Some thought she might succeed, others thought the link between Fishbowl and the bombing, still unproven, was too tenuous to create a generalizable case. Eventually the senator had her press spokesman put out a statement welcoming Mr Koss's intent to cooperate and saying that Senator McKenrick was following very carefully the investigation into the role that Fishbowl and, indeed, other social media sites, might well have played in the taking of the lives of 300 American citizens in Denver. It suggested that if the executives running these sites, as Mr Koss had confessed, were aware of their potential to offer a medium of conspiracy to terrorists, then maybe the time had come for them to do something about it.

And then she waited to see what kind of reaction her statement was going to get.

The noises out of the press at the right end of the spectrum were encouraging. McKenrick decided to push things a little further. She appeared on a couple of politics shows to say that she was looking for responsibility, not restriction. But if restriction was the only way to enforce responsibility, then perhaps some kind of restriction would need to be considered. Or perhaps some other means of ensuring that the next pair of deranged fanatics wouldn't be provided with the medium to do what Hodgkin and Buckett had done. When asked what she had in mind, she replied that there were steps that Congress could take, and they were all under consideration.

Andrei and the rest of the Fishbowl leadership didn't even register a vague statement made in Washington by a senator they had never heard of, amidst all the predictable noise from a thousand sources about the dangers of social media. McKenrick and her team, for their part, watched the reaction from the right-wing press and the hard core of the Republican Party, her natural constituency. There was interest in what she had said. It was high time that someone got control of the anti-life, anti-gun and anti-Americanism that passed for normal on so much of the internet, and if Diane McKenrick thought she could do it, then she ought to come on out and tell the nation how.

The senator talked to people whose support would be critical if she decided to take things further. She concluded that enough of them were behind her.

Two weeks after the Denver bombing, Diane McKenrick stood up in front of a press conference, waved a copy of Andrei Koss's statement, read the first sentence, and said that someone in Congress had to take a stand. She then issued a five-point plan for regulation of social networking sites, involving higher levels of transparency, increased accountability, and, most radically, the holding of officers of social networking companies personally answerable for enabling criminal activities that could be demonstrated to have been planned or promoted by use of the site. She announced that she was sponsoring a bill to put her proposed measures in place before any further catastrophes befell the American people.

McKenrick's proposal was challengeable on at least three constitutional grounds and, in normal circumstances, wouldn't have merited discussion. But in normal circumstances, Diane McKenrick, who was as wily an operator as any three-term senator, wouldn't have put the proposal forward. Challenges would take years. If her legislation did make it through, only to be struck down later, it would make little difference to her. By then the election would have taken place, and she would either be the US president or still have another four years in her term as senator. And if the legislation didn't make it through, she would still cement her place as the champion of the hawks and have a host of targets amongst her rivals to beat up on security grounds as she made her run for the presidency.

If Diane McKenrick was hoping to touch a chord on the national stage, she did, to an extent that not even she could have envisaged.

Her proposal polarized the nation. Emotion was pent up after Denver on all sides of the political spectrum, just waiting for a valve to vent. Hardcore users of social networks – disproportionately young, educated and affluent – came out against the senator with visceral revulsion. Light or non-users of social networks – disproportionately old, poorly educated and blue collar – swung behind her. The committed right, bruised by the fact that Buckett and Hodgkin had emerged from their own shadowy fringe, saw in McKenrick's attack a way of shifting the blame towards a target they could excoriate. The committed left saw it as an assault on freedom and diversity. But in those early days after Denver, it took courage to make a case that people should be free to say what they chose and exchange whatever information they desired without being castigated as soft on terrorism. Many liberal politicians spoke softly or went to ground. Right-wing politicians felt empowered to raise the volume, telling hair-raising stories of things that had been done and said on social networks that were severely distorted, if not entirely fabricated. The first amendment was in retreat before a posse of enraged vigilantes who seemed to have the wind at their backs. Not sure which way the chips were going to fall, the president prevaricated. His press secretary announced that the White House was studying the senator's proposal.

In the furore, the facts of what Buckett and Hodgkin had actually done on Fishbowl became unimportant. Ideas of creating an American Taliban, which Buckett had aired a couple of times, were treated largely as a joke by others on the website, who failed to grasp his intent. Reading his posts carefully now, it was possible, with hindsight, to find clues that pointed to Denver, although there was nothing approaching an explicit plan that he enunciated, and the ravings of some of the other participants in these forums were even more lurid. In this world of violent fantasy, it seemed, Buckett had been a rare example of someone who was prepared to act. Nothing in his words picked him out as that person.

But someone in the FBI was leaking information to McKenrick's office and there was enough in Buckett's words for Senator McKenrick to quote him selectively, as if his remarks on Fishbowl set out nothing short of a comprehensive blueprint for the killings. She gave an interview in which she cited a few ambiguous phrases of Buckett's – ostentatiously reading from an official-looking dossier, which in fact contained a single sheet with three type-written sentences – claiming that these were only the least damning of the terrorist's postings and that the FBI was in possession of much more explicit material.

The director of the FBI called the officer leading the enquiry to ask if that was true, and when he discovered that it wasn't, he called McKenrick and asked her to desist. The senator responded by threatening to call the FBI director before the Committee for Homeland Security to explain what progress his inquiry had made so far in accounting for the FBI's dereliction of duty in failing to identify Buckett and Hodgkin as potential mass murderers.

On social networks themselves, numerous group pages were set up in which people registered their opposition to McKenrick's campaign. Some were more inflammatory than others, but all had in common a view that free speech had to be protected and that website operators shouldn't be called to do the work of the police. Mass e-petitions were organized against her. McKenrick turned that to her advantage, disparagingly representing the people who signed up to those pages as lily-livered liberals and mocking them as housebound sociophobes whose idea of action was a click of a mouse. She seemed to welcome each report of more people joining group pages against her, as if their abundance proved her case. A few group pages were set up supporting her as well, but never garnered many users. McKenrick cited the number of pages, but never the number of participants, and somehow made them out to be red-blooded Americans when a large number of them were actually government-sponsored users from repressive foreign regimes with a strong interest in seeing social networks curtailed.

Fishbowl hired a PR consultancy to help it fight back. So did other social networks. They were all in danger if McKenrick managed to introduce the principle of criminal responsibility for activities that took place on their websites. But they were all speaking over each other without coordination or intent. It took a tech CEO in Silicon Valley to see that he and his rivals were shooting off too many shotguns in too many directions. If they could come together and speak with one voice, fire with one aim, they could convert their scattergun defence into one booming, targeted attack, which at least would give them a chance of countering the force that was sweeping towards them.

He was a 41-year-old, ex-New Yorker called Jerry Glick and he ran Charitas, a social network that specialized in providing a community for workers in charities, aid agencies and other NGOs. He took the unprecedented step of convening a meeting of some of the most prominent tech CEOs in the country. Since the crisis had been sparked by the alleged involvement of Fishbowl in the planning of the Denver bombing, Andrei Koss was invited as well.

24

HALF A DOZEN people were already in the conference room at the Palo Alto Sheraton when Andrei arrived. Jerry Glick came over and shook Andrei's hand, then introduced him to the others. Andrei knew who they were – a collection of the biggest names in Silicon Valley. Even though by now Fishbowl was often spoken of in the same breath as their companies, Andrei, who avoided any kind of public appearances, had never met any of them or mixed in their circles. At the best of times, he was terrible at making small talk. Now he found himself standing awkwardly, watching these icons of the internet, saying nothing.

The last few CEOs arrived, Mike Sweetman among them. 'You're with the big boys now, huh, Andrei?' he said, without extending his hand.

Andrei shrugged.

'We'll see,' growled Sweetman.

They sat. The CEOs were ten men and one woman, a ratio that would have surprised no one who knew the tech world. A pair of lawyers was also in attendance to take records of the meeting and ensure there could be no later allegation of trade collusion amongst the participants, many of whom were competitors with each other. Glick opened the meeting. The first thing he did was ask Andrei, as the leader of the company most under fire, to say a few words.

Andrei hadn't prepared anything. He tried to gather some thoughts.

'Well, first,' he said, 'I think I should say that I feel like the least qualified person to speak in this gathering.'

He looked around. Every eye was on him. Faces that he knew from photographs. The notion that they were all watching him, waiting to hear what he had to say, was so incongruous that his throat almost dried up.

He coughed. 'I'll guess I'll just say what I think. I'm not trying to do anything but build Fishbowl into a strong, flourishing operation, I guess like all the rest of you with your ventures. This campaign by Senator McKenrick affects each of us in the same way. She's focused on Fishbowl but her bill takes in all of us. You probably all know that I put out a certain statement when Fishbowl was first identified as being possibly involved in the planning of the Denver bombing, and the senator has made quite a lot of that. I admitted we might have been the medium for some communications. Looks like we weren't, not in any significant way. I know this may sound kind of odd, but even so, I don't regret writing that. I think it's important we admit it. If we don't, it becomes the gorilla in the room. The truth is, stuff gets said and talked about on our networks that none of us would approve of.

'I've been cooperating with the government in the investigation after the bombing, but there's a world of difference between that and prior restraint. The reason I've been cooperating is because I think that's the price you have to pay for *avoiding* prior restraint. Either we fight to the death to allow free speech on our networks, or we become agents of the state. That's not why I founded Fishbowl. It's not a fight I would ever have particularly wanted to have, and not now, but I guess it's one that's always been coming to all of us. And me, if it's about free speech ... I'll fight to the death.'

'I couldn't care less if you fight to your death,' rumbled Mike Sweetman ominously, 'but you're fighting to ours too. Did you get any legal advice before you put that statement out?'

Andrei didn't answer.

'Well, you screwed us all with that one. Damn right we're all in the same boat – and it's your statement that put us there.'

'Mike,' said someone else, 'he's right. It's a fight we were always going to have.'

'And I don't think this is the time to start allocating blame,' said Glick.

'When is the time, Jerry?' demanded Sweetman. 'We're fighting for our lives here. We're fighting for our independence. If McKenrick's bill gets through, you and I and probably every other person in this room will end up in jail unless we shut down. Laws get passed in the heat of the moment that allow the government to do terrible things and no one gets around to changing them back. You remember the Patriot Act? And who do we have to thank for this thing now? Mr Koss. That statement he seems to be so proud of is being used over and over and over against us, and the truth is, what Mr Koss over there runs is a parasitic excuse for a business that lives off the back of the business that I've built and you've built and half a dozen other guys in this room have built . And so he comes along and sits on the back of us and shits all over us with his statement. Only thing is that he shits on himself as well, which, frankly, is quite a feat.'

There was silence again, part embarrassed, part supportive. There were a couple of nods around the table.

'I don't accept the insinuation,' said Andrei quietly. 'Much less the imagery.'

Sweetman shrugged in disgust.

'Are you saying, Mr Sweetman, that the same kind of communication that Buckett and Hodgkin were said to have had on Fishbowl – which, by the way, they didn't – couldn't have happened on Homeplace?'

'Of course I'm not saying that.'

'Then what are you saying?' said Andrei. 'I don't understand your point.'

'You don't have to come out beating your breast like Robert-frigging-Oppenheimer and saying "Oh, my God, I have been the medium of evil."'

'"I am become death, the destroyer of worlds,"' murmured someone. 'That's the quote, Mike.'

'Who gives a fuck?'

'That isn't what I said,' said Andrei. 'You should read the statement.'

'I have read it. Made me puke.'

'I think we should take responsibility. It happens. That's the kind of business we run.'

'No, that's the kind of business *I* run. You just sit on the back of it.'

'Mike,' said one of the other guys, 'maybe your attitude here is a little influenced by your ... you know, your business attitude towards Andrei.'

'Hell it is!' said Sweetman – but the opposite was true. He had tried to ruin Fishbowl, he had tried to buy it. Most recently, he had tried to compete with it. That was probably what was hurting him most. The Denver bombing had nipped his relaunch of Worldspace in the bud and so far, in the furore that had followed, there hadn't been any point in even trying to get it back on the agenda. It now languished with a couple of million active users that were reducing in number by the day, and everyone knew it. The brand stank so badly that it probably never would be salvageable. It was Sweetman's first significant business failure since he had conceived of Homeplace a decade earlier. 'I just want to know what value he thinks he adds.'

'Mr Sweetman,' said Andrei, 'I have three hundred million people who think I add some kind of value.'

'You've taken my users and Jerry's users and Ed's users and the users of half the people in this room, and done nothing to originate them yourself.'

'I offer them something different. It's a deeper connectedness than you offer.'

Sweetman snorted in disgust.

'OK, guys,' said Jerry. 'This isn't getting us anywhere. This isn't what we're here for. If everyone wants to sit here attacking each other then, frankly, I'm going home.'

Sweetman snorted again. 'There's only one person who needs attacking.'

'All right, Mike. Enough, OK? You've made your point. Take it outside if you want to continue.' Glick paused, looking around the table. 'Does anyone else want to take a shot at Andrei? Because if that's what you're all here for, maybe we ought to call it quits. Look, I took a risk getting you all together so, seriously, if that's all this is about for you guys, I'm going.' He waited. 'OK. So let's try and be positive. Whatever the role of Andrei's statement, whether this was a fight that was always coming or whether the statement brought it on us – whatever – the statement's been made. Nothing in it was false or misrepresentative. Each of us might have an opinion about whether it was better to have made that statement or not, but it's been made. And right now it's one piece of ammunition – only one piece – that's being used against us. And I want to know, do we think there's any way that we as a group, as an industry, should respond? If you guys feel that, no, we should continue individually, then thanks for coming and grab a bagel on your way out. But if there is a way, then now's the time we should talk about it. You know, if this is a fight we always had to have, maybe we can turn this around and use it as the opportunity to win it.'

For a moment no one spoke, as if everyone was deciding whether they wanted to leave or to give the meeting a chance.

Then Marc Edwards, CEO of a video and file-sharing site called Hoola, cleared his throat. 'Our problem is we have all these people who are strongly opposed to what McKenrick's doing, millions of people, but they're posting messages on their home pages, they're joining group pages, they're blogging … it's all inside the online community. But the people who are driving this, they're outside that community. So they don't hear it or see it, and if they do, somehow the fact that it's online kind of robs it of credibility. And the people we have to persuade, those people aren't in that community, either. They're the soccer moms and the judo dads that McKenrick and her like need to get re-elected. They're the people McKenrick is talking to. And I think the outrage that's happening amongst our people, our community …

it's not getting through to them. So at the moment for that big group, it's the McKenrick argument, it's the panic security argument that they're hearing.'

'Marc, soccer moms and judo dads use our networks,' said someone else.

'Sure, Raj, but they're deep in what they're doing. They're not sitting there reading the comments every day. They're exchanging photos, they're sending recipes! As far as they're concerned, they don't care if we're forced to shut down stuff that some agency in government deems subversive. They're not about to do anything wrong. And if that keeps little Johnny or little Susan safe, they're happy. McKenrick is winning this argument.'

'So what's our counter?'

'Well, its free speech, right? You shut the medium, you shut down the exchange.'

'No one's talking about shutting it down.'

'Which is exactly why McKenrick's argument is winning. Because she's not talking about shutting it down. She's talking about using criminal responsibility on our part as a lever to create censorship.'

'Which is absurd,' said someone else. 'Stuff gets said on the phone every day that's more obscene and abusive than anything that happens on our networks. Has anyone ever talked about holding phone companies responsible?'

'People are really concerned about this kind of restriction,' said Andrei. 'I'm seeing it on Fishbowl all the time.'

'But we have to get it out of Fishbowl!' said Edwards. 'We have to get it out of Homeplace and Charitas and Hoola and get it right into the faces of the soccer moms and judo dads so they can see that people *are* concerned about this, people like them, and that if this happens, this is a fundamental change to our way of life. And the people in Denver didn't die for that. They didn't die so some senator could rip up one of the greatest freedoms underlying our Constitution.'

'That's it,' said Jerry, snapping his fingers. 'That right there, Marc. I really like the way you put that. They didn't die so some senator could tear up the Constitution. That's exactly the point – so how do we make it? Because it's the truth, right? That's what the bombers wanted to do, tear up the Constitution. McKenrick is continuing the job of the bombers – she's just doing it by different means.'

'She's using them.'

'How do we get that message out?'

'I've got a great PR agency.'

'No, how do we *really* get it out? Into the real world.'

There was silence.

'We can't be the ones to say it,' said Mandy Rikheim, the only female in the room. 'It's got to come from *people*.'

Glick nodded. 'How? *How?*'

Someone suggested a petition, someone else a concert.

'What about a march?'

All eyes turned to Bill Rosenstein, CEO of a major crowd-sourcing site.

'My mother marched in Selma in 1965,' said Rosenstein. 'She bussed in from Philly. Twenty-two years old. I don't know how many times she told me about it when I was a kid. It was the formative experience of her life. And that was what brought the message home to the nation, wasn't it? That march in Selma.' Rosenstein paused. When he resumed, his voice was quivering with emotion. 'That was about freedom. That was about the Constitution. Isn't that what this is about? I say we march. We march to commemorate the Denver victims. We march to protect the freedoms they died for.'

'Where, Bill?' said Rikheim. 'Denver?'

'Everywhere. In every city where we can organize it. It's, what … six weeks now, since the bombing? Let's say on the eight-week anniversary, if we can get it organized that quickly, we march.'

'We could never organize it that quickly.'

'What about July 4?' said Glick. 'People will be out already. Let's use that, let's channel it. Let's show the soccer moms and the judo dads that this really matters, that people are concerned enough to come out on the streets to protest it, that the country their kids are going to grow up in is going to change if they don't do something to stop it.' He looked around the table. 'What do we think?'

'I like it,' said Rikheim. 'It would be awesome if it works.'

'The tricky part is to bring the two things together,' said Edwards. 'What was done to those poor people in Denver with what McKenrick is trying to do. The thing is, is it in poor taste?'

'Why did they die, Marc?' replied Glick. 'They died because they were federal workers doing their job to uphold what this country is about. They died because they were firemen and ambulance drivers and policemen and public servants who came to the aid of their fellow citizens. What's in poor taste, what's appalling, is Senator McKenrick trying to use their deaths to do the exact opposite.'

'I'm not arguing with you, Jerry. I'm just saying that we need to get that across.'

'That I agree with. We need to build it up like that. We need to find speakers who will make that point. We need to make sure we get all that across.' Glick paused. 'So what are we saying? Are we saying this is it? Are we saying we're with Bill? We organize a march to commemorate the victims?'

'And defend our constitutional freedoms,' said Rikheim. 'The best way we can commemorate those people is to defend our freedoms.'

'Right. So that's what we're saying?'

'We should talk to our lawyers,' said Mike Sweetman.

'Sure, we talk to our lawyers, but apart from that … is it a yes?'

Someone nodded. Then someone else.

'Andrei,' said Glick, 'what about you?'

Andrei nodded. 'Fishbowl's in. We'll help organize. We'll do anything.'

'Mike?'

'I've got to talk to my lawyers.'

'Sure, but ... yes or no?'

Everyone in the room waited on Sweetman's answer. His network alone had more than double the number of users of all the others combined. Homeplace's involvement would be critical both to give credibility to the marches and to stimulate turnout. He was, by some measure, the most important person in the room.

And Sweetman, who knew it, didn't want to have anything to do with Andrei Koss or anything in which he was involved. Just allowing Koss to be associated with him, he felt, gave Koss a status he didn't deserve. But Sweetman also had a very clear understanding of the needs of his business, and he felt that his network, in the current fevered environment, faced a genuine existential threat from Diane McKenrick. Even if the full extent of her absurd proposals wasn't implemented, Congress might compromise on constraints that would severely impede his growth and profitability. And the idea they had just come up with to counter her, he had to acknowledge, was smart. There was almost a touch of genius to it.

At length he turned to Jerry and nodded.

Glick gave a smile of relief. 'So what do we call it?'

'Just what you said, Jerry,' said Rosenstein. 'We're defending freedom. July 4. Let's call it the Defence of Freedom marches.'

Rikheim smiled. 'Let's see McKenrick oppose that. Let's see her stand up and say she's opposed to defending freedom.'

'You know, there is a risk,' said Sweetman. 'There is a way this could actually work against us.'

'Which is?'

'We're sitting here all excited in this room, we think it's going to be another Selma, and then we do it, we organize it, we hype it, we build it up – and no one turns out.'

There was silence.

'We'll look like idiots.'

'People will turn out,' said someone.

'Let's not kid ourselves, it's high risk. We're upping the ante. Just so we're aware. If the turnout's low – McKenrick wins.'

25

THREE-QUARTERS OF a million marched in Denver. The city that had lost so many of its sons and daughters two months previously gave itself over to a great sighing catharsis of grief. It wasn't the biggest rally in the country, but it was by far the most emotional. *Denver Honours Its Martyrs* proclaimed one banner stretched behind the podium in City Park where the march ended. *Denver Says No To Senator McKenrick* said a second.

The nation joined with Denver. Over a million wound their way through Central Park in New York, while 800,000 converged on Washington, bussing in from all over the country. Los Angeles saw an estimated 600,000; San Francisco a similar number. In Chicago, a million descended on Grant Park. Houston saw 400,000. In Oklahoma City, where the wounds of Timothy McVeigh's bombing were never far from the surface, it was estimated that 40 per cent of the city's population thronged the area around the Oklahoma City National Memorial. In cities and towns across the country, Fourth of July celebrations were transformed into Defence of Freedom gatherings. Speaker after speaker on podium after podium, in parks, in stadiums, in fairgrounds, in front of town halls, said that the only fitting memorial for those who had died in Denver – people whose basic and most fundamental constitutional right, the right to life, had been snatched away by Buckett and Hodgkin – was a reaffirmation of the constitutional freedoms guaranteed to all Americans.

Around 300,000 turned out in Papago Park, in Diane McKenrick's home town of Phoenix, to affirm that message. Combatively having accepted an invitation to speak, she was listened to in stony silence until a wave of slow handclapping built up and drowned her out.

That day marked the turning point of public opinion. The sight of 20 million or more Americans marching in avenues, malls and parks across the country had an impact, and not only on soccer moms and judo dads. Politicians from the left who hadn't distinguished themselves for their courage began to find their voices on podiums from which the sight of people who had come out in their masses emboldened them to say more than they had intended. The president, being given reports of the numbers descending on Washington, suddenly found time in a schedule that had been too busy for attendance at the rally to speak live by videolink to the crowds in the Mall. At a pre-scheduled press conference with a visiting head of state the next morning, he described the day as one of the proudest in American history, when the American nation had affirmed both its deep compassion and its unshakeable fidelity to the constitutional foundations that were still as right and relevant as when the Founding Fathers had first enunciated them.

The sentiment spread in the following days. While the more extreme elements of the right wing of the Republican Party and their media sympathisers sneered at the lefties who had turned out to provide aid and comfort to terrorists, more moderate Republicans sensed that the time had come, if they had ever been on McKenrick's bandwagon, to jump off quietly. In sight of the sheer number who had turned out, it just wasn't tenable to say this was a loony minority. Just about everyone in the country had a friend, relative, workmate or acquaintance who had marched.

In private, Diane McKenrick began to get apologetic calls from people who, only a fortnight previously, had been encouraging her to push ahead. In public, their silence was deafening.

But the thing that really did for McKenrick, more than the number of people who turned out or politicians on the left finally finding their voices, was a single image – the image of her standing on a podium, a suddenly small, impotent figure with a look of confusion on her face, struggling to be heard. Those who saw footage on the news that night heard the rounds of slow handclapping reverberating like thunder in the natural amphitheatre of Papago Park. Those who didn't see the footage saw the image, which was carried on the front page and website of just about every newspaper the next day. Some papers carried it as part of a montage of images from around the nation, others displayed it in isolation. The paper edition of the *New York Times* had it in a six-column box, judging that it summarized the upshot of the marches better than just about any other photo that had been taken that day.

Sometimes an image is so powerful, so evocative, that it tells not only what has happened but what is about to happen. Comparing it to the 'Ceausescu moment' of 1989, when the Romanian dictator, who would survive only another four days before being summarily executed along with his wife, was photographed staring in perplexity at the unprecedented sight of a crowd of his downtrodden people jeering him to his face, the *Times* editorialized that it would be surprised to see Senator McKenrick's bill last another week and that, to all intents and purposes, her presidential bid was over before it had begun.

Her bill, in fact, lasted another two weeks before it was formally withdrawn. Her bid, as she knew herself, was finished before she had even stepped down from the podium in Papago Park and the sound of the slow handclapping had stopped echoing in her ears.

The CEOs who had come together with Jerry Glick to organize the marches on that Fourth of July didn't speak at the rallies. In the runup to the day, hostile voices from the right of the political spectrum had, as expected, accused them of exploiting the tragedy of Denver to garner publicity for their businesses. As part of their strategy to defuse the claim, they stayed in the background and allowed the event to speak for itself. The message came from others, from local leaders impassioned to speak out. But the CEOs did march, not in Silicon Valley, but dispersed across the country, back where they had come from, in the places where they had grown up.

Andrei marched in Boston, his home town. It was the culmination of two weeks of frenetic activity, during which he and half the Fishbowl organization had taken on the responsibility of organizing the marches in fourteen states.

Sandy Gross marched with him. They were at the front, in a row with Boston celebrities and Democrat politicians who were leading the march. Andrei's presence hadn't been publicized in advance for fear of alerting disgruntled Fishbowl users who might want to stage some kind of protest at his compliance over the investigation of Buckett and Hodgkin, but as the march went on, news began to spread that the Fishbowl founder was in the crowd.

As the march moved into Boston Common, where a stage and screens had been set up for the speeches, order began to break down. The front rows, flanked by security guards, were overtaken by others pouring into the common. Someone yelled that he could see Andrei Koss. Suddenly there were people all around him. Sandy grabbed hold of his arm to keep from being separated from him. Two of the security guards who had accompanied the front row of marchers were with them as well; they managed to hail over a couple more guards, who came pushing and shoving their way through the crowd.

Andrei and Sandy came to a stop, surrounded. People were holding up phones trying to get a picture of Andrei.

'Talk to them,' said Sandy.

Andrei looked at her uncomprehendingly.

'Talk to them, Andrei!'

She pushed two of the security guys slightly apart, reached out a hand and pulled someone through. He put up his hand towards Andrei for a high five. Instinctively, Andrei hit it.

'Andrei Koss! You rock!'

Someone else came in. Then someone else. Then a couple of people together. Soon the security guards were moving people through as if they had planned to do it all along. Most of the people just yelled, 'Hey Andrei,' or something like it and took a photo or grabbed his hand. There seemed to be no ill will over his policy after Denver – on the contrary, everyone just seemed excited to see him. Some wanted to talk, trying to tell him what Fishbowl meant to them as the security guys tried to move them on. They had stories about someone they had met, a connection they had made. Others had an idea for what they wanted from the site. Sandy was the master of ceremonies, holding the security guys back until they were done, then reaching out a hand for someone else.

Andrei didn't know what to say or do. Mostly he nodded and shook hands and bumped fists and said it was great to meet them and tried to smile as they took a photo on their phones. There were students, office workers, stay-at-home moms, off-duty cops – a kaleidoscope of the city passed in front of him, all wanting to touch his hand, say a word, hear his voice, make some kind of connection.

Then a big man of around thirty with a blond goatee came through the ring, grinning widely.

'I'm Barry Diller, man!'

For a second Andrei didn't make the connection.

'Barry Diller, Andrei!'

Andrei got it. The Dillerman.

'Andrei Koss!' Diller put both his hands around Andrei's head and planted a kiss on his forehead, then grabbed him in a hug.

'Hey!' yelled one of the security guys.

'It's OK,' said Andrei.

'Giving data to the Feds,' said Diller, standing back from him. 'That was a dangerous thing, Andrei.'

'It was only—'

'I know. I stood up for you. You had to do it. I know you'd never betray us.'

Suddenly Diller reached into his jacket. For a split second Andrei remembered the warnings he had had about disgruntled users. He had an intimation of danger. Everything seemed to happen in slow motion. Diller's hand clasped something in his jacket. Out of the corner of his eye, Andrei saw a security guy lunging at him. Then Diller's hand was out and the security guy had an arm around his neck and Diller held up a ... phone.

'Hey!' he yelled angrily at the security guard. 'What the fuck are you doing?'

The security guy let go of him.

Diller put his arm around Andrei's shoulder, thrust the phone out in front of them and took a photo. He looked at the screen. 'Cool.' He looked back at Andrei and clenched a fist, second and fifth fingers raised as if at rock concert. 'Fishbowll! To me, it's always got two *l*s!'

'OK,' said the security guy. 'Come on. Let's move.'

Barry Diller held up his hands. 'I'm going.'

He took a step, then looked back into Andrei's eyes. The two fingers of his fist were extended again, pointing straight at Andrei's chest. 'Don't betray us, Andrei.'

That day in Boston was the first time Andrei had come across the users of the service he had created in any number. He knew better than anyone that Fishbowl had 300 million registered members, but that was just one number in a long series of ever-increasing numbers on the Fishbowl growth curve. The people on the streets of Boston that day were only a tiny minority of that membership – thousands, not millions – but they were real people, right there, in front of him.

He had known they were out there, but he had never *felt* what that meant. Fishbowl was a real, living thing in their lives. Their passion for it was palpable. To see it was humbling. Fishbowl wasn't his, Andrei felt – it was theirs. He was its custodian. He felt an enormous sense of responsibility, so overwhelming that it was scary. Ensconced within the office in Ramona Street, he had never been confronted by the extent to which he had, like it or not, become a public figure. He had never intended to be one. But now he saw, like it or not, how his deeds were watched, scrutinized, evaluated, by the people into whose lives he had put the connectedness of Fishbowl.

It had been the most powerful experience of Andrei's life.

That night, he rang Ben, who had marched in New York and had been equally swept up by the extraordinary sense of community he had felt in Central Park. Andrei told him that what had been most striking was the way people had been desperate to speak with him, if only for a second, the way they had wanted physically to touch him. What could they possibly have got out of that?

To Ben, who actually knew something about human psychology, it was no surprise that people wanted to have some kind of contact with Andrei, no matter how trivial. He could hardly believe that he had to explain it. But, then, Andrei was Andrei. 'You've done something important in their lives,' he said. 'You've given them something that's meaningful.'

'Sure, but what difference if they shake my hand?'

'They crave a sense of personal connection. Some of these people will remember this for ever.'

Andrei shook his head. It still made no sense. 'I met a friend of ours, by the way. The Dillerman.'

Ben laughed. 'Really? What's he like?'

Andrei thought back over the incident. 'He's … intense.'

'That's a surprise.'

'He said a funny thing,' said Andrei, suddenly remembering. 'To him, "Fishbowl will always have two *l*s". What do you think that means?'

'I don't know. Two *l*s? I guess he wants it to be pure, like it was.'

'He told me never to betray them.'

'Who?'

'I don't know. "Us", he said. "Don't betray us."'

'The greater the love, the greater the danger,' said Ben, laughing. 'They're the ones you have to watch.'

'He said he understood about sharing the data after Denver.'

'There you are. Come on, it sounds like it was a great day.'

'Ben, it was awesome. It was totally, totally awesome. The people ... I mean, I still don't know about this personal contact thing, but Fishbowl ... it's alive, Ben. What we've done ... I don't think I understood it until today.'

'Sounds like it's made an impression on you.'

'Ben, it's beyond an impression.'

Andrei knew that he couldn't ignore what he had experienced. He had never wavered in his commitment to bringing the greatest possible depth of connectedness to his users, but now he felt this commitment to be even more rooted, as if it had fed and hardened on the zeal of the people he had met.

With that, something else changed for him as well.

Chris and James had both been telling Andrei for months, even before the Denver bombing, that he had to be more visible. The company needed a figurehead who was accessible and, so long as he was the CEO, he had to be that person. Andrei had evaded the responsibility, but even before the march he had suspected that he wouldn't be able to do that much longer. Now he knew not only that they were right but what it would mean to do it. It wasn't any less intimidating – if anything, after the fervour that he had experienced on Boston Common, it was even more daunting – but the march forced him to accept that, if he wanted to be the CEO of the company, he would have to face up to this part of the role.

But if he was going to be more visible, now wasn't necessarily the time to start. If anything, now was a time to stay in the shell. Not just for him, but for everyone in social media.

The collapse of the McKenrick witch hunt left social media in a strong but at the same time potentially vulnerable position. Their role as an enabler of free speech had been vindicated, and although it had not been formally tested in a court of law, officers of companies providing social media now seemed to be nestled in the protective shadow of the first amendment. On the other hand, the potential for that medium of exchange to carry obnoxious content had been admitted and exposed, and it was anyone's guess what would happen if another Denver occurred that could be definitively linked to a social network in the planning phase. A second atrocity might bring back the McKenrick argument stronger than ever and make people think twice about the right to freedom of expression if it appeared to be measured against the right to life.

The PR people in the tech industry and the Washington lobbyists they employed were virtually unanimous in recommending that this was a time for steady, quiet responsibility, keeping heads down, tightening policies on acceptable behaviour, abuse, hate speech and incitement, and increasing monitoring of some of the most egregious communications on their services. It was no moment for bragging or grandstanding. If tech companies were seen to be triumphalist, public opinion, which had moved in their favour, might just as soon move back again.

For Fishbowl, however, keeping heads down was not so easy a proposition. From a network that was already the destination of choice for the socially adventurous and internationally minded, McKenrick's campaign had now definitively made it a household name, familiar from New York to New Mexico, from the netizens of San Francisco who never left their apartment without a tablet computer to coal miners in West Virginia who couldn't tell a tablet computer from a plate of hash browns. Interest in Andrei was intense. The company was under virtual siege by journalists bombarding it with requests for an interview.

Fishbowl was close to two years old. Three hundred million people used it. Almost unbelievably, the only media interview

Andrei had ever given had been the one to to a student journalist at the *Stanford Daily* when he had still been living with Ben and Kevin in Robinson House.

Andrei decided that, if he was going to accept the responsibility of being more visible, he had no choice. The time had come to open himself to an interview again.

26

THEY TOOK THE photographs first. The interviewer, Deborah Handel, was a senior features writer for the *New York Times* and had flown out for the interview. Andrei was in his usual T-shirt, jeans and sneakers. The Fishbowl communications person, Alan Mendes, had wanted him in something with a little more gravitas – not a suit, but maybe a Steve Jobs-style roll neck – but Andrei said he'd think about it, and didn't. They shot him sitting on the edge of a desk and standing against a wall. He felt awfully wooden and didn't know what to do with his face. They told him to smile, then to look serious, then thoughtful. The photographer shot a glance at Handel and rolled his eyes.

Coaching had been arranged for Andrei. Alan Mendes had organized two days of training, but even before the end of the first day Andrei had had enough. He and the coach, a retired features writer for the *Los Angeles Times*, had started by agreeing the things Andrei wanted to get across in the interview, and then the rest of the coaching, as far as Andrei could glean, was designed to make him appear in a certain light, while at the same time making him appear not to be trying to do so. 'Remember, be yourself,' the coach kept saying every time she asked him to say something in a way that was totally not himself. It seemed irrational and self-contradictory, and Andrei had had the strong feeling that the longer it went on, the more confused he was going to be when he finally sat down to answer the questions. Midway through the afternoon of the first day, he sent the coach home.

Now, as Deborah Handel invited him to take a seat, he frowned, waiting for the first question to hit him.

'Tell me about Fishbowl,' she said.

Easy. Andrei talked fluently and at length about Deep Connectedness, about his perspective on the world as clusters of ideas and values, about the way the world would change as facilities like Fishbowl made that model of the world a reality.

Handel's eyes glazed over a little, but he didn't notice.

'Tell me about the way it started,' she said.

'I just had the idea for it, as a way to get more connectedness. I had this idea that it would be a good thing.'

She waited. 'But where did you get the idea? Did something spark it off? What happened?'

Andrei shrugged. He remembered Guy from Colombia and *Aguila Roja* but he didn't feel he should talk about that. It was too nerdy, and he didn't spend any time in chat rooms any more.

'OK. Well, when was that?'

'Around two years ago, in my junior year at Stanford.'

'And you had this idea of Deep Connectedness? That was the idea back then?'

Andrei nodded.

'And did you think it would ever be as big as it is?'

'We're not as big as we could be. We're still growing. There's a hunger for Deep Connectedness, and my job is to find ways to help people to find it.'

'You talk so much about Deep Connectedness. Do you really think it's so important?'

Andrei stared at her, wondering what exactly it was that she didn't get.

'Why Deep Connectedness? Why this obsession?'

'Do you use Fishbowl?'

Handel smiled. 'No, I don't. I mean, I've looked at the site.'

'But you registered, right?'

'To be honest, Andrei, I just looked at as part of the background for this interview.'

'And you don't use it?'

She shook her head.

Andrei frowned. 'That's interesting. Do you use other social media?'

'Sure. Homeplace.'

'What about Worldspace? Sorry, I mean Openreach..'

'No.'

'You see, when I hear that, and when you tell me you went onto Fishbowl but you don't use it, it makes me wonder what I can do to make the experience more appealing for you, so you have the motivation to explore Deep Connectedness. Tell me what it is that I can do.'

'Maybe I just don't need it.'

'Everyone needs it.'

'Maybe not.'

'We've always been able to find people with your interests, but what if we had a function that could take your profile and select what we would consider to be the most fascinating people for you among them? They could be anywhere in the world. What about that?'

'I guess that might be quite interesting.'

'Not just those who are most similar or dissimilar to you with your particular interest, which we can do already, but those who, by our algorithms, we identify as those you would find the most fascinating – or the most influential, or the most educated, or the most vocal. Or anything. You could set the parameters. For example, you could be looking for us to find the most interesting of the most influential people among those with different views than your own about whatever it is you're interested in. You might want to try to understand them, debate with them. You know, for a journalist, you might find this quite useful. What are you interested in?'

'Orangutans,' said Handel, citing the most outlandish thing that came into her head to see where it would go.

'Cool,' said Andrei, taking her seriously. 'Conservation, I guess? OK, say you're interested in orangutans, but you want to find people whose view is that we shouldn't be spending money on conservation. You want to understand their argument, maybe so you can combat it. What if we could get to that level of specificity, so we'd be able to find you people in the countries you've specified with an interest in orangutans but opposed to conservation efforts, *and*, of those, the ones we think would be most interesting for you.' He paused. 'Would that function be useful to you?'

Handel smiled. 'I guess so. If you could do it.'

'We're working on it. Now, how about this? What if we could provide you with photos, videos, text from public sources that are directly relevant to what you're talking about with someone *as* you're talking to them? Instead of having to try to remember where you saw something, it would be there for you right away.'

'You'd be reading what I'm saying?'

'No, no one's reading anything. It's totally automated. Just think, how cool would that be. It's a form of connectedness not only to the present but to the past. To things people have said or photographed or whatever. If you're talking about orangutan conservation, for example, there'd be data and pictures right there, as you're talking. You wouldn't even having to go looking. Now, as a journalist, wouldn't that be useful? If we could do that? Would that change your mind?'

'Maybe.'

'What if we could …?'

Handel watched him as he reeled off another idea Fishbowl was working on, and then another, wondering whether he really was interested in exploring what would make her use the site or whether it was just a way to avoid talking about himself. It was obvious that he was comfortable talking about Fishbowl, his vision for it, its functionality, but she was about as interested in that as she was in finding out about his grandparents – actually, she was more interested in finding out about his grandparents. She didn't want to know about Fishbowl, she wanted to know about him. As he spoke, Handel wondered how best to get around his defences, get him talking about himself. Asking about Fishbowl, she thought, but about something that had a personal angle was probably the best way to put him off his guard.

'I understand you have a motto at Fishbowl,' she said, when he paused for breath. '"Don't make the world a worse place."'

Andrei nodded. 'Kind of. It's something we use as a measure of what we're doing.'

'Has it served you well?'

'I think so.'

'Give me an example.'

Andrei talked through an example of a functionality they had rejected because they considered it would make the world worse.

'Don't you think that's kind of unambitious?' she said, interrupting him.

'What?'

'That motto, about not making the world worse. I mean, most people want to do something positive, not just avoid something negative.'

'It's not about avoiding something negative.'

'It sounds like it. I guess you're not a risk taker.'

'Why?'

'It's safety first. Don't make the world worse. That's like, "The first thing to make sure is that I don't mess up." Is that how you've always been? When you were a kid, for example?'

Andrei gazed at her. 'That's an interesting way of looking at it.'

'Tell me what you were like when you were a kid. Was it always safety first?' Handel waited. 'Maybe it's got something to do with your background as an immigrant – being uprooted at such a young age?'

Andrei ignored the question. His mind was still working on how Handel had perceived the motto. 'I think you've misunderstood it. First of all, when you're doing what we're doing, building something totally new, not making the world worse is something you've got to beware of. It really is. And the second thing is, there are so many things that we could do, the idea is let's try as many as we can as long as they're not going to make the world worse. Let's throw them out there. And then we'll find the ones amongst them that people want.'

'And what does it mean about you, that that's the approach you take?'

'No, let me just go back, because this is really important if you want to understand Fishbowl.' Andrei frowned. 'We want to make the world better. Absolutely. But *I* don't know what's going to make the world better. I have ideas, but I might be wrong. Or my definition of "better" might be different from everybody else's. So the best I can do is put stuff out there for the world to react to. We develop all kinds of things. We develop functionalities that people love, we develop function-alities that people look at and say … "Meh". And that's fine. If no one ever said "Meh", then I'd know for sure I'm not trying enough stuff. So what I have to do is throw as much as I can out there. And what we're saying is, the only things we're not going to offer is stuff that will make the world worse. Otherwise, we'll offer you anything you like, and you decide if you want it. And I think that makes the world better.' He gazed at her.

'That's what the principle means. It's absolutely not safety first. It's about throwing as much at the world as we can for the world to choose. And we take risks with that. Absolutely we do. And it costs money to do that – to have a bunch of really smart programmers and inevitably some of them are working on stuff that we think is cool but is going to end up "Meh". But you've got to do that if you want to do anything new. So it's not about not taking risks – the way I see it, it's about taking as many risks as you can, but also taking responsibility for not making the world worse. And we could. We really could. If we're not careful, we could definitely do things that would make the world worse. You know, our advertising, we've really worked hard to make sure it doesn't degrade the user experience – in fact, we hope that it actually contributes to it – but there's all kinds of stuff we could have done that would have been just horrible and would definitely have reduced the connectedness we want to provide.'

'So if you think about that approach, Andrei, about trying anything as long as it doesn't make the world worse, what do you think it is about *you* that makes you take that approach? Tell me how—'

'Maybe that's what the motto should be: "Try anything, as long as it doesn't make the world worse."' Andrei glanced at Mendes, who was sitting on a chair by the wall, then he looked back at Handel. 'You know, that's quite an interesting way of putting it. I'm going to think about that. Thank you.'

'A pleasure.' Handel smiled briefly, as if she really meant it. That approach hadn't worked in opening Andrei up. She decided to try something more direct. 'OK. You've been described as a boy-wonder of the internet. How does that make you feel?'

Andrei shrugged. 'It doesn't make me feel anything. It's seems kind of ridiculous, to be honest.'

'Then how would you describe yourself?'

He shrugged. 'I'm just, you know, very focused on Fishbowl at the moment.'

'So tell me about yourself. Tell me about Andrei Koss.'

Andrei looked at her, then glanced at Mendes. Inside, he was frozen. He had known that question was bound to come, but he didn't know what to say. The answers he had tried out with the coach had seemed ridiculous, contrived. There was nothing in his life, he felt, that anyone other than a fellow nerd would find remotely interesting. That was how he had felt for as long as he could remember. Anything he said could only disappoint.

'Let's start with where you were born,' Handel prompted him. 'You're Russian, right? That must have an effect.'

'We came to States when I was four.'

'So you don't remember Russia?'

'Not really.'

'So you don't think being Russian has made a difference?'

'To what?'

'To you.'

'It's very hard to say. I've never experienced anything else.'

'But if you had to say ...?'

Andrei frowned.

She waited.

'Andrei,' said Alan Mendes, 'you can talk a little about yourself. It doesn't have to be just Fishbowl.'

'I don't think being Russian's got anything to do with it,' Andrei said to him.

'That experience of being uprooted,' said Handel, 'even if you don't remember it, surely it must have an effect. Don't you think so? Even in family dynamics.'

Andrei looked at her blankly.

'OK ... ummm ... what do you do for fun?'

He continued to stare at her.

'Do you go out? Clubs? Concerts?'

'I'm ... really busy with Fishbowl.'

'I'm sure you are but ... what else? What else is there to Andrei Koss?' Handel paused, praying there was something. 'Video games?'

'I don't play much.'

'What do you play?'

'Nothing really.' The image of him sitting in front of a video game was definitely something Andrei didn't want people to have. Besides, he really didn't play much any more.

'Nothing?'

'I like movies.'

'What sort of movies?'

'Big movies. Epics.'

'Like ...?'

'*Troy. 300. Kingdom of Heaven.*'

'Historical epics,' said Mendes.

'Right. Why? What is it about them that interests you?'

'I don't know,' said Andrei. 'I just like them.'

Handel smiled. 'You're a thoughtful guy, Andrei. You must be able to say more than that.'

'Something about them appeals to me.'

She watched him for a moment, then couldn't help laughing.

Andrei wondered what was funny.

'Do you have a girlfriend?'

He nodded.

'What's her name?'

'I don't want to drag her into this.'

'"Drag her into this"?'

'She's a private person. Fishbowl's got nothing to with her.'

'But I'm interested in *you*, Andrei, not only Fishbowl.'

Andrei frowned. 'I don't think I should talk about her.'

'There were pictures of her with you at the Defence of Freedom march.'

Andrei nodded.

'Doesn't that make her kind of a public figure?'

'I don't think so. She had the right to march.'

'So you're not going to tell me her name?'

Andrei shook his head.

'Not even on background?'

Andrei looked at her uncomprehendingly.

'We can talk about that later,' said Mendes.

'OK. Well … what does she think about the fact that you're a very wealthy man?'

'I'm not a very wealthy man,' said Andrei. 'If I told you what I had in my bank account, you wouldn't be impressed.'

'How much do you have in your bank account?'

'Ah, I don't think we're going to answer that,' said Mendes.

Handel smiled guiltily. She hadn't really expected to get away with that one. 'Let's go back. Maybe you don't have a lot in your bank account right now, but you will. You'll be a wealthy man. People say Fishbowl's worth many millions and you own the majority of it, right? That makes you a wealthy man.'

'Maybe. I don't really think about that.'

'Does your girlfriend?'

'I don't know. You'd have to ask her.'

'But you won't even tell me her name.'

Andrei nodded.

'Look, I guess one of the things I'm asking is, you're a young man with a very big future in front of you, one that involves a lot of wealth, so I'm interested if you find that that influences the kind of women you meet and the relationships you have.'

'I've been with my girlfriend from before I started Fishbowl.'

'So then ... let's say she wanted to break it off, do you think your potential wealth would stop her?'

'That would be kind of sad, wouldn't it?'

'It does happen.'

'I hope it wouldn't happen with her.'

'Do you think it would?'

'If I thought it would, I probably wouldn't be with her.'

'Have you got plans with your girlfriend?'

'Plans?' said Andrei, deadpan.

'I think she might mean ... marriage,' said Mendes.

'Oh.' Andrei shrugged.

Handel sighed. 'OK. What about going out? Umm ... where do you go to eat?'

'I go to Yao's a lot. You know Yao's, on University Avenue?'

She shook her head.

'It's this noodle place I found when I was at Stanford. It's kind of where we have our meetings.'

'You mean Fishbowl meetings?'

'Yeah.'

'At the noodle place?' Handel clutched at the straw of colour that had suddenly floated into view on what was otherwise turning out to be a drab, grey stream of an interview.

'It's kind of, like, we never had anywhere to really meet, and we didn't have an office – even now the office is completely open – so we'd go to Yao's.'

'For dinner?'

'Lunch, often.'

'What do you eat?'

'I usually have the fried prawn and chicken noodles.'

'Is it good?'

'I'm no expert, but I have eaten at a number of noodle establishments, and I think, yeah, it is pretty good.'

'What else do you eat there?'

'Actually, I only ever have the fried prawn and chicken.'

'You've never tried anything else?'

'I don't know.' Andrei frowned. 'I think that's the first thing I tried there and it was pretty good. You know, I usually have fried prawn and chicken when I have noodles. Not just at Yao's.'

'I like beef noodles,' said Handel.

'Really? You should try the fried prawn and chicken if you go there.'

'I will. What kind of meetings have you had there?'

'Meetings ... you know ...'

'Can you give me some examples?'

'Well, the meeting where I suggested to Kevin and Ben that we should set up the company, that was at Yao's.'

'That's Kevin Embley and Ben Marks,' said Alan Mendes. 'Andrei's co-founders. I'll get you the spelling.'

Handel glanced at him and nodded, then turned back to Andrei. 'Was that when you were still at Stanford?'

Andrei nodded.

'What did you say to them?'

'I told them I couldn't do it without them.'

'Is that true?'

'What? That I said it to them or that I couldn't do it without them?'

'Both.'

'Yes. They're both true.'

'What did they bring to the company that you didn't have?'

'Ben's good with people. He understands the way people think.'

'And surely you don't think that you don't?' asked Handel, her tongue firmly in her cheek.

'Not like Ben,' replied Andrei seriously. 'And Kevin, Kevin's a great programmer. And he's a Stakhanovite.'

'Meaning?'

Andrei explained.

'Do you guys work hard?'

'Pretty hard.'

'Tell me what it was like in the early days. You started the company in your dorm, right?'

Andrei nodded. He talked easily again, back on more comfortable ground. Handel talked him through the first months of Fishbowl, using Yao's as a point of reference, always asking what had happened there, who had been present, what had been decided. She could see the noodle restaurant running as a theme through the piece.

Later, she asked Andrei about the impact Fishbowl's suspected involvement in the Denver bombing had had on him and the company. As she expected by now, she got very little on the first and much on the second. But then Andrei opened up a little, talking about the experience of meeting people at the Defence of Freedom March on Boston Common and the sense of responsibility he felt. He went on to talk about how that sense of responsibility reinforced his commitment to building Deep Connectedness, and then he was back on to that, and by the time Handel tried to steer him back to the personal aspect of the experience, the door that had opened for a moment, unguarded, had closed again, and it was too late

Handel finished with the concluding question that she had planned, asking Andrei how he saw Fishbowl's future, what he hoped to achieve, what he considered would be his greatest challenges, and was treated to another long investigation of the idea of Deep Connectedness and its capacity to change the world.

At the end, Deborah Handel couldn't decide if Andrei's obfuscation on the personal front came out of some kind of sense of superiority, or whether he was just a shy, vulnerable guy who didn't have the personal confidence to let anyone get inside his head. She thought it was probably the latter. When he had talked about the experience on Boston Common, she had felt she had got a glimpse through a chink in the armour, and what she thought she had seen was someone who was bewildered, almost naive, about the public position into which he had been thrust. It would have been easy to paint him in the nerd stereotype, easy to mock the belief he had in Deep Connectedness. But she wasn't sure that did him justice. On more familiar ground, when speaking about Fishbowl, she had found him thoughtful, insightful, even visionary. The idea of what he could do with an interest in orangutans had impressed her. She could see all kinds of ways she could use Fishbowl as a journalist, and wondered how she hadn't realized this before.

But what she had heard was relevant to more than journalism. Deborah Handel was no tech expert, but she wasn't sure that Andrei's idea of Deep Connectedness really didn't have the capacity to change the world, at least a little.

For some reason, as she sat down later that day to look over her notes and record her impressions of the interview while they were still fresh, Handel found herself liking him. Perhaps because he had seemed, in a way, to be honest.

She went onto Fishbowl again and spent some time navigating through the world that it opened up to her. She registered an interest in orangutans, took some Baits, and followed the trail that immediately opened up into the world of pongophiles. The next day, she went to Yao's and talked to the owner, Tony Yao, and a couple of the waiters. She had the photographer take some pictures. She even had a dish of fried prawn and chicken noodles to see what Andrei was talking about.

When her piece came out a month later, there was less in it than Handel had planned about Andrei, and more about Fishbowl's vision and evolution. And about orangutans. And Yao's, which was the quirkiest thing she could find to add interest to the story.

Any reader would have been forgiven for imagining that every important decision about Fishbowl had been taken at the restaurant and that if you wanted to find Andrei Koss, all you had to do was go down there at lunchtime any day of the week.

27

FOR FISHBOWL, THE effects of Denver were far-reaching. Andrei received approaches from the FBI and even more shadowy agencies in the intelligence community on the mistaken assumption that his cooperation after the bombing meant that he would be keen to cooperate in other, less overt ways. There was talk of 'back doors' and 'mass data transfers'. Andrei rebuffed them all and eventually they stopped contacting him, presumably reverting to their usual ways of snooping. Although security on the site had been a priority ever since John Dimmer had turned up with Fishbowl's first National Security Letter, Andrei had a team get to work on developing even more sophisticated levels of encryption.

A more important effect was that user registration skyrocketed, at first out of solidarity from the inhabitants of cyberspace as Fishbowl came under McKenrick's attack, then due to the internet multiplier phenomenon as awareness of Fishbowl entered truly popular consciousness. 'Fishing' and 'Baiting' became words in general use, even amongst people who had never opened Fishbowl – and they weren't talking about rod and reel.

As user numbers rose, advertising revenues continued to surge, and investment interest in Fishbowl intensified. Valuations of the business were now heading north of a billion dollars. At its core, the advertising model was that which had been developed by Andrei in the early days of the 4Site contract, continuously improved and refined by a team overseen by Kevin. Andrei himself took little interest in it now. As far as he was concerned, the advertising operation merely provided the funds for server space and salaries to drive the development of all the other functionalities that his programmers were working on. None of the other meta-networks that had been set up to try to capitalize on Fishbowl's success came close in their capabilities.

Eventually, Andrei got a call from Mike Sweetman

For the second time in Fishbowl's short history, Sweetman asked if Andrei wanted to sell. This time the offer was for $1.5 billion, raised immediately to $2 billion when Andrei's response was negative.

Andrei had no interest in selling. Fishbowl was in the almost unprecedented situation of being a start-up that had reached mega proportions without recourse to venture capital. Chris Hamer's investment of $1 million aside, and excepting the few tens of thousands that each of the founders had put in, Fishbowl had financed its own growth.

When Andrei said he wasn't going to sell, Sweetman asked if Andrei wanted to explore a partnership, offering to discontinue Openreach as part of any deal. It wasn't as big a concession as it sounded – it was an open secret that Openreach had failed, and its continued existence was something of an embarrassment for Homeplace. A series of meetings ensued. Andrei, Chris and James sat on one side of the table, Sweetman and his chief financial officer on the other side. But although there were many potential synergies, no matter how Sweetman pitched it, at the core of the partnership there always seemed to be some kind of preferential ranking or treatment for Homeplace users. Andrei couldn't see how that was going to enhance Deep Connectedness in general, or the experience of Fishbowl's users specifically, and he couldn't see how a partnership that didn't privilege Homeplace in some way could be in Sweetman's interest. The negotiations came to an end without agreement.

After the final meeting, Chris sat down with Andrei and told him that the time had come to deal with Homeplace. Mike Sweetman had thrown everything he could at them – now it was time for Fishbowl to turn the tables.

Andrei thought about it. Fishbowl was already capable of offering most of the functionality that Homeplace offered for people who wanted to network with their friends and acquaintances, and with a dedicated development programme it could relatively swiftly fill in the gaps and offer everything Homeplace had. Beyond that, it already provided the Deep Connectedness that Sweetman had tried and failed to replicate. It was thus a relatively small step to merge the meta-networking capabilities that were the core of Fishbowl with the services of a home network for those who chose to use it in this way with friends and family. The difficulty would be getting people to switch – at present, if you left Homeplace, you would lose everything – text, photo, video, audio – you had ever posted or received there. If Fishbowl could develop a seamless protocol for importing data from Homeplace – and *if* that protocol could get access to Homeplace's user data – they could make it as simple as a single click for a user to cut links with Homeplace and transfer everything to Fishbowl. But the second 'if' was a big one. Sweetman would fight tooth and nail to prevent any such protocol having access to his users, yet that didn't mean there wasn't a way to force him, if one was prepared to work at it. Scrutiny of Homeplace's behaviour by the Department of Justice hadn't gone away, and the locking-in of user data was often cited as an example of its anti-competitive approach. Sweetman had already been forced to make a number of minor concessions. With smart lobbying and a concerted, persistent campaign – over years, if necessary – it wasn't beyond the realm of possibility that Homeplace could be forced to open up entirely to data transfers.

James agreed with Chris. As he had shown over Denver, James's Christianity was of a muscular, if not bruising type and didn't mean limitless compassion – certainly not in business. And as long as Homeplace continued to be a force, he said, it would always be scheming against Fishbowl.

Discussion continued over a period of weeks. Andrei wasn't persuaded. He hadn't started Fishbowl in order to put other people out of business. And what they were talking about was simply reproducing what Homeplace already offered.

'We won't be offering anything new,' he said. 'Why would I want to do it? Out of some kind of grudge?'

'You're not sure what he might try next to hurt us,' said James.

'I'm not worried. I think Sweetman's the one who's worried about us.' Andrei didn't fear Mike Sweetman any more. He felt that Fishbowl had seen Homeplace off, and saw Sweetman's desire to partner with him when he couldn't buy him out as a sign of weakness. 'Guys, honestly. Let's forget about it. Why would we bother?'

'Efficiency,' said Chris. He paused to let the word sink in. 'Sweetman's never cared about his users, Andrei. Everything they've developed over there, they've developed so they can gather data and sell advertising. Every single thing they do, we can do more efficiently. We can give users more efficiency *and* more connectedness. We won't be offering the same service – we'll be offering something better.'

Andrei watched him thoughtfully, then glanced at his watch.

'Take a look at Homeplace,' said Chris. 'A good look. And don't tell me we can't do things better.'

Chris had no particular aspect of Homeplace in mind when he said that, but he thought, if Andrei Koss couldn't take a look at a website – any website – and find ways to do things more efficiently, then that website probably didn't exist.

Andrei looked. A few days later he sat down with Chris and James again.

'OK,' he said. 'Let's do it.'

Additional programmers were employed and a cohort of publicity consultants and lobbyists contracted. Fishbowl began a long fight to force Homeplace to open up to a transfer protocol that would spirit its users away with a single tap on a screen.

As it approached its second anniversary, Fishbowl had entered a new phase of its existence It was no longer one of a myriad start-ups jostling and bumping in the primordial soup at the foot of the internet ladder where companies surfaced and sank with remark-able rapidity. It had definitively exited that morass and risen to the rungs of companies that were seen as fixtures of the space.

Andrei had started to live less like a student unexpectedly let loose from the dorm, if not quite in the style of a tech baron. He had left the house in La Calle Court, having to pay a hefty five-figure sum to undo the damage that had been inflicted during almost a year and a half of frat-house occupation, and moved into a condo off University Avenue. He had gone online and ordered a bed, a sofa, a table, chairs and a desk for his computer, which he thought pretty much filled his needs. Anything else in the place had been put there by Sandy, who was in her senior year at Stanford and spent about half of her time in the condo and half in the dorm. She got him cutlery, plates, mugs and other kitchen basics. She bought towels and bed linen, and most of his clothes as well.

Andrei was now increasingly visible as the face of Fishbowl and more accessible to the media, albeit in small and controlled doses. He had been dissatisfied with his performance in the inter-view with Deborah Handel and, as a result, he undertook a serious programme of coaching in order to improve. He tried to define what aspects of himself he was prepared to expose and to find ways of being comfortable in talking about them.

As the months passed, he began selectively to accept invita-tions to speak at conferences and his utterances were listened to and reported. His confidence grew. He was mixing with heavy-weight internet entrepreneurs in whose company he was increasingly seen to be a natural member. As a result of the McKenrick campaign, he had been invited into their upper circle and found that he was not only able to hold his own but that he was taken seriously. He had worked closely with a number of fellow CEOs in the Defence of Freedom campaign and had, in particular, struck up a friendship with Jerry Glick during that intense, hectic fortnight. Now he and Sandy went to Jerry's for the barbecues that Glick liked to hold on the weekends at his big house in Palo Alto Hills, where Andrei met more of the aristocracy of Silicon Valley.

Fishbowl now employed almost four hundred people and had moved to a new space on Embarcadero Road, this time taking three floors of a regular glass-and-concrete office block. There were no individual offices but, for the first time, there were meeting rooms where people could have private conversations. As always, an aquarium stood opposite the entrance, this one larger and stocked with more fish than the one in the Ramona Street office. In Ramona Street, anyone who felt like it had cleaned the tank and fed its occupants, resulting in an informal roster, murky water and a high turnover of fish. Now a man from a professional agency came in three times a week to see to the aquarium and the water was always sparklingly clear. The fish also had a noticeably longer life span.

The original advertising deal with 4Site had come to an end and was not renewed. Ed Standish, who had come across to join as Senior Vice President for Advertising, was constantly expanding the team. Eighteen of them occupied a section of the second floor on Embarcadero, with another twenty-plus based in an office in New York.

As always, the original tight core of programmers who had been with Fishbowl since the early days resented the arrival of what seemed to be ever-increasing cohorts of business types, as did the other programmers, who were joining in growing numbers. One of the benefits of Fishbowl's rising profile was that it could attract software engineers of the highest calibre, often luring them away from jobs in the iconic companies of Silicon Valley. The cult of us-the-programmers-who-are-the-only-ones-who-know-what-this-website-can-really-do versus them-the-business-guys-who-dumb-everything-down-and-don't-get-the-point-of-anything was strong. Kevin was mischievously guilty of propagating it and this caused considerable friction with James, who was trying to hold everyone together.

Andrei, whose natural inclination was to side with the cult, knew that he had to rise above it, yet everyone knew where his sympathies lay. Theoretically, he wasn't supposed to be programming any more, but at least a couple of times a month he couldn't stop himself heading over to Geek's Grotto, as the programmers had proudly named the fifth floor, and taking in a wheelspin that often turned into an all-nighter. It would end with high fives and yells of 'Stakhanovite!' and then a bunch of them would go out and invade Yao's.

Andrei's forays into programming were only one thing that made his relationship with James tricky. By themselves, James probably would have overlooked them, but trust between the two men had been badly eroded by the Mea Culpa statement, as Andrei's message to the Grotto after the Denver bombing had come to be known. James believed that Andrei had reneged on an agreement they had reached the night they had met at La Calle Court, according to which he would not say or do anything until they met again with the lawyer the following morning. Andrei accepted that he had ignored James's request not to do anything before speaking to a lawyer, but didn't believe he had ever explicitly agreed to it. The issue had lain dormant during the turbulence and extraordinary intensity of the weeks that preceded the Defence of Freedom marches, when they had forced themselves to work together for the sake of the company. But it was only dormant – not resolved. Eventually, during a stormy meeting, James demanded that Kevin, Ben and Chris say in front of Andrei whether Andrei had actually agreed to say nothing that night in La Calle Court. James claimed that he had asked and Andrei had said yes. The actual word: yes. No one else was sure if he had said it, or at least wasn't prepared to say that they were, but they agreed that the general understanding, when they had broken up that night, had been that Andrei would accede to James's request.

Andrei accepted that he might have given that impression, even while being undecided at the time about what he would do. He apologized for that.

For his part, Andrei was aggrieved at the things James had said to him the following morning and the anger he had shown. James had called him stupid. He knew for a fact that people in the office had heard James blow up at him on the phone. James accepted that he shouldn't have said certain things, and even without those things, that he shouldn't have let people hear the conversation and promised not to allow it to happen again. Andrei didn't think it sounded like a very genuine apology.

Andrei was beginning to wonder whether James was the right man for the job. He was supposed to be the adult in the room, and Andrei knew it couldn't be easy for him to play that role, part of which meant controlling Andrei himself. Andrei was still his boss and by a large margin the majority shareholder. Yet some of the things that had come out of his mouth the morning of the Mea Culpa statement had suggested that he wasn't really comfortable in the chaos of Fishbowl, and Andrei didn't know if that was going to change. James had managed to put some order into the place, but Andrei wondered if he would be satisfied only when he had put in more order than Andrei wanted, stifling the unpredictability and somewhat uncontrolled creativity that Andrei felt was at the heart of Fishbowl. On the other hand, Andrei valued James's judgement. Maybe yet more order was needed, and Andrei was just going to have to learn to live with it.

He talked to Chris, who had been closely involved in recruiting the COO. Chris thought that James had turned out a little more corporate than they had hoped, but he also thought that neither he nor Andrei could have brought the kind of order and organization to Fishbowl that James had done. Andrei didn't dispute it.

'You ask me,' said Chris, 'this isn't the time to get rid of him.'

While Andrei was considering whether James should stay, the COO was focusing himself on readying Fishbowl for an initial public offering, or IPO, in which a percentage of the shares of a company are released on a stock exchange such as the NASDAQ, raising cash to fund growth and at the same time realizing fortunes for those lucky enough to own stock. Unless Andrei chose to sell the entire company, or chunks of it to venture capital investors, this was always going to be the route to realizing the value he had created.

Everyone more or less assumed that an IPO was on Andrei's mind. But even if he retained majority control, it had downsides. Once the company was listed, a duty was owed to the public shareholders who held stock. Fishbowl would need to publish extensive, open accounts and be accountable to financial regulatory authorities and to the demands of the markets. This would not only take considerable time and resource but would also also constitute a significant restriction of freedom. Important decisions would need to be justified to the markets, and their results would be followed. There would be less leeway to try new things, experiment, fail. Andrei didn't know if he was ready for that, or ever would be. Fishbowl was still funding its growth from its burgeoning advertising revenues and the company had no need for cash from a public offering. Andrei had enough trouble dealing with James and the business approach he applied to Fishbowl without having to worry about another thousand people constantly analysing the business from the outside.

But Andrei didn't say anything to stop James. He buried himself in the stuff that he enjoyed – ideas, projects – and the stuff that he didn't enjoy but as CEO had to do – external representation of the company – while leaving the COO to manage the business.

James was making sure that the cost base of the company was under control even as it expanded, that the record of advertising and revenue growth was healthy, that regulatory compliance was in order – all things that investors would scrutinize closely. For an IPO to succeed, for the shares to be taken up and the price to be high, he knew that the company had to look mature and stable enough to be taken seriously as a long-term business with sustainable sources of revenue and exciting potential for growth. He also knew that timing in an IPO was everything. The business had to look right, but the market also had to be receptive, with plenty of investment cash looking for a home. Fishbowl definitely looked a strong, sustainable business – much more so than many others that had gone public. And the market seemed to be eager for it.

Andrei couldn't continue to ignore the question of the IPO for ever. He turned to Chris for advice about it. In general, Chris was becoming more of a sounding board for him. Although Ben was now back at the company full time, having finished his degree at Stanford, the year in which he had been away had marked a shift in Andrei's relationship with him. Even if Ben had sometimes been in the office, he had been much less involved than before and his grasp of what was going had been limited. His mind had been on his studies and he had seemed somehow detached from the business. Sometimes, Andrei had got the feeling that he begrudged Fishbowl the time he spent there. The long conversations that they used to have had petered out – the last one Andrei could remember had been after Denver, when he had agonized over cooperating with the investigation, and they had been a rare event for some time before that. Many of the things on Andrei's mind now related to the business side of Fishbowl, about which Ben had no expertise, but to which Chris could bring a fund of experience.

Chris thought the timing for an IPO was probably pretty good, but he also didn't think there was a rush. He believed Fishbowl was going to keep rising in value and there was no sign of the market heading into one of its periodic bouts of aversion to internet stocks. He thought they should do the IPO some time in the next couple of years but it didn't have to be right then. James was more eager, arguing that the market was hot for Fishbowl after the publicity it had attracted, and the price of the stocks would command an added premium. After the complaints he had heard from James on the morning after the Mea Culpa statement, it occurred to Andrei that James might have been so enthusiastic because he wanted to cash out and leave the company. He had

1.75 per cent of the stock. At $2 billion – the price Sweetman had offered – that would value his stock at $35 million, and by now Sweetman's offer was probably low.

Over a beer in Andrei's condo one night, when he was up in Palo Alto, Chris suggested that they talk to a couple of investment banks to get their view.

'They're going to say do it, aren't they?' said Andrei. 'They're investment banks. That's what they do.'

'We could talk to a couple of VCs. They have a good grasp of when to go to the market.'

'Why would they tell us?'

'They might think they're going to get a piece of it. We could always let them think that. Why don't we talk to Robert Leib over at LRB? I could set up a meeting.' Chris paused. 'Do you want me to?'

Andrei didn't reply, musing on the beer in front of him. There was a dream he had had intermittently since he had been a child. In it, he was somehow bouncing like a rubber ball, bouncing higher and higher, even though he knew that a person couldn't bounce like a ball and at some point he would have to crash back down. In the dream, he was always anxious and scared, wondering how the bouncing was going to end as he flew higher and higher – and then he would wake up. Sometimes he had the dream recurrently, sometimes not for months.

In the past few weeks he had had it at least half a dozen times.

Suddenly he looked up. 'Chris, do you think this is really going to work?'

'What? The IPO?'

'No, Fishbowl. The business.'

Chris laughed.

'I'm serious.'

Something inside Andrei made him wonder if it could be this easy, if it really was possible to go from nothing to a company worth in excess of a billion dollars, starting out of a college dorm, with no knowledge of business at all, in two years. Somewhere, surely, there had to be a flaw. And if there was a flaw, then the IPO process would uncover it.

Not that he didn't believe in Fishbowl. He did, passionately. He believed in everything he had written in the black notebooks when he had first begun to think deeply about what it represented. He had stopped writing in the notebooks, but had kept them. Andrei had come to believe in Deep Connectedness as a natural human desire and a fundamental need, and he believed that Fishbowl's success was proof of that. He also believed in it as a powerful force for good – monsters like Andrew Buckett and Walter Hodgkin apart – and that it would help make the world a better place. But that didn't necessarily mean that, long term, Fishbowl would be the financial success it appeared to be. In fact, it seemed to him almost paradoxical. Something that was a force for good surely didn't make money.

What if it was all founded on air in a way that he didn't understand? After all, what did he really know about business? What if he was surfing the skin of a bubble and at some point the bubble was going to burst and he was going to find himself hitting the ground with a thud?

'Sometimes I can't believe it,' he said. 'This life … is it mine? Sometimes I feel like I'm back in the dorm at Stanford and this must be some kind of a dream.'

'Andrei, this isn't a dream.'

'I think to myself, it can't really work.'

'It's working,' said Chris. 'What else do you need to see?'

'What if it doesn't last?'

'*Doesn't last?* Andrei, I think you've got something here that in another year or two is going to be established as one of the truly iconic things on the internet.'

'I bet you thought that about FriendTracker.'

'No, I never thought that about FriendTracker. FriendTracker was ridiculous. It came out of a bet between me and this guy I worked with on one of my other ventures, Josh Henkler, about who could come up with the most repulsive, slimy, disgusting internet idea and make it work – "work" being defined as the first to reach a hundred thousand users. And I thought what could be more disgusting than a program that rates your friends?'

Andrei looked at him sceptically. 'You never told me that before.'

'It's true. I'm not proud of it. I ask you, is that what friendship's about? Rating people? But you know what? People loved it. People wanted this hideous thing. And what for? Not to show someone how good a friend they were. No, it was, like, I'm going to use this to get rid of the friends I don't really like. I'm going to show them how much I despise them and hurt them as much as I can in the process. I'm going to alienate them from all their other friends and leave them bereft. That's when it really took off – when people started using it to piss their friends. We had suicides, Andrei! And you know what? With every suicide, we got more users! What kind of a world, huh? I had to promise to keep doing stuff to tone it down, but I never did. We'd do something cosmetic and say we'd made sure it would never happen again. No one really wanted me to do anything except the moms and dads of the kids who'd killed themselves, and they didn't use the site, right? Everyone else who made a noise forgot about it after ten minutes. But it was a fad. It wasn't a sustainable business. The Ukrainian idiots who bought it had no idea. Getting a return out of that business, *that* was about timing. All timing. That was all there was to it.'

'Aren't you scared the Ukrainians are going to come break your legs some day?'

Chris laughed.

'Seriously. You should talk to my father. He could tell you some stories about Ukrainian gangsters.'

'Look, Andrei, Fishbowl isn't FriendTracker. Believe in this thing that you've made. It's real. It's awesome. It's not going away.'

Andrei didn't reply. What if the issue wasn't Fishbowl, but him? What if he didn't have what it took to lead it? Maybe it should be someone who had some experience. Maybe it should be Chris.

'I think James is right,' said Chris. 'The market's hot for us right now, but that doesn't mean you've got to do the IPO. You have time. Fishbowl's not going away. You have the most targeted offering for advertisers in the world. They'll pay in blood for your data. Andrei, what we've got is a whole new model. That's what you've built here. That's as solid as a rock.'

Andrei watched him doubtfully.

'The IPO ... you can take your time.' Chris paused. 'Let me set up that meeting with Bob Leib. He's a good guy. They're all vampires, but Bob's the best of them. I mean he's not always out to suck your blood. Occasionally, he looks up from the carcase for a second. Let's hear what he's got to say. He's a very good judge of the market.'

But a week later, when Chris called from LA, he hadn't set up the meeting. And he hadn't set it up a fortnight later, or a month later. He hadn't even called Leib to try. As it turned out, that meeting wouldn't take place for another year.

Instead, Chris set up another meeting – with Andrei, James, Kevin and Ben. He had had an idea, one that had nothing to do with a possible IPO. An idea that at some level had been perco-lating in his mind ever since a certain evening watching ping pong with Ben during the first, wild summer of Fishbowl in La Calle Court.

28

'EDGAR ALLEN VANDER,' said Chris. He looked around the meeting room at Andrei, Ben, Kevin and James. 'Ever heard of him?'

They stared back at him blankly.

'I've heard of Edgar Allen Poe,' said Ben.

'That was his great-uncle.'

'Really?'

'Not sure. Would you like him to be? With Edgar Allen Vander,' said Chris theatrically, 'anything is possible.' He paused, enjoying the showmanship. Everyone could see he was on a high. He opened his computer and hooked it up to a projector. A Fishbowl page came up on the wall. 'This is the Vandernarianism School page. Ignore the posts – yada, yada, yada … See that box on the right? That's the sign-up box for the Edgar Allen Vander conference in San Diego next March. See that number. We've got … Wow! It's up to two hundred and sixty-four registrations.'

'Dude, what the fuck is this?' said Kevin.

'Oh, of course. You don't know about him. Edgar Allen Vander, who, I've just been informed, was Edgar Allen Poe's great-nephew, founded a new age religion called Vandernarianism twenty-three years ago in Redwood, right here in California.'

'That makes him way too young to be Edgar Allen Poe's great-nephew,' said Ben.

'Great-great-nephew, I think. Anyway, the point is, Edgar Allen Vander did, so far as is known, create Vandernarianism, the four tenets of which are, as we all know ...' He clicked on a button on the School page. 'One, own only what you can. Two, display only what you must. Three, leave only what you have. Four, discern only what you see.'

The others stared at the list of commandments.

'What is less well known is that Edgar Allen Vander, who authored these famous tenets, was himself created by a short Armenian man called Nicholas Kervakian.'

'You mean that was his real name,' said Ben.

'No. What I mean is, Nicholas Kervakian created him.'

'You mean like God,' said Kevin, with a falsely innocent tone, knowing that would rile James.

'After a manner of speaking. Because what no one knows – apart from me, that is, until this moment – is that Nicholas Kervakian himself ...' Chris paused and brought up a Fishbowl home page '... is me.'

The home page on the screen showed a set of Photoxed images of Chris with moustache, dark hair and about thirty more pounds in weight.

Kevin grinned. 'You sly beast.'

'Thank you, sir. In six months, gentlemen, using nothing more than four tenets, eight invented biographical facts, and a keyboard – and the mighty Fishbowl, of course – I created a cult. A bona fide, all-ends-up cult that is meaningful enough for two hundred sixty-four people to register for a conference about a man that didn't exist.'

'Sounds like Christianity,' murmured Kevin.

James glared at him.

'Oh, no,' said Chris. 'That took years. Although to be fair, Jesus didn't have Fishbowl. I simply wanted to see what was possible. Starting from nothing, nothing but an idea and a keyboard and the awesome power of the mighty Fishbowl. And the gullibility of human beings, of course. Their awful need to believe. Wouldn't want to forget that.'

'The point being ...?' said James, in a tone of intense irritation.

'Two hundred sixty-four people. That's at five hundred dollars a head *before* accommodation and travel expenses. That's one hundred and thirty-two thousand dollars.'

'*You took their money?*' James's face was red with rage. 'You took these people's money? What is this supposed to show? That you can commit fraud on Fishbowl? You think after McKenrick this is what we need, to show that you can hoodwink—?'

'I didn't take anyone's money. They registered. No money has been sent. Tomorrow they'll be informed the conference is cancelled.'

'But they'll still believe in this Vander person.'

'Maybe I'll tell them it was a joke. Maybe not. I mean, the tenets aren't so bad. They're essentially meaningless. I made them up pretty much randomly, but they're not exactly telling anyone to go out and kill somebody. And who am I to stop it? Who am I to say Vandernarianism doesn't exist?' Chris raised an eyebrow. 'Maybe it does.' He clicked on an online encyclopaedia and brought up an entry for Edgar Allen Vander.

Kevin laughed uproariously. 'Dude! Stakhanovite!'

'I did not write that page,' said Chris. 'I promise you.'

James shook his head in exasperation. 'What is the *point* of this—?'

'Dude, what's the point of the Mona Lisa?' retorted Kevin. 'What's the point of the Taj Mahal? It's genius.'

'It's puerile!'

'Genius is puerile,' said Chris. 'Let's look at something else that's not so puerile. Bali.'

'Oh, for heaven's—'

'Bali,' said Chris again. 'Yoga.' He clicked at his computer and brought up the website of a luxury yoga retreat called The Imperial. 'Take a look at that. Pretty cool, huh? Not cheap. It'll cost you twelve thousand dollars a week to do their programme. But it's a great place. Haven't been there myself, but I know someone who has. Raved about it. Totally awesome. And that, gentlemen, is all I said.' He clicked again and brought up the home page of another Photoxed image of himself, this one slim, taut and toned. 'OK? That's *all* I said.'

'To who?' asked Ben.

'To the eight people who decided to go there over the past three months as a result of me telling them that. One from France, two from Germany, one from Australia and four from right here in the States.'

Kevin grinned. 'You did a Cooley.'

Chris cocked a finger at him. 'Now you get it. A Cooley. Only not with a pair of sneakers or a wet suit, Tonya, my pretty little friend. With a twelve thousand dollar yoga retreat.'

'What's a Cooley?' demanded James.

'When you get someone to buy something,' said Kevin, 'preferably against their previous preferences.'

'And it took you three months to get eight people to sign up,' said James dismissively.

'Spending half an hour a day, max.'

'*Eight* people.'

'There are more on the way. It takes a little time to build up a head of steam. The next three months, I'd say it will be twenty.'

'Twenty,' snorted James.

'Twelve thousand each, James. What if it was cars, yachts, skiing holidays, designer clothes, designer goods? Anything high end, anything expensive? Let me ask you a question. What's the best form of advertising? Let me answer it for you. Word of mouth. Fishbowl is the mouth, gentlemen. A mouth wired directly into the ears of hundreds of millions of people, and only Fishbowl knows exactly what they want to hear and when they want to hear it.'

Ben glanced at Andrei for a second, then turned back to Chris. 'You're saying we do this? We go to businesses and say we can target your potential customers with a virtual personality that persuades them to buy their product?'

'Correct,' said Chris. 'Although *persuades* is a strong word. Think of it as raising awareness. You raise awareness at the right moment, and you don't even need persuasion.'

'And what? We have people sitting here doing it?'

'Correct again. This will only work for high-end goods. My rough calculations say that anything that sells for over five to seven thousand dollars – very roughly – will be a financially viable object for this kind of marketing. Think about those eight people who are going to Bali. Do you remember where they came from? The States, France, Germany, Australia. Think about it. Three continents, four countries. How much advertising would you have had to throw out across the *world* to find those exact people, at the exact right time when they're ready to consider going on some kind of retreat, with the exact right idea? But me, hey, I'm sitting there talking to them! I don't have to go finding them – they tell me when they're ready! And all I have to say is, I've heard of this great place. That's it! And, yes, in case you're wondering, every one of those eight, when they come back, when they've had that experience, become advertisers themselves. Word of mouth. Word of mouth building on word of mouth. We prime it and we keep it going. You sell this idea to an advertiser, and you do it so you get not only the commission on the sale but the commission on the expected value of the sales the word of mouth will generate. That's a significant multiple.'

'Have you done that?' demanded James. 'Has this resort in Bali been paying you?'

'Not yet. It was an experiment. At the moment, they have no idea why they're experiencing such a surge of interest.'

There was silence.

'Cool,' said Kevin.

Andrei was staring at the picture of the yoga retreat, frowning. Chris sat down and let him think.

Since the summer in La Calle Court when Chris had begun collaborating with Kevin on personas, he had become increasingly fascinated with the thoroughness and commitment of Kevin's approach to something that, like a butterfly, might last only a number of weeks and then disappear. Kevin constructed lives and, like a freewheeling cyber magpie, stole whatever he needed – a face there, a body here, a background, a friend, a family – to give them substance. There was performance and creativity in it as well as deep subversion, all qualities of high importance to Chris's conception of spirituality. He had seen how a personality grew and took on a life of its own, a life that had a logic beyond the intentions with which it had been launched into the world. He had experienced how it was to inhabit that life, snippets of time in which he was excised from his real-world existence and translated into another.

In some ways it was similar to having an avatar in a virtual world, but there was a difference in knowing that he was talking to real people, not other avatars, and being seen as a real person, that made the experience all the more compelling. Sometimes he spent the whole day in front of his screen, inside the skins of his personas. He could talk to people in ways he had never talked, hear them in ways he had never heard. The mixture of the real and the virtual was heady, so heady that sometimes the line blurred. To Chris, it echoed his experiences of the disembodied yet obviously all too real experiences of Peruvian *chamans*, or of the Australian aboriginal Dreamtime. In exploring the cyber world through these constructed personalities, he felt he was crafting a new and intensely meaningful form of these experiences. He came to see the creation and inhabiting of these personalities as something fundamental and important, perhaps a defining act for the still-emerging cyber world, a world in which physical appearance, life experience and identity itself, were fungible.

But the cynic and the entrepreneur in Chris, so intertwined as to be almost indistinguishable, were never far from the mystic. The germ of the idea he was putting in front of Andrei and the others had been in his head since the moment Ben told him about the Cooley experiment – it had simply taken time to find shape as he explored and inhabited his world of constructed personalities. How far would people's gullibility and willingness to believe allow him to take them? Could he reliably reproduce the Cooley effect? To find out, he had created a 42-year-old, expatriate

American yoga enthusiast who lived in Singapore and had heard about a luxury yoga retreat in Bali from a friend, and set himself a task. How many people could he stimulate to go on the retreat? Then he had got the idea of doing something even more subversive. What if he could create not just a personality who spoke about something that existed but both a personality and something outside him that didn't exist, and get people to believe in that as well?

From there it had been a relatively short step to the persona of an enthusiast of a prophet – randomly named Edgar Allen Vander – and his religion of four random tenets. He had worked the Fishbowl Schools, seeding them with tantalizations to visit the Edgar Allen Vander School page and its links to the tenets of the faith and the biography of the prophet. It turned out that the simplicity – if not total vacuity – of the four commandments that he had invented was a stroke of genius. People could read anything they liked into them, and they did. Before long, the School page was alive with what Chris perceived as sad, damaged, needy, searching people, seriously discussing his empty aphorisms and mining them for meaning. Articles on Vander appeared in online encyclopaedias. He had planted the seed, then sat back and watched as the tree grew. Yet the success of Vandernarianism had taken him by surprise. It was far in excess of anything he had anticipated. To Chris, it was awe-inspiring.

But he wished now that he hadn't started the meeting by talking about Vandernarianism. That was one for Kevin. The yoga foray, on the other hand, was a straightforward Cooley experiment – Chris hadn't known just how important an experiment until the conversation a month earlier, when Andrei had told him about his doubts over whether Fishbowl would last. Chris had said to Andrei that Fishbowl had established a new model of advertising, but afterwards it had struck him – that wasn't true. Fishbowl merely offered a better version of the existing model that tried to identify people's interests from their online activity and aim advertisements at them that seemed to match those interests. What Fishbowl was doing was more powerful not because it was different but because in Fishbowl people identified themselves by the one or two things that were top of their list of interests, and an advertiser could be reasonably certain that they would be interested in what they had to sell them. In other words, it was only the old model more powerfully applied.

During the month that had followed since then, the number of people signing up for the Bali resort had shot up from two to eight. Chris had thought he would be doing well if he could get three. He had also had the idea of seeing what would happen if he announced a Vandernarianism conference – and found 200-plus people eagerly signing up. He realized then that a new model of advertising really was possible – not merely the old one better applied. A new model that, because of the quality of Fishbowl's targeting and the ability of a constructed personality to enter the discussion flow, gave them a unique advantage.

'This isn't serious,' said James again. 'You're saying we hire people to make personalities—'

'Palotls, James.'

'*Palotls?*'

'That's what these personalities are called.'

'Aren't they avatars?'

'No, an avatar is an online incarnation of a person who exists in the real world. A palotl is an individual who exists only in cyberspace. From *papalotl*, the ancient Mexican word for butterfly. The Aztecs thought butterflies were the souls of dead warriors. A palotl is a fragment of our soul brought to life, as it were, in cyberspace.'

'Cool,' said Kevin.

James looked at him in distaste. 'I don't care what you call it. We're not going to have people creating these things and then trying to sell stuff.'

'That's not how I'd put it.'

'I don't care how you'd put it. We're not doing it.'

'Why not?'

'Why not?' James looked at him in disbelief. 'Do I have to tell you? OK, there are about a thousand reasons. For a start, you're not telling people you're advertising.'

'So? When a celebrity goes on TV and says he uses a product, does he announce that he's advertising it?'

James stared at him in disbelief. 'Everyone knows he's advertising it.'

'Really? Do children know? He doesn't say, "I'm advertising, kiddies. I'm being paid so ignore every word I say." There's no announcement that says, "This is an advertisement."'

'People know.'

'Do they? Look, this is legal. I've checked it out.'

'No, Chris. It's not illegal. There's a difference.'

'Oh, are you going to pull morality on me, James? Listen, you think a kid in the inner city watching some basketball star advertising sneakers thinks, This is advertising, I won't pay any attention? If you want immorality, start there. What I'm talking about here is high-end goods. These are people who have the ability to make an informed decision and plenty of disposable income. I'm not talking about pushing sneakers at kids whose parents can't afford to put food on the table. If you want to get on a high horse, James, get on your high horse about that.'

'We don't push sneakers.'

'Don't we? It's going on all the time under our noses. You ought to spend a little time on the Schools pages once in a while. Every corporation is in there doing it, getting people to boost them. Unidentified, as it happens. Recruiting kids and tossing them a sneaker or a download if they're lucky. It's called viral marketing, James. Maybe you've heard of it.'

'But *we* don't do it.'

'Exactly,' said Chris. 'That's our problem. With the data we collect, we can do it so much better than them.'

James shook his head in disgust. Chris stared right back at him, smiling at his discomfort.

'So what you're proposing,' said Andrei, 'is that we … hire a bunch of people to create palotls and sell that service to advertisers?'

'In a nutshell … yes.'

James snorted in contempt.

'What?' demanded Chris.

'What about our reputation?'

'We're providing information. I told you, I told no lies. And I don't propose that we would. Factual information only.'

'But biased, partial, selective.'

'Whose information isn't? At least it will be factual. Have you ever read *any* of the stuff on the Schools pages, James? Most people are talking out of their ass. What's better – partial but factual information or complete nonsense?'

'This is not about Deep Connectedness.'

'That's a matter of opinion. I happen to think it is. Does it make the world a worse place?'

'Obviously it does.'

'Really? Obviously? Those eight people who are going to Bali didn't think so. Five have already been and you should see what they said when they came back. The people who had jobs at that resort because of them didn't think so. So in exactly what way was the world worse because of this, James?'

Langan threw up his hands in the air. 'This is *not* about Deep Connectedness! This is not about any of the things Fishbowl is here to do. Andrei, this goes against every single thing I believe in. It goes against my faith. It goes against the way I do business. This idea isn't worth the time we've already spent on it.' He looked at his watch and got up. 'I've got a wife and kids. I see too little of them already to waste my time with something like this. You guys can keep talking about it as long as you like. In case you're wondering, I'm a no on this. No, no, no, no, *no*! This is not happening while I'm COO. Not on my watch.' He left, not quite slamming the door but closing it a little too loudly behind him.

There was silence for a moment.

'You know, the weak point in all this,' said Kevin, as if James had never even been there, 'is that you're using people's faces in your home page – images you've taken off the net. Doesn't matter how much you Photox them, we still couldn't do that.'

'True. Ideally, we'd use computer-generated images.'

'I don't know of any software that's good enough to create images that will stand up to scrutiny.'

'I don't either.' said Chris, relishing the changed atmosphere in the meeting room. With James gone, it suddenly felt as if they were back in La Calle Court, throwing around ideas for whatever merit they might have without consoring themselves because of what a guy in a suit would say. 'If we did this, the people we hire would have to agree to have their images used. But we could manipulate the images so they wouldn't be recognizable. It's an issue, but we could get over it.'

'I'm not sure this is about Deep Connectedness,' said Andrei.

'I dispute that,' said Chris. 'You've always said we need to have a broad conceptualization. I think this fits that envelope. At the moment, we have a broad conceptualization of what Deep Connectedness can be but a relatively narrow one of who it can be *between*. You guys started off thinking of it as connectedness between two unique and irreproducible individuals who exist physically in the world. OK, Kevin already pushed us beyond that with palotls, which were his idea – and Andrei, you backed that, rightly, because a broad conceptualization required you to do that. So you expanded the idea to connectedness between as many manifestations of one self as an individual wants to project into cyberspace. And I'm saying, let's expand that further into connections that include corporate entities, multi-person entities, if you will.'

'Companies,' said Ben.

'In this case, but it could also be other entities. It could be charities trying to get you interested in the cause. It could be consumer groups trying to inform you of your rights. Other social networks allow corporate entities on.'

'We've never done that,' said Ben. 'We've always said no.'

'And I'm saying we should reconsider. Not because others do it – because it's a way of extending Deep Connectedness.'

'So that companies can sell stuff.'

'In the case of the example I gave you, but it won't be in every case. But even if it is, we already do that. We already have advertising. Guys, let's be honest. We wouldn't be here today if we didn't.'

'When we have Sponsored Baits,' said Ben, 'people already know it.'

'Does that make a difference?'

'Of course it does.'

'Why?' said Chris. 'And how do you know that's not a bad thing? We know that some people won't click on a Bait simply because it's sponsored. What if that's depriving them of seeing stuff they actually would want to see? Wouldn't they be happier if they didn't know it was sponsored, clicked on it, and then did see it?'

'That's their decision.'

'How can they make that decision if they have an irrational bias against Sponsored Baits? In fact, the very fact that we identify them as such means that we're recognizing this bias and encouraging it.'

'Chris, come on …'

'No, seriously, Ben. We don't require any other Bait to have an identified motive, and, let's face it, a lot of people's motives are exploitative. Some people will click on a Bait because they think the person looks hot and they want to hit on them, or because they want to get some kind of information they might use to their advantage, or because they want to see if they can sell you something, or because they want to convert you to a religion … It's only advertisers where we say, you've got to identify your motive.' He looked at Andrei. 'Singling out advertisers is not consistent. Let's go back to our principles. If we do what I say, does it make the world worse?'

'Not for me,' said Kevin.

'Andrei?'

Andrei was silent. Instinctively, he would have said that it did. But as Chris had reminded him, it was one of his principles to be open to challenge on the scope of Deep Connectedness. 'I'd have to think about it,' he said eventually.

Chris nodded. 'Let me add one thing. Companies like us, we all survive through advertising. That's reality. We allow advertising and that gives us the money to keep building the great services we want to build. And you know what? The way I see it, the advertising we do is a form of Deep Connectedness as well.'

'That's a new one,' said Ben.

'No. I've always thought so. We enable companies to connect with their customers in a way no one else can. And to me, if you have a broad conceptualization of Deep Connectedness – both of what it can be about and who it can be between – then that's a form of Deep Connectedness like any other. But the truth is, however good we are now, the most efficient model of advertising will always win. At the moment, we target better than anybody else, which is why our advertising revenues have always been so strong. But the way we do advertising, that's already yesterday's model. The model I've described, that's tomorrow's model. If we don't do it, someone else will. And I would hate to see that happen. Not only because of what that would do to the value of the five per cent that I own of this fine company, but because I think Fishbowl does and will do Deep Connectedness better and more efficiently than anybody else will ever do it. I think we're more honest and more transparent. I don't think anyone else would have had the *cojones* to write the Mea Culpa statement, Andrei. That was a Stakhanovite thing to do. But if we don't lead, if we don't develop the model of tomorrow, someone else will take our place. To me, that's another perspective on thinking about why this is about Deep Connectedness. It's about making sure we're the ones still here to provide it.'

'We're doing pretty well with what we've got,' said Ben.

'Ben, this model of advertising will carry us through some way yet, I grant you that. But not in the long term. Of course, you could ask people to pay – we don't have to be a thirty or fifty billion dollar company. We could be a five billion dollar one. That would be OK, right? All we'd have to do is ask the five hundred million users we'll have in a year's time to pay, say, ten dollars each year. Ten bucks. How many would do it?'

'Some would,' said Ben.

Kevin smirked. 'You and your grandmother.'

'Some would,' said Chris. 'Maybe once. But you know what else would happen? Someone would come along and provide our exact same service for "free", by doing exactly what we're talking about tonight, and create the thirty or fifty billion dollar company we could have been. And not even the ones who were prepared to pay their ten bucks first time round will pay it the second year, and then we're nothing. That's human nature.' Chris grinned. 'Never fails to disappoint.'

'I don't care about how much we're worth,' said Andrei.

'What I'm saying is that if you're not worth a lot, you're going to be worth nothing.'

Kevin grinned.

'Forget that,' said Andrei. 'Let's say this is a way of extending Deep Connectedness – I need to think about that, but maybe it is. Why do we do this now?'

'Why would we wait? We want the most Deep Connectedness, in the broadest sense, don't we? We've never waited before.'

'Maybe James is right. Maybe this will kill our reputation.'

'Andrei, James is dead wrong.'

Everything Chris had ever seen had convinced him that people couldn't care less what use was made of them or their data on the internet, as long as they didn't have to pay for it. They wouldn't care about this either, he was sure, or at least not enough to do anything about it. But he didn't put the argument quite that bluntly.

'People don't like change, even when it's bringing them even better Deep Connectedness. It'll take some time for them to see its benefits. So, yeah, there'll be people who scream, but after a while they'll stop.' Chris paused. 'Let's do an experiment. Let's sell this concept to a couple of advertisers, do it for a while – four, five months – see if it works on a commercial basis, then leak the fact that it's been happening. There'll be a shitstorm. We'll say we don't know how it happened, we're shocked, we're going to investigate, yada, yada, yada – then let's assess where we are a couple of months after that. If there's been a sustained impact on the user base, I'll concede. I still think this is the future, but I'll accept we shouldn't be the first mover and we should wait for someone else to blaze the trail.'

'Dude,' said Kevin, 'no way James is going to let you do that. You heard what he—'

'James doesn't make the decisions!' snapped Chris. 'Kevin, James is the COO. He executes what he's fucking told to execute.' Chris looked at Andrei. 'James doesn't get it. This is start-up mode, Andrei. This is trying something new and radical. Come on. You and I both know James doesn't get that stuff. But this is what Fishbowl is for. To do the big stuff, the groundbreaking stuff. Look, we don't need to use anyone from the commercial team. We don't even need to tell Ed Standish. I'll find someone to help me and I'll do it from LA. I'll keep you informed. You'll have a veto over the decisions. And I won't tell any lies. I didn't tell any lies about Bali – you'd be amazed how little I had to say. Guys, this is legal! And we can do it totally the Fishbowl way. Don't make the world worse – don't tell any lies.'

Andrei watched him. To do this without James knowing went against everything the headhunter had told him when he had hired the COO. She had urged him to make sure James was included in all the important decisions, even the technical ones. There was no way to undermine a business operator more quickly in a tech company, she said, than to cut him out of those.

And Chris had been there when she had said it.

'You're not even making a decision,' said Chris. 'It's just an experiment. Even if it works, you can still say you don't want to do it.'

'And if it goes wrong?' said Ben.

'Blame it on me. We'll say it was a rogue act and the company is severing its ties with me. Andrei, come on.'

Andrei didn't reply.

'You know what?' said Chris impulsively. 'How much is my five per cent of this company worth? Fifty million? A hundred million? If I'm wrong, I'll not only take the blame, I'll sell every last share back to you for the million bucks I paid.'

29

CHRIS'S OFFER TO sell back his shares for a million dollars if his experiment went wrong didn't sway Andrei. If anything, it made him wary. A good idea shouldn't have to be accompanied by a bribe.

Ben found Andrei the next day and asked if they could talk. When they had closed the door of a meeting room behind them, he told Andrei that he felt strongly that they shouldn't proceed with the kind of activity Chris was suggesting.

Andrei already knew Ben felt like that from what he had said during the meeting. But in Andrei's opinion, Ben had never had a particularly broad conceptualization of Deep Connectedness. Andrei heard him out but said little in reply, and Ben came away from the conversation frustrated and depressed. He went back to his desk and sat down, not sure what to do next. In general, he had too little to do. He was still Chief Mind Officer, but since James had joined as COO his role had become as nebulous as his title. When he had still been studying at Stanford that hadn't been a bad thing, but now that he was back at Fishbowl full time, it left him underemployed and embarrassed at the thought that people must be wondering what he did all day. He had mentioned it to Andrei a couple of times but nothing had happened to change the situation.

From Andrei's perspective, it wasn't that he necessarily disagreed with Ben about Chris's proposition. In fact, he wasn't naturally in sympathy with the proposal, either, but he was determined to look past his own prejudices and view it through the lens of a broad conceptualization, one that was willing to constantly examine, challenge and, if necessary, change his assumptions about what Deep Connectedness meant. This conceptualization had moved a long way since the days in Fishbowl's first year when he had baulked at putting conventional advertising on the site, and would have been unrecognizable to the Andrei of that time. Had he stopped to consider it, Andrei would have regarded that evolution in his thinking as a positive. He was also determined to view Chris's idea from a starting point of inclusiveness, the principle of trying things as long as they didn't make the world worse rather than having to be sure from the start that they would make it better and that people would want them. Andrei believed that this approach had been one of Fishbowl's most important strengths from its earliest days in Robinson House. He was determined to remain open to challenge and willing to try new approaches, conscious that it was all too easy to start believing that the way you currently thought of things was the only way they could be understood.

Andrei felt that Chris had challenged him in two important ways. First, why should Deep Connectedness be restricted to connections between individuals or their online personifications? Throughout their lives, people had important relationships with organizations. And organizations were, after all, collections of people. Why, therefore, should Deep Connectedness not involve organizations as well? And if it should involve organizations, why should it exclude organizations that were trying to sell things?

Second, why should corporate entities be identified as such? If people could have palotls, as Chris had named them, why couldn't companies? And if people could have undisclosed motives, some of which related to personal gain, again, why not companies?

In fact, who was to say that companies weren't doing this for themselves already, undisclosed? If people were capable of doing it – as Kevin had demonstrated – surely corporations were?

James had found that all of this had needed hardly a moment's thought. He had closed his mind immediately to the apparent deceit of representing companies by palotls. But to Andrei it wasn't necessarily a deceit – it could also be seen as a natural, perhaps inevitable manifestation of the opacity that was an intrinsic part of online connectedness, and which had been present from the moment the very first person on the internet had decided to use a pseudonym. It had never been Andrei's mission to eradicate that. Focused on constantly exploring and expanding his conceptualization of Deep Connectedness, and determined to prevent instinct ruling his thinking, he saw these challenges as serious questions, not to be answered glibly.

It was these challenges, rather than the potential for a new model of revenue-generating advertising, that interested Andrei in what Chris had said. Fishbowl's revenues were already suffi-cient for the needs of running and developing the company, even with the added costs from the effort they were making to rival Homeplace's services with a suite of more efficient func-tionalities and to force Homeplace to allow unfettered data transfer, which was an ongoing project. There was a growing pile of cash in the company's account.

As far as advertising was concerned, Andrei still told himself that it was a means to an end, a necessity in order to be able to respond to user needs and continuously improve the efficiency of the Deep Connectedness that Fishbowl provided. Even if you saw it as a form of Deep Connectedness in its own right, as Chris had suggested – and Andrei had to admit that there was a case for that – you didn't need every last cent of revenue that you could get, as other major internet companies seemed to want. So many founders had started out with altruistic intent – or so they claimed – to facilitate access to knowledge or information sharing or social interactivity, and had ended up gathering all the personal information on their users that they could acquire and packaging it for advertisers in order to build multi-billion-dollar companies. Andrei didn't see himself in that light and found them sickeningly hypocritical. They still spoke as if they were actually trying to do something for the world.

In any event, Andrei didn't think Chris's suggestion would generate much in the way of revenue. Even if it succeeded, the returns from any model requiring people to manually work the Fishbowl network, no matter how lucrative on a per-person basis, would surely pale in comparison with the automated click-auctions from which Fishbowl currently earned its money, not unless they could employ hundreds or even thousands of sales people.

To Andrei, this wasn't about money. It was genuinely about Deep Connectedness. It was a test of his willingness to stick to his principle of having a broad conceptualization, of his preparedness to embrace challenges to his thinking. Despite his own bias, which told him that this was something he didn't want to do, he was determined to force himself to face the challenges Chris had made. And perhaps it was partly because of this bias – his awareness that he had instinctively veered toward rejection coupled with his determination always to test his instincts – that he eventually made the decision that would prove to be so momentous in shaping the creature that Fishbowl was finally to become: to go ahead with the experiment and let the chips fall where they would.

Andrei had once said to Chris that the surest way for Fishbowl to become irrelevant was for three guys sitting in Yao's to try to tell the world what it could do. He still believed that.

Chris came back up to Palo Alto the following week. This time he and Andrei had dinner alone at Yao's.

'I was hasty last week,' said Chris.

Andrei looked at him quizzically. 'You don't believe what you said about this new model?'

'No, I do.'

'You don't want to do the experiment? You want to tell James?'

'Shit, no! Tell James? Are you out of your mind?'

'Then what is it?'

Chris hesitated. 'I've supported you for two years, Andrei. I saved your butt that first summer when you were going to burn yourselves alive.'

'I know.'

'I've put in ... I don't know how many months of work over that time and never drawn a salary.'

'Do you want one? I always thought you wanted to be an investor.'

'I don't want a salary.' Chris hesitated again. 'Look, what I'm saying is, I got carried away last week. I made an offer to you that I didn't really mean ... I mean, I hadn't planned it. It was the heat of the moment.'

'You mean about your shares?'

Chris nodded.

'That was a big bet.'

'Yeah,' said Chris. 'Something just ... I don't know, I didn't mean to say it.'

'What do you want to do about it?'

Chris shrugged, gazing at him for a moment, then looked away.

Andrei watched him. For the first time in the two years he had known him, it didn't feel as if Chris was the one who knew everything and he, Andrei, was the novice. Suddenly, Chris seemed a lot smaller and more limited.

Andrei could have told him to forget about it. He didn't need the extra 5 per cent of shares back. With 65 per cent of the company still in his ownership, they were irrelevant. But something stopped him doing that. Chris, he felt, had to honour in some way what he had said. He knew that was harsh, but he found himself wanting Chris to pay some kind of a price over this.

'If we go ahead,' said Andrei, 'let's make it half. If you do it, and you're wrong, you sell back half your shares for half a million. You get to keep two and a half per cent.'

Chris stared at him. There wasn't exactly a smile on his face.

'Or we can call it off,' said Andrei.

'No. I'm right. You'll see.'

'I'm not sure if the risk you're running is worth the payoff.'

Chris shrugged. Part of him just wanted to see if he was right. There was nothing more fascinating to Chris than seeing how low people would go. Would they bother to resist this? He doubted it. But he didn't say that to Andrei. 'If I'm wrong, I lose two and a half per cent of the company. That's not an insubstantial amount, I grant you, but the other two and a half per cent still gives me plenty of a return on my investment. But if I'm right – and I'm pretty sure I am – I have five per cent of a company that will be worth an order of magnitude more. So if this is the only way to get you to do this, then that's how we'll do it.'

'An order of magnitude?' said Andrei. 'I don't think there's going to be that much revenue out of it, even if it works.'

Chris smiled knowingly. 'One step at a time, my friend. Let's see if it works. Let's prove the concept. Then let's see where it goes.'

After a moment Andrei shrugged. 'OK. It's your risk.'

'But the IPO's off while we do this. There's no way we can do an IPO while this is going on.'

Andrei nodded. He was relieved. Now he had a reason not to do the IPO, which he hadn't really wanted to do anyway. 'I guess I'll have to talk to James.

'What will you say?'

'I don't know … I'll say I don't think the market's right.'

'He won't like it,' said Chris.

'Have you changed your mind about him? Last time, you said now's not the time for him to go.'

'He's not a start-up guy, Andrei, but he knows how to run a business.' Chris shrugged. 'It's okay to have James around as long as he doesn't get it in the way.' He looked at Andrei meaningfully for a moment. 'OK, back to the topic – there's something we need to get clear beforehand. What's the measure of success? We're going to get a lot of people – or what will seem like a lot of people – saying they don't want this. It won't really be a lot, it will be an infinitesimal fraction, but they'll make a lot of noise.

It's not the noise I'm interested in, it's what people actually *do*. Do they leave Fishbowl? Do they stop using it? Those should be our metrics.'

Andrei nodded again. Chris was right: it wasn't the noise that mattered. Andrei had seen so many storms of apparent resistance blow up, only to finally reveal nothing of lasting substance beneath the sound and the fury. And Chris was right about another thing. This was what Fishbowl was for, to ask the big questions, to put them to the world, and then to objectively and impartially view the answer.

'If I'm putting fifty per cent of my share on this, we need to be clear.' Chris grinned. 'We'd have to be clear anyway, but now we have to be really, really clear.'

'Which means what, in practice?'

'Which means, when we do it, when we announce it, we don't listen to the noise. We look at the numbers. Registrations and deregistrations, visit frequency, the usual parameters. And we look at it for a couple of months. Whatever happens, Andrei, we give time for the initial effect to wear off and see what people are really doing before we make a decision.'

'That's fine.'

'That means you're going to take the heat as the CEO. When people are crying out for someone to take action, when the 300 are going postal in the Grotto, they're going to be aiming at you. I'll be OK. No one knows who I am. You're going to be the one who needs to hold out.'

Andrei gazed at him. 'That's fine,' he said again.

'Don't kid yourself. It'll be tough. Two months. We look at the numbers. Do we have a deal?'

'Not if we have litigation. If we have litigation or a serious threat of it, then that's another story.'

'OK. A serious threat. Not verbiage. Not just vague talk about the possibility of some kind of action.'

'And if the numbers are bad,' said Andrei. 'If the numbers are bad, that's it.'

'That's fine. If the numbers are bad. Let me give some thought to what that means. I'll suggest the metrics.'

'OK.'

'But otherwise,' said Chris, 'if we don't have litigation, and the numbers don't tank below levels we agree – then you hold out for two months, no matter how much noise there is. And then we decide.'

'And you tell no lies.'

'Absolutely. That's the principle. Tell no lies. Put a search and store on everything I do so a third party can audit it.' Chris leaned closer. 'Now, deal or no deal?'

Over the next weeks, working out of LA, Chris drafted in a free-lance advertising consultant, prepared a pitch, took some flights, and did deals with a luxury yacht builder in the Netherlands, a top-brand Swiss-watch maker and a high-end safari operator in South Africa. Chris – or his palotls, to be accurate – would give people links to dedicated web addresses to claim a discount so the clients could track the sales due to his activities. Fee levels were agreed at various sales thresholds. To capture the word-of-mouth effect, mentions of the brands in an agreed range of media would also be tracked and there were structured payments if the rate of mentions rose. Chris flew to Palo Alto and met Andrei and Kevin in Andrei's apartment. He showed them the briefs from the advertisers and the profiles of the palotls he proposed to construct. Together, they agreed what he could and couldn't say to adhere to the principle of telling no lies.

Kevin flew back to LA with Chris, where they worked together on constructing the palotls. Then Kevin went back to Palo Alto and Chris set to work.

For the next four months, Chris flew to Palo Alto fortnightly and met Andrei and Kevin in Andrei's apartment to review the results.

James Langan wasn't involved. Neither was Ben.

30

FOUR MONTHS LATER, over the Easter weekend, James Langan took his family to a church retreat in Colorado that they had been attending annually for six years. He came back refreshed, re-energized, at peace with himself and determined as an evangelical to do what he could to share that inner peace with the people he knew and worked with.

The mood lasted for around half an hour, which was the point at which Langan looked up to see the head of the customer service team approaching his desk.

'James, there's something you need to see,' he said to Langan. 'Do you mind if I use your screen?'

James pushed his chair aside and let the other man get to the keyboard. A minute or so later, the head of customer services stood back. He pointed at a post on the Sunken Wall of Atlantis. 'That one there. Right at the top.'

James read.

'I'm assuming someone's made some kind of mistake or it's some kind of a sick joke, but there's a shitstorm like you wouldn't believe—'

'It's not a joke,' muttered James, staring at the words.

'Huh?'

'It's not a joke,' said James, abruptly getting to his feet and pushing past the other man.

He walked over to Andrei's desk. 'You got a minute, Andrei? Let's go in there.' He pointed to a meeting room and walked off without waiting for Andrei's response.

The walls of the meeting room were made of glass. Everyone on the floor was watching.

'Is it true?' said Langan, after he had closed the door behind Andrei.

'Is what true?' asked Andrei.

'There's a post in the Grotto saying we've had people working secretly on Fishbowl to promote products. Watches, apparently. The post says we've been doing exactly what we agreed not to do when Chris came up here that time.'

'When Chris came up here that time, we didn't agree not to do anything, James. You walked out of that meeting, as I recall.'

'And you never said anything different.'

'You never asked.'

'You mean you *did* it?' demanded James.

'I'm not saying that. I'm saying you walked out of the meeting and never even asked later what we decided.'

'That's because the idea is so repulsive that … You don't seem surprised by this.'

'The post on the Sunken Wall? I've seen it.'

'It went up, like, twenty minutes ago.'

'Twenty minutes is a long time in this business.'

'And it doesn't worry you? You didn't think you wanted to come and talk to me about it?'

'I was trying to find out what I could.'

'And what have you found out?'

Andrei shrugged.

James leaned closer. 'If someone's been doing this, Andrei, I won't stand for it. I don't care who it is. *Whoever* – they're out.' James gazed at him for a moment, then stood back. 'All right, we need a statement. I'll get Alan to draft it for you.'

'No, I'll write it.'

'I want to see it, Andrei. And I want our lawyers to see it. No more Mea Culpas – not unless we really have something to apologize for. Don't admit anything until we know for sure.'

'OK.'

'And we need to investigate this. Properly. I'll do it.' James paused. 'I've got a pretty good idea where to start.'

An hour later Andrei showed James the statement. It was five lines long, saying that he was aware of the rumour, would ensure that it was fully investigated, and would say more when there was more to say.

'Where's the rest?' said James.

'I thought we should keep it low key. I don't think we should act like it's the end of the world.'

'Do you have any idea of the shitstorm that's going on out there? Have you checked into the Grotto in the last hour?'

'I've been writing the statement, James.'

'This took an hour?' retorted James sarcastically. 'Do you have any idea of the effect this is going to have on our reputation?'

'Don't catastrophize, James.'

'Don't *what*?'

'We don't even know if it's true.'

'Something doesn't have to be true to stick. And Senator McKenrick? Remember her? Wake up and smell the coffee, Andrei! This is going to drag us into the mud.' He glanced at the statement again, shaking his head. 'You don't even condemn it.'

'I thought you said no Mea Culpas.'

'Condemn it,' said James. 'Say that Fishbowl unequivocally would condemn such activity if we find that it has taken place. Say that as part of our response to this, even if no such activity is proven, we'll do everything we can to put in place safeguards to ensure that it can't in the future. Go back and add that.'

Andrei didn't move.

'Do you want me to do it? Do you want me to type that out—?'

They were interrupted by Alan Mendes, Fishbowl's head of communications, who told them they had already had their first interview requests and wanted to know if they had a line and who was going to do the talking.

'No one's talking,' said Andrei. 'I'm about to issue a statement.'

'Is it ready?' asked Mendes.

Wordlessly, James passed it to him and watched as Mendes scanned the lines.

'Andrei's going to condemn it,' said James. 'He's going to add that we're going to take measures to minimize the risk that anyone could do it in the future.'

'Well, that would help.'

'I'm not adding anything,' said Andrei. 'That's the statement, Alan. Send it to the lawyers and tell them I'm going to post it in an hour.'

James stared at him.

'That's the statement. That's it.' Andrei left the statement with Mendes and walked out of the room.

James took his eyes off Andrei and looked at Mendes. 'Send it to the lawyers,' he muttered, through clenched teeth.

Mendes left. James stayed behind in the meeting room, fuming. He felt humiliated, excluded, isolated. Something was going on, he was sure of it. He felt radically and irreversibly undermined. He was so angry he literally didn't know what to do. He closed his eyes and tried to pray, for patience, for understanding, for anything, but his rage was so intense that he couldn't do it. That was the worst of it, he told himself, what this had done to his inner state of mind. He had arrived that morning full of the peace of Christ's grace, and now he was filled with anger, fury, hate.

On the other side of the sixth floor Andrei sat down and opened his screen to the Grotto. A monumental shitstorm was in progress. The fanatics, the cynics, the idiots and the conspiracy theorists were out in force. Many of all persuasions seemed to be saying that the rumour was no surprise because social networks had been exploiting their users for years, probably in this very way.

Andrei was struck by that. They already thought Fishbowl was doing this – and yet they used the service? What was wrong with them? People might be yelling and screaming all they liked, but if they really believed what they were saying, and they had been using Fishbowl despite that all this time, were they going to stop now just because their fears had been confirmed?

At around four in the afternoon, Chris walked into the office.

James had been calling him every quarter of an hour and had had all his calls go to voicemail, which had merely enraged him even more. He confronted Chris directly on the open floor of the office.

'I just want to know,' he said. 'Yes or no?'

'Yes,' said Chris, staring him in the eye.

James watched him for a moment. Then he turned and marched across the office to Andrei. He pointed at the meeting room again.

'I don't believe you didn't know,' he said to Andrei, when the door had closed. 'Tell me right now that you didn't know. Look me in the eye and tell me.'

'I'm not saying I didn't know,' said Andrei.

'And Kevin and Ben?'

Andrei gave a slight shrug. Kevin, of course, had been involved in the experiment from its inception. Ben hadn't taken part in the fortnightly meetings in Andrei's apartment. In fact, after he had told Andrei he was opposed to the idea, Andrei had never explicitly told him that he had agreed for Chris to go ahead. When Ben had become aware of the post in the Grotto that morning, however, he hadn't been surprised. He realized that he had guessed it was happening all along.

'What would have happened if it didn't happen to leak?' demanded James.

Andrei didn't reply.

'You can't run a business like this! You go off with Chris to Yao's and I don't know what you're plotting! It's him or me, Andrei. Chris is finished with this company. He's got his shares, he's still an investor, but we don't see him – or I'm gone. What's it going to be?'

Andrei glanced through the glass wall at Chris, who was sitting on the edge of Kevin's desk. Chris was someone who had ideas. James was just a guy who knew how to run a business. And Andrei had had his doubts about him ever since his outburst over the Mea Culpa statement.

He looked back silently at him.

James waited a moment longer for an answer. Then he nodded. 'Fine. I'm out of here. If this is the kind of business you want to build, you go ahead and do that. Count me out.'

'James, I don't want you to leave. I really hope you'll reconsider. We have to be prepared to think broadly about Deep—'

James had walked out. He marched across the floor and went to his desk, pulled out a drawer, swept his personal effects into it and headed for the exit.

'Every step into the future leaves behind those who want to live in the past,' called out Chris as James went past him.

James stopped, his back to Chris.

'You never really got it, did you, James? We made a mistake with you. You're not really a Fishbowl kind of guy.'

James put down the drawer on the nearest desk. He stepped back to Chris.

'I'm a Christian,' he said.

'What does that mean?'

'This.' James drew back his fist and socked him in the jaw.

Chris staggered back. James turned around again and picked up his drawer.

Kevin laughed. 'James! Dude! Stakhanovite!'

31

THE DEPARTURE OF James Langan as Fishbowl COO didn't pass unnoticed, partly because of James himself. The Christian inner peace of which he had been forcibly stripped that morning showed no sign of returning by the time he got home with his drawerful of personal effects, and he signed off the day by posting a spiteful, ill-tempered blog announcing his resignation. Although he stayed carefully within the bounds of his confidentiality agreement, he made it abundantly clear that he had departed because of unhappiness at certain activities that had taken place within the company. Coming on the day that the rumour of secret marketing activity within Fishbowl had surfaced, and Andrei's less than ringing rebuttal, it wasn't too hard to add two and two together and get four. Most of the analysts who tracked what Fishbowl was doing – and there were a lot of them – were pretty good at basic math.

By the next morning, the shitstorm had spread far beyond the Grotto. TV news reports carried stories of the rumour and verbatim texts of Andrei's Grotto post. Alan Mendes was almost constantly on the phone, as were the other people in his team. He wanted Andrei to make a stronger statement than the one he had issued the previous day. Ideally, a denial. If that wasn't possible because Andrei's investigation was still under way, then at least a strong condemnation and a promise to get rid of whoever had been responsible

Andrei called him into a meeting with Chris, Kevin and Ben. Andrei also called in Louise Steinberg, James's number two, who had become de facto COO when James had walked out. There were certain truths they needed to know.

Andrei told them that he couldn't issue a denial or a pledge to act because there was some truth in the rumour. He said that an experiment had been in progress over the past few months, with watches, as the rumour suggested. He didn't tell them about anything else that Chris had been doing.

'So what happens now?' said Louise.

'We wait to see what happens – if the furore dies down.'

'And if it doesn't?' asked Louise.

'Then we admit that it happened, issue a condemnation, like Alan has been asking for, and stop.'

'And one of us loses a hell of a lot of money,' added Kevin with a grin.

'Look, James left over this,' said Andrei to Louise and Alan. 'You have the right to do that as well. I don't want to lose you, but if this isn't OK with you guys, you can go. I don't know what the situation is with your stock options, whether you've been here long enough to retain them, but actually, I don't care. You can keep them. I don't want you to stay for the wrong reasons. To me this isn't about money. It's about Deep Connectedness and about being brave enough to explore it in all its forms. I need people here who are excited by that and are honest enough, brave enough, to want to stay on that journey wherever it leads. That's what we're doing here. If you stay, I want you to stay because you want to be part of that, not for a bunch of stock options.'

Alan and Louise glanced at each other.

'Anyway, what do you think?' asked Andrei. 'Are we going to see mass defections?'

'To where?' asked Alan rhetorically. 'Worldspace?'

'We've already got a dozen School pages that have been set up against this thing,' said Louise.

'That's not defection,' said Chris. 'That's loyalty.'

'I think we're taking a huge risk. Can we do this kind of thing? Is it legit?'

'We're a private company,' said Chris. 'Everyone who holds a voting share is sitting in this room. We can do anything that's within the law.'

'And this is?' said Louise. 'Do we know that?'

'We've had advice.'

'Like I said, if you're not comfortable, Louise, you can leave,' said Andrei. 'You too, Alan. This is a challenge to my thinking, but that's what I want Fishbowl to be. A place where our thinking is challenged. Every single person in this company needs to be totally cool with that. If it's too uncomfortable for you, I understand. No hard feelings. You'll keep your stock options. You'll have to abide by your non-disclosure clause, that's all.'

There was silence for a moment, then Alan shrugged. 'I don't know, this is kind of interesting. What do we do next?'

'You can see why I can't issue the kind of statement you want,' said Andrei.

'Then I guess you'll have to admit it. You can't keep evading it.'

'Everyone in the company is confused,' said Louise. 'They're talking. Fifty people must have seen the way James left yesterday and ...' She nodded towards Chris and his bruised face. 'They need to know what's going on.'

Andrei looked out of the glass walls of the meeting room and saw dozens of pairs of eyes quickly averted.

'We've got to get a meeting room where not everyone can fucking see everything we say,' muttered Chris. 'Any of those guys lip read out there?'

'Probably,' said Kevin.

'I'm serious, Andrei,' said Louise. 'You've got to talk to them.'

That afternoon, Andrei gave an all-hands talk in the office, standing next to the aquarium in front of the 400 and some Fishbowl employees who now inhabited the office on Embarcadero, with a videolink to the Fishbowl offices that had recently been set up in New York and London.

It wasn't a situation in which Andrei instinctively felt comfortable. His natural connection was with the tech guys but he knew that in front of him more than two-thirds of the people were commercial. His anxiety level was also raised by the fact that he was not going to be telling the truth – or at least not the whole truth. Six or seven people might just about be able to keep things confidential, but hundreds wouldn't. Someone would talk, whether inadvertently or otherwise. And the stakes were even higher because the response of Fishbowl's people was just as much a part of the experiment as the response of Fishbowl's users. For the moment it looked as if Alan and Louise were staying, but they only knew about one of Chris's experiments. There were still two more to be announced. If highly talented, creative people – the kind of people Fishbowl had increasingly been able to attract – didn't want to work for a company that provided that form of Deep Connectedness, then it wasn't viable, whether users wanted it or not. Fishbowl's employees had just as much opportunity to put an end to this as did its users.

First, Andrei addressed the topic of James Langan's departure. He attributed it to differences that had been developing between them for some time, particularly over the speed of Fishbowl's possible IPO. He admitted that James was also concerned by the rumour of a new kind of marketing but had chosen not to stick around to investigate it. Technically, that was true. Second, Andrei addressed the rumour itself. He said that, as he had said in his Grotto posting, it needed to be fully investigated, but that whatever came out of the investigation, every necessary action would be taken to protect Fishbowl's reputation and position it even more strongly for success, and if anyone had any thoughts on that, he wanted to hear from them personally, either then or any time in the future. Then he took questions.

The first one, naturally, was what he would do if the rumour about the selling of watches proved to be true.

Andrei had rehearsed his answer to this question with Alan, but still he hesitated. Anything he said now would be remembered by the entire company. He had to lay the groundwork for events that were going to follow, not put himself in a position of having to change direction later, and certainly not say anything that could eventually be interpreted as a lie.

'That would depend,' he said. 'It would depend on how our users respond.'

'I don't understand what that means, Andrei,' said the questioner.

'I think everyone's assuming that if this has really happened, then our users are going to be unhappy about it,' said Andrei carefully. 'I'm not sure if that's true. All I'm saying is, if it has happened, then rather than guessing what they want, let's see how they respond. I'm not going to lay down any kind of law about what they do or don't want, what they can or can't have. Fishbowl has succeeded because we've never done that. We've always been willing to listen, to adapt, and not tell people what they can and can't do. I think that's one of our great strengths. So let's do the investigation, and if we see that it's happened, let's see what our users say.'

'Our users are already saying a hell of a lot.'

'Let's see what they say when the facts are known.' Andrei caught Louise's eye and saw her watching him solemnly. 'And let's remember, the most vocal users are not necessarily the most representative. Let's be careful to understand what all our users are saying.'

There was silence as people took this in.

'So are you saying, Andrei,' asked someone on the videolink from the New York office, 'that if the users said, "Actually, we like this," then we'd let this keep happening?'

'Who are we to say we shouldn't?'

'So if they say, "We love being duped by people we think are our friends but are actually just cold-hearted salesmen," that's OK?'

There was a smattering of laughter in the crowd.

Andrei caught Louise's eye once more. 'First of all, I don't think anyone's been duping anyone. Let's investigate and see what's been said about these watches, but if it's all been factual, then the question of duping doesn't come up.'

'It's still duping someone to make you think they're a friend.'

'OK, let's not argue about the words. Friend, acquaintance, online contact, whatever. I think you have a serious point. Let's say people say, "You know what, we like this. This is a form of Deep Connectedness that we like, between us and various companies, and we like the fact that it happens in a way that is kind of natural, like you're talking to your friend." And, by the way, it's not only companies who could use this, it's NGOs, it's civic organizations ...'

'But it's companies as well.'

'Hear me out. I'm not saying people *will* say they want this, but I'm saying *if* they do, are we saying we shouldn't give it to them? Are you saying we should exercise some kind of censorship over what they can and can't have? That Andrei Koss should stand here and say, "No, you can't have that, because I don't think you should"?'

'What if they say, give us child pornography?'

'Now I think you're going a little far. Would that make the world worse? Definitely. And I don't think the majority of our users, or any kind of significant group at all, are going to be asking for that. Not to mention the fact that it's illegal. Let's keep this in perspective. All I'm saying is we need to find out what our users want. But let me ask you this. We have Sponsored Baits, right? Some people don't click on them just because they're sponsored. So they're excluding themselves from information that they may very well want to have.'

'Don't they have a right to choose?'

'Absolutely. Yes. But Sponsored Baits are the only time we ask anyone to state a motive. Why do we do that? Lot's of other stuff is going on out there with all kinds of motives that aren't declared, including commercial activities. So if we're going to be consistent, I'm not sure that companies paying to use our service should be the only ones who have to declare their motive. And you know what? Like I said, companies who *aren't* paying us are doing stuff all the time themselves – viral marketing, using our network. We all know that.' He paused. 'Look, the point is, I'm not the final authority on Deep Connectedness. Neither are you, and neither is anybody in this room. I don't know all the forms it can take. I try to have a broad conceptualization. That's my principle. I'm prepared to be challenged and think fresh. It's a constant journey of discovery and if we think there's a new form of Deep Connectedness that we can support, then it's our obligation to find out if our users want it, and not just assume that we know. And anyway, before we jump to any conclusions, let's see what the investigation shows.'

A week later, in a post to the Grotto, Andrei announced that there had indeed been some activity of the type alleged, apparently involving high-value timepieces. He said that a review of the data showed that statements made in the course of this activity regarding the products had been purely factual in nature and didn't involve any misrepresentation that he was aware of. He added that a number of people who had bought the watches in question had been contacted and were perfectly satisfied with their purchases. Now this had been discovered, he wrote, he would wait to see whether the user community wanted this kind of activity to continue before taking any further steps.

The user community reacted with uproar. Hundreds of thousands of e-signatures appeared on petitions set up by outraged Fishbowl users. The announcement made prime time news. Mike Sweetman, locked in battle with Fishbowl over his users and beset by allegations of monopoly behaviour, demanded a probe into Fishbowl's marketing practices. The Santa Clara district attorney announced that she was opening an investigation into potential charges of fraud and mis-selling against the company. In Washington, unknown to Andrei, the cyber crime division of the FBI opened a file on Fishbowl.

The number of names on petitions rose. After three days, Alan Mendes told Andrei he thought the verdict was clear. 'You said you wanted to hear what the users thought. I think they've spoken.'

'I'll issue a statement.'

'Good,' said Mendes.

Steeling himself to push the experiment to its limit, Andrei issued a statement reiterating that the activity had taken place amongst buyers of extremely high-value watches who could be expected to have the ability to exercise independent judgement and that no misrepresentation had been involved.

'Andrei, that's just going to make things worse,' said Mendes.

It did. The levels of abuse aimed at Andrei from the Grotto reached new highs – or lows. Jerry Glick called and told Andrei that if everything he had heard was true, he couldn't approve of what Andrei was doing. Mike Sweetman again publicly condemned Andrei for the approach he had taken, stating that it gave succour to the enemies of internet freedom, who would now have another stick with which to beat the internet community. The DA announced ominously that she would pursue her investigation with all vigour. In the office, Alan Mendes and Louise Steinberg were at him every day, saying he had to issue a condemnation. Ben, of course, thought they should stop.

By now, Andrei himself wanted to declare the experiment over. But Chris was in the office every day as well, reminding him of the deal they had struck, reminding him that this was exactly the pressure he had told Andrei that he would experience.

The argument came to a head late one night towards the end of the second week of the crisis when Chris, Andrei, Kevin and Ben met to discuss the situation.

Ben had said little since learning of Chris's activities. Sometimes he wished he would just blow up over his exclusion from knowing about the palotl experiment, as Kevin would have done, but that wasn't the way he was. By nature, he couldn't help searching for reasons for the things people did. One part of him was angry and alienated over that exclusion, but another part of him saw that it could be interpreted almost as an act of kindness on Andrei's part, a decision to spare him involvement in something he didn't support – provided you believed that Andrei was capable of that kind of sensitivity. Right now, given how Andrei had ignored his frustrations over having too little to do over the past several months, he wasn't sure that Andrei was.

The sense of alienation lingered in Ben, even though he had been finally brought into the loop. He couldn't help feeling that since Andrei had cut him out earlier, he would just have to solve the problem for himself. It was a childish attitude, Ben knew, but it wasn't easy to overcome. Anyway, his opposition to Chris's experiment had been clear from the start, and Andrei probably knew that that hadn't changed.

But tonight Andrei asked him directly what he thought. Ben said that, in his opinion, it was obvious that the users didn't want what Chris was offering and they should stop it.

'It's not obvious,' retorted Chris, who didn't dislike Ben, but thought he had long outlived his usefulness to the company, if he had ever actually had any.

'Even the Dillerman's saying he's not sure this is right,' said Ben.

'I don't give a fuck about the Dillerman!' snapped Chris. 'Andrei, listen to me. We always expected an uproar. We always expected the point one per cent of vocals to drown out the ninety-nine point nine per cent of couldn't-care-lesses. I know you've got people shouting at you, not only from outside but from within the company. Forget about them. It's just noise.'

'What about the DA?' said Ben.

'What about her? More noise. She's up for re-election. What has she said that's solid? Nothing. Legally, we're strong and she knows it. Let's wait until she comes up with something real. That's what we agreed. In the meantime, let's look at the numbers.'

Andrei glanced at Kevin.

Kevin nodded. 'Dude, the numbers are awesome.'

*

Chris's three experiments had already yielded $200,000 in revenue for Fishbowl over the past four months, and, even if he did nothing more, the revenues could be expected to rise from the seeds he had sown. But those weren't the numbers he was talking about. What he meant were the user metrics he had discussed with Andrei at the start of the operation. What they showed was that the people protesting most on the School pages that had been set up in response to Chris's experiment were heavy users of Fishbowl. But they weren't using Fishbowl less heavily – they were using it *more*. The place where they were protesting was Fishbowl itself. It wasn't the behaviour of a group of people who were going to defect – even if there had been an equally extensive, independent meta-network that they could have defected to.

Light to medium users of Fishbowl showed no discernible change. Chris commissioned a survey and found that most of them weren't even aware of the controversy. Those who were aware fell mostly into the 'Don't care' or 'Oppose somewhat' categories of the questionnaire. Unlike the heavy users, for whom Fishbowl was so important that they couldn't leave, for light users, Fishbowl just wasn't important enough for leaving even to be on their minds.

But the awesome part of the numbers, as Kevin described it, came out of the registration figures for the website. New registrations were actually rising. People apparently were looking at Fishbowl out of curiosity – and staying.

The next day, Andrei showed Alan and Louise the numbers.

'So what do we do now?' asked Louise.

'Well, Chris has actually told us he's been doing the same thing in another product category,' said Andrei.

Louise stared at him. 'This is going to get everything started again.'

'Probably.'

'Which product category?' said Alan.

'Yachts.'

The third and final revelation came a fortnight later, a month after the initial rumour, when Andrei announced that they had discovered that they had been promoting luxury South African safaris. By now the response was cynical. What a surprise! But it was growing weary as well. There were only so many times someone would sign an e-petition without seeing it have any effect.

For the first time, Fishbowl went public with its line that it would follow its users' preferences but would be sure to listen not only to the vocal minority but to the silent majority as well. Fishbowl, Andrei added, would always err on the side of the broader, more generous interpretation of Deep Connectedness and user preference. This was widely interpreted as meaning that Fishbowl would persist with the practice.

An 'Andrei Koss is a Traitor' School page was started on Fishbowl. Overnight, membership exceeded half a million. Funnily enough, that didn't shake Andrei in his conclusions but strengthened them. Half a million sounded like a lot, but it was less than one in 700 of Fishbowl's users. They were getting more new users than that every day. The lesson Andrei had learned previously when he had introduced advertising, when he had issued the Mea Culpa statement – that you could seemingly do just about anything you wanted and it would provoke nothing from the users but a roar of protest that would soon blow itself out – etched itself more firmly than ever in his mind.

A couple of days later, Fishbowl was subjected to a denial-of-service attack from a previously unheard of group called Spring Uncoiled. For the first time in its history Fishbowl went offline. It was seven hours before it was up again. The infrastructure guys went into crisis mode and when the next attack came, twenty-four hours later, they were ready for it. Over the next week they were subjected to numerous attacks of various sorts, but the site didn't go down again.

Jerry Glick went public with his previously private repudiation of Fishbowl's new line of activity. A number of tech heavyweights echoed his line. Chris said they were probably already trying to work out how to replicate the idea themselves. In Washington, Diane McKenrick followed events closely, toying with the idea of going after the industry again. But it was deep into primary season for the presidential nomination – a nomination she had once dreamed might be hers – and there was no support from anywhere in the Party to reopen that can of worms with the unpredictable effects it might have on voter patterns.

Andrei met the DA at her office in San Jose with his lawyers and explained exactly what Fishbowl was doing. He was confident from the advice the company had taken that there was no ground for a prosecution. The DA knew it, too. Even if she could have conjured up something that might have prolonged the saga, she was a smart political animal with ambitions for higher office. In public, tech companies were condemning Fishbowl, but she knew that wouldn't necessarily translate into support for her if she tried to force the issue. Curbing the money-making potential of an up-and-coming internet business wasn't going to prove strong grounds for re-election in a district dominated by tech companies and their employees.

The mainstream media lost interest. The protests died down. Barry Diller posted a message in which he had managed to persuade himself that this was part of the broader, more generous interpretation of Deep Connectedness to which Fishbowl was committed. The 'Andrei Koss is a Traitor' School dwindled to a few tens of active users, the last resort for the irreconcilables. Privately, Chris thought it was hysterical. Not even they could tear themselves away from Fishbowl, preferring to bitch and moan on a page provided by the very website they professed to hate so much.

Fishbowl did lose a couple of employees at the height of the controversy, while the recruitment people reported that some candidates had turned down offers from Fishbowl, or at least had delayed giving an answer. But that effect quickly dissipated. The candidates who had delayed their answers scrambled aboard when told they had a week to decide or the company would withdraw its offer. Fishbowl was an employer of choice for the cream of the Valley's programmers – it would obviously take more than this to change that.

Two months to the day after the rumour was first leaked, Chris turned up in Palo Alto and took Andrei, Kevin and Ben to Yao's, where he asked Andrei to state explicitly that he had been right.

Andrei didn't feel totally at ease about the outcome. He had been prepared to have his conceptualization of Deep Connectedness challenged and let the chips fall where they would – but there was still a part of him that would have preferred it if the users had risen up in revolt. But they hadn't. A tiny percentage of them had blustered, but even that had petered out. And in the meantime, the publicity had brought in new people in their hordes. Fishbowl's users had accepted the innovation. If this was a new form of Deep Connectedness, then he had a responsibility to provide it, so long as it didn't make the world worse and so long as a large group of the users accepted it. These were propositions that someone like James Langan, and even Ben, would have rejected, but which Andrei, under his principles of broad conceptualization and inclusiveness, felt obliged to accept.

The next morning, Chris arrived in the office with a couple of guys carrying crates of champagne and glasses. He had the crates put down in front of the aquarium. He climbed on one and called everyone over, then proceeded personally to uncork the bottles and pour the glasses. People wanted to know what they were celebrating. Chris told them to ask Andrei. Andrei wandered across reluctantly. Word had spread in the office and people were arriving from the other floors. Someone had set up links to the other Fishbowl offices. Chris put a glass of champagne in Andrei's hand. Before he knew it, Andrei was standing on a crate in front of the company.

'Ummm ... what I want to say is, this has been a tough couple of months. I want to thank you all for sticking through it.' Andrei paused, trying to get his thoughts together. 'Looks like we've discovered a new form of Deep Connectedness, one between individuals and corporations. Some people didn't like it and they made a lot of noise. But the vast majority of our users have accepted it and, more importantly, some forty million people joined after it was made public. Now, it feels as if a lot of people protested, but we've looked at the numbers and it was a lot less than forty million. So we got a lot more people saying "I like Fishbowl with this" than saying "I don't". So, guys, this is here to stay.' Andrei raised his glass. 'To Deep Connectedness, in all its many colours.'

There were murmurs from around the floor. Some people put their glasses to their lips, others stood watching, still not sure what they were celebrating.

Andrei was conscious that he probably hadn't sounded very excited. Part of his job, he knew, was to inspire people. 'Guys, this is cool! And I just want to say, if you're wondering … no, I don't see a conflict between this and what Fishbowl is here to do. I see it as part of our mission. I was doubtful at the start, but I was prepared to be challenged. If we're going to keep evolving, if we're going to stay the meta-network of choice, we have to always be prepared to be challenged. Like I said, I was doubtful, but I kind of like what we've done now. Is this advertising? Or is it a service, a way of bringing people's attention to stuff they might need at exactly the right moment – giving them factual informa-tion, not randomly but when they actually need it? To me, that's kind of cool. And it's totally new, and that's what Fishbowl should be doing. Things that are totally new. And although it's a form of Deep Connectedness that's between people and corporations, it's a form that's natural, human and user-friendly. In other words, it's Fishbowl. And who knows where it will lead? There are other organizations than businesses. There are other things people need to know about than products, and other things you can do than sell them. You all know we have the principle of don't make the world worse. Well, let's add a second to that – don't tell lies.

If we stick to that, then I think what we have here is a new and exciting form of Deep Connectedness, which is what Fishbowl is all about – Deep Connectedness in all its forms.' He raised his glass and drank. 'OK! Thank you.'

Andrei walked away. People came forward to get more of the champagne. Chris followed Andrei back to his desk.

'Well said.'

Andrei shrugged. 'Thanks.'

Chris rubbed his hands. 'Let's get to work.'

32

A SECOND OFFICE was rented four blocks from Fishbowl's existing office on Embarcadero. It was soon staffed with a team of advertising executives to sell the new service, a tech group to develop palotls, and an ever-expanding team of sales representatives learning how to use them. Chris, with the help of the human resources head, took ownership of recruitment. He sold the job to likely sales people as being like piloting a drone compared with being in the cockpit of a plane – a lot quieter, a lot more of a desk job, a lot more effective. And with a hell of a lot less travel.

It was probably only one in ten people he saw who had anywhere near the capabilities for the job. Chris looked for mature, experienced people who had worked with high-end goods and knew the kind of clients who purchased them. As he had learned through his experience over the previous months, it was the ability to appear to be just another guy with a couple of good stories to relate – the exact antithesis of a high-pressure sales person – that succeeded in these circumstances. They also had to be prepared to stick to a set of strictly factual remarks, knowing that all their conversations and postings might be monitored. Nothing Fishbowl's palotls said could be construed as misrepresentation.

As for the businesses the advertising executives approached to use this new form of promotion, many were initially sceptical. But their scepticism was tested when they were shown the results of the initial palotl experiments, and since the use of a link restricted to Fishbowl-generated customers would enable them to define precisely the results of the campaign, Fishbowl could offer entirely results-based deals which represented no risk to the advertiser. The numbers of companies using the service soon grew exponentially.

Fishbowl's employees knew what was happening. There was no reason to hide it. Someone coined the term 'Fish Farming' for it, and the second office soon became known as the Fish Farm.

Andrei spent very little time there. It was an entirely commercial place without a software engineer in sight. He was far more at home in the office at Embarcadero, which had expanded to occupy all five floors of the building. A new COO, Jennifer McGrealy, had been brought on board to replace James Langan, retaining Louise Sternberg as one of her executives. She had a strong commercial background in a number of tech firms and was fully aware of operations at the Fish Farm when she came on board. Jennifer saw it as a fascinating new revenue stream and, as part of her remuneration package, negotiated a deal that gave her a percentage of its growth.

Chris had been right – Fishbowl users seemed to have accepted that this was the shape of the world now. And he was right about the more efficient model crowding out the less efficient, just as the more efficient species in evolution crowd out the others. Rumours were circulating of other social media companies experimenting in Farming. Once someone started doing it, it seemed, everyone would. In addition to selling products, information gleaned from conversations on Fishbowl was fed back to the advertising companies, allowing them to tailor and improve their offerings. Naturally, companies were willing to pay for feedback of this quality. Jenn McGrealy soon saw the opportunity and built a lucrative business in customer intelligence.

Andrei didn't keep track of the mounting revenues that Farming was bringing in. For him, all of this was merely a facet of Deep Connectedness, with information flowing in both directions, and the additional revenues it generated merely provided even more funds for Fishbowl to continue refining and improving the service. When interviewed, he spoke as if the massive valuations that were regularly put on the company were a side issue in comparison with the mission of delivering Deep Connectedness. To listen to him when he spoke at tech gatherings, it would have been easy to imagine he was still a dewy-eyed novice running a start-up in a dorm room without a cent of revenue to its name.

Sandy Gross, who was now in graduate school at Stanford and living with Andrei in the condo, supported what he was doing. If what wasn't illegal was legitimate, and if this was the most efficient model – as the rumoured efforts to copy Fishbowl suggested – there was no reason to hold back.

In other respects, however, Andrei did pay something of a price. Farming had made him a controversial figure, and many of the internet moguls who had befriended him were now wary of being seen with him. His weekend visits to Jerry Glick's barbecues came to an end. But Jerry, he thought, had always had something of the holier than thou about him, and Andrei had already been getting a little tired of him. Andrei was starting to build a small but vocal following in the tech press and amongst other young internet executives who saw him as a brave, radical visionary of the new world that the net was inevitably ushering in. It was hard not to begin to think of himself somewhat in this way.

Only one thing happened in the months after the Farm was set up to disturb his equanimity. And that came not from outside the company but from within.

By the time the Fish Farm had been set up and was functioning fully, it was over a year since Ben had finished his degree and been back full time at the company. One night he called to see if he could come around to Andrei's apartment. He arrived at about ten o'clock. Sandy had gone to a club with some friends. Andrei opened the door for him in shorts and a T-shirt and found Ben holding a large, flat package wrapped in brown paper.

'What's that?' asked Andrei.

'It's for you.' Ben walked past him into the apartment, still holding the package. 'Want a beer?' he said, opening the fridge and helping himself.

They sat together with a beer each on the only sofa in the huge living room of Andrei's condo. By now the paucity of furniture had become a source of pride for him.

Ben handed him the package.

Andrei looked at it warily. 'What is it?'

'The convention when someone gives you a gift is that you open it to find out.'

Andrei put down his beer and unwrapped the package. It was the napkin from Yao's on which he had written his growth projections back in the January after Fishbowl was founded, the day he had asked Kevin and Ben to buy into the company. Ben had had it framed, with a brief description of the event and the date inscribed underneath.

'I'm going to leave the company, Andrei.'

Andrei continued to gaze at the napkin, then put it down on the floor.

'Andrei?'

'I heard you.' He looked at Ben. 'Why?'

'I'm done. I don't really feel I offer anything. I don't even know what I'm supposed to be doing.'

'You offer a huge amount. Ben, we wouldn't have got anywhere if you hadn't been there. Right at the start—'

'That's a long time ago now, Andrei.'

'I still need you.'

Ben gave a short laugh. 'You've got Chris.'

'Chris isn't the same.'

Ben shrugged. 'Could have fooled me.'

Andrei felt a slight sense of panic. There had never been a time when Ben hadn't been a part of Fishbowl. Even during his senior year at Stanford he had been involved. Andrei knew that Ben's earlier functions at the company had dissolved and that he should have found a more concrete role for him. Ben had told him that he wanted more to do, and James Langan had talked to Andrei about the need for Ben to have defined responsibilities. Ben had no team, unlike Kevin, President for Getting Things Done, who was responsible for the hardest of the hard core of programmers, coding the most challenging innovations that went on the site. James had had Ben sit in on meetings of the customer intelligence team, and he had come up with ideas from time to time and overseen the research that followed. Some of the ideas eventually made it into practice, but that wouldn't have justified the position he held or the salary he earned. But none of that, or that fact that Ben and he no longer spoke as they used to in the old days, meant that Andrei was ready to lose him. He had never even contemplated a time when Ben wouldn't be around. He was one of the original three, the founding Stakhanovites. That was a bond that could never be broken.

'We can be more specific about your role,' said Andrei. 'I know I should have done that.'

Ben shook his head.

'We'll give you some people. You can have a team.'

'To do what?'

'To do ... I don't know ... stuff ...'

'Andrei, there are other things I want to do. I want to be a therapist.'

'You want to listen to people whine about what their parents did to them when they were in diapers?'

Ben smiled. 'You want to tell me?'

'You really want to do that?'

'Yeah, I really do. That's why I finished my degree. I've got postgraduate training to do. It's, like, it's time for me to do it, Andrei. I've organized a place in New York on a doctoral program. And, to be honest ... I'm just not that interested in Fishbowl any more. It's not my thing like it's your thing. It never was. I mean, it's been a hell of a ride. I wouldn't have missed it and I'm grateful you gave me the chance. Really. The day you wrote that thing ...' he gestured to the framed napkin on the floor '... the day you asked me to be a part of this ... you only get one chance at something like that in life. In many lifetimes, and that's if you're lucky. You gave it to me. Not to mention nine per cent of … what was the latest valuation I heard? Fifteen billion?'

'Something like that.'

'How much is nine per cent of that, anyway?'

'Around one and a third billion.'

'I think I'll be comfortable.'

'You could have had fifteen per cent if your folks could have raised another twenty thousand.'

'You know what? I'm not going to lose any sleep.' Ben looked around. 'And buy yourself some furniture.'

'I'm OK.' Andrei sighed. 'You really want to leave?'

Ben nodded.

'Let me ask you the Chris question. Is being a therapist the ultimate, absolutely most important thing you can do?'

'I never liked that question. I don't think anyone can really answer a question like that. There's no one answer. There's multiple answers.'

Andrei looked at him blankly. He didn't see why there couldn't be one answer.

'Look, Fishbowl has been a hell of a ride. Really. It's been awesome.'

'OK, so if there are multiple answers, is Fishbowl one of the most important things?'

Ben sighed again. Andrei was looking at him as if it was desperately important that he said yes.

'Is it?'

'Maybe. Yes, OK, it is, one of them. But right now there are other things that have risen up the scale.'

'So maybe Fishbowl will rise up again.'

Ben shrugged.

'So maybe you'll want to come back.'

'Nothing's impossible.'

'So you should stay involved. That way, when you're ready to come back, you can just step back in.'

'Andrei, I can't stay involved. I mean, we can always talk, I'll always be there. But I have to be able to concentrate on other things. I have to be able to put my whole mind to it.'

'You did that in your senior year and you stayed involved.'

'No, I didn't. It was hell. I was constantly torn. I couldn't do anything properly. I hated it. I don't know how I got through. I shouldn't have come back. I should have left then. I knew it, actually. It's my fault.'

Andrei was silent. He gazed down at the framed napkin. For some reason he thought of the notebooks in which he had written his thoughts about Fishbowl. He hadn't looked at them since putting them away after the move from La Calle Court.

'Hard to believe it was only three years ago,' said Ben, glancing at the napkin as well. 'It feels like longer. It's like we've lived a lifetime.'

Andrei frowned. It felt like yesterday to him.

'I just thought it wouldn't hurt for you to have the evidence of how wrong Andrei Koss can be. A memento mori, if you will.'

Andrei didn't smile.

'That came out wrong. Look, I just thought you might like to have it. We don't have much from those days. We should have kept the aquariums. Where did they get to, anyway?'

Andrei shrugged. Robinson House, La Calle Court, Ramona Street, they had each had an aquarium.

'Is this because of Farming? said Andrei suddenly. 'Is that why you want to leave?'

Ben shook his head.

'I'm sorry I didn't involve you. You just didn't … you didn't want to know about it.'

'It's fine. I'm over it. I didn't want to be involved. You did the right thing.'

'But you don't like it.'

Ben shrugged. 'Andrei, it's your company. It's always been your vision—'

'It *is* because of Farming! Ben, we always said we'd debate freely and move on. That's what always made it work.'

'I have moved on.'

'I don't mean like that.'

Ben sighed. 'It's not Farming. OK. I mean, it's not only Farming.'

'People had the chance to say no and they didn't.'

'A lot of them did.'

'No, not a lot. A tiny fraction. And they *said* it, but they didn't mean it. They weren't prepared to do anything about it. It's a form of Deep Connectedness. We gave them a chance to say no and they didn't.'

Ben watched him. 'Andrei, do you really believe it's about Deep Connectedness?'

'Yeah. I do. Your conceptualization of Deep Connectedness was always a little too narrow.'

'Don't you think there's a deceit involved?'

'What deceit?'

Ben almost smiled. Yes, which deceit? The deceit involved in Farming, or the one going on inside Andrei's own head? Could he really believe that this was about nothing but Deep Connectedness?

'Ben, people know they might encounter palotls. What difference does it make if it's a person or a company? If people don't like it, they'll leave.'

'It's not that easy.'

'Sure it is. It takes about a minute to deregister.'

Ben took a deep breath. That was Andrei, he thought, no emotional intelligence. When you talked to him about deregistering, he thought of the series of mouse clicks involved, not the barriers inside someone's head. But, still, Ben didn't dislike him. They went back too far, and he genuinely admired Andrei for all that he had achieved. Ben didn't want to dislike him, even if there had been moments in the past year, as Farming had been unveiled and it had become clear that Chris had finally supplanted him as Andrei's confidant, when he had felt that he might start to.

'Look, even if it is about Deep Connectedness,' said Ben eventually, 'you didn't have to implement it.'

'That would be hypocritical,' replied Andrei, with no apparent irony. 'It's not my role to tell people what they can and can't do. It's my role to give people what they want as efficiently as I can.'

'Andrei, you've got to have more of a moral yardstick than efficiency. You did after Denver.'

'I was the same after Denver as I always am.'

'You insisted on giving the content to the FBI when everyone was telling you not to. That had nothing to do with efficiency.'

'Yes, it did. It was most efficient for the business.'

'You said it was about responsibility.'

'Exactly, and taking that responsibility was most efficient for the business.'

'You said you'd only give it about something like that, not about a lesser crime. Isn't it hypocritical to do it in one case and not the other?'

'It was a business decision, Ben.'

'James argued the opposite.'

'Well, James was wrong. The best thing for the business was to hand over that data. That was the most efficient way of exonerating ourselves. And it worked.'

'So, that was the only reason, was it? Because it was best for the business? Because it was efficient?'

'Yes,' said Andrei.

Ben gazed at him, remembering the phone call the night Andrei had written the Mea Culpa statement, the way Andrei had been agonizing. No matter what Andrei said now, it was the one time, Ben thought, that he had seen him driven by something other than efficiency, consistency, logic. Something deeper, he was sure, had been at play.

'You're better than that, Andrei,' he said quietly.

Andrei looked at him blankly.

'Andrei, you've got to have a measure that's better than saying that what people want, they get. Sometimes people want the wrong thing.'

'How can that be?'

'Look at the country you were born in!'

'The people didn't want the wrong thing – the Communists didn't let them say what they wanted. I've always said Fishbowl isn't something three guys at Yao's impose on the world. The Communists were the epitome of three guys at Yao's, Ben. They were the exact opposite of us.'

Ben sighed. 'Fishbowl's just a business now, Andrei.'

'No! Don't say that! Money? How much do I need? How much can one person use? It's about Deep Connectedness, Ben! Fishbowl will always be about Deep Connectedness! Farming is part of that. That's the thing you can't see. You know what the proof is? If it was about money, I wouldn't have bothered with Farming. It's high-end goods. It's niche. For the trouble it's worth, it doesn't make enough. I'm bothering because it's about Deep Connectedness. My responsibility isn't to protect people from themselves. It's to offer them Deep Connectedness in its truest and most varied forms. It's exactly the same responsibility I had after Denver, which was to do what I had to do to keep the Deep Connectedness of Fishbowl alive. They're two aspects of the same thing. It's not only to keep Deep Connectedness alive, but to make it as big and multifaceted as I can. And I don't know how you can say we haven't succeeded.'

'I'm not saying that.'

'Look at the people who talk to each other! Look at what happens when they get together! We're changing the world, Ben.'

'I told you, I'm not saying I disagree with that.'

'So how can there be anything more important? How can you say there's anything else you would rather be doing?'

'Maybe I don't want to change the world. Maybe I just want to help people change their lives a little bit at a time.'

Andrei was silent for a moment. 'Why did you say it's just a business? Take that back.'

Ben shrugged. 'There's a lot of business about it.'

'Take it back, Ben!'

'All right. Whatever. I take it back.'

'It can't be avoided. Deep Connectedness comes at a cost.'

'I know it does.'

'So I don't understand your issue.'

'Andrei, I don't have an issue.' Ben sighed again. 'Look, it's just time for me to move on.'

Andrei opened his mouth to say something, but didn't. He glanced at his watch.

Ben didn't want to depart in bitterness. When he said he was grateful for the chance to be part of Fishbowl, he meant it, no matter how unsatisfying the last year had been. He had much more to thank Andrei for than to complain about.

'We've had some good times, Andrei. La Calle Court ... that was crazy, That was a once-in-a-lifetime experience ... You remember when Mike Sweetman offered you a hundred million dollars?'

Andrei didn't reply.

'Come on, Andrei. That was a hell of a day.'

'That wasn't when were at La Calle Court,' muttered Andrei. 'We were still in the dorm.'

Really?' Ben laughed. 'Was it that early? Amazing. I'll never forget it. We're at Yao's and you're sitting there telling us Sweetman's offered you a hundred million – just like that – and you said no, and Kevin and me are sitting there thinking, *What the fuck?*'

'You think I should have sold?' asked Andrei.

'No.'

'But back then? Did you think so?'

'I don't know what I thought. A hundred million dollars. That was like ... Is this serious? Is this for us? Tell me the truth. Were you tempted? You must have been tempted.'

Andrei shrugged.

'I bet you were!'

'A little.'

Ben laughed. He sucked on his beer, then he put it down. 'That was before Chris came along.'

'Yeah,' said Andrei. 'That was before him.'

'You know, about Chris – you should watch out.'

Andrei looked at Ben. 'What does that mean?'

'I just want to be honest with you. As a friend, someone has to tell you. I don't know if he has the same vision you have, Andrei. Fishbowl's yours, not his. You built it to what it is. Just remember that.'

'Is this about Farming again?'

'It's about lots of things. He's not … he's not serious.'

'Chris? What are you talking about? Do you know how much time he's put into this?'

'That's not what I mean. It's a game. Everything's a game to him.'

'Look, Chris has his faults. OK? I know that. I don't think of him like I used to. I used to be a little in awe of him. Not any more.'

'You should think about whether he's the right kind of person to be involved.'

'He has a lot to offer, Ben. He shares more of my vision than you think. And he isn't *leaving*.'

There was silence.

'I'm just saying—'

'Don't go! Look, Ben, don't leave now. Please. Something's about to start. Something totally awesome. I want you to stay and be part of it.'

Ben waited for Andrei to tell him more, but he didn't.

'What is it?' asked Ben eventually. 'What would I do?'

'You can't leave now. I'll give you a team. I'll talk to Jenn. We'll make sure everyone knows exactly what you do.'

'What's this amazing thing you're talking about?'

'It's an idea Chris and I have been thinking about.'

'Chris and you?'

'We still haven't got it all worked out, but we're pretty close.'

Ben waited again to hear what it was.

'Look, don't leave, Ben. You'll regret it. Just wait. The ride's not over. It's only beginning. At least think about it. Will you think about it?'

'I have thought about it.'

'Think about it some more. Let's talk about it again.'

'Tell me what this thing is you're thinking about.'

Andrei hesitated. 'I will. I promise.'

Conversations between Andrei and Ben continued for the next few weeks, but Ben couldn't be persuaded to change his mind and Andrei, for some reason, didn't reveal the big idea he had hinted at. When Ben asked Kevin if he knew what it was, Kevin claimed that he didn't.

Eventually, Andrei grew reconciled to the prospect of Ben's departure. He tried to accept that becoming a therapist was more important to Ben – at least at this point in his life – than continuing at Fishbowl. The night before Ben left, Andrei went with him and Kevin for one last meal at Yao's. Lopez served them, just like in the old days, and when Tony Yao heard that Ben was leaving, he came out of the kitchen to say goodbye. Andrei had his usual noodles, but he didn't have much of an appetite. It was the passing of an era.

The next day Ben was gone.

Within a week Andrei had sat down with Kevin and Jenn McGrealy to let them in on the big idea that he and Chris had been hatching.

33

THE IDEA HAD germinated early in Chris's mind, even before he flew to Palo Alto to propose the first experiments in Farming. At that point the notion was barely formed, embryonic, but if it hadn't been in his head in some shape, he wouldn't have bothered with the experiments. On Andrei's side, the idea occurred to him later, as the experiments neared their end and he began to focus on the possibilities they opened up – and also the limitations.

For both of them, Farming, in the form in which it had been put into practice in the Fish Farm, was a sideshow. It was labour intensive, requiring a highly skilled, emotionally intelligent sales person to spend his or her time behind a palotl, developing and working a network in order to encourage awareness of a particular brand. Any one person could manage only five or six palotls at a time, so the model would only ever work for high-value items, for which each individual sale generated a substantial revenue. If that was all that could have been achieved with Farming, neither of them would have thought it was worth the effort. It might have been a new model of advertising on the net, one many more times effective than the existing model for the products to which it could be applied, but it would never take the place of the existing model because those products were so restricted. The really interesting questions were: what if it could not only complement the traditional model but displace it? And what would it take to do that?

Naturally, they saw the first question differently. For Chris, what they had achieved was proof of user acceptance for a radical new model of marketing – but the real prize would be a form of selling that could extend across all goods and services, no matter how low in value, from bubblegum to soda. For Andrei, what they had was a limited and inefficient form of connectedness between organizations and individuals – but potentially the harbinger of a radically new form of connectedness with a scale and reach never seen before. Where their interests converged was in the second question.

The answer to it was clear: what was required was the development of an automated program that produced and managed palotls indistinguishable from those of the manually operated palotls of the Fish Farm. A program that could scan the network, identify people who were potentially responsive to a particular message, create customized personas indistinguishable from real people to engage those individuals, develop connections, hold conversations, build relationships and deliver the message in the most effective way and at the optimal moment calculated to achieve a positive response. Set free in the Fishbowl environment, with a defined set of objectives, it would be independent, capable of learning by itself, adapting, developing. As Chris might have put it: create that program and you could sell anything, whatever its value. As Andrei might have put it: create that program, and you could create connectedness between an individual and any organization, whatever its size.

The common objective of developing an automated palotl program meant that they were never forced to confront each other's divergent conceptualizations of what such a program would be for. In fact, each of them thought that they were in control of what they were about to do.

It was Chris who first broached the idea of trying to develop a palotl program during one of his fortnightly trips to Palo Alto, during the Farming experiment. Typically, he regarded the prospect as both unprecedentedly momentous and belly-achingly hilarious. The idea of a program that could rifle unseen through the electronic world, listening, morphing, talking, asking, answering and selling stuff as if it were a regular person was so abominably horrendous that it titillated the cynic in him like nothing else he had ever known. But if they could pull it off, it would also be the greatest technical advance in his adult lifetime, with the prospect of wealth on a scale almost unimaginable.

After two years of working with Andrei, Chris honestly didn't know the extent to which Andrei really didn't care about the money that Fishbowl was capable of earning, just as he still didn't know if Andrei's remarks sometimes betrayed a parchingly dry deadpan humour or utter, naive seriousness. All Andrei ever talked about was Deep Connectedness, and he professed indifference to Fishbowl's commercial success as long as it generated enough cash to keep funding its development. Was that real or put on? Andrei would have been far from the first tech CEO to hide his true commercial aspirations behind such a pretence. Chris was sure that Deep Connectedness was the only thing that had mattered to the Andrei he had first met over dinner at Mang, but he found it hard to believe that nothing had changed as Fishbowl generated ever larger revenues and its valuation climbed. Yet even if Andrei was only affecting his dorm-boy altruism, Chris knew that, as a result, he couldn't openly appeal to an interest in money – he would have to leave that to Andrei, who was smart enough to see the potential, and let him work it out for himself. So in proposing that they try to develop a palotl program, Chris emphasized what he knew Andrei would openly respond to: the size of the challenge, the magnitude of the technical advance, the gain in efficiency.

Andrei, for his part, thought that he had stepped out of Chris's shadow. He rarely had moments now when he wondered if he was the right person to lead Fishbowl and, when he did, he wouldn't have considered handing over to Chris, as he had sometimes considered in the past. Chris's offer to return his shares when he had proposed the Farming experiment had been a kind of trigger that changed the way Andrei saw him. It had struck him as impulsive and immature, and Andrei now thought he could see those traits in Chris going all the way back to when he had first met him. The way he had behaved towards James Langan had been unnecessary and spiteful – they had all gone behind James's back, but there had been no need to taunt him with it at the end. Chris deserved the punch he had got. And in retrospect, the way Chris had behaved during the first summer of Fishbowl's existence in La Calle Court had been more frat-boy than any of them. Chris also had an unsavoury habit of hitting on young Fishbowl staffers, which had already resulted in a couple of settlements for sexual harassment costing significant sums of money.

But Andrei wasn't considering cutting his ties with Chris. He no longer needed him for his business acumen, having a team of people with more of it than Chris would ever have, but he still valued Chris's curious, restless mind, his iconoclasm. Fishbowl could never have too much of that. As long as he knew Chris's faults, he thought, he would be able to take the best of what Chris had to offer for Deep Connectedness while preventing him from doing any damage to the business.

But Andrei's understanding of human nature was never his strong point. After two years, he still hadn't grasped the complex and changing mix of drives that impelled Chris Hamer – and he had no idea that he hadn't grasped them. Chris was fascinated by big ideas, and had been genuinely bowled over by Andrei's vision of connectedness when he had first come across Fishbowl. But even then, at the very start, he had sensed the commercial potential, which was always of interest to him. As that potential had got bigger, with no sign of tailing off, it had become more important to Chris. And at the same time, in Farming, the mischief-maker in Chris found himself with the opportunity to put something so cynical, so exploitative into the world that not even Mike Sweetman at Homeplace had ever thought of it. And the best thing about it was … the more mischief he made, the more money he stood to earn! It was like FriendTracker again, but a thousand times bigger.

So under a mutual misunderstanding of who was leading whom, and why they were doing it, Andrei and Chris began working together to sketch out the project that would be Fishbowl's greatest advance yet, and arguably the thing that would change the nature of the internet for ever.

The size of the challenge was beyond daunting. Automated programs to converse electronically, or chatbots, had been around since a primitive prototype called ELIZA was unveiled in the 1960s. What Fishbowl would be attempting to achieve was exponentially more sophisticated than anything that had been developed since. Anyone looking carefully could identify existing chatbots without much difficulty, even the most advanced. And a palotl needed to be much more than a chatbot. It had to have pictures of itself, family, friends. If you weren't going to use Photoxed images of real people, you would need image-generation software that was hugely more advanced than anything that was currently available. The program would need to learn and adapt. The artificial intelligence integrated in it would need to be at a level that was far beyond anything yet created.

Investigation of the possibility of achieving all of this started as Chris's Farming experiments drew to a close. Each fortnight, Chris came to Palo Alto to meet Andrei and Kevin to review progress, and usually stayed over at the condo. The next day, he and Andrei would go to Yao's and, over noodles and kung pao chicken, out of view of anyone else in the company, they began to outline a picture of what the future would look like. They continued after the Fish Farm was set up, spending hours at Yao's talking through the problem, identifying the needs, roughly architecting the outlines of a solution. As their ideas developed, Andrei's early thoughts about the breadth and power of the potential benefits of this type of Deep Connnectedness began to crytallize. He realized that it could be used for far more meaningful objectives than selling. It could play a transformative role in medicine, education, legal services – anything that could be done remotely but required the empathy and adaptability of a fellow human being.

Between meetings, Andrei spent time investigating chatbot engineering to try to determine how far away from that solution the current state of technology was. He read up on artificial intelligence and came to the conclusion that, eventually, the necessary advances would be made to enable such a program to be created. It was only a question of time – but how much of it? If Fishbowl got enough smart people together, could the problems be solved in a reasonable period, or was it something that would take decades of painstaking, plodding work as one advance built slowly on aother? In other words, if they decided to take on the challenge, was it only a question of how much money they were prepared to spend?

Andrei didn't know.

Chris was desperate to get Andrei to go ahead. If he could have funded the work himself, he would have, but he knew he wouldn't be able to raise anywhere near the money required. He needed Fishbowl to do that. It wasn't a program designed purely for selling stuff, Chris kept reminding Andrei. While that was a legitimate form of Deep Connectedness, it would receive the earliest attention only because it was needed in order to repay the costs of the program's development. Then there would be all the other uses they had been talking about. Imagine bringing medicine to a billion people in Africa. Imagine bringing education to every slum in Asia and every favela in South America. These were new forms of Deep Connectedness just waiting to be developed. To the extent that they even existed today, they were hopelessly inefficient.

Nonetheless, Andrei had his doubts. There was no guarantee they would succeed. And even Fishbowl's coffers didn't run deep enough to fund this by itself. They would need to raise money. And it certainly wasn't something they would want to do as a public company under the beady eye of Wall Street's analysts, which meant they would need to find the money elsewhere.

That wasn't a problem, said Chris. By now, there wasn't a venture capitalist in the world who wouldn't have been interested in taking a stake in Fishbowl. As he had a year earlier, before the

Farming experiments had diverted him, Chris suggested they should go and see Bob Leib – this time not to get his advice but to get his money.

But Andrei still wasn't sure whether, however much money they threw at it, it would be enough. Fishbowl had grown through steady, incremental, multi-faceted innovation. Throwing a huge sum at one specific project in the hope of a Great Leap Forward wasn't something he had ever done before. His procrastination went on for weeks. These were the same weeks during which he was trying to persuade Ben to stay at the company, when he kept hinting at a huge project that he and Chris were planning.

Andrei was still caught in two minds when Ben left. Somehow, his departure seemed to intensify the need to decide.

Andrei met Chris again at Yao's.

Chris had made all the arguments before: 'Someone's going to do it,' he said to Andrei. 'If we've worked out that this is the future, so will someone else. The prize will fall to the one who dares to try.'

'Do you know how much we're talking about spending?' said Andrei.. Every other project he had taken on, every problem he had set out to solve – he had always believed there was a solution in reach. It was only a matter of being smart enough to find it quickly. But in this case, no matter how much they spent, they still might fail. They might not get the program to the level of sophistication required within years or even decades.

'Andrei, Bob Leib is going to bite your hand off when we make him an offer. He'll be getting a stake in Fishbowl, which he *dreams* about getting, and at a *mother* of a discount from its value even as it is today. So even if we blow all his cash and nothing comes of it, there'll be enough in the future from what we *already* do to give him a return he doesn't deserve. Don't lose any sleep over Bob Leib.' Chris leaned closer. 'If we succeed ... the returns will blow his head off. He'll be on his knees thanking you for taking this chance.'

That was another thing that worried Andrei. Chris had told him to keep talk of their plans vague and not mention the idea of developing a palotl program if and when they went to Leib. 'We should tell him,' said Andrei.

'Not if you want to get this done. He'll only thank you in retrospect. Tell him up front, and you'll spend the next six months working out a business case to get him to agree and you'll be giving him and his boys a progress report at every board meeting to get them to release the next bunch of funds, which will only be a quarter of what you need. You want to try to run this project like that, go ahead, tell him.' Chris laughed. 'Trust me. That's how these guys are.'

Andrei watched him doubtfully.

'Don't worry about the money. Just think about what it would be like to solve this motherfucker. It's going to be like nothing else we've done. This kind of thing happens once in a generation. Once in a century. That's what Fishbowl is for. The big stuff. The stuff no one else will do. We're going to do something that would take fifty years if we left it to the rest of the world to find a way. And we're going to invent Deep Connectedness in a way that no one has ever seen before. It's a quantum leap in efficiency. It's not about advertising. It's about education, it's about medicine, it's about changing anything you want to change. And are you telling me that's going to make the world worse?' Chris smiled. 'Are you seriously telling me that? Andrei, I'd go further. We can't *not* do this. We've got a responsibility to try.'

Andrei hesitated. The sum they were considering spending was so large. The chances of success, he estimated, were no better than fifty-fifty. Perhaps less.

But he couldn't say no. He just could not bring himself to walk away. The challenge was too tempting.

So, after three years of avoiding the entanglements of venture capitalists, Andrei Koss finally found himself driving the two miles into the very heart of their lair in Sand Hill Road and sitting alongside Chris Hamer in a meeting room at LRB, pitching Fishbowl to Robert Leib with the help of a salmon-fishing palotl.

*

The $300 million injection that Robert Leib agreed to provide took six weeks to finalize after the meeting at the LRB office. Leib organized a syndicate with two other venture capital firms to raise the money. He could have had his choice of two dozen. There wasn't a venture capitalist on earth who wouldn't have jumped at the chance of getting a piece of Fishbowl, especially at a valuation that came in at around a quarter of the consensus valuation of the company. Leib had had his analysts comb through the company books and had calculated that Fishbowl was worth even more than that.

Andrei met the investors in the syndicate. Chris's strategy was perfect. Blinded by the gift that Andrei had seemed to place on a platter for them, they demanded remarkably little detail about the specific projects for which the cash was earmarked. Andrei told them that he needed it to fund further web service development and other expansion activities, and gave some examples that had nothing to do with the palotl project that he and Chris had in mind. He used a lot of technical language that only someone with an advanced degree in computer programming would have understood. It was good enough for Leib and his partners. Despite having made multiple tech investments in the past, none of them knew any specifics about the costs of developing programming improvements – other than that it cost a lot – and weren't in a position to judge whether the projects Andrei mentioned required the sum they were putting in – or a tenth as much, or ten times as much. Once you decided to make an investment, Leib believed, you had to trust people, tech people above all. In his experience, you got the best out of tech people by letting them do what they did best and making sure they had good commercial people around them to monetize the product. If you tried to understand the detail, all you'd do was stand in the way. As an investor, all he wanted to know was that there was going to be a way to turn great programming ideas into revenue. With Fishbowl, Andrei Koss had already demonstrated abundantly that he was able to do that.

With outside investment came the need, for the first time in the company's history, to set up a real board. Andrei made it a condition of the deal that he retain control. His lawyer devised a dual class stock arrangement that gave a certain class of shares – the ones Andrei would continue to hold – amplified voting rights, so he would effectively retain control of the company unless his holding fell below 10 per cent of the total stock.

Normally, Robert Leib wouldn't have stood for a provision that effectively gave indefinite control of the company to the founder of a start-up. But Fishbowl was no ordinary start-up and Andrei was no ordinary founder – and the likely returns Leib was going to make on this investment were no ordinary returns. The statutes of the company were changed accordingly, and the new stock structure implemented. The board had six seats. Andrei took one, nominating Chris and Kevin for another one each. Robert Leib, representing the VC syndicate, which now held 4 per cent of the stock and an option for a further 3 per cent in a year's time, held a fourth seat. The fifth seat went to Pete Muller, an internet entrepreneur whom Andrei had met and respected. He left the sixth seat vacant.

Andrei could still vividly remember the day that the first half-million dollars from 4Site had hit his bank account, back in the days when Fishbowl had still been run out of the suite in Robinson House. It was a measure of how far he had come that the day Leib's $300 million was wired to the Fishbowl account didn't stick in his memory at all. It was simply an amount of money he needed in order to do something and, when it arrived, he could forge ahead. His chief financial officer put his head around the door of the office that Andrei now occupied and told him the funds had arrived. Kevin was with him at the time, deep in discussion about the project for which those funds were required. Andrei simply nodded at the CFO and turned back to Kevin.

A team of headhunters was already at work for a multi-million-dollar fee. Their brief over that winter was to lure the world's best talent in artificial intelligence and linguistics programming. MIT,

Stanford, Imperial College in London, and the dozen other top academic software labs in the world were targeted, with the inducement of multi-million-dollar salaries and generous reloca- tion packages to California. It didn't prove too hard to tempt away brilliant young associate professors earning a fraction of that sum, with the additional prospect of life-changing sums in stock options and the prospect of working alongside the most outstanding brains of their generation. To add to the academic talent, the most creative programmers in Seattle and Silicon Valley were offered a doubling of their existing remuneration package and a bundle of stock options as well. Hollywood and video games developers were raided for the leading talents in visuals. Altogether, a team of sixty-eight of the world's most gifted researchers and program- mers was recruited and relocated to the Bay Area.

The project was to run under strict secrecy. Jenn McGrealy found an office away from the rest of Fishbowl in a nondescript block on Manhattan Avenue in East Palo Alto, just south of Route 101. The people recruited were instructed to tell their spouses that they were working in a private academic research institute, which was strictly true, since a private institute, sepa- rate from Fishbowl, had been incorporated under which all salaries and expenses were paid. The institute was owned by a Cayman Islands-based holding company, which in turn was confidentially owned by Fishbowl, so no casual association would link Fishbowl to the work being done there. Non-disclosure clauses in the employment contracts were draconian. Administration and infrastructure was to be run by a small team within the office on Manhattan Avenue that was unconnected with Fishbowl's support services. Besides Andrei, Chris, Kevin and Jenn McGrealy, no one in the wider Fishbowl organization knew that the project existed.

By March, Fishbowl's new employees and their families were flying in to Palo Alto at the rate of twenty a week. After six months of recruitment, the team assembled for the first time on Manhattan Avenue. They were greeted by Andrei, Chris and Kevin.

Andrei gave a welcome speech in the atrium of the office, standing in front of the obligatory Fishbowl aquarium. He told the assembled cohort that the work they were going to undertake together in that place would one day be looked back upon as having changed the world. There were no smirks, no rolling of eyes. This was a collection of men and women of such talent that a comment like that didn't seem to them in the least hyperbolic.

'What's this project called?' asked one of them, when Andrei had finished.

Andrei glanced at Chris. They had been referring to it simply as the Farming Project, which wasn't very inspirational. 'We thought we'd leave it to you to come up with a name. There ought to be enough brainpower here to think of one.'

A ripple of laughter ran through the group.

'What about the Manhattan Project?' said a Spanish accented voice from the group, citing the name of the Second World War project that had spawned the atom bomb. 'We're on Manhattan Avenue, no?'

'That's right,' said a third voice. 'And, like you said, Andrei, we're changing the world.'

Chris laughed. 'Let's just hope we don't blow it up.'

34

THE PLAN WAS for Kevin to be in charge of the project. He relocated to Manhattan Avenue, leaving Fishbowl's projects in the hands of two senior programmers who became joint heads of development.

Initially, Andrei planned to drop in from time to time to check on progress, but he soon found that he couldn't stay away. The office on Manhattan Avenue housed the smartest, sharpest group of people Andrei had ever come across, passionate about knowledge, about their own areas of expertise, about breaking new ground. Just walking in there gave him a buzz. The thought that he had brought this group together made him feel both uniquely privileged and proud. He would go over to Manhattan and sit there for hours, listening, immersing himself in the detail. As people from so many varying disciplines came together, there was much shared education. There were long discussions about the nature of linguistics and its programmability and what amounted to seminars by the artificial intelligence gurus as they explained their field to everybody else. People from different disciplines brought new perspectives that opened up new ideas. The place was a hothouse of creativity.

And yet nothing much happened. Weeks went by, then months. Despite the sharing of so much knowledge, communication about the actual work underway seemed poor. Andrei knew about individual pieces of investigation that other people in the office seemed to be unaware of. He heard about collaborations that started, then stopped. Work was being done, interesting work, but it was going in a thousand directions.

After three months Andrei asked Kevin to organize a week-long seminar in which everyone would present the work they were doing. He asked Chris to join them. Chris didn't care too much about the detail of how the problems were being solved and hadn't spent much time in the Manhattan office, so most of it went over his head, but certain things were clear. At lunch on the second day he said to Andrei: 'This is all over the place. These guys are running amok. And you can see they don't think shit of Kevin.'

That was what Andrei had been thinking. The Manhattanites were treating Kevin with disdain. It was obvious that they didn't respect him – at least partly because Kevin, from his side, didn't seem to have put any kind of order into what they were doing and appeared to be waiting for it to emerge by itself.

The following week, Andrei went to the Manhattan office for a talk with Kevin. Kevin's response made it the toughest conversation he had ever had. He asked Kevin to go back to Embarcadero and take up overseeing other projects again, while he, Andrei, led the Manhattan project personally. Kevin asked for more time, then begged for it. Andrei said he couldn't give it to him. The burn rate on the project was in excess of $10 million a month and, every month, Jenn McGrealy would ask him what was happening out there. Even if it had been a tenth as much, he would have done the same thing. He had assembled the smartest team of people that probably existed anywhere on the planet at that point in time. He couldn't waste that firepower.

Kevin left and Andrei moved in.

Andrei had already realized that the ways he had conceptualized the problems to be solved in the months prior to setting up the project were simplistic. They were much more complex. If the project was to have any hope of solving them, it needed structure. It couldn't be run in the informal, fortuitous way that most things at Fishbowl were run. In that respect, Kevin had been the worst person Andrei could have chosen to head the project. He had a taste for anarchy that was normally compensated by a group of senior programmers who knew his foibles and ensured that projects were completed despite him. But these lieutenants were lacking at Manhattan Avenue.

Fortunately, despite what had happened under Kevin, Andrei still had an opportunity to recover the situation. He had the respect of the Manhattanites. They knew better than anyone that the project had been going nowhere under Kevin, and removing him showed decisiveness. Although each of them was far more knowledgeable than Andrei in his or her field, they were impressed by the way he had spent time sitting and listening, by the questions he had asked, and by the engagement with their answers that he had shown. They also recognized that he had envisioned and built what was clearly by now one of the world's great websites, and had also envisioned this project of which they were lucky enough to be a part. And every one of them, no matter how gifted or arrogant, did feel lucky to be a part of it, and not only because of the money they were earning and the stock that was accumulating in their options accounts. To be part of a group like this was a once-in-a-generation experience, given to very few. The departments they had come from could only dream of pulling together this concentration of talent and expertise. All of them had often imagined what they could achieve, what apparently insurmountable obstacles could be overleapt, if only the whole range of talents could be brought into the room. And here, on Manhattan Avenue in East Palo Alto, thanks to Andrei, they had been.

The first thing Andrei did on taking over was to organize a second seminar. He had everyone outline what they thought needed to be done to develop the Manhattan programme and what role they saw for themselves. There was vigorous, often passionate debate out of which emerged key themes, if not consensus. Then he worked with groups of people from within and across each of the disciplines in a series of wheelspin-type sessions to rank the issues and shape them into a work programme.

There was unhappiness about some people being chosen to work directly with Andrei and others not, but a hierarchy of sorts was emerging. Project leaders were named and teams were formed to work on each of the issues. They reported back to each other in an all-day Friday session each week.

Andrei found his new role both incredibly stimulating and extraordinarily challenging. He was constantly talking to people, identifying problems, trying to find ways to solve them. In that respect, he was like a kid with a toy box. But he was also constantly at the very edge of the envelope of his knowledge – or even outside it – with people whose minds were razor sharp. And, in many instances, those minds came with egos to match. He loved it and at the same time it scared him. He had never felt more alive.

Slowly, progress began to be made. Problems were solved. Solutions converged and new issues emerged. The progress got faster. In what seemed to Andrei like the blink of an eye, a year had passed. Already, $100 million dollars had been spent.

The rest of Fishbowl was running largely without Andrei. His tendency to bury himself in the fun stuff, which had started back in the days of James Langan, took over. At one point he hadn't appeared at Embarcadero for over a month and Jenn McGrealy found herself having to physically go over to Manhattan to get things done. She insisted that he agree to spend at least one day in the Embarcadero office every week, and she set out to look for premises that would unite all the Fishbowl offices with space for the growth that was still taking place.

Andrei agreed for her to find somewhere new and to bring the Fish Farm onto the same campus, but he refused to move the Manhattan Project. Here groundbreaking work was being done, work that would have application, he knew, way outside Fishbowl. For Andrei, this had nothing to do with business. Here, a revolution was taking place, and it was going to stay in splendid isolation until it was done.

*

The bulk of the groundbreaking work in the Manhattan project was done in the first two years. Soon after that, as the focus shifted towards developing user applications, a number of the original members of the team left. Some were disgruntled at what they foresaw as the excessive commercialization of their work, although what else they imagined would be done with it, considering that the project was being funded by a private company, was unclear. Most of the leavers were academic linguists whose work was done anyway. Others were replaced by new people. The project's secrecy held. None of those who left broke their non-disclosure agreements, probably motivated by the thought of stock options that wouldn't vest for a further two years.

The two external members of the Fishbowl board, Robert Leib and Pete Muller, remained in ignorance throughout the project, just like the rest of the world. As far as they were aware, the escalating spend that they saw in the company accounts to the Caymans holding company, which they were told was being directed to the 'Institute for Technical Science', were payments to a Fishbowl-owned incubator which had been set up for tax purposes and was developing Fishbowl's cutting-edge functionalities. Since neither Leib nor Muller knew enough about the way a meta-network of Fishbowl's size and stage of development operated its R&D to question the magnitude of the spending, few questions were asked. As far as they were concerned, the spend on the institute could have been $10 million or it could have been $100 million. A year after his first investment, Leib organized a second syndicate to exercise the option of taking another 2 per cent of Fishbowl for a further $300 million dollars, and counted himself lucky.

During this time, Fishbowl established itself as one of the unquestioned giants of the internet world, a feature of the landscape so ubiquitous and influential that it became hard to remember what internet life had been like before it existed. Constant focus on delivery and improvement of functionality was its hallmark. Jenn McGrealy proved herself to be a superb executive and leader, controlling not only the day-to-day operations of the company but also helping Andrei exert a discipline over the programmes run by the two heads of development that he wouldn't have imposed by himself. Andrei came to rely heavily on her judgement on how to allocate his time outside the Manhattan office.

In Palo Alto, Fishbowl now had over 1,900 employees housed, with the exception of the Manhattanites, in an interconnected pair of buildings on University Avenue, and a further 600 employees worldwide. Its IPO was eagerly awaited and rumours regularly swept the market that Fishbowl was about to announce its public offering, which was expected to be amongst the highest ever to come to the market. Homeplace, once the monster of the social media world, was in steep decline, its user base having largely migrated to Fishbowl after it had been forced to open access for data transfer. The money spent on the political lobbying to force the move, and on developing services to outshine Homeplace's, had paid off. As a combined network and meta-network, Fishbowl was the second most visited site on the net, its user numbers topping one billion. Its advertising revenues, both from what was regarded as traditional internet advertising and from its high-end Farming, escalated accordingly. Farming was being widely copied by other networks, many of which had lined up to condemn Andrei when Fishbowl had blazed the trail. Now they were scrambling to catch up.

About a year after Andrei moved Kevin off the Manhattan Project and back to Embarcadero, Kevin left Fishbowl in order to purse a new venture of his own. Although nominally still the Vice President for Getting Things Done when he came back to Embarcadero, Kevin had never recovered his previous position at the top of the programming tree. The two heads of development who had been nominated when he had gone off to lead the project, jointly selected by Andrei and Jenn, were able, organized and disciplined. Development ran more smoothly under their command. Although Kevin didn't formally report to them, they controlled the development programme, and he found himself sidelined, allocated only specific projects with smaller teams. Kevin had his own ideas about what he wanted to do, and they didn't necessarily fit into the Fishbowl framework. After years in Andrei's shadow, he had also decided that he didn't want anyone else controlling them.

Kevin had never lost his interest in palotls, and was keen to do something with them in the social media space. His ideas were vague but he could afford to blow a few million figuring out what those ideas were. On paper, Kevin was an immensely wealthy man, and once Fishbowl came to IPO that wealth would be realizable.

To help get him started, Andrei had Fishbowl buy back a fraction of his shares at a generous valuation and acquire 5 per cent of Kevin's new company to give him extra capital. Kevin still held almost 15 per cent of Fishbowl and could have staked a claim to keep his place on the board, but he was more comfortable off it. He spoke to Andrei from time to time but their conversations about Fishbowl didn't run very deep.

Andrei didn't find Kevin's departure anywhere near as wrenching as Ben's exit. He had been more or less expecting Kevin to leave since he had moved him off the Manhattan Project. The days when the three of them had wheelspun in the dorm at Stanford were ancient history, barely credible when he walked into the sprawling Fishbowl campus on University Avenue, and Ben's departure had already put all of that behind them. Besides, although different in nature, the fierce locus of energy in the Manhattan office was every bit as consuming for Andrei as Robinson House and La Calle Court had been, and filled whatever gap they had left.

Chris's involvement waned somewhat as the Manhattan Project dragged on. He was eager for the results, but not for the fastidious, specialized work that was necessary to get them. Board meetings brought him to Palo Alto on a bi-monthly basis. At other times, he would come up and hang out just to see what was happening. Eventually Chris took off for the New Guinea Highlands. It was the first spiritual quest he had taken since becoming involved with Fishbowl.

Chris was away in New Guinea for six months. When he got back he came up to Palo Alto for the weekend. He was thin, suntanned and buzzing with energy. At the condo, he regaled Andrei and Sandy with stories of what he had seen in New Guinea, until Sandy made up some kind of excuse to get away. Andrei took Chris to Yao's.

'So what's happening with Manhattan?' said Chris. 'Are we finished?'

'Not quite.' Andrei told Chris where they were up to.

'Sounds like you've got the basics,' said Chris.

'There's more to do.'

'There'll always be more to do. It doesn't need be perfect, Andrei. It doesn't need to do everything right now that it might be able to do in the end. It only needs to work.'

'It can be better.'

'Remember how you started Fishbowl. If you'd waited until it was as good as it could be, you still wouldn't have launched.'

That was different. When he had started Fishbowl, Andrei had had nothing to lose. 'There's no video functionality,' he said. 'And the audio functionality is crude.'

'You don't need either. Plenty of people just write. That's all the Fish Farmers do right now.'

'We need more. You can't teach a kid to read if he has to read everything you say when he's teaching him. You need someone who can talk to him.'

'And that might take you another ten years. What you've got already is awesome, Andrei. It's more than awesome – it's fucking Stakhanovite! Let's use it and get the money to do the rest of the development. Stages, Andrei. Putting in place the next model of advertising was always the first step. We do that, and that gives us the funds to develop the rest.'

'I guess so.'

'You need to start testing it.'

'We test all the time.'

'Externally? On Fishbowl?'

Andrei shook his head.

'Start.'

Andrei knew that it was time. He didn't need Chris to tell him that what he had was just about good enough as a starting point. He had been prevaricating over unleashing the program. Something was holding him back. Maybe it was just that this thing was so big, so special, so precious, that he didn't want to take the risk of it failing until it was pefect.

'This is it, Andrei!' Chris grinned. 'Watch out. You're about to change the world.'

They started testing on Fishbowl. Four months later, they were done. Watched by Chris, Jenn McGrealy and the Manhattanites, Andrei symbolically switched off the lights in the office on Manhattan Avenue.

The Manhattan Project ran for a month shy of three years, a fearsomely short period for what it accomplished. It cost just over half a billion dollars, and left each of its researchers a multi-millionaire.

Andrei Koss was twenty-seven years old. It was not quite seven years since he had founded Fishbowl. His two co-founders had moved on from the company. He was known to the outside world as a brilliant, visionary, somewhat introspective tech leader who appeared at selected conferences, occasionally gave an interview, and had an intense manner in private conversation that some people saw as passionate and others as arrogant. His company, Fishbowl, was a big beast of the internet jungle, one that was setting the pace in the world of social media and hadn't been scared to introduce the controversial Farming approach, which was fast becoming the standard on the net for high-value products and services.

People thought they knew what the company was about. But no one, including two of Fishbowl's own board members, was ready for what it was about to unleash now.

35

ROBERT LEIB GLANCED at Pete Muller, who looked back at him with a frown of disbelief. Andrei had started the board meeting by saying there was a project he wanted to tell them about. Then he had proceeded to describe a project that had been running, apparently, for years, and which had cost ... which had cost a sum that must have included a mistake with a decimal place. Or two.

Apart from Andrei and Chris, Muller and Leib were the only ones at the board meeting. One of the seats had never been filled and a second had been vacant since Kevin Embley had left the company almost two years earlier.

'*When* did you say you started this project?' demanded Leib.

'Three years ago,' said Andrei.

'Was that after we joined the board?' demanded Muller.

'Around that time.'

'I don't know what's worse,' said Leib. 'If you started after we joined, or took my money without even telling me it was already happening. Chris, I assume from the fact that you haven't said anything that you knew about this?'

Chris nodded.

'And you were happy that Pete and I were told nothing about this?'

'It was a software development project,' said Chris. 'Fishbowl has hundreds of development projects running. I can't recall you ever having wanted the details before.'

'I don't think it has hundreds that cost … what did you say, Andrei?' said Muller. 'Five hundred and fourteen million dollars? Is that what you said?'

'Cheap,' said Chris.

Muller ignored him. 'Is that what you said it cost, Andrei?'

'It's complete now,' said Andrei. 'I expected that we might end up spending even more, but the team we pulled together exceeded expectations.'

'And what team was this?' demanded Leib.

'Linguists, artificial intelligence experts, graphics experts, programmers. For artificial intelligence and linguistics we drew on the most advanced academic labs in the world. MIT, Stanford, Imperial College, Cambridge—'

'It was a who's who,' said Chris. 'Plus we got seven of the nine top programmers in the Valley.'

'How?' said Muller

'Why do you think this cost five hundred million?'

'And what exactly did you achieve?' demanded Leib, who was trying to balance the anger he could feel boiling away in him with the knowledge that if Andrei Koss spent half a billion dollars on a project then there was a good chance that something rather useful had come out of it.

'I think that's what Andrei was trying to tell you.'

Andrei nodded. 'The Manhattan Project—'

'The *what*?' said Muller.

Andrei shrugged. 'We had an office on Manhattan Avenue.'

'We're changing the world,' said Chris. 'Oppenheimer did it with a bomb. We're doing it with something infinitely more powerful.'

'I've never met an internet entrepreneur who didn't think he was changing the world,' retorted Muller.

Chris grinned. 'Listen to this, Pete, and tell us if we're wrong.'

Muller exchanged another glance with Leib.

They listened as Andrei took them through a summary of the Manhattan Project. Leib was expressionless throughout. Muller sat with his arms folded, a frown lingering on his face.

When Andrei was finished, there was a moment of awestruck silence.

'You were right,' said Leib eventually. 'If you really have managed to do this, you'll change the world. Question is, what's it going to look like once it's changed?'

'Buckle up!' said Chris. 'We're about to find out.'

'And as far as the business is concerned …?'

'Can you imagine how hard it will be to replicate this? The days of advertising in any of the ways we know it today are gone. This is the future, gentlemen, and we're the first ones to arrive.'

'And we can use it for other things,' said Andrei. 'It's not just for advertising. There's a whole range of applications.'

'Sure,' said Muller, 'but are you certain people are going to be prepared to use a website where they don't know whether they're talking to a real person or a sales program?'

'Farming didn't stop them,' said Chris.

'But this is on a mass scale.'

'To the individual, it's still on an individual scale. We see the mass. They don't.'

'Is it legal?' asked Leib.

'It's no different in principle to Farming,' replied Andrei, 'which we know is legal.'

'Maybe on this scale it isn't,' said Muller.

Andrei looked at him. 'Why not?'

'Because it's automated?'

'That's irrelevant. We have to stay factual and not mispresent. If we're doing that, this is a service, Pete. It's about bringing relevant information to people at the exact time when they want it. Look, to me this is about Deep Connectedness – extreme, radical Deep Connectedness. Advertising is only one small aspect of it. There are all kinds of other stuff, all kinds of other forms of connectedness it can facilitate. But if you want to focus on advertising, fine – think about advertising as we know it, and it's full of deceit. It tries to create emotional attachments to things that have no emotional content. We're doing the opposite. We're putting factual information out in a way that's relevant to the interests people have told us they have.'

'That's what you say.'

'That's what it is.'

'But it looks like it's coming from someone they know. An actual person who exists.'

'Is an endorsement from a celebrity any better?,' said Chris. 'They're made to look like the celebrity likes the thing he's advertising and has maybe even used it. Well, that's legal. It happens all the time.'

Robert Leib heaved a deep sigh and shook his head a couple of times. 'Well, I have to say, this would have to be the most dysfunctional board I've ever sat on—'

'I wouldn't even call this a board,' muttered Muller.

'If you two guys think it's OK to spend five hundred and fourteen million dollars in cash – most of which, I assume, came from me and my partners – without even so much as telling me or Pete here what was going on over a period of three years, I don't know what you'd think isn't OK. Andrei, I'm going to tell you, I've never been treated like this. So I'm angry. I'm damn angry.' Leib paused. 'But on the other hand, if you and your team have done what you really say you've done, then all I can says is ...' Leib threw up his hands. 'I'm speechless.'

'The future's arrived, Bob,' said Chris. 'The future's right here.'

'Let me show you an example,' said Andrei.

He projected his computer on the screen and pulled up two home pages, side by side. 'One of these is a person's real home page. The other is a program palotl's.'

'That means a computer program generated it,' said Chris. 'Not a person. This is what we call a PP, a program palotl. A program independently generated everything you see there, including the photographs.'

Leib and Muller peered closer.

'Here's a conversation between them,' said Andrei, switching to a chat trail. 'Again, one of them is a PP. Can you tell which one?'

Leib read down the screen.

Pete was still chewing over the way he had been treated. 'Why weren't we told?' he said suddenly. 'I'm assuming you had a reason, Andrei. I'm assuming it didn't just slip your mind.'

'We didn't think you'd believe it could be done,' said Chris. 'We thought—'

'Chris, I asked Andrei,' said Muller. 'Do you want to let him answer?'

'I'm giving you the answer.'

'Let him answer. Just shut the fuck up, Chris, and let him answer.'

'What the fuck's wrong with you, Pete?'

'Just fucking let him answer.'

'Guys!' said Leib. 'Andrei, do you want to answer Pete's question?'

'It's like Chris said,' said Andrei. 'I thought that if you thought your money was being used on this, Bob, you'd try to make me end it or be less aggressive, cut back on the spending somewhat, or you would have tried to track it against some kind of business targets, which would have fatally compromised the project. I apologize if I was wrong.'

Leib shook his head thoughtfully. 'No, you're not wrong,' he murmured.

Andrei glanced at Muller. 'That's the reason.'

'Well, I don't know if I can serve on a board where this kind of thing happens,' said Muller.

'I agree,' said Leib. 'It shows a basic lack of trust and respect.'

'I apologize again if that's the impression,' said Andrei. 'On the other hand, Bob, what you just said to me is that you had a basic lack of trust in me, a lack of respect for my judgement, and you would have tried to get me to scale back on the Manhattan Project, or even shut it down.'

Pete Muller stood up. 'I can't work on a board like this. If you don't want me to help think through the big decisions – and I can't see one bigger than this – then I don't see that I really have a role.'

'I'm really sorry to hear you say that, Pete,' said Andrei.

'Pete, sit down,' said Chris.

'Don't tell me to sit down!'

'Pete, don't be so petty.'

'So *petty?*'

'Look at the bigger picture.'

'Shut the fuck up, Chris!' shouted Muller, hands clenched in fury.

'Don't tell me to shut the fuck up!' yelled Chris, getting to his feet too.

'You ought to have known better.'

'What ought I to have known better?'

'No, you're right. Why would I expect you to know better? Why would I expect Chris-fucking-Hamer to know better?'

'You fucking moron, Muller! Andrei has just stewarded this motherfucker of a project through from concept to completion in three years, and even though you know what the implications of this are, all you can think about is whether you were fucking *told!*'

Muller stood staring at him for a moment. 'If I want to be told about stuff when it's done,' he said through gritted teeth, 'I'll read about it in the newspaper.'

'I'll be sure to send you one,' said Chris, sitting down and turning away from him. 'Hard copy, which is what you probably still read.'

Muller turned to Andrei. 'I resign from your board, effective right now. From the way you run your company, Andrei, it doesn't look like you need one.' He looked at Leib and stood for a moment longer, then shook his head in disgust and walked out.

The door slammed. A pregnant silence followed.

'Are you leaving too?' asked Andrei, looking at Leib.

'That depends,' replied Leib. 'Is there anything else I don't know about?'

'Nothing significant.'

Leib smiled wryly. 'Would you have described this as significant?'

'Yes,' said Andrei.

'And is this going to happen again?'

'I don't have any plans for anything on the same scale.'

'What if you did in the future?'

'Would you trust me that I know what my team is capable of?'

'You're not omniscient, Andrei. You can make mistakes. You can overreach yourself. Anyone can. That's why you have a board – not to tell you what to do, but to help think things through, even challenge you occasionally.'

Andrei frowned. 'That's fair enough.'

'What I can say,' said Leib, 'is that, having seen this, I would have a different attitude. I might not be quite so quick to assume that something can't be done. I'd give you more of a hearing than I probably would have. So I need to think about how I would have reacted. But you need to think about the way you behaved, too. You really, really need to think about the way you handled this, Andrei. It doesn't become you.' Leib paused. 'You know perfectly well that you have the votes on this board. No one can stop you doing what you want to do. That means you can behave like a dictator if you want. It's up to you. For what it's worth, I don't think that would be a very wise approach. I don't think it would show a lot of foresight. The reason Pete and I – well, me anyway – are here is that we might be able to give you some advice. We might have some thoughts. But we can't give you thoughts if we don't know what we're supposed to be thinking about.'

'Who needs Pete's thoughts?' muttered Chris. 'He's a complete fucking moron.'

'He's not a complete fucking moron.'

'An incomplete fucking moron, then.'

'Andrei, when you get to a situation when you've got a guy like Pete Muller walking away from your board, that is not something to be proud of. I'm going to be blunt with you. That's a reflection of mismanagement on your part.'

Chris snorted.

'I'll see if I can get him back.'

'If he's so smart he would have seen this achievement for what it is.'

'Chris, enough!' shouted Leib. 'Shut the fuck up!' He turned back to Andrei. 'Personally, what I'm saying is, I need to know about something like this. I need you to show me that trust.'

Andrei was watching him. He had listened to everything Leib said, absorbing it, without saying a word.

The venture capitalist considered his next move. He didn't want to leave Andrei's board, whether or not he was told everything he should have been about the Manhattan Project. For a start, he had a lot of his investors' money – and his own money – tied up in Fishbowl, and he was keen to do what he could to make sure it earned the best return it could. But, more importantly – because he had no doubt he would make a spectacular return on his investment, whether or not he had any personal involvement from this point on – Robert Leib had the feeling that Fishbowl was only beginning, and that somehow the combination of Andrei Koss and Chris Hamer – the visionary and the iconoclast, as he thought of them, the thinker and the rebel – had the power to do things that really would change the world, or at least shake things up in quite interesting ways.

Bob Leib had reached a stage in his career where he had made so much money and had so many opportunities to make more that there was only so much of a buzz to be had from yet another boost to his bank account, however many zeroes were on the end of it. Fishbowl was doing stuff – meaningful, risky, extraordinary stuff – and so long as he was on its board, however unconventionally it operated, he would have a ringside seat.

He smiled. 'So what happens now? Do we go public with this?'

'Duh ...' said Chris. 'I don't think so.'

36

PETE MULLER DIDN'T return to the Fishbowl board, despite Bob Leib's attempts to get him to reconsider. Approximately six months after the board meeting at which he walked out, following further testing and refinement, Andrei Koss clicked a mouse on a button that sent FishFarm 2.0 live.

Four brands had signed up as the first to be Farmed. Within forty-eight hours, the mention count of the four brands was already ticking up across a range of media that were being tracked, indicating word-of-mouth awareness spilling out of Fishbowl. Within a week, the mention count had doubled. At the first monthly review with the advertisers, the average rise in sales was 2.2 per cent, an unprecedented monthly uplift in mass-market retail. Fishbowl account managers were soon on the road, visiting the world's biggest companies with the numbers in hand.

The Farming that Fishbowl had pioneered after Chris's initial experiment had been artisanal in scale – this was industrial. The program scanned, Baited and insinuated itself as palotls into conversations with millions of people and groups, looking and chatting like any other person, but primed to identify moments of purchasing readiness and implant awareness of the product being advertised at the perfect moment. It could be used to sell anything, no matter how trivial. The program could construct palotls to personify a brand's qualities, actually bringing the brand to life – a fun-seeking teenage girl for marketing a boy band's records, an urbane fifty-something with a touch of grey in the hair for a single malt whisky – with different interpretations of the brand for different market segments. Picking up on cues in conversations with each user, palotls would continuously tailor their life stories and aspirations to become the most powerful source of word-of-mouth recommendation – someone just like you. In the reverse direction, the quality of the market insights the program was able to collate, analyse and feed back was a quantum leap ahead of anything available through traditional market research. An additional group of marquee names was soon added to the initial four brands using the program.

Chris was frequently in Palo Alto as the program was refined and then moulded after launch. Bob Leib had also become more engaged with Fishbowl, often driving over from Sand Hill Road to the University Avenue campus and spending hours hanging out with Andrei and Chris. He was fascinated by what they had achieved, their drive and vision, and by the vast experiment that he considered FishFarm 2.0 to be. He was beginning to feel that the day Andrei Koss and Chris Hamer had come through his door to pitch Fishbowl had been the luckiest day in his life.

Andrei, for his part, was beginning to value Bob as a more considered and solid counterweight to Chris, whose capriciousness seemed to have increased since he had come back from New Guinea and Farming 2.0 had become a reality – or perhaps the break from Chris had simply made Andrei see him in sharper focus. In any event, he found Chris increasingly irritating. It was a long time since he had first felt that he had stepped put of Chris's shadow, but now he was beginning to think that not only had he stepped out of his shadow but that he had outgrown him. Chris's advice to keep the existence of the Manhattan Project from Leib and Muller, Andrei believed, had been poor counsel, and he regretted acceding to it. His behaviour at the end with Pete Muller had been aggressive and gratuitous, much like his behaviour with James Langan, betraying the same petulant streak. Andrei was also thoroughly sick of Chris's hitting on staffers, or Fishettes, as Chris liked to describe them, which he continued to do despite being warned repeatedly by Fishbowl's head of legal affairs.

FishFarm 1.0, the original operation targeting consumers of high-end goods with live sales people, continued as before, aided by some of the Manhattan Project technology such as automated palotl construction and updating. FishFarm 2.0 wasn't yet sophisticated enough to take the place of real people for the high-priced products that FishFarm 1.0 was designed to sell. Typically for Andrei, once the initial version of FishFarm 2.0 had been developed, he was obsessed with driving it to maximum efficiency. Development of the advertising functionality therefore didn't stop. On the contrary, it accelerated, as real-world operations provided a constant flow of new data from which to improve it. The team had merely transferred from the now defunct Manhattan Avenue office to the sixth floor of the office on University – which was predictably dubbed Los Alamos, after the facility in New Mexico that had been home to the original Manhattan Project and which continued thereafter as a nuclear weapons lab – and kept working.

Another problem that remained from the original Manhattan Project was the challenge of having the program engage in voice and video interactions – a necessity if it was to have the applications in education, medicine and other fields that Andrei foresaw. The project had focused on getting the basics of written communication right, an immense achievement in itself, and FishFarm 2.0 was limited to that. If a contact suggested a call, the program responded as someone who wanted to keep communication in written form. To create the capability for voice and video would require a step change in voice and animation technology that was at least as big, if not bigger, than the step change the Manhattan Project had already taken. Even by Manhattan standards, expenditure would be large – but Chris was as much in favour of attempting to do it as Andrei was. The return would be immense. People were naturally inclined to trust others more if they could see and talk to them. Having voice and video capability would take marketing effectiveness to a whole new level, with a commensurate monetary payoff.

This time, Andrei was open with Bob Leib about his aspirations. Hundreds of millions from the burgeoning revenues that Fishbowl was making were earmarked for the development of the next phase, FishFarm 3.0. Occasionally Leib stepped back and asked himself if he had drunk the Kool Aid, but he supported Andrei's ambition. The Los Alamos team swelled to 80, then 100 people, then up to 200 people, spilling off the sixth floor and taking over the seventh. Headhunters scoured Hollywood animation studios and video game developers, luring them with the same package of inducements that had tempted the first Manhattan Project team. Leib was stunned by the sheer quantity and quality of talent and the things he saw on the super-high-definition screens scattered around the sixth floor whenever he went to visit Andrei there. He joked that if the building was ever hit by a plane, America would have to go begging to other countries to lend them some brains. Andrei replied, deadpan, that there would be no one for other countries to send because Los Alamos already had them all.

In retrospect, even within the constraint of written communication, the launch version of FishFarm 2.0 was relatively crude, barely a pale forerunner of what the program would later become. Anyone looking for some kind of automated palotl program would eventually begin to identify it. Limitations on its artificial intelligence capability meant that there was too much repetition of the same remarks in the same situations, and there was a tendency to mention the products too often when selling them, making it seem like a sales pitch was in operation. Even as the Los Alamos team learned from the data and worked continuously to iron out the problems – improving the artificial intelligence capabilities to allow responses to evolve better, or developing a more subtle approach to product mentions – suspicions surfaced amongst the most tech-savvy of Fishbowl's users that some kind of automated program was in operation. Never short of conspiracy theorists, the Grotto had been full of such claims for years. But now there was a greater tone of certainty. Rumours began to spread, some of them well founded. Someone wrote a 'Spot the Bot' app that had a reasonable success rate in identifying program palotls – the Los Alamos team itself downloaded and harnessed the app, which it developed and improved, as a testing tool. Within a few months of launch, the denizens of the Grotto were certain that some such program was operating, and demanded to know the truth.

Andrei posted a brief announcement in the Grotto announcing a new form of Deep Connectedness that would serve to bring relevant products to the attention of Fishbowl users, but with little detail about how it worked. He reiterated the FishFarm motto: Don't tell lies.

The predictable storm ensued. Andrei didn't even bother to find out what was being said. He had long stopped caring about what went on in the Grotto, and especially what was said by the remaining stalwarts of the 300, who had their own chat stream. Apart from Barry Diller and a handful of others, for whom Andrei could do no wrong, they all seemed constantly opposed to anything he did, usually in the most abusive terms, and never seemed to ask themselves whether they might occasionally – or even just once – show an inkling of appreciation for the service he had built for them.

But the furore wasn't restricted to the Grotto. It widened rapidly to the blogosphere and then to the mainstream media, engulfing Fishbowl in a hurricane of vituperation. But by now the lesson was deeply engrained in Andrei that he could do just about anything he wanted, and apart from a passing roar of noise, nothing much would happen. He knew there would be the usual School page campaigns that would sign up millions of people who thought that clicking a button to add their name to a page was some kind of meaningful activism.

He knew that every crazed right-winger who wanted to shut down free speech on the net, every crazed libertarian who wanted to lift every restriction on the net, and every crazed left-winger who actually had nothing to say about the net would come after him. He knew that prosecutors would look for legal avenues of attack to boost their profiles, politicians would look for demagogic means of attack to boost their re-election chances, and competitors would look for commercial means of attack to boost their profits. As far as Andrei was concerned, they could do and say what they wanted. He had been through so many battles pursuing his evolving vision of Deep Connectedness that by now he believed that no one really understood what he was trying to do – so he had stopped listening.

He knew that the average Fishbowl user – each of the 1.4 billion people who had no particular axe to grind and just wanted to get on to Fishbowl each day and share stuff with the people they connected with – was going to log on just like he or she had logged on before, vaguely aware, perhaps, of the controversy, but after the first day or two, finding that their experience on the site hadn't changed one bit, not giving it another thought.

In the office, the mood was a little more perturbed. The number of people working for Fishbowl was much larger than the number when Farming 1.0 had been launched four years previously, and few had been through anything like this before. There was a small number of resignations. On the site, user numbers and visits did drop slightly. Mike Sweetman, now running a much-reduced Homeplace that had been gutted by Fishbowl, promised never to introduce such a program.

Chris laughed when he heard of the pledge. 'Like anyone cares.'

There were denial-of-service attacks and a rise in the frequency of hacking attempts but, after the experience with Farming 1.0, the infrastructure guys had been working for months to get ready for them. There were speeches from politicians and outrage from across the political spectrum. And then the storm began to abate.

Unable to provoke a reaction from Andrei, with the website not imploding, as so many pundits had predicted it would, interest began to wane. Just as the storm had spread from the Grotto to the blogosphere to the mainstream, now it reversed direction, contracting from the television studios and newspaper websites to the blogs to the Grotto, where the last band of hardcore zealots, like the original 300 in the film that Andrei had used to watch, fought a shrill and increasingly hopeless battle.

In Andrei's opinion, the 300 were self-important, self-appointed guardians who had come to a party to which no one had invited them. When once he would have listened to them, and tried to mollify them, now he had no patience for them. 'Leave if you want to leave,' he wrote in a terse post in the Grotto. 'No one's making you stay.'

The hurricane blew itself out, but Fishbowl wasn't quite the same afterwards. Internally, externally, everyone knew that it had morphed into something different. It was impossible to ignore its sheer size and the power it now wielded, and the fact that this power was being put to use in such a commercial way.

Over time, there were more resignations from among the core of old-time Fishbowl staff people who had joined when Deep Connectedness had been the sole manifest vision of the company, advertising had been a necessary evil, and not even FishFarm 1.0, let alone FishFarm 2.0, had been a glimmer in Andrei's eye. They took their stock options and left. In their place came executives who joined in the full knowledge of the goals that Fishbowl had set itself and the kind of revenue-generating machine that Jenn McGrealy had constructed.

But Andrei himself wasn't really aware of this. As Fishbowl had grown, he had become distant from his staff. The company now employed over 4,000 people and had offices in New York, London, Mumbai, Beijing, Sao Paolo and outposts in another dozen cities. While Andrei was still involved in the major hiring decisions, he had no real involvement or input into the process below the top level. Jenn McGrealy was an extraordinary operating executive and had learned to manage in a way that left Andrei free to spend his time in the areas that most interested him – which overwhelmingly was Los Alamos. His office was on the sixth floor and half of his time or even more was spent with the teams as they grappled with the enormous challenges that confronted them in developing the FishFarm 3.0 that he envisaged. He would emerge from the sixth floor to give interviews or appear at conferences, where he spoke passionately about the ideal of Deep Connectedness and was frustrated by the cynical questions he always seemed to get about profits, control, monopolization and, of course, the integrity of a site that quite unashamedly operated palotls. But then he would ask, by way of response, whether the questioner was a Fishbowl user, and the answer was always yes.

All people could think about, it seemed, was money. And yet, Andrei told himself, that was the least important thing to him. He didn't understand how they just couldn't see that he was changing the world.

But he was wrong. Some people could.

37

FARMING 2.0 WAS the second time Fishbowl had left the FBI red-faced. Andrew Buckett's ravings on the site prior to the Denver bombing, while not involving any actual planning of the attack, had highlighted the Bureau's failure to identify the threat posed by him and Hodgkin before they could act. This time, while less public, the effect of what Fishbowl had done on the Bureau's reputation inside the Beltway was potentially far more damaging. Despite having had Fishbowl on its watch list since the day Farming 1.0 had become known, the Cyber Division of the Bureau had failed utterly to realize or even suspect that Farming 2.0 was under development. Like the rest of the world, they only found out when rumours began to spread. But, once the cat was out of the bag, they knew they were dealing with something momentous.

Ed Garcia, a 34-year-old graduate of Duke University's Computer Science programme who had joined the Cyber Division seven years previously, was the agent with the deepest knowledge of Fishbowl. He immediately recognized the quantum leap in capability that had taken place if the rumours were true. He scanned the Grotto, got hold of the Spot the Bot app, spent some time on the network, and was soon convinced that some kind of artificial intelligence program was at work. He wrote a report that went via his boss to James Monk, the head of the Cyber Division. In it, Garcia didn't pull his punches about what he considered to be the full range of uses for such a program.

Monk reflected on the report for a couple of weeks, wondering if its conclusions were exaggerated. He got another couple of agents in the division to validate it independently. By then, Andrei had posted his enigmatic statement in the Grotto that more or less confirmed that the rumours were on to something. The agents reported back to Monk that Garcia's conclusions, if anything, were conservative. The report went to the FBI director, and from him to the Department of Justice, where its conclusions were read by the attorney general. The attorney general had the legal issues investigated by the Office of Legal Counsel.

Six weeks after the furore erupted, when the first blizzard of public outrage was dying down and Andrei Koss and the Fishbowl team were imagining that the worst was past, Ed Garcia found himself with James Monk, the FBI Director and the attorney general in the Oval Office, meeting the president and his national security advisor.

The president listened as Monk outlined the issue. The frown on his face, which was familiar to the more senior people in the room, suggested that he was having a little difficulty grasping the nature of the computer program that they were talking about. One after another, the national security advisor, the attorney general and the FBI director chipped in.

'You!' said the president, cutting across them and pointing at Ed Garcia. 'Tell me what this is about.'

Garcia froze.

'I thought you're the expert,' said the president irascibly. He had a cold that he had picked up on a G20 visit to Berlin, where he had been forced to spend a dinner sitting beside the German Chancellor, who had spent the whole evening sneezing into a disgustingly moist handkerchief. The president's fuse, always short, was already smouldering. 'What's he doing here, Frank?' he demanded of the FBI director. 'Didn't you say he was the expert?'

Garcia coughed. 'Simply put, sir ...'

'Yes, put it simply,' said the president sharply. 'And remember, when I went to school, we used things called pens and paper.'

'Well, simply put, sir, it's a program that talks to you like it's a person.'

The president stared, his look of incomprehension turning to one of incredulity.

'It can talk to millions and millions of people at once. Potentially, if they've built it right, it can make itself look different to different people, working out what kind of apparent person is most likely to gain an individual's trust. It's intelligent – what I mean by that is it can learn and evolve. From what you say, it can identify what you're interested in, what's bugging you, and it can respond to that in a way that will draw you in. You'll think you're talking to a person. But you're not. You're talking to a program that can figure out just which of your buttons to push to make you its friend.'

'And it's used to sell stuff? Is that it?'

'That's the obvious use, Mr President. You could set it up so it's looking for people who would be interested in a particular product and to find opportunities to recommend it. That's not our worry. What we're concerned about is that, in theory, if it can promote a product, it can promote anything – an opinion, an idea, an ideology. It could be used to radicalize people. It could be used to sway public opinion about an issue. It could be used to have an effect on an election.'

'Ah …' The president got it now. He had no idea how such a thing could work, but he understood the implications.

'That's if it exists.'

He looked back at Garcia. 'We don't know if it exists?'

'The CEO of Fishbowl has more or less admitted it, but not explicitly, and the company hasn't released any details about it. There are definitely patterns of chat on Fishbowl that are highly suggestive that something like this is in operation.'

'On the other hand,' said Monk, 'it's possible that he's consciously allowed the speculation to get ahead of the reality. Stoked it, if you will. The general expectation is that Fishbowl is getting ready for an IPO. If you want to boost your stock price before a possible IPO, you might lay down the tracks that you've made this kind of advance – and make no mistake, Mr President, it would be a groundbreaking advance – while preserving deniability for later.'

'Have we talked to this CEO to find out if it exists?' demanded the president.

'Not yet,' said the attorney general. 'We've been trying to determine first what the legal position is.'

'And what is the legal position, Sue? Surely something like this can't be legal? Even if they just use it to sell stuff, surely it can't be legal.'

'Actually, it is.'

'We can't stop it?'

'No, sir. Not under current law.'

'So someone can just go out there and sell something without saying who they are?'

'Our laws are generally about *what* you say – misrepresentation, fraud – and not who says it.'

'So they can do this without saying who they are?'

'Yes, sir. People do that all the time.'

'And the people who use this Fishbowl thing, they don't mind that?'

The attorney general looked at Garcia for an answer.

'Apparently not, sir.'

'Jesus Christ,' murmured the president. 'What kind of a world is this?'

No one chose to answer that question.

'What if they did try to use it for political purposes?' asked the president. 'That would have to be declared, right?'

'Only if it's being funded,' said the attorney general.

'So if this CEO decides he simply wants to put a message—?'

'Nothing to stop him doing that.'

'How many people does this thing talk to?'

'One point four billion,' said Garcia.

'Jesus *Christ!*' The president sat forward. 'Is there any evidence that the Democratic Party funded the development of this program?'

Garcia looked at him quizzically. 'No, sir.'

'Check that out, Frank.'

'As far as we understand,' said the FBI director, 'this was developed for commercial purposes—'

'Just check it out, Frank.'

'Mr President, we would also have to check out whether the Republican Party was involved.'

The president was silent for a moment. 'Better let me ... have some conversations.'

The FBI director nodded.

'Now, what if this thing fell into the wrong hands?' said the president. 'What if someone steals it? Could someone steal it?'

Everyone looked at Garcia.

'I don't think that's the issue,' said Garcia.

'Why not?'

'It's not a *thing*, Mr President. It's not like a gun you can walk in and steal. It's pages of code. Thousands and thousands and thousands of pages.'

'You seem to know an awful lot about something when you don't even know if it exists.'

'Well, it would be pages of code, sir.'

'What if you stole the computer it's on?'

'There's no—I mean, there wouldn't be any one computer it's on. It would be distributed and replicated across a bunch of computers that are linked together.'

'What if you took control of the place where they are?'

'They wouldn't be in one place. They'd be distributed. That's both for security and redundancy. There wouldn't be any one facility that, if someone took it over, they'd have control of this program.'

'What if someone ... hacks into it? Is that the term?'

'Well, I would imagine that would be very hard to do. I would imagine that Fishbowl, with the resources it has available, would have about the best security out there.'

'So does the Pentagon, theoretically,' muttered the president.

'And every schoolboy and his dog seems to be able to hack into there.'

'Potentially, in theory, yes, someone could hack into this program,' conceded Garcia.

'And?'

'They could mess with it, but probably only for a short period of time until the intrusion was discovered. What I mean is, they could probably disrupt it, but they couldn't take control of it. It would be very doubtful they could do that, certainly not in a way that wouldn't be immediately discovered.'

'Well, if it can be disrupted, that sounds like that's something we should make sure we're able to do.'

Garcia and Monk glanced at each other.

'So what you're saying,' said the national security advisor, 'is that you can't steal it, and you can't hack it so that you can control it ...'

'But you could sell it,' said the FBI director. 'Or license it. To an Islamist group, for an example.'

'Jesus Christ, this thing's a fucking nightmare!' The president yanked a handful of tissues out of the box on the coffee table in front of him and blew his nose angrily, then dropped the used wad on the rug at his feet. 'Can we restrict that? Can we restrict their ability to license it?'

'If Fishbowl wants to license it to a foreign entity,' said the attorney general, 'then theoretically we could control it by making it subject to export control, but there are difficulties with that. Export controls are largely for defence-related items for military use, and this program hardly falls into that category. At a pinch, we could try to make an argument that it's dual use – meaning that it could have both civilian and military applications – but whether a court would agree with that is another question. I mean, if Al Qaida uses PowerPoint for their propaganda, do we ban Microsoft from exporting it?'

'What if they sell it to a US entity?' said the national security advisor.

'Our laws aren't supposed to restrain trade, they're supposed to encourage it. So long as we have no legal grounds against the program, we have no grounds to restrict its distribution.'

'So a foreign regime could set up a company here and buy this program and it wouldn't be subject to any kind of control.'

'It starts to get quite complicated. If the purpose was to circumvent an export control, and we could show that the US entity was actually controlled by a foreign party, then I think that they wouldn't be able to do that – provided of course, that we can get an export control in the first place. But what if nothing is actually exported? What if the third party uses the program residing on servers in the United States? Have they exported something or not? We'd work on the assumption that it's an export, but it's not clear what a judge would rule. The export control system was set up to deal with transfers of physical goods – missiles, rocket parts, nuclear fuels, nuclear blueprints – not for a program that might never actually leave US soil. It's grey. It's very grey. And in terms of selling it to any bona fide US organization, we have no ability to control that. The legal situation—'

'Hell, Sue,' said the president. 'Bottom line is, this thing's not illegal, right?'

'Not at present.' The attorney general shrugged. 'It's not clear how we could make it illegal. Anything that applies to Fishbowl has to apply to everyone. It's not clear what that legislation would have to look like without making illegal just about every sales and advertising operation in the country. And that's before a first amendment challenge, which would certainly follow.'

'So it's not illegal. OK. Let's put that aside.'

'We're still looking at it but, for the moment, yeah, let's assume it's not.'

'So tell me, if a political party here in the United States, for example, wanted to use this program in an election campaign, then this company would be free to license it and there would be nothing we could do until such time as they actually used it.'

'I'm not sure there'd be anything we could do even if they did use it. Not unless it was used to say something defamatory or fraudulent.'

'They'd be seeking to influence an election.'

'Everyone seeks to influence elections, Mr President. If they declare, for instance, that they're from the Democratic Party, I don't see that it would make a difference if it's a program using a palotl – that's the name for the virtual personalities they create – or if it's a real person. If you have an animated figure in an advertisement, you don't need to state that it isn't human.'

'People can see that it's not!'

'A blind person can't. There's no law that states that you have to say, "I'm from such and such a party, and I'm a real human being."' The attorney general smirked a little at what she had just said. She didn't know many politicians who would be able to pass that test.

The president saw the smirk. He grabbed another handful of tissues and testily blew his reddened nose. 'Setting elections aside, it sounds to me that if you guys are right, this program is the biggest propaganda or misinformation or whatever-you-want-to-call-it tool we've ever seen, and this company can use it pretty much to do what it likes or sell it to whoever it wants. Is that right? Is that what you've come here to tell me?'

'That's what we've come here to tell you,' said the attorney general.

'And you had no idea this was being developed?' demanded the president, turning to the FBI director.

The FBI director bit his lip.

'Shit, Frank! What the fuck are your guys doing over there? How long would it take to develop something like this?'

Garcia coughed. 'Years, I would imagine.'

The president shook his head in disgust and grabbed a fistful of tissues.

'So it seems like this thing comes down to what this company is going to do,' said the national security advisor. 'The CEO ...'

'Andrei Koss,' said the FBI director.

'What kind of guy is he? Is he a Democrat?' demanded the president.

'He's not politically affiliated, as far as we know.'.

'What *do* we know about him?' asked the national security advisor.

All eyes turned to the FBI director, then followed his gaze to Garcia.

The agent shrugged. 'Not a lot. He's a geek. He doesn't say a lot in public. When he does, he talks a lot about what he calls Deep Connectedness, which is what he says Fishbowl offers.'

'Sounds like the name of some kind of cult,' muttered the president.

'It's a fancy word for people being able to find others who share their interests anywhere in the world.'

'What does he believe in? What drives him?'

'Apart from that? Nothing that's obvious. Koss is evangelical about Deep Connectedness but that seems to be about it. We do have one other data point. After the Denver bombing, when his network seemed to be implicated, he cooperated fully with us. I mean, beyond what he had to do by law. He gave us whatever we wanted. And we didn't have to push him – he kind of volunteered it. Afterwards, we pushed him to cooperate on a more continuing, covert basis. I think the NSA did as well. He drew the line at that. But ... he doesn't strike you as the kind of guy who's out to bring down the state, as it were.'

'Is he the kind of guy who's out to earn as much money as he can?'

'It's hard to say. Not from his persona. He lives pretty under-stated in a condo. He's not into houses and cars.'

'Women?' said the national security advisor.

'If you're looking for leverage,' said Garcia, 'there's nothing we know about.'

'What about money?' said the president again. 'Is that his thing?'

'He's built a company that's worth a conservative fifty billion dollars, Mr President. Some analysts say that when they do their IPO, it could go as high as a hundred billion. And he's built that on the back of a very smart and very ruthless insinuation of advertising into the business, culminating in this latest thing, which is potentially more lucrative than anything the internet has seen before. And on the way he's more or less wiped out his biggest competitor, Homeplace, who, five years ago, you would have said could never have been beat. But then when he speaks, he says that he really doesn't care about the size of Fishbowl or its revenues and as far as he's concerned, the money it makes is just there to allow him to give his users the service they want.'

'And he owns how much of this company?' asked the national security advisor.

'Around a half.'

'So that makes him worth twenty-five billion to fifty billlion? And none of this is about money ...' The national security advisor glanced at the president, eyebrows raised.

'I'm not saying we believe him,' said Garcia. 'He's just been very good at developing this public persona of the guru of this Deep Connectedness thing, detached from commercial concerns, that sort of thing. To be honest, everyone thinks it's beginning to wear a little thin.'

'But he's not going to go out and put this thing at the disposal of Al Qaida?' said the Attorney General.

'No. I don't think he's going to do that.'

There was a knock at the door and the president's chief of staff came in. He glanced meaningfully at the president and then took a seat.

The president glanced around at the assembled officials. 'OK. So what do we do?'

'We talk to him,' said the national security advisor. 'If we can't dispossess him of this thing, then we try to make him an ally. Let's see if the security on this thing is tight. Let's see if he'll cooperate and make sure it isn't used for anything but commercial purposes.'

'And let's scare the shit out of him about what we might do if he puts a foot out of line,' said the president. 'Tell him we're going to be watching every damn thing he does. Tell him when he's on the can, Uncle Sam's going to be watching him wipe his ass. And if we don't like the way he does it, Uncle Sam's gonna come after him and wipe it for him. I'm serious. Make sure he understands he can do things the easy way, or we can make his life hell.'

'We'll talk to him,' said the attorney general.

'Tell him.'

'We'll say whatever we legally can, Mr President.'

'What else?' said the president. 'Sue, you're still checking the legal possibilities, right?'

The attorney general nodded. 'You know, this company has gone out and built this program – which seems to be a program of enormous power, an absolutely exceptional piece of software engineering – and, frankly, I've got to say, it's something the United States government should have done for itself. Someone was always going to do this. It should have been us, Mr President. Instead of spending whatever we spend on fighter planes and aircraft carriers that have no one to fight...' she glanced pointedly at the national security advisor '...because no one else's fighters and carriers are anywhere near as good as ours, we should have spent some money on this.'

'How much did it cost?'

'A few years back they went out for investment capital and took in around six hundred million,' said Garcia. 'I'm guessing that's what it was for.'

'Six hundred million,' said the attorney general. 'What is that? Nothing. Not even a speck in the defence budget. This is like ... it's like leaving a bunch of college kids to invent the atom bomb. It's absurd. The idea that—'

'It's done,' said the president impatiently. 'What's your point, Sue?'

'You ask what the government should do, Mr President? Simple. It should buy Fishbowl.'

The idea wasn't taken seriously. To the extent that he even considered it, the president had no intention of taking the political hit for spending up to $100 billion of US taxpayers' money to gain control of a program that had cost barely half of 1 per cent of that sum to develop.

Andrei Koss was invited to meet James Monks and the deputy attorney general. The Fishbowl legal team wasn't surprised by the request. While there was nothing illegal about FishFarm 2.0, they had warned Andrei that it might well garner attention from the Department of Justice, who would probably be interested in the rectitude of Fishbowl's commercial operations.

Andrei went with Jenn McGrealy and two of the Fishbowl lawyers. A good part of the conversation was devoted to questions about the nature of the program: what it was being used for, and its security arrangements, most of which Andrei was happy to answer. There were questions about himself, his political leanings, his personal beliefs, which the lawyers tried to intercept but which, again, he was prepared to answer. There were questions about whether he planned to license the program or even sell the company, the first of which he had no intention of doing and the second of which he had not even contemplated. Yet nothing was asked about the clients of Fishbowl that were using the program or the products being advertised or what was being said about them, which was what the lawyers had told him to expect and which they had decided that he would decline to answer. All in all, Andrei and everyone else on the Fishbowl side of the table found it a somewhat puzzling meeting. At certain moments they were aware of a sense of menace in the air, with opaque references to close scrutiny from the Department of Justice and undefined lines that couldn't be crossed.

As Andrei met the Department of Justice officials, debate about Fishbowl was dividing the security establishment. The

United States political process, even aspects of its national security, it seemed, were now potentially hostage to the whim of a 27-year-old Stanford dropout who found himself with virtually unlimited funds at his disposal, the seemingly most powerful propaganda tool the world had ever seen, and the free choice of how to deploy it. And there seemed to be no legal way to get it out of his hands. Some within the security establishment leaned towards a strategy of robust containment, leaving Koss free to deploy the program commercially but pressuring him to ensure that other uses would be neutral with regard to domestic politics and aligned with US government policy abroad. Others saw a policy of containment as a temporary fix at best and, at worst, one that would allow Koss the time to develop and refine the program so that it became even more dangerous. They were actively seeking a way to control it.

Diane McKenrick, six years on from Denver, was still a senator, was still chair of the Senate Homeland Security Committee, and was therefore fully aware of the debate.

38

AS THE FURORE over FishFarm 2.0 receded from the Fishbowl campus on University Avenue, the question of Fishbowl's IPO came surging back. For years Andrei had refused to answer publicly questions about his plans for an IPO. Internally, in the years when the palotl program was under development, he and Chris had consistently told Pete Muller and Robert Leib that they wanted to wait until further software development was complete. When that wore thin with the two board members, they had said they were waiting for the decimation of Homeplace to be complete, since that would add value to Fishbowl shares. But now, both within and outside Fishbowl, everyone assumed that Andrei had been waiting for the launch of the palotl program, and with that complete, the sale of Fishbowl stock through an IPO was only a matter of time.

Robert Leib, who knew as much as anyone about timing an IPO, argued that the time was ripe. Chris said that if Bob believed it was time to float, it probably was. Controversy over Farming 2.0 had died down, Leib pointed out, but it was still new enough to be exciting, and experienced analysts would realize that future revenue streams from the new program would be colossal. The buzz around it would lift the offering into the realm of an iconic, perhaps unprecedented internet float. The market for tech stocks, he also felt, was reaching one of its periodic peaks. If an IPO of the magnitude of Fishbowl's was going to achieve its full price, there had to be plenty of cash looking for an investment home. Time it wrong and that cash would be locked up elsewhere, with the result that the IPO would come in under-priced. The market was perfect, awash with cash. Wait another year or two and that might change.

Andrei respected Leib's sense for the market. But Bob Leib, after all, was an investor, with an interest in extracting the maximum return on his stake. Andrei had other considerations. He talked to another couple of tech CEOs he had got to know and they didn't dispute Leib's assessment, but they did advise Andrei to think carefully about whether he wanted to lead a public company. They had gone the IPO route and while they now each held shares worth $1 billion-plus, they emphasized the impact it would have on the way he ran Fishbowl. The company, and Andrei himself, would be under microscopic scrutiny day in, day out. And whereas now he could simply shrug his shoulders and ignore such scrutiny, he wouldn't have that luxury once Fishbowl was listed on an exchange. There would be a legal minimum of information that he would be obliged to provide and that minimum was a lot more than Fishbowl was accustomed to giving out. He would have legal duties towards his shareholders. If anyone told him it made no difference to be publicly listed, they said, they either had no experience of it or they had an agenda of their own.

Their words weighed heavily with Andrei, as heavily as Leib's recommendation in favour of an IPO. If Andrei did float the company, he would realize at least a billion of the value of his shares as a cash dividend on the day of the IPO, with many billions more in the value of the stock that he held. But he didn't need those billions of dollars. He still lived with Sandy in the condo off University and had only a couple more pieces of furniture than the day he'd moved in. The car he drove was five years old. Having that kind of money in the bank would just complicate his life. Neither did he need the thrill – or the burden, as he envisaged it – of turning up in richest-people-on-the-planet lists. What he did value was his freedom to run Fishbowl the way he chose, and steer it towards the vision he had for all of the things that it could do in the world – a vision that had expanded dramatically with the creation of the palotl program and the non-commercial uses to which it could be put once it was further developed.

He called Kevin and Ben to ask each of them what they thought. They both had large stakes in the business and, although they didn't have seats on the board, he thought they had a right to be heard. Even without the IPO, both of them had reaped rewards from Fishbowl ownership and were now wealthy men. Fishbowl was awash with cash and Andrei had arranged multi-million dividend payouts in the last couple of years, largely to ensure that they both had something to show for their early years at the company, since he himself had no need for the even bigger dividends that washed up in his bank account.

Kevin's own venture, which had morphed into a palotl-based social gaming application that ran on top of Fishbowl and other networks, was also starting to earn some revenue, although it was a long way short of profitability. He was the more enthusiastic about an IPO. He told Andrei that he agreed that the market was hot and said that Andrei should go ahead. Ben seemed unconcerned either way. He was getting towards the end of his PhD in psychotherapy and had started his clinical training, and spoke with detachment about Fishbowl. Listening to him, Andrei had a sudden, painful recollection of the night Ben had come over and told him he was leaving. Ben didn't give a direct answer about whether he thought Andrei should do the IPO. He seemed more interested in understanding what it meant to Andrei, whether he was ready for it, whether he was doing it for the right reasons.

The ongoing conversation about the IPO between Andrei, Chris and Bob Leib continued over the next few months. Every week or two Leib would produce some new snippet of market information that supported his contention that now was the time for the IPO, Andrei would hesitate, while Chris told him that they were already under the scrutiny of Wall Street and it wouldn't be so different anyway. Leib and Chris grew closer as they pushed for the IPO. To add to the financial rationale, Leib argued that Andrei had an obligation to go public, that this incredible thing that he had built had become established so deeply within the infrastructure of people's lives that they had a right to own a part of it, just like they had a right to own their own house.

Andrei looked at Leib sceptically when he heard that one. It was the first time he had seen this apparently sentimental, philosophical side to the venture capitalist, and reminded himself, as he found himself increasingly having to do, that LRB and its partners had a 6 per cent stake in Fishbowl and stood to make a return of 1,000 per cent from a successful float, not an insignificant portion of which would accrue to Robert Leib personally. Leib's wealth hadn't been accumulated through sentimentality. Besides, when the feeding frenzy of the float was over, the vast bulk of the stock, as Robert Leib knew better than anyone, would be in the hands of investment funds, institutions and wealthy individuals like Leib himself. At best, only a tiny portion of Fishbowl's users would own stock, and Andrei didn't think that would make any kind of a difference at all.

Perhaps Leib sensed Andrei's scepticism. 'Look,' he said the next time they spoke, 'there's also the question of what this means for you personally, Andrei. Being CEO of a publicly quoted corporation is not the same as being CEO of a private concern – especially if you're the CEO of one of the most valuable corporations in the world. There's a certain prestige that goes with that. A certain status. You're putting yourself forward for public scrutiny, that's true, but in return, that buys you a platform – the right to be listened to in a way that you'll never be listened to now. Andrei, you have a vision for the world. You should have that platform. Your vision deserves it.'

Sandy, now an anthropology fellow at Stanford, thought he should get on with it. At some point, she said, there was going to be an IPO. Everyone said the timing was good. May as well bite the bullet. She grew increasingly impatient as the issue dragged on and they had a number of terse conversations. In part, these were an outlet for other frustrations that she hadn't voiced.

Sandy had been with Andrei for eight years, since before he had founded Fishbowl. She had been living with him in the condo for almost half that time. There had been moments when she had been on the verge of walking out, and she didn't think that Andrei was even aware of it. Friends were asking why she put up with him – those who didn't ask assumed it was for his money. Sometimes, Sandy didn't know herself. Andrei had always kept her away from any limelight that Fishbowl might have thrown, which was OK with her, but she felt that she had put so much into supporting him as he built Fishbowl from the very beginning, and she didn't know if he recognized that. He took no real interest in what she was doing. He asked her about it, but a month later he'd ask her the same thing and she could see he had forgotten. Yet she knew that she would never meet anyone like Andrei again, and she understood why sometimes he was so preoccupied that he barely knew she was there. Perversely, that was part of his attraction. She thought that she did love him, but had begun to wonder if that love was actually a manifestation of some kind of Florence Nightingale complex that she had developed towards him. If they did stay together, she knew, she would always be the one putting in more. Sometimes she doubted he could survive without her. That probably wasn't a healthy thing in a relationship.

Yet she hadn't walked away. And it was eight years now. Eight years and not once had they talked about marriage.

In the meantime, since the markets were expecting the announcement of an IPO, the analysts beadily watching Fishbowl interpreted whatever they saw as preparation for it. Fishbowl had a war chest heaving with cash. Andrei acquired a crowdfunding site called Playstarter for half a billion dollars in cash and stock. Robert Leib regarded it as an overpayment, and even Chris was doubtful. Playstarter had never made a dime and it was unclear that it ever would. Andrei argued that crowdfunding – the practice of raising funds for new ventures by pre-selling product to willing purchasers – was a form of Deep Connectedness, and that FishFarm could radically improve the efficiency of the operation by bringing awareness of the offerings to millions more people than Playstarter had ever been able to.

He also went after a small competitor site called Finder, which had developed an interesting model of connectedness based on an innovative compatibility algorithm. Fishbowl tried to replicate the service and put Finder out of business, but the other site had developed a growing following that wouldn't budge. It was easier to buy them out. The founders were a pair of MIT students a couple of years younger than Andrei. Remembering his response to the $100 million offer Mike Sweetman had made him – not small enough to persuade him that Fishbowl had no future but not big enough to seduce him to sell – Andrei got on the phone and offered a billion dollars for their creation, arguing that they would never have the scale to be anything other than niche. They took the cash and the Finder network was merged into Fishbowl.

The market viewed both of these acquisitions as overpriced, but with everything being assessed through the prism of an upcoming IPO, they were generally viewed as housekeeping operations designed to strengthen Fishbowl's competitive position. It would have taken more than a couple of questionable acquisition prices to put a dampener on the Fishbowl story.

Yet Andrei still hadn't decided on the IPO, and the discussions within Fishbowl went on. He could have put an end to them if he had adamantly refused to consider the matter further, but Leib's argument about the platform for his vision that an IPO would give him was one that had stuck, and if he wanted that platform, he couldn't help wondering if Leib was right in saying that now was a moment in the market that might not return for another five years.

Chris was talking to investment banks. Andrei was aware of it but didn't know what Chris was saying to them. He only knew that he was constantly being asked to join meetings that Chris had set up with Goldman Sachs, J.P. Morgan, Morgan Stanley, Mann Lever, Merrill Lynch, Deutsche Bank ... The routine three guys in suits would turn up with bound copies of their pitch book outlining why they would do a better job of taking Fishbowl to the market than any of their competitors – who had already turned up, or were soon to turn up, with near identical pitch books in their hands. Chris started talking about J.P. Morgan as being the natural choice and Andrei got the feeling that he was continuing to meet with them and was becoming friendly with one of their executive directors, William Larkin, whom he referred to as Billy. He was always quoting Billy's views about the state of the market.

In the financial press, speculation over a Fishbowl IPO was constant. It had moved from speculation about whether the IPO would happen to talk about the likely level of the share price. The IPO was the only thing Andrei got asked about. He never gave a lot of interviews but now he stopped altogether.

Eventually, at a meeting of the board – which consisted only of Andrei, Chris and Bob – Leib told him that he had to decide. The speculation was starting to damage the company.

'How can it damage us?' replied Andrei irritably. 'It's got nothing to do with what we actually do.'

'If you let it go much longer,' said Leib, 'if and when you do decide to go to IPO, people will wonder whether there was a problem that made you uncertain. They'll wonder what's happened to that problem now. They'll think you're trying to do the IPO before everyone can see it.'

'I've already said a couple of times publicly that my only concern over an IPO is whether it will be good for the business and our users.'

Leib shrugged. 'That's what you say. Doesn't mean that's what they believe.'

'Well, that's only damaging if we eventually choose to IPO,' said Andrei pointedly.

'True. It also means that, right now, attention out there is being diverted from the business and all the great things you're doing to this question. That's not good for growth.'

'Growth in Fishbowl is viral,' said Andrei. 'It's always been viral. Doesn't matter what a bunch of puffed-up analysts say.'

Leib threw up his hands. 'You know what, Andrei? I don't care any more. I'm sick of arguing about it. I've told you a thousand times, I don't think the timing will be as good again for another five years. We've been talking about it so long I think now you've only got six months, twelve months tops, to get it done. After that, you never know what the appetite of the market will be. You might only get eighty per cent of what you'll get today.'

If it hadn't been for Leib's comment about an IPO giving his vision a platform, Andrei would have told him that he didn't care. Andrei didn't know if it was just another argument Leib was using to help unlock the fortune he had locked up in Fishbowl, but even if it was, he couldn't help feeling that Leib was probably right. If you really wanted to change the world, if you really wanted to be a player, at some point you had to step out of the shadows and present yourself publicly to the scrutiny of your critics and your peers. That would buy you a level of respect and credibility that you would just never have as the leader of a private company.

But wasn't Fishbowl changing the world anyway – not through what he said, but through what it did? And wasn't that more important than anything he could say? The financial side of the IPO didn't interest him at all. Did he really want to take on the responsibilities and scrutiny that came from leading a public company? It was the status, the platform, that resonated with him. But did he really need it to help make his vision of the world a reality?

As with so many of the big choices he had had to make recently, Andrei procrastinated. Decisions seemed to have been easier in the past, when the stakes had been so much lower. On this one, one set of arguments balanced the other, and he couldn't decide.

39

DIANE MCKENRICK HAD given up her presidential ambitions – or so she told herself. Despite the debacle over the Denver bombings, she had retained her Senate seat when the time had come to fight for it again five years later. But her best shot at the presidency, the natural point in the arc of her career, had been back then or during the electoral cycle that followed. However, with a Republican incumbent running for re-election at the following cycle and no appetite within the party for a challenge, she had sat that one out. The upcoming nomination would be wide open, but now she was too old – or so she told herself. The light burns hard in some people, and they don't understand it's all over until they're on their last flight home from Washington and have to face the fact that they don't have a return ticket. Sometimes a voice in her whispered that if she did win the presidency at the next election, she would still be only seventy-two when running for a second term. Ronald Reagan had been seventy-three.

Fishbowl. The name haunted her, the more so for its puerility, as if some little child from which she should easily have been able to defend herself kept poking her in the eye with a stick. She still didn't understand exactly how Andrei Koss and his minions had managed to trump her argument after Denver, when the dangers of unregulated social networking had been so clearly manifest. Who had had right on their side – she or the Denver murderers? Somehow the liberal-internet complex, as she called it, had managed to divert attention from that question to a bunch of civil liberty side issues that in her opinion didn't amount to squat in comparison with what the Denver bombers had done.

And now this. It was as if he was thumbing his nose at her, at the government, and the whole country. *Look at me! I'm Andrei Koss and I can do what I like and watch me make a hundred billion dollars into the bargain!*

As Chair of the Senate Committee on Homeland Security and Governmental Affairs, McKenrick had seen the FBI report that went to the attorney general. She listened to the debate that was rustling through the undergrowth of the security establishment: Containment vs Control. The Containers said that as long as nothing could be legally done about Fishbowl, as long as its program and its application violated no statutes, the best that could be done was to keep Koss in line with a combination of dialogue and threat, making it clear to him that the Department of Justice would come down on him like a ton of bricks if he made the wrong move. The Controllers said that waiting until he made the wrong move was waiting until it was too late, and something needed to be done now to make it impossible for him to make that move in the first place.

McKenrick tried hard to distinguish the resentment that still festered within her towards Fishbowl from her genuine security concerns about its latest program. Resentment, she knew, wasn't a sound basis for political action. Was this new program as dangerous as it seemed? If she understood it correctly, it gave enormous powers of influence to whoever controlled it. If it could sell products to people by making them think it was the guy next door, it could sell political ideologies as well. It could sell propaganda, misinformation, indoctrination. It could sell Denver-style terrorism, jihadist terrorism and any of the other terrorisms that haunted McKenrick's nightmares.

Or could it? The senator wasn't sure she did understand it properly, so she told her chief of staff to find someone who could explain to her what this thing was about. The chief of staff arranged for a briefing from James Monk, who confirmed her fears. He was squarely on the Control side of the debate, although he didn't know what action could be taken. But he was sure that something more was needed than to keep an eye on Andrei Koss and hope he acted like a good guy – which was, he thought, in light of the threat, not quite enough.

Diane McKenrick thought it wasn't enough either. Well, the Chair of the Senate Committee on Homeland Security and Governmental Affairs did have certain powers at her disposal. For a start, she could hold investigative hearings. She could get Andrei Koss and others like him and drag them into the light, put them on oath and force them to expose what they were doing to the whole world. And then ... McKenrick didn't know exactly how things would play out then, which was the problem. She didn't expect to uncover illegality, only irresponsibility. But somehow she felt that if people could see that irresponsibility – irresponsibility that verged on immorality – and if she could tie it to the obscene wealth that people like Koss seemed to be able to accumulate, it might generate a wave of revulsion that would rise and swell and drive away the smugness with which she imagined Andrei Koss went about his business in the world. He had marched against her for freedom, which apparently she had been attacking; well, now others could turn on him. No freedom without responsibility. That's what she would say.

Opinion amongst the other senators on the committee was divided. They straddled both sides of the Contain vs Control debate, but even those who were on McKenrick's side were wary of associating themselves too closely with her on this. Her last foray against her so-called liberal-internet complex had hardly been an unadulterated success, and they questioned the wisdom of helping her have a second tilt. They questioned her motives. Was it a quest for payback? Was it going to be more successful than last time? McKenrick had to work on them, all the time asking herself the same questions.

The president, with whom she discussed the matter, said that his hands were tied. There was very little he could do unless

Andrei Koss took a step that was either criminal or at the very least constituted a material threat to national security. He didn't oppose her plan to hold hearings into the matter, although he doubted they would accomplish a great deal.

That was the concern that kept niggling at her, preventing her from making up her mind. She was sure that to force Koss, under oath, to divulge what he had done would be a good thing. She was sure he would squirm and wriggle, and from her personal perspective that would give her a great deal of satisfaction. But if what he was doing was legal – and everyone said it was – she wasn't sure just how high, if at all, the wave of revulsion would rise. And if there was no wave of revulsion, the hearings would achieve very little.

She considered it at length with her most senior staffers. Best case, they thought, Koss would say something careless that showed up the danger of the power he had accumulated or which cast doubt on his fitness to hold it. He might say something that would enable her to draw connections to the Democratic Party or foreign governments or other shady entities. Any of this might be enough to turn the spotlight on the security threat that Fishbowl now posed and force Congress to take notice or possibly, in the very best case, set off the wave of public and legislative revulsion that would force Koss to withdraw the program altogether. And worst case? Worst case, Koss would hold up under questioning and the hearings would be a damp squib.

She didn't think that was such a bad downside compared to the upside, as long as they didn't build the hearings up too much, or set them up so anything short of an admission by Koss that he was an agent of the Chinese government would be seen as a failure. She wouldn't make the same mistake she had made last time. This time, she would start off low key, at least until Koss said something, and take it from there.

One of her staffers pointed out that Fishbowl was thought to be readying itself for an IPO and, in that context, being involved in a Senate hearing, even if it revealed nothing, could be damaging. The mere sight of Koss being sworn in before a Senate committee would make him look as if he had something to hide and might knock quite a few billion off the hundred billion the company was reputed to be worth. Other things aside, McKenrick liked the sound of that. While she had been careful to ensure that the motive for the hearings, if she chose to hold them, wasn't revenge, she couldn't deny that putting a spanner in Andrei Koss's works, even if she achieved nothing else, would give her a modicum of satisfaction.

She got support from Monk when she called him to ask if he thought that committee hearings might be useful. Bring it out in the open, he told her. Get the Bureau a mandate to do something.

But she would be the one taking the risk, wouldn't she? Not the FBI. How foolish would she look if the hearings yielded nothing? Even if she didn't build them up? The picture and the words on the front page of the *New York Times* the morning after the Denver marches still haunted her. Her Ceausescu moment. She was determined never to have another one of those.

But didn't she have a responsibility to do it? Set aside the personal aspect and the prospect of hitting Fishbowl just before its IPO. When McKenrick was honest with herself, she knew that very little that she had done in her eleven years on the Senate committee could really be said to have made a difference. Most of the committee's time was spent scrutinizing what other people were doing, and if the committee found mistakes, it was almost always after the damage was done and the intelligence chiefs had already acted. Here was a chance to do something active, to lead. The security chiefs were asking her do to it. She wanted to do it. For the sake of her country, didn't she *have* to do it?

But she might fail. Andrei Koss might manage to humiliate her again. Time and again she thought, why take the risk? Then a voice inside her would say: 'But you might succeed.' And then what? She couldn't help wondering. Was she really too old?

After all, Ronald Reagan had been seventy-three when he ran for his second term, and she would be only seventy-two ...

40

THE REPORT THAT broke the impasse inside Fishbowl made its first appearance on the *Wall Street Journal* website. It claimed that Wall Street sources had confirmed that Andrei Koss had finally decided on Fishbowl's IPO and had appointed J.P. Morgan to lead the offering. It also gave the date of the IPO as July 12, a little over four months away.

Within an hour of the report going up, it was all over the media. The Fishbowl press office was besieged with calls seeking confirmation.

Chris rang from LA. 'Is this true?' he asked.

'No,' said Andrei.

'What are you going to say?'

'I'm not sure.'

'We're going to have to say something.'

'I know,' said Andrei. 'For a start, I'm going to get Alan to call the *Journal* and complain.'

'If Alan calls, they're going to tell him it's true. If he says it's not, we're issuing a denial. Is that what you want to do?'

'Yes.'

'Andrei, think about it,' said Chris. 'If you deny it, forget the IPO, at least for the next year. You can't deny today and then turn around in a month and say we're going ahead. The market will see you as either indecisive or an outright liar. You don't want them seeing you as either when you're about to go to IPO.'

'We'll say it was speculation.'

'No, it's too specific. It's got the name of the bank, it's got the date of the launch. It's going to look like this was all set and now you've changed your mind. People are going to think something's wrong with the business. That something's happened and now you're reneging.'

'I'm calling Bob.'

'Call Bob. He'll say the same thing.'

Leib did.

The report put Andrei in a bind. He would have to come out and say what he actually intended to do.

Andrei told Alan Mendes, Fishbowl's head of communications, to hold off the press as best he could. That night, Sandy Gross told him to go for it, as she had been telling him for the past few months. She was actually glad it had happened. He had been bounced into it, but now he would be forced to make a decision. He should do it now or announce that Fishbowl was *never* going to do to an IPO and put the idea away for ever.

Once again, the seemingly unending IPO saga got Sandy thinking about her own situation with Andrei.

Andrei sat up virtually the whole night pondering the decision he had to make. Sandy's remark that he should be glad that someone had done it stuck with him. Someone *had* done it, and they must have known the effect their action was going to have. But, right then, the question of who that was was a distraction. He had to decide, one way or another.

There were no new arguments to consider. It was the same old set of pros and cons jostling in his mind.

Chris caught the six o'clock flight from LA the next morning and was in the office before Andrei. He started giving Andrei the usual arguments for doing the IPO. Andrei didn't want to hear them again. 'Let me know when Bob's here,' he said, and walked off to kill some time with the guys in Los Alamos.

Leib arrived and they got together in Andrei's office.

'Well?' said Leib.

Andrei was silent for a moment. He looked at each of the two men. 'All right, let's do it.'

Chris whooped, fist punching the air.

Andrei didn't crack a smile.

'It's a yes?' said Bob.

'It's a yes.'

Leib shook Andrei's hand. 'That's a good call, Andrei.'

Andrei shrugged. Then he glanced at Chris. 'I'm not doing it with J.P. Morgan.'

'Andrei,' said Chris, 'Billy's done a whole bunch of work on this and—'

'I don't like them.'

'He says that if we talk about licensing the palotl program to other websites for advertising, we'll add a fifty per cent premium to the value we achieve.'

'I don't want to talk about licensing it. I've told you before. Is that what you've been telling them? That we're going to license it?'

'Andrei, they're good to go.'

'Is that what you told them? Is it?'

'It's an IPO, Andrei! They're doing what any banker does. They're looking for the angles.'

'I said I don't like them.'

'You hardly know them.'

Andrei didn't respond to that. For some reason, he didn't want to give Chris the satisfaction of using J.P. Morgan.

'Andrei, listen—'

'OK, Andrei,' said Leib. 'It doesn't need to be J.P. Morgan. Who do you want to go with?'

'I'm not sure. Let's get them back in.'

'Then at least let J.P. Morgan pitch again,' said Chris.

'I'm done with them. OK, Chris?'

'How am I going to tell Billy?'

'I couldn't care less. As I said, I'm done with them. I don't even want them in the syndicate. Now let's get Alan in here so we can draft a statement and get it out.' Andrei glanced at his watch. 'I've got a meeting in Los Alamos. Get someone to come get me when there's a statement to look at.'

He headed out. Chris followed him.

'Andrei,' he said as they walked, 'what's this thing about not liking J.P. Morgan?'

'What do you care?' demanded Andrei.

'Billy Larkin's a good guy. He'll do a good job.'

'They're all the same, Chris.' Andrei stopped. He faced Chris directly. 'Let me ask you something. Did you leak that report in the *Journal*?'

'No.'

'Did your friend Billy leak it?'

'Why would he do that?'

Andrei watched him. He was sure that Chris was lying to him. He was sure that Chris or Billy or someone connected to him had leaked the item to force the issue.

'I swear to you,' said Chris, 'if someone leaked this, I know nothing about it. And if it was Billy or one of his guys, then absolutely you couldn't trust them with handling the IPO. But let's at least let them—'

'Forget it,' said Andrei. He looked around. They were standing near a gaggle of desks, thrown together without any obvious pattern of arrangement – as was the Fishbowl way – and the programmers who occupied the desks were watching them. He turned back to Chris. 'Billy's out. J.P. Morgan's out. OK? I'm not talking to them. Get on the phone and tell him.'

'What will I say is the reason?'

Andrei shrugged. 'Say what you like.' It gave him a perverse pleasure to imagine Chris having to hold that conversation. 'I'm going to be in Los Alamos. Tell Jenn what's going on and get someone to find me when the statement's ready.'

That afternoon, Fishbowl issued a statement repudiating the *Journal*'s report and saying that while the IPO was going ahead within the next four to five months, it had not yet set a date and was in the process of nominating its bank.

Two weeks later, after a beauty parade of hopeful firms, Fishbowl announced that it had appointed Mann Lever to lead the issue. The next day, Senator McKenrick announced that the Committee on Homeland Security and Governmental Affairs would be holding a series of hearings to investigate the risks to national security posed by programs creating human impersonations, otherwise known as palotls.

41

IT WAS CLEAR who McKenrick's Senate hearings were aimed at. The only palotl program operating anywhere in the world, as far as anyone was aware, was Fishbowl's. An hour after the announcement, Leib and Andrei were on a video call to New York with Didier Broule, the senior Mann Lever banker on the IPO who had been appointed only twenty-four hours previously.

The IPO date, not yet revealed, was widely expected to be by the end of July. Andrei's immediate reaction was to announce that they were delaying the setting of the date until the hearings were done.

Broule was opposed to the idea. 'If we delay, Andrei, it looks like we have something to fear. It looks like we feel that our IPO is dependent on whether this Senate committee gives some kind of green light. If you do anything to give the market the feeling there's political risk in this business, you can halve your valuation.' He snapped his fingers. 'We need to be firm and say, no, we're going to the market.'

'Surely the market's going to feel there's political risk from the fact the Senate's holding hearings.'

'Not necessarily. These hearing are set for ... when is it?'

'Week of May eighteen,' said one of the junior bankers on the call with Broule.

'If the hearings weren't going to conclude until after the IPO, then I think we'd have to say, yes, we push it back. We're planning on the twenty-first of July, right? By the time these hearings are over, we'll still have time to do our roadshow and get the buzz going. It's the last two weeks that are golden. Sure, in the meantime, the market will be looking at the hearings, but you'll make our job a lot harder, Andrei, if you say we're not going to do anything until the Senate is done. It will sound as if you don't know yourself whether you're a risk to national security and you're waiting to be told. And that's an impression that will stick. Even if the Senate committee says actually there's no issue here at all – which is what we would all expect them to say – investors are always going to associate you with a certain degree of political risk. Andrei, my job is advise you how best to get the highest valuation for your business consistent with a sustainable share price. Your best course here is to go ahead strongly and by doing that separate yourself from the political situation.'

'What if the committee does come up with something that prejudices the IPO?'

'Well, if it comes up with something, we can always pull it. We don't have to go ahead. You can pull an IPO the day before if you have to – and if you have to, you have to, although it's not something I'd recommend. What's important now is not to prejudge that, not to make ourselves a hostage to fortune. We should go ahead with our heads held high.'

Andrei was silent, conscious that Mann Lever had $120 million of fees at stake in the Fishbowl IPO, and that the banker on the screen in New York probably stood to take away a not inconsiderable proportion of that sum as a personal bonus. There was no way he was going to give advice that would put that IPO in danger.

Andrei was right. Broule knew, as did every banker on Wall Street, that Andrei had procrastinated for months over agreeing to the IPO in the first place. At this point, a delay that might turn into a rethink that might turn into decision to forget about the IPO altogether was the last thing he would suggest.

Leib pressed the mute button on the computer. 'I agree, Andrei. Let them hold their hearings. We'll cooperate in any way we can. But we're loud and proud and we know our business is totally above board and we're going to do this IPO. That's how we should approach this.'

'Guys?' said Broule from New York, 'I can see you but I can't hear what you're saying. Have we lost sound or are you muting?'

Leib hit the button. 'We were muting, Didier. Just wanted to think about what you said.'

'That's fine, guys. Just checking. Take your time. Mute again if you want.'

Leib glanced questioningly at Andrei, who shook his head.

'No, we're OK,' said Leib.

'Andrei,' said Broule, 'what are your thoughts?'

Andrei's thoughts were that he wished he had never agreed to the IPO in the first place. But pulling the plug on it was a big step, and in a way Senator McKenrick's announcement made it even harder for him to do it. He couldn't help but recognize the truth in what Broule and Leib were saying, even if both of them did have a degree of self-interest at heart. There would always be an association of some kind of national security problem with Fishbowl if he backed down. And the ramifications of that for Fishbowl and his vision of what it could achieve were difficult to estimate.

'I'm going to think about it,' said Andrei.

'OK, but in the meantime we'll keep going like we planned. The timelines are tight enough.'

'That's good, Didier,' said Bob Leib. He glanced at Andrei. 'They should keep going.'

'Gentlemen, there's another way of looking at this,' said Didier. 'This could be quite positive. These hearings are focused around your palotl program, which we all know is the thing that is really unique and revolutionary about Fishbowl. It's unparalleled. When we start going out to talk to investors, that's what we need to get across to them. The unparalleled revenue capability that this gives you. Now, what's going to be happening is that just before we do that, we'll have had a Senate committee sitting there day after day sending that message across. That this is a powerful, important, revolutionary program. Does a Senate committee do that if the thing they're investigating isn't pretty important? No. So effectively, we've got a third party – the US Senate, no less – saying this is an enormously powerful program. Kind of helps make our point for us, doesn't it?'

'But they're saying it's a threat to national security,' said Andrei.

'But we all know that's not true. We all know it's a program with huge commercial application and this threat to national security business is just some senator with a pretty hostile track record trying to big herself up for a hopeless run at the next election. That's a line I'm very comfortable with. That's a line our media guys will be taking when the moment's right, and which we can put out to investors. Given Senator McKenrick's track record, I think we'll get a pretty good hearing. As for the power and potential of this program, the senator's helping us make our case.'

Leib glanced at Andrei. 'What do you think?'

Andrei shrugged. It made a kind of sense. But so, he suspected, would the opposite argument.

'Let's just hope they call you to testify.' Broule laughed. 'I guess they'll have to. How can you investigate something without talking to the person who has the only living, working example of it on earth?'

Andrei stared at the banker's face on the screen. He *hoped* they'd call him?

'You think that's going to help?' said Leib.

'Absolutely. A lot's going to depend on you, Andrei. You'll need to give a strong, confident, robust performance at the committee. You'll need to be charming, natural, likeable.'

Andrei felt ill.

'We'll strategize this. We'll get you the best coaching we can get. That's what we're here for. I'm not talking about some washed-up reporter trying to make a few bucks in his spare time. This is why you hired Mann Lever, Andrei. I can get you a dozen ex-senators to put you through the exact experience of what a

Senate committee hearing is. There won't be a single question McKenrick's committee asks you that you won't have answered before.' Didier paused. 'When it comes down to it, this is how it's going to play out. You're the man with the program. You know it like nobody else knows it. You know what it can do, you know what it can't do. You control it. Which means this so-called threat to national security … Andrei, in the end, it's you. Show us that you're not a threat – and the threat's not there. All that's there is one very smart, very likeable guy and the enormous commercial power of what you've created. The American dream, in short. All that's left of these hearings is a witch-hunt by some bitter, technophobic, has-been old senator against the embodiment of that dream. Now, if we succeed in putting it across like that – and remember, we'll be working the press around this – then in the court of public opinion, who wins?'

Robert Leib nodded. 'Didier's right.'

'Of course I'm right,' said the banker. 'And that's why I'm going to get you a market capitalization of a hundred and twenty billion dollars in four months' time, Senator McKenrick or no Senator McKenrick. You know what? She's not an obstacle – she's a godsend. We just need to make sure your performance when you go in front of that committee is pitch perfect.'

42

ANDREI WOKE EARLY on the morning of the hearing. He had breakfast sent up to his hotel room. As he ate, he studied the text of the oral statement that he was going to make. It was the final text that had been approved by his legal team but he made a couple of slight changes nonetheless.

His parents had come from Boston to Washington to see him the previous night, and they had had dinner together. He wished his father had some advice to help him out, but there weren't too many lessons from Moscow in the nineties that were going to be of much use in front of a US Senate committee.

Now he was too nervous to want the breakfast, but ate anyway. He had been told by his lawyer to make sure to get something into him because it might be a long morning.

At around eight, one of the Fishbowl legal people who had travelled to Washington with him called to see if he wanted to go over anything. Andrei said he was fine. He spent some time doing emails and then went to have a shower and get ready. Someone had organized a suit for him and it was hanging in the wardrobe, ready for him to put on. The tie proved a little harder and in the end he gave up.

He read over the statement again. A couple of words still worried him and he tried out alternatives but couldn't find anything that was better. He scrolled the list that he had been given of the committee members. The bankers had pulled together background on each of the senators, although Andrei found it hard to remember who was who. He had some kind of mental block about it. For days he had kept telling himself there'd be time to get it straight but now there was no more time and he still hadn't got it.

He watched the time move towards 9.15. When it got there, he stood up and went to the door. Suddenly he felt nauseous and clammy. He stopped for a moment, leaning against the wall, and took a deep breath. Then he opened the door and caught the elevator down to the ground floor, where a car was waiting for him.

The lawyer who would be with him in front of the committee joined him for the ride, together with Alan Mendes. While Mendes put his tie on for him, the lawyer ran over the procedure one more time. There would be TV cameras in the room. Committee hearings were often half-empty but he was the star witness and it was likely that all the members of the committee would be there, hoping to score whatever point they wanted to score. He would be sworn in and then would be invited to read his statement. After that he would face questions. There was no limit to the time he could be in front of the committee, although it was unlikely to be more than a couple of hours. Finally the chairman would thank him and he would be excused.

In answering questions, he should be polite, to the point and at all times calm. It was likely that hostile senators would seek to provoke him. He also should try not to appear vexatious or get into a confrontational exchange. If a senator insisted on a view contrary to the one he had presented then he shouldn't be argumentative. If he felt it was absolutely necessary to resist, he should push back moderately and only once, but finally desist by saying, 'That's your opinion, Senator.' Not that that was guaranteed to bring a line of questioning to an end: the senator might easily riposte with something like, 'So you're saying it's not your opinion?' and try to provoke a bite-back. Again, if absolutely necessary, he should also refuse to answer a question, although he could expect a vigorous response if he did that. The lawyer would be with him to give advice. He had to remember that every senator dreamed of producing a soundbite that would have him or her on the evening news.

The car pulled up. Andrei saw the dome of the Capitol rising into a muggy May morning. He and his entourage were guided by a Senate staffer to a small room adjacent to the committee hearing chamber.

He waited until he was called in.

'Raise your right hand, Mr Koss.'

Andrei raised it.

'Do you swear that you will tell the truth, the whole truth and nothing but the truth?'

'I do.'

'Please be seated.'

Andrei sat. Arrayed across the raised bench in front of him was the full committee complement of sixteen US senators. Behind him was a seating area packed with journalists and spectators.

'Mr Koss,' said Senator McKenrick. 'Would you care to address the Committee?'

Andrei cleared his throat. 'Yes, Senator.'

'Go ahead.'

Andrei took the folded pages of his statement out of his suit pocket.

'I founded Fishbowl along with two Stanford roommates of mine, Kevin Embley and Ben Marks, seven and a half years ago,' he began, sticking strictly to the text. He spoke about the vision behind Fishbowl, its early days, its growth, its evolution. He explained his idea of Deep Connectedness and the part it could play in bringing the world closer together, making it more convergent, exposing the superficiality of differences and the depth of commonalities. He described his role as seeking to understand what forms of Deep Connectedness his users wanted and meeting those needs in the most efficient way. He talked about Fishbowl's employees, their skills, their involvement in their local communities through company-sponsored programmes, their commitment to

Deep Connectedness. Altogether he spoke for nine minutes, and in those nine minutes he gave as clear and succinct an account of the vision and aspiration of Fishbowl as he had ever given before.

Then the questions started.

The first to speak was a Republican senator from New Mexico, Mario Sim, who Andrei seemed to remember from his briefing notes as having been described as a hawk.

'You've given us a very complete account of your company, Mr Koss,' Sim began. 'And yet I believe you have omitted something. Something that I believe you call "Farming". Something for which I believe you have developed a program.'

'I believe you're referring to what we call the intelligent adaption program, or IAP,' replied Andrei. 'I did discuss this in my written submission.'

'But not in the oral presentation you just gave us.'

'I'm very happy to, sir.'

'Well, that's kind of you, Mr Koss,' said Sim. 'Tell me how this IAP of yours works.'

Andrei had practised this. 'The IAP is a program that aims to bring factual information to the attention of our users through a person-friendly interface.'

'This is what you call a palotl?'

'We use that term to describe what appears to the user. Obviously, there's a considerable body of programming that sits behind that.'

'Could you explain more to us about that?'

'Certainly.'

Andrei spoke for a few minutes about the program, giving a broad overview of its functionality and the diversity of its potential applications, trying to hold himself back from getting too technical. The bankers had told him that the senators would interpret that as an attempt to evade the point.

'So what this all really means, Mr Koss,' said Sim, when he had finished, 'is that you make people think they're talking to a real person when they're talking to a program that's selling a product.'

'That's not how I see it, sir,' said Andrei, carefully trying to avoid antagonizing the senator.

'How do you see it, Mr Koss?'

'The IAP is artificially intelligent, which means it learns as it goes. Just like a person who gets to know you, if it's engaged in a dialogue with you, over time it learns about you and it learns how to understand your needs and be more effective in communicating with you.'

'Which makes it more effective at selling stuff.'

'Which makes it more effective at doing anything it's doing. It's not about selling—'

'It's not about selling? Excuse me for interrupting, but are you saying it's not being to used to sell anything?'

'No, it is, but—'

'So, to put it plainly, the idea is it learns about you and gets more effective at selling you stuff.'

'What it does is learn to know what you need and when you need it,' said Andrei, 'which, if you want to talk about selling, I see as a lot more helpful than some kind of advertising where you might end up with impulse buys that you're never going to use. I see it less as selling or advertising, Senator, and more of a service.'

'A service?'

'Yes, sir. A service that tells you about stuff only when you really need to know about it and only when it's relevant to you. Because the program knows that. It makes it much, much more efficient, and makes it much less likely you're going to spend your money on something you don't really want.'

The senator stared for a moment. 'I just wonder, Mr Koss, whether you really believe what you're saying? Whether you really have managed to persuade yourself that what you just said is true?'

Andrei stared back at him.

'Because if you have, then, if you'll excuse me for saying so, that's a very idealistic view of what you're running. Delusionally idealistic, Mr Koss. I doubt very much the people who are paying to use your program would see it like that. I doubt they would say this is a way to cut out impulse buys of their products.'

'You would have to ask them, sir.'

'Tell me, Mr Koss, does this IAP of yours identify itself as a program?'

'No, Senator. That would defeat the purpose.'

'That would defeat the purpose,' repeated Sim slowly. 'The purpose being to deceive people into thinking they're talking to another person.'

'The purpose being to provide a friendly, human-type inter-face for whatever interaction is happening.'

'Do people realize they're talking to a program?'

'Most of them do not.'

'Most of them do not,' repeated the senator, letting the words linger in the air. 'What if they do realize?'

'Our research shows that most people continue to have a dialogue with it.'

'I find that hard to believe.'

Andrei shrugged. 'That's what we find, Senator. At Fishbowl, we look at the numbers, sir. What our users do, how often they do it, anything that helps us understand how we can serve them better. Numbers don't lie. People begin to treat it like they would treat anyone else on the network.'

'So you're saying this program becomes a kind of a friend?'

'It depends how you define "friend". What it does is it connects with people. I make no assumption about whether people want to connect with a program or not. If they do, why shouldn't they? Fishbowl is about Deep Connectedness, Senator, in all its many forms. I believe with the IAP we have helped develop a new form.'

There was silence for a moment. Then the senator shook his head theatrically and heaved a deep sigh. 'Mr Koss, I don't know what's worse. Selling by deception or making people think they've got a friend when it's just a collection of wires.'

Andrei hesitated, wondering if the senator really didn't get it. 'The intelligent adaption program is a lot more than a collection of wires, Senator. The people who developed it are probably one of the world's greatest collections of intellectual talent in their chosen fields ever brought together in one place.'

'Mr Koss, I cannot tell you how sad that makes me feel. That such a collection of talent should have been brought together, as you say...' he paused, with a sneer '... for this. To sell stuff through such deception.'

'But this isn't just about selling stuff. What I was trying to say before is the IAP has all kinds of other applications. Medical, educational, all kinds of remote services.'

'Have you implemented any of these services?'

'We're working on further improvements that are necessary for these applications.'

'Really?' asked Sim disbelievingly.

'Yes.'

'Yet you manage to have implemented the program for selling purposes without them.'

'The required functionalities are different. The other services need better audio and visual functionality.'

'Mr Koss, I understand you're in the process of an IPO. Surely if you plan to launch a new range of services with your Farming program, your investors will want to know about that.'

'The prospectus covers everything we're planning to do, Senator.'

'This prospectus, Mr Koss?' The senator held up a brick of a document, a copy of the Fishbowl IPO prospectus that had been released a fortnight previously, in keeping with the bankers' schedule for a July 21 IPO. Then he slapped it down with a resounding thud, for effect. 'I find very little in here on those functions you just described.'

'If you turn to page eighty-seven, Senator, I believe you'll find them.'

Sim turned the pages. 'Oh, yes, I find a short paragraph saying that certain services of the company may in the future be deployed in telemedicine, education, legal advisory and other

such fields. *May* be deployed. One paragraph in …' – he checked
the end of the document – 'three hundred and twelve pages. I
find an awful lot more than that on the revenues from advertising. Would you say that's a fair summary?'

'Quantitatively, probably.'

'Well, I thought you look at the numbers, Mr Koss,' said the
senator sarcastically. 'I thought you said that numbers don't lie.'

Andrei took a breath. 'Senator, the IAP is an enormous
advance. I can say that because I didn't develop it. I watched it,
and it was extraordinary to see. It was an honour to bring the
team together, an amazing team of linguists and artificial intelligence experts and brilliant programmers, many of whom are
still with us and continue to develop the program today. In the
future, others will take that knowledge and they'll develop it
further. The techniques and technologies we have developed will
spread. Many of the individuals who worked with us have already
moved to other labs. As Newton said, each of us stands on the
shoulders of giants.'

'Are you saying you're a giant that others will stand on?'

'No, sir. I meant—'

'Are you comparing yourself to Newton?'

'No, sir.'

'Are you comparing your program to gravity?'

'No, sir. Newton didn't develop gravity, as we have developed
a program. He perceived and codified its laws.' Andrei paused.
That didn't sound right. It was as if he was saying that his
achievement was more original that Newton's. He tried to correct
the impression. 'Newton developed differential calculus. Nothing
I have ever done would have been possible without that.'

Senator Sim stared at him, then shook his head again. 'All this
talk of giants, Mr Koss. All this talk of world-shaking advances.
But all it really comes down to is a way of selling stuff. Selling
stuff to people who don't even know who's talking to them. I
don't know how that makes you feel. If it was me, I'd feel sick
every time I looked in the mirror.'

Andrei bit his lip, remembering what he had been told. This was going to be an exercise in swallowing hard and turning the other cheek. He was also aware that the senator was creating the exact impression the bankers sought from this hearing. They had told him that his job was to create an image of Farming as a commercial program, both as a way of protecting himself from accusations over national security and as a way of getting investors interested in the IPO. The senator from New Mexico was doing a fine job of it.

Diane McKenrick was getting impatient for exactly the same reason. She wasn't interested in the commercial side. What committee did the senator think he was sitting on? Commerce?

'Anything further, Senator?' she asked pointedly.

'No,' said Sim.

'Senator O'Brien? I believe the floor is yours.'

O'Brien, a tall, gaunt Democrat from Rhode Island, launched right into it. 'How much money does Fishbowl make from advertising?'

McKenrick rolled her eyes.

'I believe all the relevant numbers are in the prospectus,' said Andrei, as he had been told to say in the coaching sessions he had received.

The senator, who also had a copy of the prospectus in front of him, ostentatiously turned the pages. Finally he stopped and jabbed his finger with a theatrical flourish. 'So that would be ... five point six billion dollars over the last year.'

'I believe that's our total revenue, Senator.'

'In your oral statement, Mr Koss, you said nothing about advertising.'

'Well, it's in the prospectus, as I said. Naturally, we do make some money from advertising, that's true.'

'Some money? Approximately how much of that five point six billion in total revenue is from advertising?'

'I believe all the relevant numbers are in the prospectus.'

'So that would be five point one billion?'

Andrei nodded.

'Let's call it an even five billion, Mr Koss. Would you be happy if we called it an even five?'

'If you want,' murmured Andrei guardedly.

'I wouldn't say five billion is "some money". I'd say it's a whole lot of money. How much more do you think you'll make once you license your IAP for other companies to use as an advertising vehicle?'

'I don't know, sir. I haven't done that calculation.'

'But it's in your prospectus, as you seem to like to say. It says that you may license it.'

Andrei nodded. It did say that in the prospectus. Everyone seemed to assume that the program would be licensed, even though he had never planned to do that. He hadn't wanted it mentioned in the prospectus, but the bankers had insisted it had to be listed because it was possible that Fishbowl would license it, and if the possibility was under discussion, it had to be included. It was only under discussion, Andrei had replied, because the bankers had insisted on discussing it. But the lawyers had said that unless he had decided irrevocably not to license it, now that it had been discussed, the bankers were right. If it wasn't mentioned, and he did license the program, Fishbowl would be open to litigation from anyone who could concoct some kind of grievance over it.

'You know what?' said O'Brien. 'It doesn't matter. Even if you don't license it, I'd say what you've got is a major advertising operation. Mr Koss, why don't you come right out and admit it? All this talk about Deep Connectedness ... No, sir – you're an advertising executive. You're probably just about the world's biggest advertising executive. Maybe you started off idealistically, really wanting to help people make connections, but at some point you've turned into a cold, hard-headed businessman, a businessmen who'll take this incredible collection of talent you've put together with the money you've got and turn them towards any commercial, profit-oriented activity you can find. That's your motto, isn't it? Isn't that what this Farming program of yours proves? You and your team—'

'I don't accept that.'

'Don't accept what?' retorted the senator, bristling with outrage.

'Anything you just said.'

'That you and your team will do anything to earn a buck? That you're a hard-headed businessman? That you're nothing but an advertising executive? What, Mr Koss? Which of those would you like to dispute?'

'All of them!' replied Andrei impulsively, forgetting everything he had been told in his coaching sessions and rising to the bait. Could the senator *really* not understand what he was trying to do with Fishbowl? Could no one see it but him? 'Advertising means nothing to me. It just—' He stopped as a ripple of laughter came from the audience behind him. He shook his head, reddening. 'Advertising just happens.'

'You're saying that five billion dollars of stuff just *happens*, Mr Koss?' said the senator.

'That's not what Fishbowl's about. Honestly, if I could do it without the money ...' There was more laughter. 'Look, Fishbowl is about Deep Connectedness, whether you think so or not. It's about finding people you never would have found, making those connections, cutting across barriers of geography and language and culture and class and any other barriers that come between the essential things that we share. That's a good thing, isn't it? The world needs that, and the more it has of it, the better. And with the IAP, we'll be able to do even more of that, in whole new ways. And that's not a commercial thing. It never was. It's about making the world more connected.'

'And earning five billion as you do it.'

'No!' Andrei paused, breathing heavily. 'That's just ...' He stopped in frustration. 'Look, it takes a lot of money to keep the infrastructure going and to reward the incredibly talented people who keep Fishbowl going. There's a cost to that.'

'Then presumably you made no profit on this five point six billion.' O'Brien made a show of turning the pages in the prospectus. 'No, actually, you did. Around three point eight billion. That's three point eight billion *more* than you needed to keep the infrastructure going, as you describe it, and to keep the incredibly talented people together.'

Andrei stared at the senator, who stared right back at him, the eyes in his gaunt face burning with a kind of fierce energy.

Suddenly Andrei felt as if the oxygen had been sucked out of the room. He couldn't get out of this. He knew he was being painted as a hypocrite and a liar, and searched frantically for a way to extricate himself, and he knew the only line he could take was the line the bankers had been pressing on him.

He hesitated, not wanting to have to say it.

'Fishbowl is a business,' he said at last, his voice muted.

'What was that, Mr Koss?'

He looked up at the senator. 'You're right. Fishbowl is a business, sir.' He took a deep breath. 'I'm a businessman.'

'You've changed your tune.'

'I'm not ashamed of making three point eight billion dollars last year.' The bankers had told him to be forthright and confident. 'That's the American dream, isn't it, Senator? To start a business, to be successful. The shareholders in my company, when we do our IPO in six weeks' time, are not going to be ashamed of me making three point eight billion for them. Perhaps you'll be one of those shareholders, too.'

'It looks like you'll stop at nothing to make that money.'

'No, that's not so. Everything we do is legal. We have a motto at Fishbowl. In fact, two of them. First, don't make the world a worse place. Second, tell no lies. In everything we do, we stick to those mottoes *and* we manage to make three point eight billion a year. I don't think that's a bad record. I think it's pretty good.'

'So it's not about Deep Connectedness, then? All that stuff before was so much hokum.'

'No, it is about Deep Connectedness. That's what we're offering.'

'Selling.'

'All right, selling. We're a business, if you insist. We sell Deep Connectedness. People want that and it's a good thing. It's a very good thing for our world. And because people want it, advertisers come to us and say, "Can we talk to people through Fishbowl?" And we say yes. And that's another form of Deep Connectedness, and they pay us for that.'

'No, Mr Koss, you were right the first time. What you're offering is Deep Connectedness. What you're *selling* is your customers.'

Andrei stared at him, his heart thumping.

'And you dupe your customers into thinking that the people who are buying them are their friends.'

'I have one and half billion users.' Andrei tried to control the quaver of anger in his voice. 'That's a quarter of the planet. Approximately nine hundred and fifty million of those people are on the site every day. If they didn't like what we're doing, Senator, they wouldn't be there.'

'So anything goes as long as people don't object?'

'Senator, I don't set myself up to tell the world what it can and can't do. I break no laws, and tell no lies. I'm not sure that everyone could say the same.'

The senator stared at him. 'Have you ever come across a conflict, Mr Koss, between the needs of your business and the ideals you started with?'

'Such as what, sir?'

'Such as Farming, sir. Mr Koss, I marched in Providence on a certain Fourth of July a few years back. Do you know to what I'm referring?'

'The Defence of Freedom marches?'

'Yes. I marched that day. Did you?'

'Yes. I marched in Boston.'

'I marched in support of the Constitution, in support of free speech, and I marched in support of your ideal, Mr Koss. I marched in support of Deep Connectedness, as you describe it, so a person in Rhode Island could find a person in Alabama who was interested in abolition of the death penalty and could work together on that. Or a person in Mississippi could find a person in Texas who was interested in improving the shameful state of our schooling system that this administration has allowed to crumble under its very feet. These are things that I know for a fact actually happened thanks to your network, Mr Koss. And I marched in support of you. I marched so you would have the freedom to pursue your ideal of Deep Connectedness – an ideal I believe in – without fear of prosecution. But you know what, Mr Koss? I didn't march in support of this thing you call Farming. I didn't march so that person in Rhode Island or Alabama or Mississippi or Texas would find someone who they thought was a person but was actually a program trying to *sell* them something.'

Andrei gazed at him, struggling for a response. 'It might be something they need, Senator. A program that doesn't just sell them stuff, but can learn about them, understand them, and present them with exactly what they need at exactly the right time. And, in most cases, at an improved price. Does that make the world a worse place, Senator?'

The senator let Andrei's words hang. Then he shook his head. 'You just don't get it, do you, Mr Koss?'

Andrei frowned. He wished he hadn't said what he had just said. Better to have stayed silent.

'That's the saddest thing about this whole sorry affair.' The senator leaned forward. Although five yards separated them, Andrei felt as if he was peering at him from inches away. 'What happened to you?'

Andrei swallowed. Nothing in the coaching sessions he had had over the past two weeks had prepared him for this. He wanted to say something but had no idea what. He felt belittled and humiliated and ashamed – but didn't know how to defend himself. He could feel his face burning.

The silence went on.

'Have you any other questions, Senator?' said Diane McKenrick.

'No,' said Senator O'Brien. 'I think I've heard about all I can bear to hear.'

'Well, I have a few,' said McKenrick, invoking her right as Chair to enter the proceedings when she chose. She had had enough of all these questions about advertising. She turned to Andrei. 'You said you tell no lies, Mr Koss. You said your Farming program only gives factual information. Is that right, Mr Koss?'

Andrei nodded, still flustered, his mind working over the previous senator's remarks.

'What if you gave non-factual information?' said McKenrick.

'I'm sorry.' Andrei shook his head, trying to put O'Brien's questioning behind him. 'I'm sorry, Senator. Can you repeat that, please?'

'I said, what if you give non-factual information?' said McKenrick impatiently.

'We don't give non-factual information.'

'What if you did?'

'We don't.' The questioning was on easier ground, and helped Andrei focus again. 'We're happy to be audited on that if anyone has a specific complaint.'

McKenrick made a show of sighing. 'Let me ask you something else. You sell products, correct? What if you chose to sell something different?'

'I'm not sure I understand what you're asking,' said Andrei.

'What if you chose to sell an idea, an ideology.'

'Such as?'

'Jihad.'

Andrei had practised this one, or something similar, a dozen times. He even had the delivery down pat.

'Senator, do I look like someone who's going to sell jihad?'

There was a wave of laughter in the audience behind him. McKenrick scowled.

'What if you chose to disseminate an ideology? You have a program that makes people think they're talking to friends. Isn't that the best way to influence people?'

'This seems like a totally hypothetical question, Senator. I have no ideology to disseminate.'

'It doesn't seem like a hypothetical question to me. It seems to me that you have developed something that could be used for dissemination of any kind of idea, and if it has the artificial intelligence you say it has, if it can learn and adapt to the people it's talking to, that must make it all the more dangerous.'

Andrei had no problem dealing with this line of argument. It had none of the emotional punch that he had found so unexpected, and disorientating, in O'Brien's attack. Always more comfortable in the realm of theory, he was again calm, methodical, unperturbed.

'Senator, I'm an advocate of Deep Connectedness, which I explained before. I've spent the last seven and a half years of my life building Deep Connectedness. If you want to call that an ideology, call it an ideology. I don't class it as an ideology any more than being an advocate of free speech is an ideology. Deep Connectedness is about allowing other people to express their ideologies, just as free speech is. So unless you're saying that free speech is a danger, then I don't understand what the danger is that you think you're pointing at.'

'Let me help you, Mr Koss. Your Farming program, or IAP, or whatever you want to call it there in your office in Silicon Valley, is an immensely powerful program. Would you agree?'

'I think it is a major advance, yes. I said that before.'

'Immensely powerful in selling products. Almost unimaginably powerful.'

Andrei didn't reply.

'Why don't you tell us how it works? In detail.'

Andrei's lawyer leaned over and whispered in his ear.

'Certain details, Senator,' said Andrei, 'are commercially sensitive.'

'I don't think we need that level of detail, Mr Koss. Tell us, in principle, how it works.'

'I believe I already told the first senator.'

'Then tell us,' said McKenrick, through gritted teeth, 'again.'

Andrei gave a summary. McKenrick listened with a show of disgust on her face. Then she asked a series of questions to elucidate some of the things the program could do.

'So if such a thing is so powerful in selling products,' she said eventually, 'wouldn't it be just as powerful in selling an ideology? No, selling's not the right word … *spreading* an ideology. Infiltrating our society, subverting it. Perhaps an ideology directed against the United States. An ideology that might directly or indirectly take the lives of American citizens.'

'Why would I do that?' said Andrei.

'It could take on the face of an Islamic preacher, couldn't it? It could radicalize our young people.'

Andrei was genuinely bemused at the suggestion. 'Why would I want to do that? Is there anything in anything I've ever done that suggests that I would?'

'So it all comes down to trusting you, does it, Mr Koss? You hold our destiny in our hands? On your whim we live or die?'

'Senator, that's very flattering but—'

'What if someone else had this technology, Mr Koss? Couldn't they do what I've described?'

'But someone else doesn't have this technology, Senator.'

'You said yourself that they will. You said yourself that you're one of the giants they'll stand on.'

'I didn't mean I was one of them. I just meant that every advance, every development, builds on previous ones.'

'And someone will build on yours.'

'I don't see what that has to do with me.'

'Without you, they wouldn't build.'

'I would argue, Senator, that without me, someone else would do what we at Fishbowl have done. If it can be done, it will be done.'

'So you do agree there is a danger?'

'I suppose, in the wrong hands—'

'Exactly, in the wrong hands.'

'But you can say the same about a gun, Senator. In the wrong hands, the gun is an instrument of terror. Are you saying you'd like to take it out of everyone's hands?'

Another murmur of laughter fluttered through the audience. Andrei hadn't intended the remark as a jibe, but McKenrick was a well-known gun advocate and supporter of the NRA. She had voted against every gun-control measure that had come up during her long senate tenure.

She was flustered for a moment. 'Do you really not see the difference, Mr Koss?'

'No, ma'am, I really don't.'

'Do you really not see the danger you bring to the community through this deceitful, underhanded program?'

Andrei was silent for a moment. He did see the danger, but not while the program was in his hands. 'No, ma'am.'

'What if a foreign government got hold of it?'

'I really don't see how that's going to happen.'

'You said yourself, others will build the same thing. Others will stand on your shoulders.'

'How can I stop them?'

'I don't think you're taking this very seriously, Mr Koss.'

'I'm taking it extremely seriously, Senator. I think it's people who think they can hold back technology who aren't being serious. Our IAP program is a major advance and I don't think there is anything else in the world that I'm aware of that is remotely comparable to it. But that won't last for ever. Nothing that can be built remains unique. We built the atom bomb and four years later the Soviets had done the same. We're working on our program constantly to improve it, to develop it, but—'

'I understand you'll license it, won't you?'

Andrei sighed.

'Of course you will. Everyone knows you stand to earn an

enormous amount of money if you do. What if you license it to people who won't use it as scrupulously as you pretend to?'

'I don't pretend anything, Senator. And I won't necessarily be licensing it. I have no plans to.'

'No plans to … That's what you tell us today. As I said before, it all comes down to trusting you, doesn't it? What you choose to do. When you choose to license it and who you choose to license it to.'

'Senator, we have laws in this country. If anyone is disseminating an ideology, as you put it, and there's some illegality about it, then surely they're the ones to target. Not me. Isn't this the same argument we were all having after Denver?'

McKenrick didn't want to let Koss turn the argument in that direction. 'Mr Koss,' she said, 'you say other people will eventually develop this kind of program even if they don't license it from you.'

'I expect so.'

'So people to whom you won't license it, because you're so scrupulous, might develop it themselves. Governments might develop it themselves.'

'Yes.'

'Foreign governments. Hostile governments.'

'I suppose so.'

'Isn't that something you should have thought of first?'

'They would have done it anyway. Someone would have done it.'

'But it's easier, now that you've done it. Don't you agree?'

Andrei shrugged. 'No one else has access to our program. We've proven the concept. I guess once a concept is proven, development tends to happen.'

'So there will come a time when everyone has it, or something like it?'

'Not everyone, Senator. It does still require some resources and talent to do it.'

'But others will have it. And others will use it for their own purposes.'

'Like others have radio, Senator, and television, and internet, and every other means of communication that we all have today.'

'Can't you see the difference in what you've created? Extend what you've said, Mr Koss. Everyone has this program. Think of the picture you paint. An internet where no one can be sure of anyone they see, anything they're told, anything they believe they can trust, because they have no idea if it's a person or a program, and, if it's a program, who's behind it.'

'Senator, in many ways, isn't that already the case? I'm no intelligence expert, but don't you think hostile governments already have people posing as regular individuals on social networks to influence opinion when it matters to them?'

'And you paint it on an industrial scale. You paint a world where every corporation, every institution, every government no matter how evil or corrupt, has at its disposal the ability to spread its opinions and ideology, no matter how vile, in a way entirely unapparent to the unsuspecting citizen.' McKenrick waited. 'Well, Mr Koss, what do you say to that?'

'That's an extreme.'

'And you're taking us there. And the only thing you can say is, "If it wasn't me, it would be someone else."'

Andrei shrugged. 'But it would be, Senator. My question is, what do you want to do about it? Do you want to censor everyone who's putting out an opinion you don't agree with, either through an IAP or as themselves? Do you want to shut the internet down? Television? Radio? Newspapers? The telephone? Where does it end? Do you want to start opening everyone's post?'

McKenrick gazed at him, suddenly wondering where to go next. She felt Koss painting her into the same anti-free-speech corner where she had ended up after Denver.

'What does that do for internet transparency?' she demanded suddenly, reverting to one of her prepared questions. 'Isn't that important? Isn't that something we need to guarantee?'

'I don't believe I've ever claimed the internet, as we have it today, is transparent, or that it even should be.'

'Haven't you?' retorted the Senator, trying to buy time as she thought of another line of attack.

Andrei looked at her, genuinely puzzled. 'No, Senator, you must be thinking of someone else. I know some people say the net will lead to a kind of radical transparency. I think that's delusion. The internet is just as much about opacity as transparency. It always has been. For some people, for many people, it's about having as many personalities as you want, being a part of as many clusters as you like, being as many people as you wish, and having Deep Connectedness between all of these and the other personalities you want to connect with. In future, why won't individuals have multiple personas, some of them true reflections of parts of themselves, others entirely fictitious? Why won't there be connectedness between humans and their online personalities and programs at a level of engagement that is utterly new and fascinating? That's where we're headed, Senator. Unless someone pulls the plug, unless someone switches the internet off, nothing that you or I can do will stop that.'

There was silence in the hearing chamber.

'That, Mr Koss,' said Senator McKenrick, knowing even as she spoke that the high-sounding but largely empty pronouncement that she was about to make was a poor substitute for the knock-out punch she had hoped to land, 'is a deeply disturbing and dystopian vision. One could say that any person holding such a vision has no place in the senior team of any internet company.'

'That's your opinion, Senator. You keep saying the IAP program is a danger. My users keep using Fishbowl. No one makes them do that.'

'So you take no responsibility?'

'For what? For bringing together a team that has made one of the greatest advances in programming since the invention of the personal computer? For employing four and a half thousand people? For giving my soon-to-be shareholders three point eight billion dollars in profit? Senator, explain to me. Which of those things am I supposed to feel ashamed about?'

McKenrick was silent. Andrei Koss had slipped away from her, wriggling through the escape hatch of an argument that whatever he had done, others would do anyway – an argument she hadn't foreseen, and didn't know how to counter without looking like a dinosaur.

After the hearing, Andrei's lawyer and Alan Mendes were effusive. Didier Broule, who had watched the stream live out of the Senate, called him minutes after he stepped out of the committee room. Andrei had nailed it. The security issue was dead, said the banker confidently, and there were some great soundbites about the commercial power of the IAP. McKenrick's hearings still had another week to run, but unless she could produce a Dr Evil with a smoking gun in his hand, they were effectively over. Andrei could forget about them. The IPO was on.

Bob Leib, Chris Hamer and Jenn McGrealy were ecstatic. Sandy told him that he had been awesome.

Broule proved to be right. In the week following Andre's testimony, the Senate committee questioned a series of CEOs, technologists, security analysts and internet specialists, but their evidence was too complex and too little was known in detail about Fishbowl's IAP to reduce to simplified soundbites. The media largely ignored the hearings. It was all too abstract, too theoretical. Where was the harm, where was the clear and present danger? Who were the victims?

But there were things from the Senate hearing that Andrei couldn't forget, things he kept hearing in his head, again and again. Not do with the security issue. Other things. Things that he had been asked – things that he had said.

43

SOMETHING HAPPENS INSIDE a management team as a company heads towards an IPO. A kind of fever takes hold. Will the shares be fully subscribed? Will the price meet expectations? The level of the work going on to be ready for the IPO is extreme. The sheer intensity stokes the flames. No one can think of anything else. Everything that happens in the business is seen through only one lens: what impact will this have on the float? No one, no matter how much they try to detach and focus on the business, can remain entirely immune.

By the time the Senate hearings closed, the IPO programme was ramping up; a month later, it was in full swing. A new, expanded board for the company had been constituted, with the bankers recruiting half-a-dozen serving and ex-CEOs from some of America's largest companies to lend their imprimatur. In order to stoke demand for the shares, a gruelling three-week roadshow was planned in the lead up to the launch – East Coast, West Coast, Chicago, Dallas, London, Frankfurt, Milan, Moscow, Delhi, Sao Paolo, Shanghai. Jenn McGrealy was signed up for the whole tour. Andrei fought off repeated demands to do the road-show but, eventually, getting caught up a little in the fever himself, he agreed to appear in Silicon Valley and New York in the final week of the campaign.

Broule said it was critical for Andrei to make one European appearance and he agreed to appear in London. China was essential as well. Huge investor funds were available though the wealth accumulated by the families of leading figures in the Communist

Party, with whom Broule's bank had assiduously cultivated relationships over a period of decades. Shanghai was added to Andrei's schedule, all in the week before the IPO.

Rooms had been booked that could hold 500, and there were inquiries from ten times that number, eager to see the legendary Andrei Koss in the flesh. Broule said he could have sold places to the presentations for $1,000 a head. 'We could forget the IPO,' he joked, 'and just do the roadshow.'

The figure of a share price that would value Fishbowl at $100 billion dollars, comfortably putting it into the handful of largest IPOs ever executed, had been in the air for over a year. The actual share price of the offering would not be set until the day before the float, when the underwriting syndicate, led by Broule and his team, would take a view about the degree of demand at various prices. Ideally they would want to go out with a number that would leave room for a bounce of 5 to 10 per cent on the first day, getting the market for the stock off to a buoyant start. It would also ensure that they could offload at a gain the stock that Mann Lever and the other underwriters were committed to take, while making a profit for favoured clients, who would receive large allocations of shares

Right from the beginning, Broule had been confident of bettering the $100 billion figure. Privately, he had been talking about a market capitalization in the order of $120 billion. By the time the roadshow started, he was talking of figures ten or twenty billion north of there, perhaps as high as $150 billion, which would make the Fishbowl IPO the largest ever seen. And the projection kept getting higher. By the time Andrei joined the roadshow in the last week before the launch, the media were speculating that the offering would value Fishbowl at $160 billion, and even at that level investors hoping for shares would be left empty-handed. Broule told Andrei that it was looking as if $180 billion wasn't unrealistic. At that valuation, Andrei's personal wealth on paper, with 44.7 per cent of the company, would stand at $80 billion dollars.

*

The first roadshow Andrei attended was in London. He sat at a table with Jenn McGrealy and Didier Broule on the podium in a huge room in the Grosvenor Hotel, facing 500 fund managers, investment managers and a select group of high-net-worth investors. He had avoided the media scrum that had gathered outside the hotel in expectation of snapping shots of him as he arrived by the simple expedient of staying there the night before the presentation.

The plan was for Didier to introduce him, then Andrei would outline his vision for the business, Jenn McGrealy would give the presentation on the company's operations that she had been giving for two weeks already, and Didier would then give his presentation on Fishbowl from an investment perspective, which was more finely tuned to the interests and concerns of fund managers and investors. Then there would be questions from the floor.

Andrei's presentation had been drafted by the bankers and modified over a few rounds of to and fro revisions. It took around twenty minutes and went off without incident. He even tried a couple of the apparent ad lib jokes the bankers had scripted for him and got laughs from the audience. Then Jenn stood up.

Andrei watched her as she outlined the operational strengths of the business, its commercial effectiveness, its technological development pipeline, its risk management, its resilience. He had never heard the capabilities of the business outlined in this way, and he was impressed. More than impressed – awestruck. At one point he found himself listening to the pitch, and suddenly thinking, as if he were someone who was completely outside it: This is a hell of a business! His next thought was: Did I build this thing? He knew that the answer was no. He could never have built what Jenn had built. He didn't think James Langan could have built it, either. Jenn was far superior. He had got one thing right, he thought. Listening to Jenn speaking, it struck him that hiring her had been one of the best decisions he had ever made.

Didier Broule took his place at the lectern when Jenn had finished. The banker was smooth, practised, credible, utterly at home in front of a crowd of investors. Careful to avoid saying anything that strayed outside the realms of permissible future projection, he put up numbers and sliced and diced them with ease, converting them to price to earnings ratios and earnings per share and other metrics that were grist to an investor's mill. For fifteen minutes he steered slickly through a stream of figures. Then he unexpectedly shut down the slides on the wall behind him and paused for effect.

'Now, here's the thing,' he said. 'Let's think about risk. I bet a lot of you are saying, fundamentally, this is a network. Networks come, networks go. Does anyone remember Homeplace?' He waited for the laugh he always got when he said that, whether it was in Chicago or Sao Paolo or Frankfurt. 'No, but, seriously, they come and go. People are fickle. They join one network today, they switch tomorrow – not that I think that's going to happen to Fishbowl, I hasten to add. Not with one point five billion users – that's a quarter of the human beings on the planet – and a growth trajectory after eight years that's still heading up. No, personally, I don't think Fishbowl's going anywhere in a hurry. By the way, that's not a forward-looking statement.' He paused for the laugh again. 'But I'm serious. You're investing for the long term. You should be asking yourself one important question. What makes Fishbowl different from the others?' He paused again. 'Here's the answer. Fishbowl is not a network. What do I mean by this? We've heard Andrei speak about Deep Connectedness. Fishbowl offers that. That's been the vision from day one. But let's say someone offers a better form of Deep Connectedness. Let's say one point five billion people run off there. Andrei,' he said, glancing at him, 'I'm not going to say it's going to happen, but let's say it does.' He looked back at the audience. 'Worst case.' He shrugged. 'Who cares? *Fishbowl ... is not ... a network.* Fishbowl is a program. That's the core of this business. The intelligent adaption program – or Farming, to you or me. Let's look at what one interested party had to say about it.'

Didier pressed a button. The screen came alive again. Andrei turned to watch.

It was a clip from the Senate hearing. McKenrick's face was on the screen.

'*Let me help you, Mr Koss. Your Farming program, or IAP, or whatever you want to call it, is an immensely powerful program. Would you agree?*'

'*I think it is a major advance. I said that before.*'

'*Immensely powerful in selling products. Almost unimaginably powerful.*'

'That's Senator Diane McKenrick, Chair of the US Senate Committee on Homeland Security. Not known for exaggeration.'

Didier played another clip.

'*I understand you'll license it, won't you? Of course you will. Everyone knows you stand to earn an enormous amount of money if you do.*'

'Now,' said Didier, 'imagine Fishbowl without its network, if you will. Take away the network, take away Deep Connectedness. What have you got left? That's right. The IAP. The most sophisticated, most targeted, most influential, most *effective* way of reaching a consumer ever – *ever* – developed. A program Fishbowl can use on its network, sure, but, more importantly, a program it can license to every network, every search engine, every chat room, every online publication, every place where people go on the net and reveal their needs. Which is everywhere. That's what you're buying, ladies and gentleman. You're buying Fishbowl. Great. You're buying a network of one point five billion people and rising, with all the opportunities that gives to direct advertising at them and all the revenue that brings. Great. But that's just the icing on the cake. What you're buying – what you're *really* buying – is a universal advertising application. Think about that. Do the math. Global advertising spend is 600 billion dollars. How much of that spend will a universal advertising application capture? The figures I showed you before, the projections, the cash flow – they're *before* that. Do the math.'

He waited, as if really expecting everyone in the room to be doing some kind of calculation. 'What you're thinking about now, the number in your head – that's all *upside*.' He paused, nodding. 'Upside. A universal advertising application. Not an IAP – a UAP. That's what you and your investors will be buying on Friday.' He paused again. 'And another thing. People say a company where the share structure gives one man a majority vote, even if he's holding only ten per cent of the shares outstanding, holds a risk. I agree. And that is effectively the structure we're talking about, let no one be in doubt. That's why we've assembled a board with some of the world's most exceptional business leaders to help steward the business. Even so, some people say it's risky to buy into a company with a voting structure like that. Maybe. Normally I'd agree. But there are exceptions.' He gestured to Andrei. 'That's the man with the vote. The man who gave us what we're talking about today, who built it in eight short years out of a dorm in Stanford, who's giving us the opportunity, with this IPO, to be part of one of the greatest examples of value creation that any of us have ever seen. It's this man sitting right here that we have to thank for all this – Andrei Koss.'

There was silence for a moment, then applause broke out in the audience. At first Andrei didn't even hear it. He was still watching Didier Broule, too absorbed in what he had said to be aware of anything else. People were on their feet, clapping, before he realized what was happening.

Didier motioned to him to stand up. Andrei stood, facing the applauding investors, not knowing what to do.

After the presentation, as they sat in the back of the car that was taking them to the private jet that would fly them to Shanghai, Andrei said to the banker that maybe he shouldn't focus so much on licensing.

Didier laughed. 'Andrei, that's what the investors are buying. No one trusts network stocks any more, not after what you did to Homeplace. But this they get.'

Andrei hesitated. The truth was, Broule and his team from Mann Lever intimidated him somewhat. Since the day they had been appointed, they had swept in and taken over the IPO process – the planning, the execution, the communications. They exuded energy and certainty. Everyone on the Fishbowl side – Leib, Chris, Jenn – thought they were doing a superb job. And they were. Andrei felt as if he was on a pounding, thumping juggernaut and there was no way of stopping it, or even diverting it slightly from its chosen course. And not even Andrei was totally immune to the fever generated by the juggernaut, the excitement of the ride. No one was.

Broule grinned. 'Andrei, trust me. I'm going to get you a market cap of one hundred and ninety billion dollars on Friday. That's what it's looking like. A hundred and ninety. The biggest IPO the world has ever seen.'

Andrei heard it all again, in Shanghai, in Palo Alto, then in New York City. The same speech from Didier Broule, the same words. The same applause from the investors, lapping it up.

And now the IPO was only two days away.

44

THE IPO OF Fishbowl Inc. took place on 21 July, seven years and eight months after Andrei Koss launched the second version of Fishbowll.com, which was destined to become one of the world's great internet companies.

The offering was priced at $48 a share, valuing Fishbowl at $192 billion dollars. Andrei rang the bell by videolink to open the trading session of the NASDAQ, standing in front of the aquarium in the main Fishbowl atrium, flanked by Jenn McGrealy, Chris Hamer, Bob Leib and the two dozen most senior executives in the company. Ten minutes later, the stock price had gone through $50, putting the company at $200 billion. A cheer rang across the fifth floor of Fishbowl's headquarters where a huge screen above the aquarium showed the stock price. The stock ended the day at $57.40 – almost a 20 per cent premium on the launch price. Andrei now held 44.7 per cent of a company valued at $228 billion dollars. Chris Hamer's $1 million stake had been parlayed into $11 billion, while 182 paper millionaires were made that day in the offices on University Avenue, with many more employees owning shares and options in the hundreds of thousands, and every employee, even the most recent, having at least some stock. Jenn McGrealy was worth in excess of $9 billion; Ed Standish, the advertising executive who had sold the original advertising deal to Andrei and then joined the company twelve months later with a grant of half a per cent of the shares, was worth $1 billion. A good number of millionaires were made outside University Avenue as well: Eric

Baumer, the infrastructure guy who had kept Fishbowl alive in the first summer on La Calle Court, had 1 per cent of the company. James Langan, now an evangelist pastor in Denton, Texas, still held the 2 per cent that he had accumulated in his year at Fishbowl, and was a multi-billionaire.

That night, Fishbowl took over the Grey Warehouse in San Francisco. Every employee was invited to the party, as well as other people who had been involved with Fishbowl over the years. Ben Marks flew in from New York. Kevin Embley made it all the way from his office on Emerson Road off University Avenue, where his own start-up was finally picking up speed in social gaming.

At ten o'clock, Alan Mendes ushered Andrei to a balcony looking down on the central lobby of the warehouse from six storeys up. A sea of faces gazed back at him from the balconies and the lobby below. Seventeen screens hanging off the walls at various heights showed the parties happening simultaneously in each of the cities around the world where Fishbowl had an office, whether it was morning, noon or night. It was an awe-inspiring sight and, for a moment Andrei, with Sandy beside him, just soaked it up. Then he took the microphone that Alan was holding for him and raised his hand.

There was a roar.

When he finally got silence, Andrei put the microphone to his mouth and said, 'You did it. *You* guys did it!' The warehouse erupted around him again. When he had silence once more, he gave a short speech. He said that what had happened that day on the stock market was testament to all the work they had collectively done in building Fishbowl. It was nothing more than they all deserved. Then he told them not to focus on the stock price, but to keep doing the things that had made Fishbowl what it was. As long as they did that, the stock price would take care of itself. The first eight years were just the beginning, he said. They had changed the world a little. 'Stick around,' he concluded. 'In the next eight years, we're going to change the world a lot.'

He handed the microphone back to Alan and, as the warehouse was filled with roaring and whooping, made his way with Sandy off the balcony.

He went through the crowd. Most people in the company never got to see him, let alone talk to him, and they crowded around him. At some point he got separated from Sandy. He glimpsed Ben and headed towards him. Later they found Kevin. Young Fishbowlers acclaimed Andrei as he walked past. They had no idea who Ben and Kevin were.

At around midnight they ended up on the roof. The three men who had founded Fishbowl stopped by the glass balustrade at its edge. The lights of the Bay glittered below them.

Kevin had a fat cigar in his hand. 'Billionaires' club,' he said with a grin.

'I don't know what I'm doing here,' said Ben. 'You two guys … you built this thing. I was just there for the ride.'

'Dude, that's why you only got nine per cent.'

'He only got nine per cent,' said Andrei, 'because he couldn't find another twenty thousand. And you weren't just along for the ride, OK? It was way more than that. I still miss you. I still want you back.'

Ben shook his head, smiling.

For a moment there was silence as they watched the lights of the Bay twinkling below them. It was over four years since they had physically been together in the same place – not since Ben had left Fishbowl, before the Manhattan Project had even started. That was more than half the company's existence. Ben and Kevin had gone on to other things. Whatever tensions had existed with Andrei around their departures were long in the past, and paled in comparison with what they had achieved together. Their thoughts went back to Embarcadero, to Ramona Street, to La Calle Court, to Robinson House, places that were the stuff of myth now, so far away in the life journey that each of them had taken, if not in distance from where they stood.

'Remember all those hours at Yao's?' said Ben nostalgically. 'Man, we practically lived at that place. Is it still there?'

'Sure,' said Andrei.

'You ever go back?'

Andrei shook his head. 'Not much. Occasionally. We actually have a couple of meeting rooms in the office now.'

Ben laughed.

'I gave him shares, though.'

'Who?'

'Yao. I gave him two million dollars' worth. And I gave two million each to the guys. Lopez and Marina and Feliciano and Wong. I gave them two million each.'

'Dude,' said Kevin, 'that's cool. Stakhanovite.'

Andrei shrugged.

'You know, everyone thinks you're there all the time,' said Ben. 'Whenever anyone finds out I was connected with Fishbowl, it's like, "Aren't you guys at that noodle place all the time?"'

Kevin nodded. 'There's like a legend of Yao's out there.'

'It was that interview I did after Denver,' said Andrei. 'I have never done an interview since where they don't ask me about Yao's.'

'You've never done an interview since, period.'

'Actually, that's not quite true.'

'Dude, that journalist should just have called that article "Yao's". I don't even know why you were in it. And there were monkeys, right? Something about monkeys.'

'Orangutans.'

'Stuff really happened at that place,' said Ben. 'Do you remember the napkin?'

Kevin grinned. 'Who can forget the napkin?'

'Have you still got it?' said Ben to Andrei.

He nodded.

'Is that where we first met Chris?'

Andrei thought briefly. 'No. We went to that Vietnamese place. What was it called?'

'It's closed,' said Kevin. 'Closed about a year ago.'

'I met Chris at Yao's when I asked him back up.'

'Without us,' said Kevin. 'That's when you sold us out, I believe.'

Andrei looked at him.

'Dude, I'm joking.'

'Is he here?' said Ben.

'He's down there somewhere with some Fishettes,' said Kevin. 'I saw him before.'

'So he hasn't changed. Follow the Fishettes and you'll find Chris.'

'Yeah,' said Andrei. 'That's Chris, all right.' He stared down at the Bay. Then he glanced at them again. 'It's good to see you guys. It's just ... it's been too long.'

Kevin took a deep draw on his cigar.

'We should do this more.'

'What?' said Kevin. 'An IPO? Sure. I'll take another thirty billion dollars any day.'

Ben was silent, watching Andrei.

'You guys sell any shares today?' said Andrei.

'No,' said Kevin.

'You, Ben?'

Ben shook his head.

Andrei nodded. 'Well, you should think about it,' he said quietly.

'Why?' said Kevin.

'You know what it says in the prospectus. There are risks and uncertainties. Anything can happen.'

'Dude, it says that in every prospectus.'

Andrei looked at them. 'I think the stock's peaked.'

'Why?'

'Trust me, I think it's peaked.'

Kevin saw someone come out onto the roof. He looked briefly at Andrei and Ben. 'I'll be back,' he said, and headed off.

'Don't poach my engineers!' called out Andrei.

'Is that what he's going to do?' asked Ben.

'Probably.' Andrei glanced thoughtfully at Ben. 'You around tomorrow?'

Ben shook his head. 'I'm on the six-thirty flight back to New York. I've got clients tomorrow.'

'Why are you taking a commercial flight? Buy a jet, for Christ's sake.'

'You buy a mansion first.'

'You really take your client stuff seriously, don't you?'

'Well, it's like the question Chris used to ask – what's the most important thing you can be doing ...'

'I thought you didn't believe in that question.'

'I thought you did.'

Andrei frowned. 'Do you remember when I said maybe we should stop?'

Ben shook his head. 'Stop?'

'Fishbowl. Remember when we were thinking about the 4Site deal. I said, you know, maybe we should just stop.'

'Instead of allowing advertising? I kind of remember. Vaguely. Yeah, you did. You said maybe we should stop.'

'Your folks had just put in thirty thousand dollars. And you said, "What's going to happen to that?"'

Ben laughed. 'Did I?'

Andrei nodded. 'If your folks hadn't put in thirty thousand, what do you think you would have said? If you had nothing at risk.'

Ben gazed at him, wondering why he was asking that. 'I don't think you should have stopped, Andrei.'

'That's because you're worth twenty billion dollars.'

'No. That money's ridiculous. I don't want it. It's way too much. I'm going to have to find a way to give it away.'

'Yeah,' said Andrei. 'It's crazy.'

'What's going on, Andrei?'

Andrei shrugged. Ben continued to watch him. Andrei gazed down at the Bay.

'You know, there's only one thing I'm really proud of,' Andrei murmured.

'What's that?'

'After Denver, when I gave the data. Everyone was telling me I shouldn't. But I did.'

'You told me that was just a business decision. The night I told you I was leaving the company, that's what you said.'

Andrei shrugged.

Ben watched him closely. 'Why did you do it?'

'It was the right thing for the business. I think we showed that, eventually.'

Ben didn't say anything. He felt as if he was in a session with a client.

'I don't know. I guess I thought it was the right thing to do. I was surprised James didn't.'

'Yeah,' said Ben. 'So was I.'

'Chris, you know … I wouldn't expect anything more from Chris. And Kevin's Kevin. But I thought James, you know, this big Christian …'

'Well, render unto Caesar what is Caesar's.'

'What does that mean?'

'Do what you have to do legally, I guess.'

'Do you remember the shitstorm we had in the Grotto?'

Ben laughed.

But Andrei gazed down at the Bay again.

Ben wondered what was going on in Andrei's mind. He had been brief and somewhat understated when talking to the crowd on the balcony, but Ben had thought that was just Andrei. The speech hadn't made Ben think that he was in a particularly introspective or downcast mood. But maybe it was natural to have a sense of deflation after the IPO, a feeling of anticlimax. It occurred to Ben that Andrei, as Fishbowl's CEO, had probably got used to putting on a façade quite a lot of the time, and that would only get worse now that the company was listed on the NASDAQ and his public commitments would increase.

'At the time,' said Ben, 'when you were trying to figure out what to do that night after the bombing, you told me it was because you had a responsibility. You said you had this special responsibility because you had brought Fishbowl into the world.'

Andrei nodded.

Ben waited. Andrei said nothing.

'You know, you're not giving yourself much credit. You have a lot more to be proud of than Denver. Deep Connectedness is real. You envisioned it, Andrei. You made it happen.'

'Yeah, but you left. You left after we started Farming.'

'I wanted to do other things.'

Andrei shrugged.

'Just think of what you've done. Just think of everything you've made happen.'

'It wouldn't have happened at all if you hadn't told me to make it a dating site for the mind.'

'I don't think I actually used that term, Andrei. I think you invented it. Deep Connectedness is a strong, strong force for good. You should be proud of that.'

'I'm only proud of Denver. And the march.'

'Defence of Freedom? Didn't you meet the Dillerman that day?'

'Yeah.' Andrei put up his hands with his second and fifth fingers extended. 'Two *l*s!'

Ben laughed. 'I wonder what he's saying today.'

'Who knows?' It had been years since Andrei had worried about what the Dillerman or any of the other 300 would say.

'Remember the Curse of the Dillerman?' Ben laughed. 'Don't worry. He'd find a way to believe you were doing the right thing.'

Andrei didn't speak for a moment. 'I'm only proud of Denver, Ben. That was the only time I stood up.'

'Stood up to what?'

Andrei didn't reply.

'Well if that's how you feel, it's never too late, Andrei.'

Andrei looked at him. 'Is that what you tell your clients?'

'Sometimes.'

'Well, you're right.' Andrei nodded to himself. 'You're right.'

'Listen, Andrei ...' Ben hesitated. 'You want me to stay around tomorrow? You know, if you want to talk about stuff ... I can stay.'

'No. You've got clients.'

'I can. If it's important.'

'No, it's fine.' Andrei smiled. 'It's good to see you, Ben. I mean that. Don't worry, I know you're never coming back to Fishbowl. But we should ... you know, we should get together more often.'

'Maybe I'll buy myself that jet.'

Andrei stood for a moment longer. 'I'm going,' he said suddenly. 'I'll see you again soon, huh?'

Ben watched him go. Maybe it was just the aura of the night, but something about the way Andrei marched off reminded him of the afternoon, eight years before, when Andrei had suddenly turned around on the way to Ricker dining hall and marched back to the dorm to turn the first Fishbowl into the thing that would conquer the world.

Sandy stayed later at the party than Andrei. When she got back to their apartment she found him on the sofa with a set of small, black notebooks scattered around him. The framed napkin from Yao's had been pulled out of the cupboard where it was normally hidden and was on the sofa beside him as well. Andrei was gazing at the huge TV screen that Sandy had had installed on the wall. He was on the screen, almost life size, dressed in a suit and tie, sitting at the table in front of Senator McKenrick's committee.

It was the same part she always found him watching: the part with Senator O'Brien from Rhode Island.

She sighed. 'You're not watching that again, honey ...?'

'What did you really think of it?' said Andrei, not looking around. 'Tell me the truth.'

'I've told you already. You were great. They didn't touch you.'

'I mean about what I said.'

'I mean about what you said as well.'

'Don't you think I came across as a phony? A hypocrite?'

'No. You came across as a smart guy who's built a great business that makes a huge difference in the lives of a quarter of the people on the planet.'

'What about when I said that I wished I could do it without the money?'

'Well, you do, don't you?'

'Then what am I doing with a company that earned four billion dollars last year?'

'Do you really think that's something to feel guilty about? Your shareholders won't.' Behind Sandy, O'Brien's self-righteous voice droned on. She picked up the remote control and turned it off. 'I've got something to say.' She came over to Andrei and straddled him, putting her arms around his neck. 'You remember how you got bounced into doing this IPO? Well, I think I need to do a little bouncing as well. Forget Senator I'm-so-self-righteous O'Brien. Here's something for you to really think about. I think we should get married.'

He looked up at her. 'Do you think so?'

'Uh-huh.'

'You're drunk.'

'Uh-huh. Why do you think I'm saying it? Why do you finally think I've worked up the courage after all this time? Have you never even thought about asking?'

Andrei shrugged.

'Of course, it's only because you're worth a hundred billion bucks.'

'A hundred and two, actually.'

'Oh, baby.' Sandy leaned forward and kissed his neck. 'You don't know how hot that makes me.' She laughed and straightened up. 'Seriously. What do you say, Andrei? Or do I go find myself another fella?'

'Are you sure you want to?' said Andrei.

'No. After nine years, I'm racked with uncertainty.'

'It's not going to be easy, being with me.'

'Oh? Something's going to change, is it?'

Andrei frowned. 'You're saying it hasn't been easy until now?'

She stared at him, then laughed.

'I just thought ...'

Sandy wondered if she was making a big mistake. But that was Andrei. He wasn't big on sensitivity to other people's emotions. He had other qualities. If you wanted to be with him, you had to accept it.

'I meant it's not going to be easy with this IPO,' he said. 'There's going to be a whole lot more scrutiny, a whole lot more pressure.'

'So you'll need a whole lot more support.'

'And you'll support me whatever happens? Whatever I decide to do?'

She looked at him quizzically.

'It's going to get tough, Sandy. It's going to get really, really tough.'

She shrugged. 'I'm a pretty tough gal. But I need to know, Andrei. I can support you through anything, but I need to know if we're solid. I need to know if this is going to be for good. And if it is, then I want to get married.' She paused. 'Because I want your hundred billion.'

'Hundred and two, actually.'

She was silent, looking into his eyes.

'I should be the one to ask if you want to get married,' said Andrei suddenly.

'What? Now you want to be the male chauvinist?'

'No. I just ... should.'

'So ask.' She threw back her shoulders and made a show of composing herself. 'OK. I'm ready.'

'In a couple of days.'

'I don't understand.'

'I'll ask you in a couple of days.'

'But you know I'm going to say—'

'I'll ask you in a couple of days. See how you feel then.'

45

AT NINE O'CLOCK the next morning, Andrei arrived in his office through a largely deserted floor. People straggled in over the next couple of hours. He worked through his emails, then sent one to Alan Mendes asking him to set up a press conference for the next day. At eleven he went to Los Alamos to sit in on a visual interface meeting. He watched a prototype of a palotl of a 60-year-old, red-haired Scotsman talking in real time to someone in the room. As a joke, the Scotsman looked as if he had been to the party the night before and had knocked back one too many. It was awesome. Scarily, scarily, awesome, right down to the slurred brogue and the reddened veins in the nose.

Andrei was back in his office when Chris walked in at one o'clock looking deeply hung over. He started talking about the party. He had gone back to his hotel, apparently, with a staffer. Andrei didn't want to hear. He had had enough of Chris treating the young females of the company like his personal pool. He had had enough of a lot of things about Chris.

'Let's have lunch,' said Andrei. 'You know what? Let's go to Yao's.'

Chris smiled. 'Yao's? How long is it since we've been there?'

Andrei shrugged. 'Come on. For old times' sake.'

They headed out of the office and down University. At Yao's, Lopez was on shift. He hadn't changed much since Andrei had first discovered the noodle restaurant as a student ten years earlier, only a little heavier and with a touch of grey in the hair. He grabbed Andrei and gave him a hug. Then he ran off to get

Tony Yao from the kitchen. By now one of the diners had recognized Andrei and yelled out his name. Everyone looked around. Suddenly someone started whooping. A moment later people were on their feet, applauding.

'Rock star,' said Chris Hamer in his ear.

'Maybe this wasn't such a good—'

'Andrei!' yelled Tony Yao, coming out of the back with his apron around him. He grabbed Andrei's hand. 'Thank you. Thank you so much.'

'It's fine, Tony,' said Andrei.

Tony kept thanking him.

'We just want to eat,' said Andrei.

'Of course. Come with me.' He took him to a table at the back and said something to Lopez. Lopez ran off and came back with a screen and set it up around them.

'Private room!' said Yao. 'Private dining at Yao's!'

Andrei and Chris sat.

'You want usual?' said Tony.

Andrei nodded.

'Chris?'

'Kung pao chicken, Tony. Don't you remember?'

Tony laughed. 'You sometimes changing, Chris. Andrei never change. You change.' He stood beside Andrei again. 'Thank you, Andrei.'

Andrei nodded. 'Don't mention it.'

'Meal on house.'

'No, Tony.'

'All meals always on house!'

Lopez came over and poured water as Tony went out to cook their food. 'Can I get you a drink?'

'Just water, Lopez.'

'I think water's what I need,' said Chris, smiling ruefully.

Lopez grinned and left them the jug.

Chris asked why Tony had been thanking him like that.

'He got some shares,' said Andrei.

'How many?'

Andrei told him.

'Good for him,' said Chris. 'And Lopez too?'

Andrei nodded. 'And the other old-timers.'

'Hey, Lopez,' Chris called out as he glimpsed Lopez going past with plates for another table. Lopez put his head around the edge of the screen. 'Why are you still working? Why aren't you out spending some of that cool dinero?'

'I haven't sold any shares. I'm not sure what to do yet.'

'Very wise. Got any plans? You could go home.'

'This is my home, Chris. I'm a citizen.'

Chris stared for a moment, then laughed. 'Sure you are. And you know what? Hold those shares, understand? This company's worth twice what they are.'

Lopez grinned and then disappeared again.

'You shouldn't say things like that,' said Andrei.

'Why not? I don't think the SEC's listening.' Chris sat back and breathed out long and slow. 'Monster of a party last night. What time did you leave?'

'Around midnight.'

'You were never much of a party guy, were you? So how does it feel, anyway? CEO of a two-hundred-billion-dollar company.'

'Fine.'

'Fine? That's it?'

'Ridiculous.'

Chris laughed. 'There's probably only ... what? Ten of you, twenty of you, in the whole world. Cool club. The share price is still going up today, by the way.'

'I know. I kind of wish it would stop.'

'You know, Apple was the first company to five hundred billion dollars. How would it be to be the first to a trillion? That would be something, huh?'

Andrei shrugged. 'It's an arbitrary number, Chris. It wouldn't mean anything to me.'

'Not even as something to aim for?'

Andrei shook his head.

Chris watched him. 'You don't look too happy. I thought you'd be, like, heading down to buy yourself a fleet of Ferraris.'

Andrei raised an eyebrow.

'No, I guess not. Come on, Andrei. Lighten up.'

'Look,' said Andrei. 'I wanted to have a talk with you. I'm going to make some changes.' He hesitated. 'Chris, I'm going to ask you to be, like, more of an investor.'

Chris narrowed his eyes.

'I don't want you coming down to the office any more. Let's have a more traditional CEO–investor relationship.'

'I've only ever been an investor, Andrei. If you wanted my advice, it was there.'

'Chris, we know that's not true. You were like a member of the management team.'

'Well, maybe you needed that.'

'I'm not saying I didn't. You did a lot of great things. Fishbowl wouldn't be where it is today or anywhere near it without your contribution. But I think the time has come for that to change.'

'How long have you been thinking that?'

'A while.'

'Since when?'

'I don't know. Does it matter? Tell me, did you give that leak to the *Wall Street Journal*? About the date of our supposed IPO?'

'No.'

'Just tell me the truth.'

'No!'

'Did your friend Billy at J.P. Morgan?'

'How would I know? And he's not my friend, I can tell you that. Not after what we did. Not even letting him pitch.' Chris shook his head in disgust. 'So what? You don't want my advice now? Is that what you're saying?'

'I do. But I want to ask for it. I want you to wait for me to ask for it. And I don't want you turning up like it's your office. You never wanted a formal role, remember? You said that wasn't the way you worked. Well, you don't work here, Chris. You're an investor.'

'I never said I—'

Chris stopped. Tony Yao came around the screen with their food, beaming broadly.

'Special treatment,' said Chris.

'You should come more often, like you used to,' said Tony.

Andrei nodded.

Chris waited until Tony had gone. 'Well, you're the CEO.' He took a piece of his kung pao chicken and ate it. His teeth continued clenching after he had swallowed. He put down his fork. 'Let me tell you something, Andrei. You would *never* be where you are if it hadn't been for me. You would have crashed and burned that first summer if I hadn't found Eric for you. You guys didn't even know enough to know how close you were to the edge. If it wasn't for me, Andrei, you'd be sitting somewhere in someone's programming department right now, saying, "Oh, there was this great idea I used to have for a website." Mike Sweetman's department, probably.'

'I'm not saying that isn't true. And you've turned your one million investment into eleven billion. So I think, you know, we can call it evens.'

Chris shook his head, steaming. 'You'd *never* have created a new model of advertising. You'd *never* have come up with the idea of Farming. That was *me*, Andrei. Me!'

Andrei was silent. He took a mouthful of his noodles and chewed it. 'I hoped you wouldn't take this the wrong way,' he said eventually.

'I'm taking it like it is, Andrei.'

There was silence again. Chris chewed his chicken angrily.

'Obviously, I hope you'll still be a member of the board.'

Chris snorted.

'You know,' said Andrei, 'I wanted to talk to you about Farming as well. I'm going to stop it.'

Chris stared at him, then put down his fork. 'What are you talking about?'

'I'm going to stop Farming.'

Chris laughed.

'I'm not joking.'

'You spent half a billion dollars—'

'More, actually. With Los Alamos, we're over a billion.'

'And you're going to *stop* it?'

'And I'm not going to license it, either. Not for advertising, anyway.'

Chris sat back. 'And what, if you wouldn't mind telling me, are you going to do?'

'I'm going to stop advertising on Fishbowl. Any kind. It's always been a necessary evil. Well, now, thanks to the IAP, it's not necessary. Fishbowl's going back to what it was.'

'What it was when you were a kid in a dorm in Stanford.'

'I'm going to license the IAP for other things – to do all the other things we said it could do. What we've developed is amazing. It's Deep Connectedness in a truly radical and ground-breaking form. Can you imagine bringing education to Africa through a palotl in every classroom?'

'It's my word, palotl! That's my word, Andrei! I invented it.'

'Do you want me to call it something else?'

'Call it what you freaking want! Andrei, listen to yourself! What the fuck are you talking about doing?'

'Think of it, Chris. Education … medical care … citizens' rights … We can bring all of that and more. Isn't that an awesome vision?'

'Every advertiser on every site across the net using our IAP, that's my vision,' said Chris. 'A trillion-dollar company, that's my vision.'

'The revenue I get from the IAP I'll use to run Fishbowl as a site for Deep Connectedness.'

Chris snorted. 'What revenue?'

'Governments will pay. Aid donors. I won't need much.'

'You're out of your mind! You want to do all that stuff? Great. Do it. But don't think anyone's going to pay you for it. Not in this world. Don't think you can do it if you stop Farming on Fishbowl.'

'Fishbowl's a sewer, Chris. It's a stinking mess riddled with selling. It's a place to sell stuff. That's all it is. It's a goddamn place to sell stuff.'

'You are out of your fucking mind.'

'I watched my testimony to the Senate committee. I looked at it and I saw myself and I saw someone I didn't recognize, someone saying things I could never have imagined saying. You know who I saw? Mike Sweetman, only a hundred times worse. I saw the sum total of every hypocritical, money-grubbing, monopolistic tech CEO I've always despised. And I don't want to be that person. I never wanted to be that person. It's a betrayal of myself.'

'And I suppose you're saying I made you that person.'

'No. I'll take responsibility for that. And it's because I made myself that person that I can unmake him. Four times I sat on a podium with Didier Broule and listened to him say that Fishbowl isn't a network, it isn't about Deep Connectedness, it's about advertising. It's a universal advertising application.'

'He's an idiot.'

'No, he's right. He's right on the money, if you'll excuse the pun. My greatest regret is that I didn't stand up in London or Shanghai and say right there that there'll be no advertising. There'll be no licensing. Well, it's not too late. I don't want to be the guy who spends his life running an advertising program. It's your question, Chris – the one you asked me the very first time we met. What's the most important thing for me to be doing with my life? Well, you know what? Being the world's biggest advertising executive, as Senator O'Brien put it, is not it. In fact, it's the worst thing I can be doing. So I'm not going to be that. I'm going to take this program and put it to use else-where and Fishbowl will be Fishbowl – a place were people connect, not some place riddled with sales where you don't know if what you think is your best friend is going to turn out to be a frigging palotl. And you know what? I'm going back to two *l*s. Fishbowll, with two *l*s, like the Dillerman said. I should never have changed it.'

Chris watched him for a moment, then smiled pitifully. 'You realize this will do nothing to stop other people developing Farming for themselves? If you leave this space open, all that's going to happen is some Mike Sweetman is going to walk on in there and take the truckloads and truckloads of money that are waiting.'

'They're welcome to it.'

'You put this thing into the world.'

'Doesn't mean I have to continue with it.'

'This gesture of yours will do nothing to stop where the world is going.'

'Maybe it won't.'

'Oh, it won't.' Chris grinned sardonically. 'Don't kid yourself, it won't. The world is getting exactly the internet it deserves.'

'Maybe so, but that doesn't mean I have to be the one to give it to them.'

'Others will. Everything on the net ends up in the same place. No one wants to pay for anything, so we all take what we know about our users – who they are, what they want, when they want it – package it up, and sell that instead.' Chris laughed. 'Don't you love it? We had this monumental thing that could have been about openness and honesty and we've turned it into this monstrous net constructed to trap and manipulate us.' He laughed again. 'And *we're* the best at it, Andrei.'

'I don't want to be the best. Not at that.'

'And you think it'll stop? At least if we're the ones—'

'Chris, don't give me that argument again. Maybe when people have Fishbowl, when they can come to a place where they're not being targeted, they'll do that instead. Maybe things will change. Maybe other sites will have to follow.'

'You're insane.'

'And your opinion of people has always been a little too low.'

'My opinion of people has been exactly what people have proven it to be. I gave them FriendTracker. They could have used it to reward friendship. What did they do? They used it to tear each other apart. More fun than the Colosseum.' Chris shook his head. 'Jesus Christ. I knew you were naive when I met you but I never thought you were still this wet behind the ears. People don't care, Andrei. They don't ... give ... a ... *fuck!* As long as they don't have to pay anything, they're happy. For the last twenty years, every single service they've used has raped them for personal data and beamed advertising straight back at them – shitty, untargeted advertising that's about stuff they couldn't care less about.

And what do they do? They keep on using the services that do that to them. At least we've found a way of getting to them about stuff they actually might care about it. Honestly, look at our pathetic species! We've all sold our souls for a home page and a search engine. And while you raise whatever pitiful sum you can get from your licensing, others will be earning a hundred times as much as you. And they'll use that to offer better services, quicker services, and all the idealistic people you think are going to hang on to your second-rate site are going to head on over without even waving goodbye. They'll keep selling their souls like they've always sold them, and Fishbowl will wither away. You're taking the greatest wealth machine anyone has ever created and you're strangling it at birth.'

'I disagree with you,' said Andrei. 'But even if you're right, it's my choice.'

'No, that's where you're wrong.' Chris stopped, looked around for a moment, and leaned closer. 'Two days ago, you could have said that. In case you don't remember, yesterday, you sold twenty per cent of your stock for forty billion dollars. That makes you the CEO of one of the world's biggest public companies. With that role comes certain responsibilities. Certain *legal* responsibilities. If you do what you're saying, the stock you sold is worthless. Nothing, zero, nada. You made promises to people.'

'I made no promises to anyone,' said Andrei. 'The prospectus says there's no certainty of anything.'

'You allowed that prospectus to say that Fishbowl earns revenue from advertising. You allowed that prospectus to say the IAP offers the opportunity for significant licensing revenues. Half the value of the company at least comes from people expecting those licensing revenues and you know it.'

'There will be licensing revenues.'

'From advertising?'

'It doesn't say that.'

'You allowed people to think so.'

'No, they chose to think so. This is a company in which I have a majority vote on the board, even if I own only ten per cent of the stock. I own forty-five per cent. Anyone investing in a company like that knows I can make a decision on a whim and there's no way to challenge it. *That's* what's clear in the prospectus. Didier Broule said it explicitly. I heard him. You invest in a company like that, you take your chances.'

'So this is a whim, is it?'

'No, it's not a whim!' Andrei stopped, conscious that his voice was raised, conscious that on the other side of the screen people must be able to hear him.

'Everything all right?' asked Lopez, putting his head around the screen.

'Everything's fine,' said Andrei. He turned back to his noodles, now going cold, and picked a prawn off the plate.

Lopez disappeared.

Chris leaned even closer. 'This isn't a whim? You could have stopped this IPO. Even two days ago, you could have stopped it. What's happened in the past forty-eight hours, Andrei? Have you had some kind of epiphany?' Chris sneered. 'Have you seen the light?'

Andrei closed his eyes. He wished he had stopped the IPO. He wished he had had the courage somehow to leap off the juggernaut and stop it. Everything about it was wrong. And yet he had let it happen.

Suddenly he looked at Chris. 'I'll buy back the shares.'

'What are you talking about?'

'I'll buy back the shares! The money's sitting in the bank. I'll offer to buy them back.'

'Andrei, those shares are now worth twenty per cent more than you were paid for them.'

'I'll pay what we sold them for. If people have speculated since then, then they've speculated. I asked forty-eight dollars, that's what I'll give for them. If they don't want to sell back, that's fine. If not, they can hold on to them and be investors in a true Fishbowl.'

'The only investor you'll have in a true Fishbowl is you.'

'And that's fine with me as well.'

'You'll be tied up in litigation for the next fifty years.'

'I'll take that chance.'

'Why did you go to IPO? If this is what you were thinking, why did you do it?' Chris's lip curled. 'You wanted the kudos, didn't you? You wanted to be the guy who had a two hundred billion IPO.'

'You don't know how little that means to me.'

'Yeah, right. Two hundred billion. It was just serving Andrei Koss's pride. And now you've done that, it's time to be holier than thou, even though it means ripping people off of the money they've put behind you.'

Andrei sighed. 'I don't know why I did it.'. He didn't know why he had done lots of things. He didn't know why Fishbowl had ended up where it was. Maybe he really had wanted the kudos, or the money. But at least he knew where he was going now. 'Someone said to me yesterday that it's never too late to stand up.'

'Stand up? To what? You should step *down*. You don't deserve to lead this company, Andrei. You ought to step aside and give it to someone who does.'

'Like you, I suppose?'

'Give me this company and just see what I could do with it!'

'Such as what?'

'Such as, for a start, not committing the most public suicide the world has ever seen. You talk about betraying yourself. *This* is betrayal, Andrei. Betrayal of millions of shareholders, betrayal of the greatest business the world has ever seen. And for *nothing*. It will change *nothing*. Someone else will simply do what you could have done. You'll be a footnote to history, when you could have been a whole chapter.' He glanced away for a moment, shaking his head, as if dazed by disbelief at what Andrei had been saying. 'You know what? When I first met you, I thought you were the visionary. I thought you were the guy who could see into that place ten or twenty years ahead. But I was wrong. All you've ever seen was what you saw sitting in your dorm room. You know, I've often asked myself, has Andrei Koss ever changed? Surely he can't believe all this sophomorish stuff he spouts about Deep Connectedness? Deep Connectedness! Shit, it's like they're the only two words you know! I'm so sick of hearing them. But you actually do believe it, don't you? You haven't changed one bit. *I'm* the visionary. I'm the one who saw the window opening up for Farming. I'm the one who proved the concept. I'm the one who saw the power of the model if we were able to program it. *I'm* the one who can see where that can take us now.'

'No, Chris,' said Andrei quietly. 'We can both see that.'

Chris stared at him. Then he snorted and shook his head again.

'I'm going to announce it tomorrow,' said Andrei. 'I've asked Alan to organize a press conference.'

'Does he know what it's about?'

Andrei shook his head.

'Does anyone?'

'Not yet.'

'Don't you think you ought to tell the board?'

'It's a formality.'

'Then as a formality.'

'As I recall,' said Andrei, 'you never seemed to be too worried about that kind of thing. But you're right. I should tell the board.

I'll get Jenn to see if she can get a call set up with them tomorrow morning.'

'Watch them sell the shares they were granted. All those captains of industry. As soon as they get wind of this, they'll be out of here like rats on a ship. And all those people who were applauding you last night, everyone who loves you so much? Watch them on the express right out of Fishbowl once they realise what their options will be worth after this.'

Andrei shrugged. The decision that he had made, which was bigger than all the others that had caused him so much prevarication in recent times, had come to him with no procrastination at all. It wasn't until he had been on the roof of the Grey Warehouse with Ben the previous night that he had had the idea of stopping Farming – but as soon as he had, he had sensed it was the right thing to do. Not only the right thing, the only thing he could do. As he was driven home, as he had sat reading the notebooks that he had written in the first, heady year of Fishbowl's existence, as he had watched himself in front of the Senate committee, that feeling had hardened into certainty. By the time Sandy had come home, he had decided.

But it was one thing to decide – another to do. Andrei felt as if a huge weight had just lifted off him. Saying what he was going to do, even to Chris, made it real. Now he knew he was really going to do it.

'You're making the world's greatest ever business mistake,' said Chris. 'I'm selling my shares.'

'Go ahead.'

'The world's moving on, Andrei. You want to hold back the tide.'

'No,' said Andrei. 'But I'm not going to be the one who brings it in.' He got up.

Lopez put his head around the screen again.

'Lopez, let me pay.'

'No,' said Lopez. 'Yao will kill me if I take your money.'

'Let's see what he'll be saying in a week's time,' muttered Chris.

Andrei went around the screen and headed for the door.

Chris followed him. 'I'd sell your shares if I were you,' he said to Lopez as he went past him. 'And tell Yao to sell as well. Today.'

On the pavement outside, Andrei stopped. He was happy. He hadn't felt like this for months. Only now – having announced his intention – did he realize how oppressed he had been feeling. Only when the weight had gone did he realize how heavy it had been. For the first time in what seemed like years he was utterly at peace with a decision that he had made.

He put out his hand. 'I hope you'll stay as one of our key investors, Chris. We can do great things. We can make this work. We really can.'

Chris grabbed his wrist. 'You still don't have to do this, Andrei. Look, I said some harsh things. We both did. Do all the other things you want to do. The medical stuff, the education stuff. Absolutely. When we started the Manhattan Project, we both knew there were all kind of good things we could do with it. Just don't stop Farming. You can do both.'

'No, I can't.'

'Andrei, we've got seven years together. Let's talk about it some more.'

'I've made up my mind. If you want to talk about it, let's talk about how you can help—'

'*Andrei?*'

They both looked around. A big man with a blond goatee had stepped out of a car that was parked by the kerb.

'I knew I'd find you here.' The man looked at him in anguish, his face was smeared with tears. He put out his arms. 'I didn't believe it, Andrei! I didn't believe it until you did the IPO. You fucking sold us out. You fucking betrayed us.'

'Andrei,' muttered Chris, 'do you know who this is?'

Andrei held up his hands to ward off the man's arms. 'Listen—'

'You made a fool of me. All these years.' He reached inside his jacket.

Suddenly Andrei had a flash of *déjà vu.*

Boston. The Defence of Freedom. A hand reaching for a phone.

But it wasn't a phone this time. There were three shots. Andrei stumbled back against Chris. The man threw down the gun and ran.

Andrei slipped through Chris's hands. He was on the pavement, legs in the gutter. A gurgling sound came out of his mouth. His neck was covered in blood, his T-shirt flooded scarlet.

Chris knelt beside him. Bubbles of blood frothed at Andrei's mouth. His eyes turned up and fixed on him. Chris knew what they were saying. He didn't want to die, not here, not now, not in the arms of Chris Hamer.

46

FISHBOWL HELD ITS press conference at the time and location that Alan Mendes had set up for Andrei on the following day. But instead of Andrei on the podium, Robert Leib, Chris Hamer and Jenn McGrealy fronted the press pack. The room was packed to overflowing.

Barry Diller had been apprehended that morning, still in the Bay Area. Driving erratically, he had crashed a rental car into a central reservation and had given himself up to a passing police unit before they had even asked for his driver's licence.

Robert Leib took the microphone to open the press conference. He unfolded a piece of paper.

'Ladies and gentlemen,' he said, reading from the page. 'Thank you for joining us today.' He took a deep breath. 'These are difficult hours, particularly for those of us who knew Andrei Koss personally. Andrei was a brilliant, insightful and, most of all, a thoughtful young entrepreneurial leader who has been cut off in his prime, and the loss is staggering.' Leib paused, shaking his head reflectively. 'Staggering. I first met Andrei in my office at LRB and from the moment he spoke I knew I was in the presence of someone truly exceptional. He was a young man of immense intelligence and talent but, more importantly – and this is what made him such a great leader – he was always willing to be challenged. He challenged himself more than anybody. I saw Andrei do great things. I expected and had looked forward to seeing him do even greater things in the years to come. Our hearts go out to his family – Sergei, Anna, Dina and Leo – to his girlfriend, Sandy, and to everyone else who is grieving for Andrei today.'

He paused solemnly.

'Well, I'm not here to do a eulogy. That's for another place and another time. There is a business to consider, and even at times like this we are forced to consider it. The board of Fishbowl convened an emergency call this morning. To lose a leader like Andrei is never easy, to lose him the day after our IPO poses an extraordinary challenge. It will take time to find a new leader for Fishbowl. A hasty appointment would be a bad appointment. The board, however, does not believe that at this time, so shortly after our IPO, we can leave the position vacant, even for a brief period. We have therefore decided to appoint an interim CEO to lead the company through this transition.

'We have, we believe, found someone who has shown by his association with the company that he thoroughly understands Fishbowl, its culture, its ethos and its aspirations. The close personal association that he had with Andrei was also critically important in helping us reach this decision. Over the past seven years he has worked closely with Andrei on all of the most important developments in Fishbowl. I have seen personally how he shared Andrei's vision and am sure that no one knows better what Andrei wanted or envisaged for the company. In fact, there is no other person, we think, who could take on this role at this time. To our great relief, he is prepared to accept this challenge. We have spoken with Andrei's family and they are in agreement with our decision. Ladies and gentlemen, I would like to present to you the new interim CEO of Fishbowl – Chris Hamer.'

The journalists watched in silence as Chris stood and came out from behind the table. Robert Leib shook his hand and held out the microphone. Chris took it and waited for Leib to take a seat.

'Thank you, Bob. I'd like to second everything Bob said. First, to Sergei, Anna, Dina, Leo and Sandy, we feel your pain. I'd like to also thank the millions and millions of Fishbowl users who have posted tributes to Andrei on School pages, in the Grotto, on blogs, and in all kinds of places. I know that this has been a comfort to Andrei's family and to all of us here at Fishbowl in Palo Alto and in our other offices.

'The Indians of the Amazon ...' Chris stopped, choking up, and took a couple of deep breaths before continuing. 'I'm sorry.' He cleared his throat. 'The Indians of the Amazon ... have a tradition that when a great chief dies each person in the tribe brings a flower, a fruit, something, and places it at the foot of a tree. That tree takes on the spiritual aura of the dead man, and by placing their offerings there each person in the tribe pays respect to his spirit. The outpouring of love for Andrei is like those offerings. Fishbowl grew rapidly from small beginnings and, in many ways, despite its size, it's like a tribe. We've lost our leader, our guide, our big brother. We're grieving.' He paused and glanced at Jenn McGrealy, who nodded, wiping a tear from her eye.

'But we have to go on. Fishbowl is a part of the lives of a quarter of the people on this planet. That's a testament to the tribe Andrei built, and he would be the last person to say that it should stop, even for a day, even for an hour, even for a minute, because he's gone. Andrei gave us Deep Connectedness. He invented Deep Connectedness. Deep Connectedness never stops. Like the Amazon, it is broad as well as deep, and it flows on.

'How do we go on? How do we do it? Two days ago we had our IPO, and now the man who brought us to this point, the man who for eight years led and built this awesome company, is gone. In the blink of an eye. When Bob asked me, on behalf of the board and Andrei's family, if I would consider taking on the role of CEO, my first reaction was "no". Not even for an interim period. It wasn't because I didn't know the company. I first met Andrei when I invested in Fishbowl seven years ago, but I think it's fair to say that I was always more than an investor. We worked closely on all the big decisions that Andrei made and particularly on the development of the IAP. Andrei used to say I was the *éminence grise* of the company. He actually put that on my business card.' Chris waited as a few people smiled. 'Yeah, that's what he was like. Who am I to try to fill those shoes? I don't know anyone who could. But Bob asked me, as the person who has been closest to Andrei in developing the business over the last seven years, to reconsider, and so I did. I was humbled and deeply honoured by the request. I came to the conclusion that I couldn't refuse. But I can't do it alone. Andrei, as you know, was both chairman of the board and CEO. Bob has agreed to serve as chairman …' he paused and glanced at Bob, who nodded gravely '… and will work closely with me. Bob has enormous experience as an investor in the tech industry, and worked particularly closely with Andrei and me in the year leading up to the IPO, so I can't think of a better person to give guidance in these difficult times. Andrei leaves huge boots to fill and I don't pretend that I'll be able to fill them, but together with Bob I'll do my best to guide the company over the coming weeks and months as we search for … not Andrei's replacement, because there is no one who could replace him, but someone who can step into the role of CEO. In the meantime, until we find that person, I'll serve for as long as needed. Andrei's spirit is with us and I'll take inspiration from that.

'So? What of the immediate future? Jenn McGrealy will continue to run the day-to-day operations of the company as she has done so awesomely for the past five years. My role is to do everything I can to make sure Andrei's vision is fulfilled. Andrei's vision for Fishbowl was unwavering, and I will be guided by my understanding of where he saw the company going in this new phase of growth that has started with our IPO. Fortunately, I was able to hear him articulate his vision just before he was taken from us. As many of you know, I was with Andrei at the time he was shot down. I was the last person he spoke to. We'd just had lunch at Yao's …' Chris frowned, swallowing hard. 'Excuse me. Just give me a second … OK … We'd just had lunch at Yao's, which was Andrei's favourite restaurant. In the early days of Fishbowl we'd often go there and some … some of the most important moments in Fishbowl's history, some of its most important decisions, happened there. On the day after Fishbowl's IPO, when Andrei had so much reason to celebrate and so much to look forward to, he asked me to go with him again to have one of those conversations like we used to have in the old days.'

Chris paused.

'I have exciting news. Andrei had made a big decision. He had decided to roll out the licensing of the IAP – or Farming, as it's sometimes called – on a wide scale. It's time to commercialize it. His vision – an extraordinary vision, a challenging vision – was of a world in which every advertiser on every site right across the net would be using the connectedness offered by Fishbowl's IAP. He asked me what I thought of that. I told him I thought it was bold, visionary, inspirational. I was a little more cautious about our ability to achieve it, but Andrei was adamant. He said we could. Not only that, he said we had to do it. This was what Fishbowl was meant to do. This was what the IPO was for.

'The first eight years had given us the ability to have that vision – our job in the next few years was to make it come true. We talked about it for a long time. I don't think I have ever seen Andrei more excited, more energized, or more certain that he was right. It was truly inspiring. I wish all of you could have heard it as well. He told me that he had one big ambition for Fishbowl. We were the first company to IPO at two hundred billion dollars – he wanted us to be the first to reach a trillion in value. He believed that licensing of the IAP for advertising across the internet would achieve that. And I believe he was right. We've got a head start over all our competitors. If we get going right now, if we use that head start, I don't think anything can stand in our way. So that's what we're going to do – start right now. And I believe we will get to where Andrei saw us getting. I believe we will be that trillion-dollar company, and probably quicker than he imagined. And when we do, that will be our monument to him, a fitting monument to everything he achieved.'

He glanced at Jenn and Bob, who both nodded emphatically.

'Ladies and gentlemen, the world of cyberspace is changing, and with it the rest of our world is changing as well. No one person can take the credit for this alone, but when history looks back, if there has been one dominant figure in the past decade, it will be seen to be Andrei Koss. He never made any apology for being in the vanguard. Andrei's gone, but his work continues.

'Since our IPO only two days ago, Fishbowl has seen another three million people sign up. Already, we have a quarter of the people on this planet. They live their lives in Fishbowl, the Fishbowl that we built over the past eight years.' Chris paused and looked up, as if the ghost of Andrei Koss was hovering above him. A slight smile played at his lips. 'Here's my pledge, Andrei – one day, the rest of the world will, too.'

NOTE ON THE AUTHOR

Matthew Glass is a pseudonym. He is the author of two critically acclaimed novels, *Ultimatum* and *End Game*.